Praise for *The Blue Team*

If you like the excitement that surrounds basketball you'll enjoy reading **The Blue Team**. It has many fascinating twists and turns that will keep your attention. I got so absorbed that I read it in just two days. I especially appreciated the many positive lessons of giving, sharing, caring and standing firm on what you believe, that were interwoven so wonderfully into the basketball story.
Norm Sonju, Co-founder & retired President/GM, Dallas Mavericks

Once I started reading **The Blue Team** I couldn't put it down. I felt like I was back at GW and part of the team. I laughed, I cried, and cheered as the story behind the story unfolded. The book spoke to my heart and most of all it spoke to my soul. When it ended, I wanted more! Well done!
Mike Jarvis - Author, speaker, and former head basketball coach at George Washington and St. John's

I finished reading **The Blue Team** a couple of weeks ago and throughly enjoyed it! I appreciate the effective weaving of biblical principles into a basketball story and personal story. Well done.
Clark Kellogg - CBS college basketball analyst

Just finished **The Blue Team** - it was tremendous! I can't tell you the last time I enjoyed a book so much. Wow, what an anointed book, Peter!!! Thank you for your diligence in being led by the Spirit from cover to cover.
Ed Schilling - University of Indiana basketball Assistant Coach

I'd like to thank Peter for putting a quality, Christian novel into the world. It's a great story, fun to read, and true to the lives of young athletes who face challenges, correction, success, and love, with a balance of service and the desire to live a Christian life. Great work!
Kevin Vande Streek - Men's Basketball Coach Calvin College

I thoroughly enjoyed **The Blue Team** as the various story lines were captivating and the Biblical points of application were apparent. In addition, the content applies to people from several genres as Peter authors a current story filled with real basketball history.

Ross Douma - Former head coach & current athletic director Dordt College

Highly recommend **The Blue Team**! The storyline reeled me in from the start and I couldn't put the book down until I completed reading it. The book is both inspiring and personally challenging.

Dan Hovestol - Former AD & Head coach at Oak Hills Christian College

The Blue Team is an intricate story of trial, tribulation, and redemption. It walks you through the life and experiences of Thomas Conner in a way that tackles life's most pressing issues. A must read for anyone who believes that the game of Basketball is about more than just putting a round ball through a hoop.

Quinn McDowell - Former college & pro basketball player

I just finished reading The **The Blue Team**. It is a very good read. Peter tells a great story, glad to have had the chance to experience this story, and I hope you will all purchase a copy of this book so that he will be encouraged to write another, and another.

Randy Pope, Founder Christian Worldview of History and Culture

It was good to read a story that included so many issues without the story getting lost in the process. I genuinely thank the Lord and you for the gift of this story...

Jerry Steele - M.A.D. House Basketball founder

I thought **The Blue Team** was fantastic. This story captures the challenges of striving for excellence in one's gifts while not losing

one's identity in Christ. This story unfolds the potential in all of us when we align our gifts for God's glory over our own.
Trish Binford - Montana State women's basketball head coach

Peter uses his own experiences as a player at The George Washington University as well as his own strong faith in God to craft a wonderful story about a young man learning to deal with new relationships, new challenges and sudden stardom; all the while trying to discover the correct path God lays out for us all.
Andrew Dixon - Government attorney & George Washington University alum

The Blue Team registers in the championship status. Peter Young beautifully weaves a great sports story with his keen understanding of the power of life lessons available to the athlete. Insightful and spot on in his description of the wonderful gifts that lie hidden for any athlete, Peter writes in the flow state with great instinct and the wisdom of a master. A great read for those who love the game.
Jim Stroker - New Jersey Hall of Fame basketball coach

THE
BLUE
TEAM

PETER YOUNG

ISBN: 978-0-9864278-0-0 (sc)
ISBN: 978-0-9864278-1-7 (e)

Lulu Publishing Services rev. date: 09/04/2018

For my family

CHAPTER 1

I WANTED TO be the next Larry Bird. He was the greatest basketball player in the world and I was going to be just like him. It was the reason I was going to college. It's what drove me on the basketball court. It was also a secret. I had never told anyone, not even my father. He was the wisest man I knew, and he understood me better than anybody else, even my mother. I'd told him everything, but not this.

Like everyone else, my father knew basketball was my passion and Larry Bird my favorite player. But wanting to be the next Larry Bird? I wanted to tell him, but I couldn't bring myself to do it. What would he say? Would he think it an unworthy goal? When discussing goals, he brought up honor before pleasure and making sure I read the Bible every day.

If I didn't tell him now, I might not have another chance for a few months. He and I stood together near the edge of a concrete platform, waiting. The next train into the station was taking me to college. He and my mom offered to drive me there but taking the train from northern New Jersey to D.C. all by myself sounded adventurous. I wiped my forehead with the back of my hand then looked at my watch. 8:30 am. It was already hot and muggy and I could feel my jeans and t-shirt sticking to my skin. My father wore one of his many dark business suits. With his hair combed perfectly and his red tie positioned just right, he looked like he had the answers to all of life's questions.

"Thomas," my father said breaking the momentary silence, "your mother and I are very proud of you. Getting a scholarship to play division one basketball is quite an honor. I have no worries that you'll work hard on the court and in the class room. And even though we're here in Jersey, we'll be with you in spirit. Just remember to trust the Lord with all your heart, not just part of it. Trust Him and continue to surrender to Him everything. Even your basketball career."

"Thanks, Dad," I replied, "I will." Then a thought occurred to me. What if the Lord didn't want me to become the next Larry Bird? By surrendering everything to Him did I have to be okay with that? I looked down and kicked a pebble with my well-worn sneakers. Wasn't I supposed to do everything to the best of my ability? Didn't it say in Corinthians that we should run in such a way as to win the prize?

"You know son," my father continued, "I love watching you play. Hopefully I'll be able to come down and see some of your games this year. And you know what I'm really looking forward to?"

"What's that?"

"I'm looking forward to seeing you mature and grow to the point where nothing upsets you on the court. I hope to see you keep your composure and not get angry if someone is trash talking or a teammate is hogging the ball or a guy like Giambalvo is guarding you."

I rolled my eyes. "That guy. What an ego! I sure hope I don't have a college teammate like him."

"Well … maybe a teammate like him is exactly what you need. That might be just the thing the Lord has in store for you as you overcome your ego. And it might not be fun but you can't conquer what you don't confront."

"I know, Dad," I said. "I'm ready to move on and leave Giambalvo and all that stuff behind."

"Good. I hope you are too. Because if you're truly humble and thankful, you'll have a great four years. You'll be successful beyond your wildest dreams."

I don't know about that. Wanting to be the next Larry Bird was pretty wild. A movement caught my eye and I squinted in the hazy morning sunshine, looking down the weed infested railroad track. The train was slowly coming around the bend on its way into the station. "That must be mine."

"Probably." He slowly shook his head and smiled. "College. Wow. Time flies. It seems like just the other day you were this little guy shooting hoops in the backyard. That hoop is going to be awful lonely without you around."

"You'll have to shoot more. And convince mom to go shoot with you. Get her out of the kitchen."

"Good idea."

The train slowed and then lurched to a stop, its brakes hissing. Others who were also waiting on the platform boarded. "Well, I should get on. I'll call you when I get there."

"Please do. And call anytime."

With that he reached out and hugged me. "I love you, Thomas." He held on tightly and I pushed back tears. "I love you too, Dad."

When he let go I reached down and grabbed my duffle bag off the platform and got onto the train. Turning to wave I said, "So long!"

He smiled and waved back. "Have a great time!"

A FEW HOURS later the train reached Washington, D.C. I navigated my way through the corridors underneath Union Station and hopped on the Metro to the George Washington University campus. It was my first time ever on a subway. Growing up in northern New Jersey I'd heard plenty about the dirty and dangerous New York City subway system but never rode in it. At first glance, the Metro seemed pretty clean. I dropped my duffle bag to the floor and sat down in a seat at the very back of the car.

An elderly man with thick glasses and a smidgen of short-cropped white hair sat nearby. He'd been reading a newspaper, but when he saw me sit down he smiled and asked, "Tall fella, you look like a basketball player. You play for any of the local schools?"

"I do. I'm a freshman at George Washington University."

"Ah, you're going to play for Coach John Thompson."

"No, not John Thompson," I said, failing to hide my annoyance. I'd heard this before. Back home when I told people where I was going to play college ball they almost always thought of Georgetown. "He coaches Georgetown. I'm going to play for the Colonials of GW."

"Yes, yes, you're right. My mistake. Thompson does coach at Georgetown. They're big deal down here, you know. They won the National Championship a few years ago. GW's never done much on the court."

"Well, I hope to change that."

"Good for you." He waved the folded up newspaper in his hand. "They could use some change at Maryland too. They're another big deal here. But now a days, for all the wrong reasons."

He opened up the newspaper and flicked it in his hands to straighten it out and resumed his reading. I saw the feature story on the front page of his newspaper was the Maryland basketball program. The summer of 1986 had not been kind to the Terrapins. First Len Bias died of a drug overdose the day after being drafted by the Boston Celtics. Then news of more drugs and poor academic standards further sullied the team. It was a mess. The death of Bias was a tragedy. He was young, strong, and talented. If he and Larry Bird could have played together, they would have made an incredible duo.

Maybe I would play with Larry Bird one day. The two of us, side by side, winning yet another NBA title for the Celtics.

That image was shattered by gasps and shrieks from the other end of the subway car. I looked over. People scurried away from one of the sets of doors, which had just closed. What was going on? A tall, beautiful woman, who looked to be about my age, walked quickly down the aisle toward me. She was dressed casually in shorts and a polo shirt and her face was white with fear.

Confused, I leaned slightly to my left and looked down the aisle past her. A man in dirty clothes violently grabbed something off the wall. Was he the reason for all the commotion? The tall woman was still coming my way.

"Can I sit here?" Her smile was forced as she gestured to the empty seat next to me. I was at the far end of the car with no one around me except the elderly man. She had passed rows of empty seats. Without waiting for a reply she nimbly stepped over my legs and sat down.

Dumbfounded, I saw the older man quickly fold up his newspaper and turn in his seat. He seemed ready to pounce. The dirty looking man stumbled toward us. The gentle swaying of the moving subway car was almost too much for him to handle. I thought he might keel over at any moment. He seemed drunk and by the way he was dressed homeless too. His shoelaces were untied, his pants and shirt soiled, and his bearded face mottled with all manner of filth.

He walked past the elderly man without a glance and then lurched right up to where I was sitting. He was tall, well over six feet, and silently loomed over me like a mute behemoth. He looked at the girl next to me, then clumsily reached for the door handle that led to the next subway car. My mind instantly flashed to scenarios I did not want to see happen: The door would open and trigger an emergency shut down of the train or, in his stupor, the man would fall between the train cars. Either way, I might get stuck in this dark tunnel.

I reacted instinctively. As the man turned the handle, I grabbed his hand to stop him and asked, "Where you going?"

He faced me, standing mere inches away, looking down at me. Blood-shot and distant, his eyes pierced through his dark black face. He reeked of alcohol and who knows what else.

He mumbled something unintelligible and thrust a torn up poster onto my lap. It was one of the many advertisements adorning the subway car walls, nearly cut in half.

"Well, that's nice," I said, "although it's barely holding together." Like he needed me to tell him that! I didn't realize being ready for college meant being ready for something like this. And what do you say to a drunk homeless guy?

I handed him back the poster and he took it. "Listen," I said, "why don't you just wait until the next stop and I'll take you to the other car? I don't think you're supposed to go from car to car while the train's moving. Okay?"

The man frowned and dropped his chin like a scolded little boy. "Just wait and I'll take you over there, okay?"

Suddenly he grabbed the handle, and, before I could react, he swung the door open and stumbled into the next subway car. The girl next to me gasped. I watched, holding my breath, as he wobbled but made it. I breathed a sigh of relief once he was safely through.

When I turned around, everyone in the car was staring at me. Many wore expressions of shock, others disbelief, and fear. A few rows away the elderly man shook his head.

I frowned. Why was everyone looking at me? I turned to the girl sitting next to me. "Are you all right?" I asked.

She was also staring at me with incredulity. It took her a moment to answer. "Oh my goodness! I was so scared!" Her voice quivered. "I can't tell you ... then you ..." She let out a deep breath. "Thanks for being here."

I shrugged. "I don't know what I did, but you're welcome." I noticed her hands were shaking. "He was kind of scary looking."

"Scary looking? I was terrified. And then when he did that to the thing on the wall ..." Leaning back in the chair she swallowed hard as if the memory was too much to bear. "Let's go and sit by everyone else, just in case he comes back."

By the time I could say, "Okay," she was already standing in the aisle waiting for me. As we walked towards the center of the subway car, everyone was still looking at me.

"Son," said the old man with disgust as we passed by, "you ain't going to live long enough to play college basketball." What had gotten him so upset?

We sat down at the populated end of the car. "So, how did you become so brave?" I could tell by her voice and the color in her face that she had regained her composure.

I felt my face redden. "Well, I don't know how brave I was. Thing is, this is my first time on a subway, and I was kind of worried the guy might do something to get us stuck down here."

"Well, you're brave in my book. I mean, he had that big knife and yet, you still tried to help him."

That big knife? That was news to me. "Hmm," I said trying to hide my surprise.

"As soon as the car doors closed, he whipped that knife out and slashed the poster off the wall, the one he handed you. That knife had to be this big." She held her hands a good eight to ten inches apart.

I had no idea! Where had he hid a knife that big when he was standing right next to me?

"When I saw him do it," she continued, "I just started walking. It was all I could do not to run. Then I prayed and asked the Lord to help me. When I saw you I made a bee line."

We pulled into the next stop. It was shaped just like a cardboard tube you wrap toilet paper around only much bigger and made of concrete. Some local policemen hurried along the monotonous gray platform to the second car. We sat and watched as a minute later they escorted the homeless man out in handcuffs. One of the policemen held the knife by his side. A chill went down my spine. It was big. Finally the doors closed and the subway started off again.

"Whew, glad that's over." The girl smiled and offered her hand. "I'm Jenae Swanson. What's your name?"

"Thomas Conner," I said.

"You new here?"

"Yes. How'd you know?"

"Well, you said it was your first time on a subway. Are you sightseeing?"

"Oh, no. I'm starting school at George Washington. I'm on the basketball team. And you?"

"Me too," she said excitedly. "I mean I'm going to GW. I don't play basketball though. I play volleyball."

"Well, I can see that. You being so tall."

"You too. Where are you from?"

"New Jersey. And you?"

"Idaho."

"Idaho! I've never met anyone from Idaho." I knew nothing about Idaho. All I had was the memory of my kindergarten teacher showing our class that the outline of the state, when turned on its side, looked like an elephant.

"Long way from home, I know. It's beautiful there." She waved her hand in a graceful arc as if pointing in the direction of Idaho. "Lot different from here. No subways, that's for sure." She let out a cute little laugh. "So, are you just getting here?"

"Yeah, took the train down this morning. Kind of a crazy first day."

"You said it. My parents flew out with me and stayed a few days before they left. Seems like months ago but it's been less than two weeks."

"Why'd you get here so soon? School doesn't start for another few days."

"Volleyball practice. We have our first match next week. Today's practice is later this afternoon, so I was doing some sight seeing."

Her blue eyes twinkled with genuine excitement as she continued on, describing her first impressions of college life in the city. When she gently brushed from her face a few strands of her long blonde hair that cascaded down past her shoulders, I was captivated.

The train arrived at Foggy Bottom, site of GW's campus, and we got off together, riding the long escalator up to street level. "It was great to meet you," Jenae said with a smile as we shook hands. "I'm sure I'll see you on campus."

"Nice to meet you too. I bet we'll run into each other at the gym."

"Sounds great," she said, "and thanks again for being here. See ya!"

She left me at a loss for words. I watched her walk down the street, her feet hardly touching the pavement.

CHAPTER 2

MY FIRST FEW weeks at George Washington University were a whirlwind. No more slashing knives on subways, just lots of meetings, classes, homework, and working out with the basketball team. I did get to see Jenae every now and then, but with her volleyball season in full swing and me focused on school and our team's preseason conditioning program, time around her was scarce. Her team had practice right before my team played pick-up games, so I made sure I got to the gym early. That way I could see her as she left the floor.

The campus gym was the Smith Center, and I was there every day. Located on 22nd Street between F and G Streets, it was a modern, blocky concrete building that, at first glance, didn't look much like a division one basketball arena. Inside, the main court sat around 5,000 people for basketball games, but tucked away in a hundred nooks and crannies were locker rooms, weight rooms, meeting rooms, racquetball courts, a squash court, a swimming pool, and athletic department offices.

Our preseason conditioning program was intense: afternoon pickup games, weight lifting, and running sprints. The lifting and running were every other day, but we played pickup ball six days a week. In addition to all that, some times I'd go back to the gym to work on my shot after dinner. Being in the gym that much was awesome. Whether it was playing games or just shooting hoops by myself, I loved being in the gym. I may have slept in my dorm room, but the Smith Center was my new home.

Today's pickup games were particularly intense. We were in our fifth game of the afternoon and the score was tied. Both teams had already won two games.

"No layups!" Jim shouted. "Hard fouls, and no layups! We can't let these young guys beat us." It was classic Jim Barger. A born leader, he was the star point guard and senior captain at GW. Lean and muscular with a mop of wavy brown hair, Jim was an excellent athlete and passionate on the court. Whenever he was in the room, no one sat around wondering what to do.

The "young guys" Jim was talking about were me and my teammates, mostly underclassmen. It was our ball and fellow freshman, Brian Patterson, took his time dribbling up court. There was a lot of hype surrounding Brian. Our coaches raved about him and Jim said he was the most talented freshman he'd ever seen. At first, I had my doubts, but as soon as I saw him play, it was obvious. He was that good.

It didn't matter who guarded him in our pick up games, he was unstoppable. Standing roughly 6'4", Brian was black and lean and well built with muscles on his muscles. He loved to slash and drive to the hoop, and his body control was amazing. His outside shot, however, was horrible, but it didn't stop him from scoring one bit. On defense, I'd never seen such quick hands. He was good and he knew it. He loved to talk about how dominant he was growing up on the tough outdoor courts of New York City. He was cocky all right, but he backed it up.

Coleman Jones, the lone junior on Jim's senior laden squad, was guarding Brian, or at least trying to. Coleman had spent most of the past two years on the bench backing up Jim and other guards who were better than him. Coleman resembled a chunky running back without running back speed.

Brian gave him a juke to his right before exploding to his left. He was past Coleman in an instant and laid the ball off the glass. Neither

Jim or anybody else on his team got there quick enough to prevent Brian from making a layup or foul him.

That put us ahead by a basket. Jim brought the ball up for his team and fed Robert Hodges in the post. GW's starting center the past two years, Robert was a wiry 6'10" defensive specialist who loved to block shots. Lanky and long armed, he had great timing and a soft touch from fifteen feet in. He was abusing the center on our team, gangly 6'11" Alex O'Neill. Alex was all elbows and knees and as graceful as a newborn giraffe. Like Coleman, he'd spent the last two years sitting the bench watching rather than playing.

Robert dribbled once, drop stepped, and dunked right over Alex. The ball shot through the net and bounced right off of Alex's noggin. I tried not to laugh but these kinds of things were always happening to Alex.

"Come on, man," Brian snapped at Alex. "Try playing some defense!"

"Shut up, freshman," he snapped back. Most of the time Alex was a happy-go-lucky guy, but from day one he couldn't stand Brian and his big ego.

Back on offense, Brian put a wicked crossover dribble on Coleman and went right by him again. Their defense collapsed to help Coleman. I was open and Brian recognized it instantly. He threw me a perfect pass and I hit the jumper. Though our styles of play were completely different, Brian and I complemented each other well. My outside shooting opened the lane for him, and his driving opened things up for me to shoot.

Jim shouted the moment I hit the shot. "Dang it! Come on, guys!" he said to his teammates. "We've got to put these freshmen in their place! We can't lose to them again."

With my made shot we were at game point. Pick up games and game point usually meant one thing: get ready to be fouled. Nobody liked losing so nobody got easy shots at game point.

We ran back on defense. Jim pushed the ball up the court. He snapped a crisp pass to Matt Davis. Matt played the same position as me and we spent most days guarding each other. He was about my height, but had 20 pounds of muscle on me. He tried to dribble past me into the lane. The last thing Matt was worried about was getting fouled. He loved to play physical and seemed to embrace the idea of getting whacked. He put the ball on the floor once, then twice, but before he could take another dribble, Brian reached over and plucked the ball out of thin air. I blinked. I know Matt never saw Brian's hand, but did I?

It was our ball. If we scored we won, again. "Hey, let's get a good shot," Brian called.

Yeah, right. I'd seen his idea of a good shot for two weeks now. It was any shot he felt like taking.

Brian lowered his upper body as if to make himself more aerodynamic. His dribble lowered as well, the ball yo-yoing between his fingers and the floor like a sewing machine. In a flash he blew by Coleman. Jim slid over to help and swiped at the ball, making clean contact, but somehow Brian held on. He took one more step into the paint and elevated five feet out from the rim.

Kevin Williams, all 6'7" and 225 pounds of him, was ready. Limited offensively Kevin was a ferocious rebounder, excellent defender, and the team's on-court enforcer. He was tough and mean-looking with ink black skin and a perpetual scowl. He shot off the floor at a trajectory guaranteed to intercept Brian. Kevin wasn't trying to block the shot. He was sending Brian a message and Brian knew it.

A split second before the two collided in mid-air Brian whipped a no look, behind the back pass to me in the corner. "Better make it!" Brian shouted, then grunted as he slammed into Kevin's rock solid torso.

"Better make it," he says? As if he could make two out of ten from this spot. I caught it and shot, never hesitating.

With Brian laid out on the floor watching, the ball swish through the net.

We won.

"Man! You can shoot," Alex said to me as he gave me a high five.

"Not bad, freshman," Jim said, slapping me on the back. His blood may have been the color of competitiveness but first and foremost he was a leader. "You and Brian are pretty tough."

"Hey, what about me?" Alex whined. "I'm tough too."

Jim laughed. "Yeah, tough as marshmallows. You just be thankful for these freshmen. You ain't ever been on a team that's beaten me three out of five."

"Nevah?" Alex said in his thick Long Island accent, a mischievous look on his face.

"Without a doubt, never. Your sorry-ass Blue Teams have never been this good. I may not be Old Man River, but I have been around a while. And let me tell you, not many freshman can play like Brian."

Wait a minute, what about me? Didn't I just hit the game winning shot?

"Yeah, but he's got a big mouth," Alex said. "Thomas, I don't know how you can stand rooming with him. He'd drive me crazy."

I shrugged. Since Brian and I were the only freshmen on the team, it was preordained that we'd room together. I got along well with all the other guys on the team, but found myself being annoyed at nearly everything Brian did. We were nearly exact opposites. Brian was a cocky, inner-city black kid who wore a Magic Johnson jersey and sung along to rap music. I was a suburban white kid who liked Larry Bird and music from the Beatles and Bruce Springsteen. But I didn't want to go into all that with Alex. I wanted to know about the Blue Team. I'd heard it bantered around a few times but never knew what it was. So I asked Jim.

He nodded. "The Blue Team, huh? All right, sit down. I'll tell you what I know."

Alex shook his head. "Dude, I know all about the Blue Team. I don't need to hear some definition."

Jim laughed. "Hey, your picture is next to the definition of Blue Team in the dictionary."

Alex walked away laughing while Jim and I sat down and leaned against the blue padded basketball support.

It was simple, really. Our practice jerseys were blue and white, blue on one side and, turn the jersey inside out, white on the other.

"If you're wearing your jersey blue side out," Jim said, "you're on the Blue Team. You're a sub. If you're wearing white, that means you're on the first team. It means you're a starter. See, the Blue and White Team is an easy way to set up teams for scrimmages and drills during practice. Blue against White. It's more official than shirts and skins, like we do in our pickup games."

He explained how the coaches use the carrot of telling a Blue teamer to "go White" when they're playing well. And if a White teamer is late for something or dogging it in practice and coach wants to get his attention, he tells him to "go Blue."

"Telling a player to "go Blue" works well. Coach uses it a lot. It's kind of like a blue badge of shame. Believe me," Jim said, his hands moving about, emphasizing certain words, "you don't want to be wearing it as a junior or senior."

I nodded, imagining myself in a white jersey on the first day of practice. I tilted my head back and took a big swig from my water bottle, letting some water run down my neck and mingle with my sweat.

"Once the season starts, those on the Blue Team don't play much. Some guys get angry and aim their frustration at the White Team. It's nothing new. Everyone thinks they should be playing."

"So, were you ever on the White Team as a freshman?"

Jim shook his head. "Nope. Freshman year I was on the Blue Team. I didn't play a lick because Chris Marcon was the starting point guard. He was a senior and only came out if he was in foul trouble or got hurt. I gotta admit, there were times when it was tough to be enthusiastic about coming to practice or games knowing I was going to sit. I was ticked off, thought I should be playing. Looking back it was obvious Chris was better. Having the competitiveness you need at this level and accepting a back up role, well ... it wasn't easy. But, I just kept working, kept telling myself my time would come, and it did. I've been starting ever since day one of my sophomore year."

Jim spread his legs on the floor and, leaning forward, effortlessly grabbed his toes. "Ah," he said with a satisfied breath, "that feels good."

I took his cue and stretched my sore legs. With tight hamstrings fighting back, my fingers and toes seemed miles apart. "So, who do you think will start on the White Team?"

"Not you, if that's what you're getting at," he replied quickly.

I frowned. "Why not?"

"Listen, I don't care how good you shoot. I've never seen Coach Ross start a freshman on the White Team the first day of practice. Never. Now, if he puts Brian there, I guess I could see it. But I still think he'll make him earn it over a week or so."

"So you think I'll be on the Blue Team?" I was incredulous. I'd been knocking down shots day after day in our pickup games. Matt Davis couldn't guard me no matter how hard he tried.

"Listen, don't worry about your jersey color. Don't let it become an identity thing. In the long run it doesn't matter. Just play."

CHAPTER 3

I LOVED WANDERING around GW's campus. It reminded me of when I was young and I'd walk downtown and get ice cream, or go to the baseball card store, or the little hole-in-the-wall shop that sold model airplanes and other toys. The side roads and back alleys of my hometown were my preferred routes, especially the alleys. It was like seeing a town without its make-up on. The historian in me loved how little updating was done to the exteriors of the old structures.

When going to shoot hoops at my beloved YMCA back in New Jersey, I would walk behind the dentist's office, cut across the weedy parking lot of the ancient library, down the stairs past the train station platform, through the narrow walkway underneath the railroad, past the bagel shop, through an alley, then arrive at the back door.

There were plenty back alleys and old buildings to explore on GW's campus. Some of the older red brick buildings had an aura of Ivy League stature. Others were huge concrete slabs disguised as buildings. I guessed they were going for the modern look, but I think they did a better job of mimicking drab government buildings in communist Eastern Europe. Buildings like Lisner Auditorium, Gelman Library, and the Marvin Center seemed so cold and uninviting, like the goal of the architect was to make you feel insignificant. The Smith Center wasn't much better from the outside, but the inside was much cozier.

GW was located in an area of Washington, D.C. called Foggy Bottom. One of the oldest neighborhoods in the city, Foggy Bottom had largely been taken over by GW's campus. To the south and west of campus was the Kennedy Center for the Performing Arts, the Watergate complex and the Potomac River. To the north was K Street where all the lobbyists had their offices. The White House was a few blocks to the east, and directly south of campus was the State Department. A few blocks further south was the Lincoln Memorial and all the other well known monuments.

Once well inside the loose GW campus boundaries you could tell you were on a college campus. Hundreds of college students walking around during the middle of the day made it rather obvious. The fringes of campus, however, were different. You could walk on and off campus numerous times a day and have no idea. Dorms, administration buildings, apartments, and small businesses all mingled together like vegetables in minestrone soup.

One of the ingredients in that soup were the homeless. It seemed like they were everywhere. There were no walls or lines on the sidewalks to segregate the dignified campus life from the gritty realities of a large city. There was nothing to keep me in and nothing to keep the homeless out.

Guys like Brian and Kevin who grew up in a city were used to seeing them, but I wasn't. We didn't have homeless people in my quiet little hometown. It seemed incongruous to have these men walking around hungry, panhandling or picking food out of trash cans while we all rushed off to our next class. At night it was awful seeing them sleep on patches of grass or concrete sidewalks while I slept in a warm bed. I wanted to help, but what could I do? There were so many of them; the problem was so big.

One day on my way to the gym, I noticed a small, disheveled looking man walking slowly towards me. His shoulders were stooped and his head hung down like a scolded dog. He wore gray pants, sneakers, and a light brown collared shirt that was pulled askew by the cheap daypack slung over his shoulder. He looked to be about my father's age and couldn't have stood more than five and a half feet tall.

Sometimes it was obvious a person was homeless, other times it was hard to tell if a guy was simply a little dirty and down on his luck. So when I saw this little man, I wasn't sure what his situation was.

As we got closer he veered slightly to his left to ensure our paths would cross. When they did, I stopped. He meekly took off his grimy baseball cap and, with eyes fixated on the concrete beneath our feet, held his hand out. "Excuse me sir," he said in a soft but clear voice, "I'm in an extenuating circumstance. Can you please spare a dollar?"

I was taken aback by his meekness. I still wasn't sure if he was homeless but life had clearly laid him low. When my father walked down the street—sharply dressed, shoulders back, head up—everybody noticed. This man was trying to hide in his own shadow. I immediately reached into my pocket and produced my wallet. I didn't have much but I could certainly spare a dollar.

I handed it to him and he quickly grabbed it. "Thank you, sir," he said then walked off.

"That's awful nice of you, Thomas, but I wouldn't make a habit of it."

I turned sharply and stood face to face with my head coach, Mike Ross. "That guy," he pointed at the small man who continued down the sidewalk, "is always in an extenuating circumstance."

I was stunned. "How did you know?"

Coach Mike Ross smiled. Like my father, he was dignified in his appearance. His brown hair had hints of gray around the temples and his face was tanned. He was dressed in khaki slacks, white shirt, and tie. For a man in his forties, he looked very fit. "That's his line," he said. "He's been using it for years. He probably does need help but giving him money obviously hasn't solved his problems."

"So, he's asked you for money too?" I was beginning to feel foolish.

"Lots of times. Sometimes I give him money, other times I don't. But don't feel bad, Thomas. Like I said, it was nice of you to do it. It shows the kind of person you are. It's one of the main reasons I decided to bring you here. Being able to shoot like you can is great, but I want guys that make good teammates. Guys that are teachable and disciplined. I saw it in you when we recruited you and it was confirmed to me when I met your parents."

I remembered when he came to our house for an official visit. It was about a year ago now. He came with one of GW's assistant coaches, Kenny Jennings. My mother made lasagna for dinner. It was her specialty and one of my favorites. I could tell by their clean plates that the coaches loved it too. My father liked Coach Ross the moment they met. He said he was straight out of the book of James—slow to speak and quick to listen. Coach Ross's demeanor commanded respect and I'd never seen him lose his composure. When he spoke, the vast majority of the time it was to teach.

He had been a good, but not great guard during his college playing days and got into coaching right after he graduated. He was an assistant at a number of schools, moving across the country from job to job like so many coaches do. GW was his first head coaching assignment. He nodded towards the gym and asked, "You headed to go play with the team?"

"Yes, sir."

We walked together and after taking no more than ten steps he said to me, "Look up."

I did, expecting to see something interesting. With nothing but sidewalk in front of me I looked at him confused.

"You've got your head down too much," he said. "There's nothing to see on the ground. Nor is there on the court. Always keep your head up when you play. It's one of the things you need to work on."

Like I said, always teaching.

MY LITTLE ENCOUNTER with the "extenuating circumstance" guy and my talk with Coach Ross got me to the gym a little later than I wanted. I was still on time to play but Jenae was already gone. Disappointed as I was, the games more than made up for it. I was on fire. Matt Davis was trying to guard me, but having no success. He simply couldn't stop me.

Matt did all the little things well. He set good screens, dove for loose balls, always boxed out, rarely took a bad shot, and was perpetually optimistic. Even though I wanted to crush him on the court, I liked Matt. It was hard not to like him. He wasn't nearly as good as Jim, but like Jim, Matt made you look good when you played with him. If Jim was the undisputed leader on the team, Matt was the loyal lieutenant. As a senior he might be the sentimental choice to start over me, but I was much better. His role would be my backup.

When we played pick up games, Jim usually picked sides. My team today was not exactly loaded with talent with Alex, Coleman, and sophomores Elijah Gleason and Tim Rogers. The other team was Brian and the four seniors. Jim mixed things up every day, making sure we all got a chance to play with and against each other. When Brian and I played together we were a formidable duo. When we were on opposing teams his intensity seemed to ratchet up a few notches. Like today.

My hot shooting lead our team to another win. We were slappin' high fives on our way over to the water fountain.

Coleman couldn't help himself from trash talking. "Hey, Brian, that roomie of yours sure can shoot, can't he?" Despite being outplayed by Brian from day one, Coleman liked his younger teammate, and the two had become buddies. "Too bad you guys can't do nothing about it. I mean, he has been pretty much unstoppable." Coleman was digging and he wouldn't stop until he hit something in Brian that set him off. Hearing the two of them trash talk with each other was common. They seemed to like it though, and it was the one thing Coleman could do better than Brian.

Coleman held up his hand and pretended to count on his fingers. "What's that two, three games in a row?"

"Four," Elijah Gleason said on cue, knowing Coleman had purposely shorted the win total. Elijah was more than Coleman's side kick. He was talented, lightening quick on defense and an excellent ball handler on offense. But Elijah would spend this year, like last, as Jim's backup. He knew it and so did everyone else on the team. In the meantime he soaked in everything Jim taught him about playing point guard. The thought of not sharing his knowledge with the guy that could potentially take away his starting spot probably never even occurred to Jim.

Coleman kept it up. "Oh, that's right. My bad. It's four games in a row. Brian, you wanna call it a day or get beat some more? I just don't know if you guys can stop him."

"Ain't nothing to stop," Brian finally replied testily. "He'll start missing."

Coleman bent over and slurped from the water fountain. When he stood up, water dripped off his ample lips and goatee. "Who'll start missing? Your roommate? The one that's been knocking down jumpers all day?"

Brian tilted his head just enough so I could see his dismissive look. "So? All he can do is shoot."

Coleman let out a mock gasp and looked at me. "Did you hear that?"

"Sure did," I said. "So all I can do is shoot, huh?"

Brian wiped his mouth off after sucking deeply from the water fountain. His big round head jutted forward from his shoulders. "You're a shooter," he said. "That's all you do. Like it ain't obvious?"

My jaw clenched. All I can do is shoot? After all that I'd done today and for the past few weeks this was what Brian thought of me?

"And it ain't even a jump shot," Brian continued. "It's a set shot. Let's go, Coleman. One more game. Get ready to have your ass kicked."

I continued to shoot well in the next game and it was Brian's team that got their butts kicked, again. We'd won five straight games. After that most of the guys were done playing for the day and started filtering out of the gym. I sat on the floor, slumped against the wall. With my sore legs splayed out in front of me, I took my sneakers off and let my feet air out. Brian and Coleman hung around and played a lackadaisical game of one-on-one that ended suddenly when Coleman remembered he was already late for a meeting with his academic advisor. "Academic *advisor?*" Brian chided. "That lady ain't no advisor. She's the one they ought to give your degree to, if you ever get it!"

Coleman brushed aside the comment and ran out of the gym. Brian walked over to me and asked, "Hey, want to play some one-on-one?"

I was exhausted but couldn't pass up the opportunity. I knew what he was thinking. He didn't need a team to kick my ass. He would do it on his own. "You're on," I said without hesitation and quickly laced up my sneakers.

I knew he was amazingly quick from all our pickup games, but I hadn't ever guarded him. Not only did I want to show him I was more than a shooter, I also wanted to see how good he really was. It bothered me how much Coach Ross talked about Brian while he was recruiting me. He made it seem like Brian was NBA material. And every time he made a fancy move in our pickup games, Coleman or somebody else would let out an "ooh" or "wow." That never happened when I hit my jump shots. Come to think of it, Brian had never given me a compliment on the court. Well, I'd just have to give him a reason to.

But from the first moment he had the ball, I couldn't stop him. He was too quick. Like a small bird talking as fast as he can, Brian's sneakers squeaked and chirped on the hardwood court with every one of his moves. I was completely exposed with no one to help me. He got past me any time he wanted. He taunted me with a jab step here, a shot fake there. My muscles twitched nervously, trying to anticipate his move. It was no use. With a grunt, he'd blow past me in a blur. My only chance was to step back a bit and hope he missed an open jumper.

On offense I could barely get my jump shot off. At 6'6", I was only two inches taller than him, but it gave me just enough of a window to release my shot. Trying to drive past him with the dribble was out of the question. After hitting quick shots over him, one after another, I could tell he was getting irritated.

"Stupid set shot," he would mutter in contempt whenever I nailed a shot. He started to crowd me even closer. Standing at the top of the key with the ball in my hands he was practically under my chin, daring me to dribble. It felt like he was nudging me closer and closer to the edge of a cliff. Another step backward and I'd plummet to my death. To move forward was to stay alive.

And I was alive in this game—barely. The more I scored and kept the game close, the more agitated Brian became. He glowered under a sweaty brow and cursed under his breath. Once I gave him a perfect shot fake. He went for it. Two dribbles later I was at the bucket for a wide open lay-up. But Brian somehow recovered in time and blocked my shot, pinning it on the backboard well above rim level. I stood there stunned. I'd never seen such an incredible athletic move!

He won the first game. I won the second. By the third I was exhausted but did my best to hide it. If he was tired, he was hiding it too. We were both pouring sweat, leaning over at the waist and grabbing our shorts in between points for a brief rest. I couldn't stop his drives to the bucket and he couldn't stop my jump shot. We didn't speak, other than the score. I had to beat him.

On game point, I was determined to not let him score, even if I had to foul him hard. I handed him the ball and got into a defensive stance, my leg muscles ready to fire at his slightest movement. My left arm extended toward him, inches from his face, palm up to distract him or maybe irritate him and goad him into a foolish mistake. His eyes seethed an angry confidence.

He juked one way and then blew by me faster than I could blink. Desperately I lunged and shoved his hip. He hit an amazing off balance floater anyway.

He punched the air with his fist and sweat flew in all directions. "Game!" His triumphant shout echoed off the Smith Center walls.

I was livid. I grabbed my ball and walked off without saying anything. How could I let another freshman beat me in one-on-one? Especially the almighty Brian Patterson from New York City, the one Coach Ross said would elevate our entire program. Now I'd just elevated his big head even more.

I stormed out of the Smith Center and marched across campus. The last thing I wanted to do was go to my dorm room and see Brian there. I turned a corner and there was the little "extenuating circumstance" man, the one I'd just given a dollar to early in the day. He was sitting on a park bench next to a filthy looking person who had straggly hair and a long, gray beard. The man's hair, beard and tattered clothes looked like they'd been used to mop the gutter.

The two were having a quiet conversation that came to an abrupt end when the little man recognized me. I didn't want to hear about his "extenuating circumstances." Not now. Every day I'm working my butt off so I can one day earn millions playing basketball in the NBA and these guys are just sitting on park benches mooching off others.

He stood up and, head bowed, approached me. "Excuse me sir," he said with hand extended, "but can you spare a dollar. I'm in an extenuating—"

"No, I can't," I interrupted, never breaking stride. "I've got my own circumstances."

The little man recoiled like I'd tried to bite his hand off. The dirty bum on the bench leaned forward and stared at me. Between his nasty, unkempt hair and thick, matted beard I could hardly see his face. He reminded me of a dirty Cousin Itt from the old black and white TV show *The Adams Family*. A sudden surge of indignation came over me and I shouted, "And tell your dirty friend over there to take a shower sometime this century!"

The dirty one bolted off the bench and mumbled something unintelligible. I walked past them, my angry strides quickly putting distance between us.

CHAPTER 4

AVOIDING MY DORM room, and Brian, I stomped around campus for a half hour. How could I let Brian beat me? I shook my head. I'd never hear the end of this.

As I walked, I kept an eye out for Brian to make sure I didn't run into him. I also made sure I didn't double back towards the homeless guys I'd just insulted. Figuring Brian would have certainly left the gym by now, I went there and showered and changed. I went to the cafeteria and ate. I wandered around campus some more. I couldn't avoid him forever. I had to go to my dorm room eventually.

When I did, Brian was there folding his laundry. His favorite singer, LL Cool J, blared from my stereo. My parents shipped the stereo to me a few days after I left for GW. I had bought it with money I earned mowing lawns while in high school. I tossed my keys onto my desk and turned off the stereo.

"What're you doing?" He shot me his favorite angry look. I knew it well by now. Mouth agape and eyes boring a hole in me. He wanted me to think I was the dumbest person on earth.

"Turning off *my* stereo," I answered trying to mock his expression.

"So that means you can do whatever you want with it?"

Okay, maybe he *did* think I was the dumbest person on earth. "Uh, yeah, it does. Buy your own stereo and play whatever you want on it. Until then, I choose what gets played and when because I own the stereo." There was a precious moment where he was silent. But it didn't last.

"Yeah, well LL Cool J is way more popular than them goofy Beatles you always listen to."

My eyebrows tilted upwards with that whopper. He loved arguing and was always trying to lure me into one. To him, there was nothing like a good confrontation. I hated arguing, but this comment was too off the wall to leave alone. "How do you figure LL Cool J is more popular than the Beatles?"

"What do you mean how do I figure?" He paused briefly, staring again, letting his words marinate. "LL Cool J is the best rapper on New York's number one radio station. New York is the biggest city in the world."

"So? The Beatles had a lot of number one hits. They had number one songs in more than one country. Shoot, they once had the top 5 hits at the same time. And they've sold more albums than LL Cool J could ever dream of."

"But they ain't number one on the biggest and most important radio station in the world."

"Yeah, but ..." I stopped myself. This wasn't going anywhere. "Oh, never mind." I sat down and stewed. Why did I have to room with this guy? I scanned my cluttered desk for something I could read that would make him stop talking to me. I grabbed my Bible.

"And you better not start preaching to me from the Bible."

"What?" I snapped back. "I've been reading my Bible every day and never said a word to you. What are you talking about?"

"My grandma used to hound us with it. Always getting on us about everything. This was a sin, that was a sin. Throwin' out Bible verses." He was sitting on the edge of the couch waving a sock around like it was one of his grandmother's Bible verses. "Drove me crazy. My dad too. Got so bad he finally left us."

Bible verses drove his father so crazy it made him leave his family? And now Brian was bothered because I'm quietly reading my Bible?

I guess the apple didn't fall far from the tree. I shook my head. "You can leave or stay," I said, "but I'll read my Bible whenever I please."

"Go ahead. Just don't be bugging me with it."

"Fine."

"That's right."

Like an echo, Brian always had to have the last word.

Disgusted, I put the Bible down on my desk, went to the little kitchenette in our room and made myself a bowl of cereal. Like going to the gym to shoot hoops, enjoying a big bowl of cereal was one of my favorite stress relievers. I did it all the time growing up. Without warning, the words of my father filled my head. Hadn't he said a difficult teammate might be just what I needed? But a teammate like Brian?

I sat down at my desk with the bowl of cereal and took stock of my day. I got furious over losing to Brian in a game of one-on-one. I was rude to those homeless guys. I go to read my Bible then argue with my roommate. Not exactly a banner day. But it worse than that. I just said I'd been reading my Bible every day but had never shared a word of it with him. Brian may be as arrogant as the day is long, but I hadn't been much of a friend either. Without building a relationship Brian wasn't going to listen to a word I said. I sighed. "So, your dad left you?"

"Yeah, he left. Moved out, but stayed in the city. He went to all my high school games, though. My mom raised me. Got a problem with that?" His eyes never left his pile of laundry.

"No ... but it kind of seems you do."

"You're damn right I do." He turned and faced me. "So I'm gonna tell you right now. I don't want you watching every single thing I do and using that book to make me feel guilty. You wanna be all self righteous and Christian, you do it on your own time. I'll do whatever I please. I've been runnin' my life ever since my old man left and I aim to keep doing it."

Unbelievable! There's no way my father could think this guy is good for me! How could this possibly be good for me?

Too angry to read, I turned the radio back on to one of my stations. John Cougar-Mellencamp's "Small Town" came over the airwaves. White, Midwestern, rock-n-roll but almost country, it was perfect. I turned up the volume. Brian tossed the rest of his laundry to the side and stormed out of the room.

A COUPLE DAYS later, after dinner at the school cafeteria, Alex and I took our time walking across campus towards our dorm. Everyone on the team lived in the same dorm. He roomed with Coleman just down the hall from Brian and me. I convinced Alex to take a shortcut through a tight alley between two campus buildings, even though he thought I was crazy for wanting to do so. "Dude, in this city, you got no idea who we're going to run across," Alex said.

"Hey, I'm not scared," I said. "I got a 6'11" bodyguard with me."

"Yeah right, a bodyguard that would outrun you at the first sight of danger."

I liked hanging out with Alex, even though he didn't take basketball as seriously as I did. He was good at self deprecating humor and always the first to compliment me on my latest made shot. In other words, he was the exact opposite of Brian.

As we exited the alley we came upon one of the many dorm buildings on campus. Just then two girls stepped out of the lobby. My heart instantly started beating faster. There was Jenae! I recognized the girl she was chatting with as one of her volleyball teammates, Holly Anderson. I couldn't remember the last time I saw Jenae outside the Smith Center.

"Hey, what's up, you two?" Alex called out in his loud voice.

"Hi, guys," Holly answered as they walked over. "We're going to get some ice cream."

Looking at me, Jenae asked, "Want to come?"

"We'd love to!" Alex said before I could answer. The enthusiasm in his voice was over the top. "You two know this good lookin' fella next to me, Thomas?" I shot him a nervous glance.

"Of course I do, Alex!" Jenae said. "You know that. Thomas and I see each other all the time at the gym. Holly, he's the one I met on the Metro."

"So you're *that* Thomas." Holly smiled as she looked at me. "Nice to finally meet you. She told me all about the subway incident."

I smiled back and wondered how Jenae described it. Was I heroic or simply lucky?

"Well, the thing that I can't get over," Alex said, arms extended, pointing at Jenae and me, "is Tom likes Jenae and Jenae likes Tom. So why don't you two go get ice cream and Holly and I will just split?"

I nearly peed my pants.

Holly and Jenae both laughed. With her face blushed and hands on her hips, Jenae exclaimed, "Alex, you're a goofball!"

Alex was indeed sporting a goofy grin as he stood there, smiling and holding out his arms. I felt like punching him in the shoulder as hard as I could. And how did he know I liked her?

"What?" he asked. "Am I wrong?"

"Why don't we all go get some ice cream?" Jenae said.

"Good idea, Jenae," Holly said. "Us ladies are going to stick together."

Like Jenae, Holly was also tall and beautiful. It dawned on me just then that the real reason Alex tried to send Jenae and I on our way was probably so he could hangout with Holly.

"And Alex," Jenae added with a mock scolding finger wag, "you just leave your matchmaking for someone else. I can handle my own affairs."

"All right, fair enough." He chuckled and shrugged as he looked at me.

What in the world should I say? My face must have been stop sign red. I was still speechless as we all started walking to the ice cream parlor.

"Thomas," she asked, "does Alex do this sort of thing to you often?"

"No." I grinned, my face flushing again. "But you're right, he's a goofball."

"Hey," Alex said, "I resemble that remark."

After a while Alex and Holly strode ahead of us while Jenae fell into step with me. I glanced at Jenae out of the corner of my eye as we walked. She was so comfortable and poised with her easy smile, expressive voice, and carefree walk. Everything about her was beautiful.

The ice cream parlor was near a small triangular grassy park, carved out by streets intersecting at angles. A few trees and park benches provided spartan accommodations for a group of homeless men. Walking by on the other side of the street it sounded like they were bickering with each other.

"It's so sad to see them living like that," Jenae said. "My heart aches for those men."

I wondered what choices led them to this point. Drugs? Alcohol? At what age did they transition from the adorable child of proud parents to an adult living on the streets? Were their parents homeless too? Were the parents even aware of the condition of their sons? "You probably don't have many homeless people in Idaho, do you?" I asked.

"No, not that I was aware of. This is all new to me. But I feel led to do something. I don't want to be scared, I want to help in some way, like you did."

"Me? When?"

"With that homeless guy on the subway. You showed you cared. You tried to help him in a small way. How often does a guy like that have people trying to help him?"

"I guess I wasn't thinking about helping him as much as I was trying to keep safe," I said. "I wonder how often we miss opportunities to help out?"

"Hmm. Good point. We can get so wrapped up in our own lives, our own goals, that we can forget about those around us who are in need."

At the ice cream parlor the conversation turned to our hometowns. After Alex talked about Long Island and Holly her home in Virginia, I asked Jenae, "Tell me about Idaho."

She lit up. "Well, it's a lot different from here. I grew up in Pocatello."

"Poca-what?" Alex blurted, sending bits of mint chocolate chip ice cream flying out of his mouth.

"Pocatello, not Poca-what or Pocahontas. It's a nice place. Small town, lots of open spaces, no subways, that's for sure." She smiled at me. "The mountains are right there. I really miss the mountains. You can go hiking, mountain biking, camping—there's all kinds of outdoor stuff to do. It even has a sand volleyball court where I used to play. And the people are real friendly. Growing up, it seemed my parents knew everybody in town. My father works at the university, so I would go to a lot of the games on campus."

"Is he a teacher?" I asked.

"Yes. He teaches math. He's good at it, too."

"Good," Holly said. "Maybe he can help me with my math class. I'm already so lost! Can I call him?"

"Sure," Jenae said, then added thoughtfully, "but be glad you're only lost in class. Sometimes I feel completely lost here."

"What're you talking about?" Holly asked. "You never look lost to me."

"I guess I question if I made the right decision, moving all the way across the country to go to school here. I wonder if it's me or where I came from, but sometimes I feel like I don't fit in. Even on our team."

"Yeah, with our seniors and their little cliques," Holly sneered, "it's no wonder."

"Oh, Holly, it's not just them," Jenae said gently as she looked down. "I think it's my faith too. Back home, with my teammates and friends, I could talk openly about my faith in Christ."

I knew there was something special about her. I was always a sucker for tall blondes, but she had a glow about her that, until now,

I wasn't sure what it was. It should have been obvious. The way she spoke, the things she said, of course she was a believer.

"But not here," she continued. "Every time I bring it up, I feel like people are shooting daggers at me."

An awkward moment of silence followed. Alex took a huge bite from his ice cream cone and Holly fidgeted with her napkin.

"I know what you mean," I finally said, rescuing her from the silence. "Sometimes it feels like being a Christian here on a city campus is like living behind enemy lines." I wanted to tell them rooming with Brian was the reason for that, but I bit my tongue.

Jenae perked up. "Tell me about it. The other day in one of my classes I mentioned Christianity and the professor practically jumped down my throat. 'This classroom is not an appropriate place to bring that subject up,'" she said trying to imitate a deep male voice. "I couldn't believe it."

"I was there," Holly added with a nod of her half eaten ice cream cone. "She's right. He acted like you insulted him."

Jenae shrugged. "Maybe I did."

"Hey, you want to insult one of your professors, just ask me," Alex said, lightening the mood. "I'm pretty good at that kind of stuff. Ain't that right, Thomas?"

I laughed. "I guess. Must be that Long Island upbringing."

"Like New Jersey ain't worse? You're the only guy from Jersey I know that's not a wise guy."

"We've all talked about our hometowns," Jenae said to me. "What's New Jersey like?"

I smiled and told them about all the huge oaks, maples, and pines around town, the thriving downtown, the back alleys, and the proximity to New York City. "And Bruce Springsteen is huge. Everybody loves him. But what I loved most," I waved my cone for added emphasis, "were the dozen or so gyms in town. Between the YMCA, the two at the high school, the junior highs, Catholic school, elementary schools, there's probably a dozen."

"Yeah, I bet you liked that." Alex turned to the girls. "You should see how much time this guy spends at the gym. Always in there shooting hoops."

"I know," Jenae added.

I was surprised. "You do?"

"Sure. Every time I leave practice you're there. Then the other night, when I had to go to my locker for something, I saw you shooting hoops by yourself."

I remembered. It was a good night at the gym, but I never saw her. My fingertips tingled with the memory of dimpled leather and made baskets.

"That's Thomas," Alex said. "Dedicated. First one in, last one out—if he ever leaves!"

I didn't want the moment to end but Holly had homework to do and Jenae said she had to get up early the next morning. As we walked the girls back to their dorm, Alex told a bunch of crass jokes that fell flat. How I wished it were just Jenae and I. One day, I vowed, just the two of us would go out on the town.

THE NEXT DAY I decided instead of wishing for it, I would make it happen. Jenae mentioned she often went to the library to study. Being right across the street from her dorm it was both safe and convenient. My idea was to go there like I was studying, sit near her and then ask her out. Simple enough. After practice I put on my favorite jeans, a white collared shirt and a dab of cologne. Dressed up, but not formal like I was going to church. I grabbed a few textbooks and walked down to the lobby of my dorm. Then I froze. I couldn't go any further. How was I going to do this? What would I say to her? What if she said no? It didn't seem so simple anymore. I needed someone to go with me for support. But who?

I did a quick mental checklist. Certainly not Brian. What about Alex? No, he'd probably try and do it for me like he did the other night. No one came to mind, so I sat down on the couch in the lobby and waited. I was sure the right person would walk in if I waited long enough.

Coleman came in. He saw me and flashed his patented toothy grin. "Mr. Jump Shot himself," he said. "Where you going?"

I panicked. I couldn't have Coleman go with me. He was too loud and unpredictable. Plus he hung out with Brian a lot. Everything that was said or done would get back to Brian. Quick, think of something! "Uh ... study group at the library." Phew, that was good.

He gave a look of disgust. "Okay then. See ya."

After Coleman left, ten minutes of toe tapping and second-guessing passed. Then Jim walked into the lobby.

Would he do? I considered it for a moment. Like me, Jim was from New Jersey. He was savvy and mature and I liked him the moment I met him. He might do.

"Thomas," he said. "What're you doing all dressed up? Going out on a date?"

What was he a mind reader? "No," I said quickly. "Uh, well, not really. I, uh ..."

His face lit up. "You're going on a date! Look at you. Little freshman, already got a girlfriend."

"I wish. You see I—"

He snapped his fingers. "Need help asking her out?"

I stared stupidly for a moment. "How did you know?"

Jim laughed. "Dude, I've been around freshmen before. Besides, it's written all over your face."

"Really? Will you help?"

"Sure. Who is it? The volleyball player?"

"Jenae. How did you know?"

"Relax. I've seen you two chat at the gym. Cute girl. So, what's the plan? You got a plan, right?"

"Yeah." I rubbed my sweaty palms on my pants leg. "I'm pretty sure she's at the library. We'd go there and make it look like we're studying together. You wouldn't need to say anything just be there. And please don't tell the other guys."

"Sounds good. Let's go."

As we walked across campus toward the library, Jim jabbered on about how he met his girlfriend when he was a freshman. I grew silent, my nerves getting the best of me. What would Jim think if I failed miserably? I didn't have much time to think about it because we arrived at the library faster than I expected.

As Jim walked through the library doors ahead of me, it hit me. "Jim, you don't have any books."

"So, do I ever?"

"We're supposed to be studying, remember?"

He shot me a dismissive frown. "All right, give me one of yours."

I looked at the bundle of books under my left arm. "I need these."

"Fine, I'll grab one on the way. So where is she?"

I shrugged. "I don't know. She could be anywhere."

He sighed. "Oh, you freshman. You're so much work. All right, let's go find her."

We had to find Jenae without seeming like we were actually looking for her. So we wandered around the first floor peering down aisles and around corners. No nook was left out. We moved onto the second floor. I was looking down a row of books when Jim elbowed me in the back. I turned and there she was. It was a perfect situation: She was sitting by herself at a large conference table. We walked over, books in hand. She must have sensed us coming, because at that moment she looked up and waved us over.

"Hey, you guys," she whispered, "there's plenty of room at this table if you'd like to join me. You two have a class together?"

We didn't. Now what? Horrified I looked at Jim.

"Naw, Jenae," Jim replied smoothly. "Just two guys on the basketball team trying to do some studying."

She smiled and said softly, "Well, good for you two."

We sat down and quietly talked for a bit more—with Jim doing nearly all the talking—before we got down to studying. After about ten minutes Jim announced that he needed to go to the bathroom and left.

"He seems like a real nice guy," Jenae said looking across the table. "He's a senior on your team, right?"

"Yes, he is, and yes, he's a good guy. Always up for a good adventure."

"Well, I don't think coming to the library is much of an adventure. Although maybe for some of your teammates it is." We both laughed a bit too loudly and then muffled our laughter with our hands after noticing the annoyed looks from other students nearby.

Still chuckling, she resumed her studying. I stared into my book, not reading a word of it, trying to come up with something else to say, some way to start another conversation—one that enabled me to ask her out on a date. "So, what are you studying?"

"English."

"Oh, are you majoring in English?"

"No, elementary education. The first year is mostly core classes. Education classes come later, so I'm told. What about you, do you know what you're going to major in?"

"History."

She nodded politely and looked at me, seeing if I had anything to add. I didn't. So much for starting a captivating conversation.

Twenty minutes of silence passed.

Then Jenae breathed deeply and folded up her books. "Well, I've been here long enough, and I have an early morning tomorrow. You staying longer?"

"Yeah, I'll probably be here a bit longer." My mind frantically tried to come up with something good to say. My window of opportunity was closing fast, but for the life of me I couldn't muster the courage to simply ask her out.

Jenae glanced over her shoulder as she stood and pushed her chair in. "I wonder if Jim deserted you, too."

I had to say something! My mind grasped for words as I squeezed the table with both hands, but no words came.

"Well, see you soon, Thomas. Thanks for joining me. Maybe Alex will set us up for more ice cream again."

"Maybe." I had to say more, something better … "Say, Jenae, why don't you and I go get some ice cream ourselves … or dinner … or something like that." Ugh. My voice sounded like I was 13 years old!

She smiled. "Oh, Thomas. That's sweet of you." I saw a light go on in her mind. "Say, how about instead of dinner, you come with me to my meeting tomorrow?"

A wave of relief flooded over me. I can do a meeting. "Sure. Where's it at?"

"The Presbyterian Church just off campus. It's the beautiful old stone building. You can't miss it. Just meet me there."

"Sure, I know where it is." I'd been there once on a previous Sunday. "What's the meeting about?"

"Well, there'll be food there. You'll see." She scribbled on a piece of paper then handed it to me. "Here's my number, just in case. It starts pretty early. We should meet at six. And you'll want to dress casual."

After she left I went and found Jim. He wasn't far, sitting just around a corner and out of sight.

When he saw me approach he closed the magazine he was reading. "So?"

I held up the small piece of paper with Jenae's phone number on it. It felt like gold in my hand. "Got her number and a date."

Jim smiled. "Not bad, freshman. Not bad."

CHAPTER 5

IT SEEMED LIKE a cruel joke when my alarm clock went off at 5:40 a.m. I whacked it quiet, then remembered why I was up so early. Jenae. She wasn't kidding when she said the meeting started early. A part of me wondered if this hour was better described as really late rather than really early. To Alex, who was often stayed out late, I'm sure it was.

I quickly got dressed, splashed water on my face, ran a comb through my hair and left.

What was this meeting she invited me to all about? She said there'd be food. Some kind of breakfast get together at the church?

I walked there alone. Without a hot shower to warm me up, I was chilled to the bone. As I stood outside the church door, just before 6 a.m., I waited for Jenae to arrive. I was surprised it was this cold, and the city so quiet. A sharp dressed businessman walked briskly down the street, a steaming cup of coffee in one hand, his briefcase in the other. As he walked south, two shabbily dressed men passed him in the other direction coming toward the church.

First Presbyterian Church was an old structure sandwiched between large office buildings in downtown D.C. Its exterior was beautiful, just like Jenae said: stone with a slate roof and large wooden doors. There was a tiny courtyard with grass and flowerbeds surrounded by a small stone wall. The rest of the neighborhood had been converted from small, old brick row houses to steel and glass office buildings. Yet

Western Presbyterian remained. It was like the one guy in the photo wearing corduroys while everyone else was in three-piece suits. There were many in the city who wanted to get rid of the building and use the spot for something else. Some of the adjacent property owners had made huge offers to the church to buy them out, including the International Monetary Fund. Yet the old church was still there, a small house of worship shadowed by buildings full of bankers, lawyers, and lobbyists. It seemed so odd to see those buildings next to each other, but the city was full of incongruous connections: modern and old buildings, the recently refurbished and the dilapidated, the gaudy and the classic, liberals and libertarians, me and Brian.

I saw Jenae heading my way. She practically skipped along the sidewalk. "You made it!" she said with a big smile. She wore her dark blue volleyball sweat pants and top and a white scarf. Even at this hour she was pretty.

I shivered. "It wasn't easy."

"Hah," she laughed. "Come on. It's down here." She pointed to an outside set of stairs leading to a basement.

"What's down there?"

She touched my shoulder. "That's right. I still haven't told you what we're doing. We're feeding the homeless. There's a soup kitchen down there."

"Soup kitchen?"

"That's what they call it. Come on."

Some of the homeless were lined up outside the basement door and along the stairs. Their faces mirrored the cold stone façade of the church: glum in the gray hour, yet many brightened as Jenae walked past saying, "Good morning."

The homeless, Jenae told me as we descended the stairs and went inside, were a mixed bag. Some men had a job but it didn't pay enough. Unable to afford rent, they were in and out of shelters or friends' places, living on the back porch of society. Others, like the mentally ill, drug addicts, or alcoholics, didn't bother trying to pay their own way. Many were lost among the weeds of an overgrown city that didn't know about them or didn't care.

The room where the men ate was large with a low ceiling and filled with fold-up tables and chairs. Near the center of the room were metal support columns. On one end of the room was a small stage with an old, faded crimson curtain as a backdrop. The kitchen was on the other end. The large tiles on the floor were polished by the years. It was oddly identical to the basement of the church I grew up in. Was there a standard blueprint for church basements?

The kitchen was cavernous with numerous cabinets, counters, fridges, ovens, and a large metal island in the middle. Each cabinet was filled with the necessities of feeding massive quantities of food.

There to serve with us were a half-dozen volunteers and the church's gregarious pastor, Paul Garzelli. Wearing a large white apron that sunk past his knees, Paul was slight of build with dark black hair. In his thick Italian accent he issued far more compliments than orders.

At 6:15 a.m. we started to make food, lots of it: scrambled eggs, bacon, hash browns, toast, coffee, and orange juice. I was asked to make the scrambled eggs and stopped keeping track of how many I cracked after 100. My right forearm got sore from the repetitive motion of scrambling. I watched Jenae as she went from job to job. First she got out the plates, cups and utensils and lined them up at the window where the food was to be served. Then she brewed coffee, filled up the pitchers with orange juice, and helped another volunteer butter the toast.

At 6:45 a.m. the doors to the basement were unlocked and an orderly procession filed past the kitchen. Some walked, many shuffled. There were lots of glassy eyed stares, sunken eyes, stunned eyes. How could life do this to men? Young and old, sick and healthy, black and white, they all shared misery, but not all felt the shame. A few were smiling and happy, as if they couldn't imagine wanting to be anywhere else. When they came by I smiled along with them and felt warm in my heart.

With aprons on, Jenae and I stood behind the large kitchen counter with two other volunteers and served. Using ladles we doled out generous portions of steaming hot food from the metal pans that lay in between us and the men. Jenae knew many by name and talked with them as they came through the line. "Good morning, Ray!" She said to one of those who seemed filled with the joy of life.

"Good morning, sweetheart. Load me up, if you wouldn't mind. I'm starving." Through his thick glasses I could see his eyes devouring the food before it ever reached his plate. He looked over at me and pointed a big bony finger. "Say, you must be the Jersey boy?"

"That's right," Jenae said, gesturing to me. "Ray, this is Thomas, the one I told you about."

"Well morning to ya, Thomas." His huge grin revealed poorly kept teeth.

"Good morning to you," I said.

"Ray, we have to keep the line moving, but come by our table afterwards so we can talk."

"Sounds good, Jenae. Sounds good." Ray nodded then continued down the line to get his bacon and toast.

"You said you told Ray about me?" I asked Jenae.

She leaned over and said, "Yes, I was here yesterday and I told him you were from New Jersey. That's where he's from too. He loves basketball so he's excited to meet you."

I looked towards the end of the line where Paul was stationed serving drinks. He and Ray were talking warmly. I noticed that Paul talked openly with Ray and nearly all the other men that came. They talked about life on the street, sleeping in poor weather, how they smelled that morning, their clothing, etc. Blunt and honest, it was evident Paul cared for every one of them. I couldn't imagine talking to the men like that, but he did it so tactfully. Most seemed to love him for it.

A minute later the filthy man whom I had told to "take a shower sometime this century" showed up in the food line. My heart raced.

Would he recognize me? And if he did, would he lash out at me or tell everyone about my derogatory comment?

I reddened and nervously stirred the scrambled eggs, trying to pretend nothing was wrong. When I looked up he was standing right in front of us. No need to wonder if he'd recognize me; he stared at me, the few features of his face not obscured by his dirty gray beard were rock hard. His hands gripped the food tray tightly, his long fingernails wrapping over the raised edge like a yard rake.

"Hi, Al," Jenae said, as if they were life long friends. "You hungry this morning?"

Al, as she called him, didn't say a word or acknowledge Jenae in any way. He stood there glaring at me. My hand trembled as I silently scooped some eggs onto his plate.

"Well, we got some good hot food here for you," Jenae said as she filled the rest of his plate with hash browns.

Al directed a short growling noise towards me—was he part dog?—and walked over to the drink tray. I gulped.

"That's odd," Jenae said with a frown. "He's usually more friendly than that. Never says much, but he'll at least smile at me. Wonder what's wrong? He sure seemed angry at you for something."

There was no way I could tell her now what I'd done. It would have to wait. But I would tell her, wouldn't I? I turned to Jenae and shrugged my shoulders. "You say his name is Al?"

Jenae spoke out of the side of her mouth as she continued to serve food. "That's what I call him. It's short for Aqualung. A.L."

"Oh, got it."

"I have no idea where he got the name Aqualung. I wonder what his real name is."

When all the homeless had been served, those serving sat down together and ate, too. I asked Jenae how long she'd been doing this.

She took a sip of tea and wrapped her hands around the hot mug. "I just started coming two weeks ago. Believe it or not, you're partially the reason I'm here."

I was? My raised eyebrows must have revealed my surprise.

"Seriously. Remember I said your performance on the subway encouraged me to help out? Well, this is what I came up with. I always knew I wanted to do some kind of service work. I just never thought it would be with the homeless. But after seeing you and that homeless guy on the subway, well, it made an impression on me. I'm often afraid of taking something on or making the effort to help if the odds don't look good. You didn't care about the odds, you just did what you thought was right. Anyway, I'm only here two or three days a week. With school and volleyball there's no way I could do this every morning."

"That's still a lot of early mornings." I contemplated getting up this early on multiple mornings and shuddered.

"Oh, that's nothing," she flicked her wrist. "Paul is here every morning. Has been for years, right, Paul?"

"Yes, I've been here awhile," he answered from the other end of the table. Without his apron on, I could see he dressed like many of the professors on campus: dress pants, collared shirt, V-neck sweater. "Not as long as some of these men, though," he said. "I've been told some have been coming here five, ten years. Can you imagine that?"

Incredulous, I shook my head and noticed Jenae doing the same. Ten years? How could that happen?

Just then Ray walked over and greeted everyone by their first name. Brown hair with tiny flecks of grey and black rimmed glasses framed a weathered face. From the shoulders up he looked to be nearing fifty. His body was a different story. He was lean and muscular and looked to be in great shape. He sat down next to Jenae and raised his cup of black coffee. "Thanks for another fantastic meal."

She raised her mug of tea and they clanked their cups. "You're more than welcome."

"So," Ray said as he rested his elbows on the table, "Jenae tells me you're from Northern New Jersey. I was born and raised in Jersey City, but I've lived in New Mexico, Colorado, Indiana—you name it. Yeah, I've ridden the rails and seen a lot of this country." He extended a finger, placed it between the lenses on his glasses and pushed them up his nose.

"When did you leave New Jersey?" I asked.

"Just after high school, in the mid 60's. It was a stupid thing to do. Foolish teenage anger, I guess. My dad and I got in a big fight. I told him off and left. Never returned. That was a long time ago. He died without me ever seeing him again. Wish I'd gone back, at least just once. But maybe it was better I left so he never knew what happened to me. I was out west when I heard the news. Spent a lot time out west. Beautiful country out there."

"In all your travels, have you ever been to Idaho?" Jenae asked.

He had and spent the next ten minutes regaling us with stories of hitch hiking across the state in the early 70's. "Whole lotta nothing out there," he finally concluded.

"Hey, that's not true," Jenae objected mildly.

"Well, Pocatello's not bad, I'll give you that. But between there and Boise might as well be the surface of the moon." He pushed his glasses up his nose again.

"Yes, but didn't you once tell me a story, Ray," Paul said, "about meeting a man there. Wasn't he the first one to tell you about the gospel?"

"Sure was. He picked me up in a shiny '65 Mustang. It was in great shape. We rode with the top down. It was hot and windy but we had a blast. Looking back, it's hard to believe he picked me up. My hair was really long and I had a beard too. I was a hippie and looked the part. But he was the friendliest person I ever met. He told me the whole story of Jesus. I'd never heard it before so I asked a lot of questions. He was patient and answered every one of them. With all that wind, we had to shout so could hear each other."

"What was his name?" Jenae asked.

"Never got it. Believe that? We rode together for a good three hours and he never told me his name. I was either too much of a jerk to ask or too busy thinking about what he said. As far as I'm concerned, that man might as well have been an angel. Anyway, he dropped me off in Boise and left. Sure wish I had taken to heart what he told me. Spent the next dozen years screwing my life up. The tragedy is, I knew the truth. He'd told me. And I knew it was true. I just kept running from it."

Smiling, Paul raised his mug of coffee. "Maybe it's time to stop running."

"Now ain't that the truth," Ray said with a laugh. He looked around the table and, seemingly uncomfortable with all the attention, changed the subject. "Anyway, Thomas, Jenae tells me you can really shoot the rock."

I blushed. "I try."

"Oh, I'll bet you more than try. The way she puts it, you're knockin' em down one after another. You know, I don't play much basketball these days, but I'd love to get in the gym and shoot."

"You should come some time. I can get you in. We'll shoot together."

"Wow, really? That'd be great. I'll show you my Larry Bird form." He raised his arms and mimicked a shot.

"You a Larry Bird fan too?"

His smile beamed. "You bet! Been watching him for years. I try to watch his form closely. I'm getting pretty close. Yeah, basketball's a great workout. Great for the cardiovascular system. Every chance I get I try and spend time in the YMCA. Mostly boxing exercises. Jump rope, speed bag, heavy bag—but I do lift as well. Lots of push-ups and pull-ups too. Got used to doing stuff like that in prison. It's the exercise of choice for most guys. Now that I'm out, I like going to the 'Y.' You know I could spend, oh man, hours there, and the thing is, well ... well, I don't have a job right now. And that's ..." He paused, searching for the right words. "That's a problem."

He took a sip and nervously adjusted his glasses.

"Ray," Paul said, "didn't you just have a job interview?"

Ray nodded. "Uh, yes sir."

"How did it go?"

Ray absentmindedly pushed his glasses up his nose again. The grin was gone, replaced by a serious look of concentration. "Well, funny you should ask. You see, I ... uh ... well, it didn't go very well."

"Why not?"

"Well, it just ..." He motioned with his hand then smacked the table. "I just couldn't believe it." Ray's forehead was red and he made a fist with both hands. "The stupid luck of it." He paused then took a deep breath into his chest and sighed as if in defeat, slumping his elbows onto the table. "This guy asks for my I.D. so he can get some paperwork going. I opened up my wallet to get my I.D. and out falls my AA appointment card." He shook his head, then looked off in the distance. "I mean, who's going to hire me after that?"

Paul thought for a moment. "So what did you do?"

"Well, I left. What do you think I did?"

"Did he say anything to you?"

"Who?"

"The man you were interviewing with?"

"About what?"

"Your AA card, you leaving the interview."

"Yeah, he asked where I was going and I told him I was going to get a drink." Ray's face reddened and his shoulders stiffened.

"But why did you leave?" Paul persisted.

"Well, that stinking little AA card fell out," Ray said in an exasperated voice. "I mean what are the odds?"

Paul extended both his hands towards Ray. "Okay, Ray. Calm down." His voice, which had a musical quality to it, never wavered or rose. "Now I ask you, what is the big deal with an AA card? It shows you go to AA meetings. Do you think we didn't tell this employer about you? Yes, we informed him of your past and of your future. Your immediate future includes the AA. So what? It also includes me and Jenae and others helping you."

Ray started to calm down.

"Ray," Paul continued, "this man, the man you were interviewing with, knew all about you. I told him myself. You could have carefully pulled out that little AA card and slapped it on his desk and still gotten the job!" Paul laughed so hard, his entire body shook. After a moment, Ray smiled too and shrugged his shoulders as if he didn't know what to say.

Once he'd stopped laughing, Paul continued. "Mistakes happen, but it was your choice to let it get to you. Take this as a learning opportunity. Next time forget about pride. Forget about making a mistake and looking silly. Be humble. Even if you spill your entire cup of hot coffee on the man, don't walk away. Don't throw in the towel and retreat like a dog to his vomit. Simply grab the man a napkin and then get on with the interview. Say to him, 'Have your pants cooled off? May I still have the job?'"

Ray chuckled and let his coffee cup linger at his mouth as he slowly took another drink.

"Right?" Paul asked rhetorically as he looked at the eyes around the table. "This is how we mature. Like Thomas here, our new friend. Say he misses a shot in a big game. What's he going to do—never shoot again? He wouldn't be much good on the court if he did that."

"Hey," Ray chipped in, "if Thomas hits half his shots that's considered good!"

"And I've seen him shoot," added Jenae as she looked at me. "He doesn't miss much."

"Excellent," Paul said. "So, Ray's going to get another job and Thomas is going to make a lot of shots. Jenae, what are you and I going to do?"

"We're going to save the world!" She playfully lifted her mug in a mock toast.

"Jenae my dear, our gracious Lord in heaven has already done that. So why don't we just start cleaning the dishes?"

"RAY'S BEEN IN and out of prison for years," Jenae said, as we walked back to campus. It had warmed up since the early morning, but it was still chilly under an overcast sky. During the time we were in the church basement the city had come to life. Taxi cabs honked as they hustled down the street and the sidewalks bustled with people.

"His alcoholism has basically ruined his life," she said.

I nodded. Despite being in shape, it did look like life had been hard on him.

"You know," Jenae continued, "if he had a steady job I think he could make it. Of course it all depends on him."

"Well, it seems he really likes you."

"Oh, Ray is great. He has his moments, like everyone else there, but there is no quit in him. I love that about him. I wish I could do more. You mentioned shooting together at the gym. He'd love that. He's always talking about his workouts."

"I'd love to. But how would I get in contact with him? I mean where does he live? He's not on the streets, is he?"

She shook her head. "Not these days from what Paul tells me. He's usually at a YMCA or homeless shelter of some kind. In the past he's been in jail or halfway houses. I think he also has friends that he shacks up with occasionally."

"That's good. On the cold nights, there are some homeless guys that sleep on this big metal grate near my dorm. I walk right by them and say 'hi.' Three, four guys are there trying to stay warm with the heat coming up from some vent below. I can't imagine what they're going to do when it gets really cold." I thought back to this morning's cold weather and shuddered. "Here I am sleeping in a warm bed every night, and these guys, who know my name, are out in the cold. It's bizarre."

"It's awful what some of those men go through."

"Does Ray have any skills, job wise? What can he do?"

"I don't know. Most times when he does have a job, he's either washing dishes or mopping floors, that kind of thing. He's burned so many bridges it's tough. He doesn't have many friends left to turn to." She sighed. "I pray for him all the time."

"You know, when you mentioned dishwasher, I had a thought. I could talk to Tony of Cortellesi Pizza. He owns the place and he's a big GW hoops fan. The coaches took me there on my recruiting visit. When he's not at the restaurant, I sometimes see him hanging out at the gym playing pickup ball. I heard him say once he's taken guys who are down on their luck and given them jobs as dishwashers. It's a long shot, but I could ask him about Ray."

"Would you?" She stopped walking and grabbed my arm. "Because that would be great. You'll really ask him?"

"Sure. I'd be happy to."

"Thanks, Thomas!"

She reached out and gave me a big hug. I was caught totally off guard. Her embrace was so full and complete. It wasn't like bending over to lightly hug my diminutive grandmother. After that, my step had a bit extra pep in it.

"You know, I'm glad you invited me. This was fun. Meeting Paul and Ray, hanging out with you."

"It was a lot more fun going with you than going alone. Anytime you want to come, just let me know."

"Thanks, but a couple days a week … I think it would just make me tired."

"Oh, come on, it's not that early!" She nudged my shoulder with hers as we continued to walk.

Smiling, I said, "I guess. Now hanging out in the gym and shooting with a guy like Ray or anybody else, I could do that every night."

"I'll bet you could."

CHAPTER 6

MADNESS. THE COLLEGE basketball season begins and ends in madness. NCAA rules allow teams to conduct official practices starting October 15th. Some schools celebrate the start of the season with a Midnight Madness event. Part practice, part party, teams start the event, usually in front of a raucous crowd, right after midnight on the morning of the 15th. It's mostly dunk contests and scrimmages, not defensive slides and other mundane drills that take up the bulk of most early season practices.

The month of March is of course when March Madness takes place. Conference tournaments, with their intense rivalries and an automatic entry into the Big Dance on the line, dial up the heat the first week of March. The NCAA tournament fills in the rest. Millions of fans fill out tournament brackets then settle in to watch lots of games on TV. It all culminates in the Final Four and crowning of a national champion.

When I arrived at GW, I highlighted October 15th on my calendar. I couldn't wait for the day to arrive. We didn't have a Midnight Madness event scheduled, so I decided to hold my own. Around 8:00 p.m. on the night of the 14th I put on my gray GW sweats, grabbed my ball and headed to the gym for an epic night of shooting.

I was halfway there when I heard a familiar voice behind me. "I know where you're headed." With the hood of my sweat top covering my head I didn't have any peripheral vision so I had to do a 180 degree turn to see Jenae standing in front of me. "To the gym, right?" She nodded in the direction of the Smith Center.

Running into Jenae somewhere on campus was about the only time I saw her these days. The past few weeks had been busy. Jenae was in the thick of her volleyball season, I had all my basketball commitments, and we had classes, homework, and midterms. How Jenae found the time and energy to still go the soup kitchen was a mystery to me. I hadn't been back since the morning we went together. I wanted to get up early and go, but most nights I got to bed too late, either because I went to the gym to shoot or I was up doing homework. With time at a premium, I always tried to make the most of these moments with Jenae. It wasn't hard. She was so easy to talk to and her smile warmed up even the coldest nights, like tonight. "Yep, going to do some shooting," I said. "And let me guess. You're headed to the library."

"Nope. I'm headed to the gym too. I left some stuff in my locker."

"I'll walk you there," I said as I pulled off my hood so I could see her better.

"Thanks. I'm not a big fan of walking on campus alone at night. It's kind of scary for a small town girl. So tomorrow is your big day, isn't it? First day of practice." It was just like her to say something without me bringing it up first.

"It is! I was so keyed up I couldn't sit still in my room so I thought I'd go get some last minute shooting in. You know, so I can be sharp for tomorrow."

"You bet," Jenae muttered under her breath. She was looking straight ahead, distracted by something or someone.

Campus was mostly quiet, but when I followed her gaze up the street towards the gym, I saw a dark, shadowy figure. Whoever he was, he was not walking but swaggering along the sidewalk. Still twenty yards away the figure waved and shouted, "Hey there, big guy! How's it going?"

Jenae recognized the voice before I did. "Ray? Is that you?"

He waved again. "Oh, hey there, Jenae. Didn't recognize you. Just saw this tall fella walking towards the gym with a basketball in hand and knew immediately who it was." He came on a bit further and stopped underneath a street light just outside the Smith Center entrance. He wore thick tan work pants and heavy work boots. An insulated red and black checkered flannel shirt served as a jacket. It was partially unbuttoned, exposing a green collared shirt and a white t-shirt underneath that.

"Where are you going, Ray?" Jenae asked with clear concern.

"Headed home." The street light illuminated an ear to ear grin. "Just got done with my shift washing dishes at Cortellesi's."

The same day I met Ray at the soup kitchen I asked Tony Cortellesi, the owner of Cortellesi Pizza, if he'd take Ray on as a dishwasher. Even after filling him in on Ray's checkered past, Tony agreed immediately. I put him in touch with Paul and between the two of them, they got Ray settled into his new job. About a week later I happened to be walking by the restaurant, so I stopped in to see if Ray was working. He was and as soon as he saw me, he bolted from the kitchen with dripping wet hands. He quickly pealed off his big green rubber gloves and shook my hand so hard it hurt. "Thanks a million, Thomas," he said. "You have no idea how much this means. Thanks a million."

I think Jenae must have forgotten that Ray worked a lot of nights because she fumbled over her words. "Oh, of course. Right. So, where is home for you now, Ray?" I was wondering the same thing.

"Last few weeks I've been staying with my old friend, Ronnie," Ray replied. "He's barely keeping his head above water. Got himself a small apartment nearby. He lets me sleep on the couch if I give him a little bit of rent money, which I can now, thanks to you," he said pointing at me.

"That's great. So, how is the job? Going well?" I asked.

"Man, It's awesome. I love it. Tony's a great guy, and it helps me stay sober, above ground, and out of jail! Thanks again."

"You're welcome. Glad it's going well."

"Say, what're you doing right now?" He clapped his hands together. "Let's you and me go shoot some hoops!"

"That's right. You and I've never shot together."

"So let's go now! You can get me in, can't you?"

I hesitated. I usually loved having someone to shoot with, but I was looking forward to having the gym, or at least a basket, all to myself tonight. I'd told Ray I would take him shooting and couldn't go back on my word. "You bet I can get you in. Come on, Ray. Let's go shoot."

"Hot dog!" Ray clapped his hands loudly.

Jenae went to her locker while Ray and I headed into the gym. It was open gym time for anyone who wanted to play. This time of night was usually busy and hard to find an empty basket, but not tonight. There was one full court game of ragged looking pickup ball going on. That left two other hoops un-used.

"Man, this is just what I needed," Ray said as he fired up a jumper that missed badly. "You don't mind rebounding for me, do you?" He stripped down to his white undershirt and removed his boots while I took off my sweat top. He was a funny sight standing there in his stocking feet with dishwater stained pants.

"Not a bit, as long as you return the favor," I said, passing Ray the ball. I looked around hoping to see Jenae, but she was nowhere in sight.

"Sounds good to me," Ray said. "Hey, let me get warmed up and then we'll go make it–take it."

Make it–take it was what I was used to growing up. If you made a shot the person rebounding passed it back to you until you missed. Once you missed a shot then the rebounder got to shoot until he missed. It was a simple solution to having one ball and more than one person wanting to shoot.

That Ray was thrilled to be out on the court shooting hoops was obvious. But it was also painfully obvious that he couldn't shoot a basketball to save his life, or he couldn't hit the broad side of a barn, or he couldn't toss it into the ocean. Take your pick of sayings, they all described Ray. I tried not to laugh, but after about five bricks in a row, I couldn't help it.

"Oh, stop your laughing, Conner," Ray said with a smile on his face. "I know I can't shoot, but just wait. I'm not fully warmed up yet."

"I'm sorry, Ray. I shouldn't laugh."

"Oh, go ahead, go ahead. We'll see who's laughing once I catch fire! I just gotta loosen up. Been doing too many push-ups and pull-ups."

He continued to miss shot after shot. He butchered nearly every technical aspect of shooting a basketball. His feet were not lined up with the basket, nor were his shoulders. His big, thick hands smothered the ball at awkward angles. Instead of following through by flicking his fingers and wrist in a smooth downward motion, he pushed the ball out of his hands, producing a wicked knuckleball that hardly rotated at all. He shot the ball right handed but positioned the ball over his left eye. Knees bent inward and his elbows out, his thickly muscled body uncoiled in a spastic explosion of arms and legs when he released the ball.

He finally made a shot after missing well over a dozen. "Okay, I'm warm now. From here on it's make it-take it."

I chuckled softly as I passed him the ball. "Sounds good. Let's see what you got, Magic Johnson!"

"Ha! You're gonna see some Larry Bird shooting right about now." He bent his knees, his stocking feet slipping on the court, corkscrewed his entire body and then shot, limbs going everywhere. His shot ricocheted off the rim and backboard.

"Okay, your turn, Conner." Ray was still smiling like a kid on Christmas morning. "Let's see it."

I stood out between the free throw line and the three point line and started shooting. I made my first, then second, then third. Pretty soon I was at eight straight from that spot.

"Aw come on, Conner. Move around a bit," Ray kidded as he passed me the ball. So I did and I kept on hitting shot after shot. My shot felt good, like actually throwing a ball into the ocean. The dimples on the ball flicked off of my fingertips with each follow through. Even if my shoulders weren't totally square to the basket, or I leaned a bit to one side, I was so dialed in it didn't matter. I could adjust my follow-through, change the arc of the shot, release the ball higher or lower. Whatever I did worked. I didn't have to think about it, I just did it. Sixteen straight, then twenty.

"Now that's Larry Bird shooting!" Ray was ecstatic. He whipped a crisp bounce pass to me. "You ain't missed yet! That's twenty in a row!" Ray started counting out loud on each shot. Twenty-one, twenty-two. When I entered the zone, it was amazing how simple it seemed. I made thirty-two straight shots before I finally missed.

Ray got the rebound and didn't know what to do. He looked at me then at the ball like something had just gone wrong with it. He shook his head. "Man, I've never seen anything like that! Conner, you've got a gift. You've really got a gift. I'm forty-two years old and there's nothing in my life that I can do that well. I mean nothing. You're eighteen and can shoot like that?" He squeezed the ball like he was going to pop it. "Man, the good Lord really gave you a gift. You're going to go places. Not my places. You're going to the NBA, fella."

The feel of the ball lingered on my fingertips. "Thanks, Ray. This was exactly what I needed."

It was Ray's turn to shoot again, and I rebounded miss after miss. "You just keep shooting," I said. "Don't worry about having to make it. We gotta work on your shot, get your form down." It was going to take some work. Hold your follow through, get the ball onto your fingertips, eyes on the rim, go straight up, not side to side—these were some of my suggestions. He was listening but nothing seemed to work. I was getting a workout running down his misses.

Finally I stood next to Ray and tried manipulating his arms into the proper shooting position while he held onto the ball. He squinted past me then said, "Is that Jenae hiding up there in the bleachers?" He waved with his left hand while the ball dropped out of his right. "What's she doing up there?"

I turned and looked up into the concrete bleacher seats. Sitting by herself, she smiled and slowly gave a subtle wave back. Had she been there the whole time? Had she just seen me make all those shots in a row? I felt my shoulders rise.

She stood up and walked down the stairs and out of sight, only to emerge through a doorway and onto the court a moment later. "Looks like you guys are having fun," she said as she walked over to us.

Ray enthusiastically recounted my shooting streak and how much his shooting had improved, thanks to my help. Considerable exaggeration was applied to both.

"I saw it all," Jenae said. "But guys, I can't stay any longer. I'm going to the kitchen tomorrow and need my sleep. You going, Ray?"

"If I can drag myself out of bed I will."

"Sounds good. See ya, Thomas. Have a great practice tomorrow."

In an instant my mind produced an old fashioned scale; stay and shoot on one side, walk Jenae home on the other. It tipped heavily to one side. "Wait," I said to her and she stopped, "I'll walk you back."

"What?" Ray asked. "We're just getting warmed up." He pushed his glasses up his sweaty nose and they fell right back down again.

Hurriedly, I grabbed my hooded sweat top that was sitting underneath the basket. "I'm good, Ray. Feel free to stay and shoot as long as you'd like. Just leave my ball at the front desk. They'll safeguard it for me. Let's do this again. And next time, I'll stick around longer."

He looked at me quizzically then the lights went on. "Oh, yeah. Got it. You should go. Escorting that lovely lady home is the gentlemanly thing to do."

Ray stood there caressing the ball as Jenae and I walked toward the exit. The moment we stepped outside, the cold night air chilled the sweat on the back of my neck. I pulled my hood up in defense.

Jenae pulled a fleece hat out of her pocket and put it on. It was multicolored with a short tassel on top and two longer ones that dripped down over her ears. Even with that goofy little thing on she was adorable.

We walked for a bit, neither of us saying a word. I don't know what she thought of the silence, but I found it unnerving. Looking for something to say, I blurted out, "Cold, huh?" Brilliant.

She chuckled. "Yes, it is."

"So, how do you get up so early for the soup kitchen during the season? Seems like by afternoon you'd be exhausted."

"At times I am, but it's so worth it. Those early morning hours are some of my most cherished moments. The smiles, the thankfulness, the humble nature of many of them, it's a contrast to volleyball practice for sure. We've got some pretty big egos on our team. Sometimes it takes the fun out of the game."

"Hmm. We got the same thing going on in our pick up games."

"I'll bet. Thomas," she said, her voice carrying more seriousness to it. "I know how much you like to come to the gym and shoot, so I think it's great you took the time to hang out with Ray tonight."

"Oh, it was nothing. It's always more fun to shoot when someone's rebounding for you. He's sure got a funny shot."

"Well, thanks anyway. It just seems so many guys couldn't be bothered with helping others. Especially athletes. We get catered to a lot and I think it sometimes goes to our heads. I'm glad you're different."

I smiled. "Thanks."

"He really likes you, you know."

"Ray does?"

"Yes. He always asks about you when I see him at the soup kitchen."

"Really? Well, I should get back there one of these days."

We walked in silence again and for a moment I entertained the idea of suggesting we go together tomorrow morning. But then thoughts of the first day of practice crowded out any other plans.

When we reached the entrance to her dorm, she turned and said, "Thanks for walking with me."

"My pleasure."

She smiled and playfully punched my shoulder. "All right, shoot the lights out tomorrow, Conner. Call me afterwards and let me know how it went."

CHAPTER 7

OCTOBER 15TH. IT finally arrived. All morning I thought about practice. Like a Presidential inauguration, this was going to be the day I made my grand entrance onto the college basketball scene. This was the day I'd show Brian and everyone else how good I was. Soon, all the colleges that overlooked me in high school would know too.

I walked to the gym imagining everyone who saw me on the sidewalk knew where I was headed and knew how important this day was. Not just to me, but to the University.

Jenae's 'shoot the lights out tomorrow, Conner,' played in my head, over and over. Shoulders back, head high, I marched into the gym, ready to conquer the world.

The first order of business was to see Max at his office outside the locker rooms. He was the equipment manager in charge of all the uniforms and practice gear. He had dark skin, a neatly cropped afro, and was quick with a smile despite working in an office that was steamy and cramped with laundry machines and shelves stacked with towels and jerseys. Max usually stood at the walk up window where he handed out all the gear. And not just to us basketball players, but the baseball, soccer, and wrestling teams too. As I approached he handed me a cloth mesh bag with shorts, jersey, socks, and jockstrap inside.

"Good luck, kid," he said with a wink.

When I walked into the locker room, I crossed the navy blue carpet and went straight to the practice schedule posted on the wall.

Jim had told me about that too. The coaches posted this sheet laying out the entire practice—what drills we'd do, for how long, and the point of the drill. It also showed who was wearing blue and white. Jim's opinion aside, I was sure I would be on the White Team.

Then I read the sheet.

White Team	Blue Team
1 - Barger	1 - Gleason
2 - Patterson	2 - Jones
3 - Davis	3 - Conner
4 - Williams	4 - Dugan, Rogers
5 - Hodges	5 - O'Neill, Dugan, Rogers

I froze. Was I reading this right? Brian's on the White Team and I was on the Blue Team?

I read it again. Brian Patterson was the only underclassman on the White Team, the rest of the starters were seniors: Jim Barger at point, Kevin Williams at power forward, Robert Hodges at center, and Matt Davis at my position.

Jim, Kevin, and Robert on the White Team made sense. They were returning starters and they'd dominated their competition during our fall pickup games. But Brian and Matt? How did they get ahead of me on the depth chart?

Matt was the kind of guy that would one day make a great coach. But he didn't play enough to command the respect that Jim did. And he was a classic "tweener"—too slow to be effective as a guard, too short to be a good forward. Yeah, he was tough, but so was I. Besides, Matt's toughness was playing through sprained ankles and bruised elbows. On the court, where it really mattered, I had clearly outplayed him.

Across the room Brian and Coleman dressed and talked in their usual loud voices. Was it me, or was Brian's voice even louder now that he had a white jersey on? The practice schedule stared at me as

I dressed. I wanted to tear the sheet off the wall and throw it into the trash.

Assistant coach Kenny Jennings burst into the locker room. "Okay, fellas," he said full of enthusiasm. "First day of practice! We ready to get after it?"

Coach Jennings was in his mid-twenties and stood just under six feet tall. I knew him well from all the time he spent recruiting me. He used to call me at my home in New Jersey and ask how my jump shot was. He was a big fan of my game and told me often. His youthful looks, combined with the GW sweat pants and t-shirt he wore, made him look more like my teammate than coach.

"You know it, coach," Brian shouted back.

I didn't say a word.

Just then the other assistant coach, Sharm Ciancio, sauntered in. "All right young men. This is it. Make sure you lace 'em up good and tight. Going to do some running today!"

Coach Ciancio was older and more reserved than Coach Jennings. Short and balding, he had a barrel chest and thick mustache. He was the only black coach we had and spent a lot of time on the road recruiting. He surveyed the room, nodded then walked out.

"Hey, let's make sure we're all up on the floor early," Coach Jennings said. "You freshmen need directions to the court? Just let me know." Coach Jennings loved to kid, but I wasn't in the mood for it. He vigorously clapped his hands as he walked out. "First day of practice! Let's have a tremendous day!"

Tremendous? Hardly. I wanted to take his "tremendous" and chuck it into the trash with the practice schedule!

Once dressed I took a long look at the photos of Larry Bird I had taped to the inside of my locker door then slammed it shut.

Humiliated, I walked onto the court wearing the blue jersey. On the Blue Team with me were Alex, Coleman, David Dugan, Elijah Gleason, and Tim Rogers. Despite being 6'11", Alex stunk. With his height and some hard work Alex had the possibility of becoming a good player. Problem was, Alex had an aversion to hard work, or any kind of work for that matter. This drove the coaches nuts. He belonged on the Blue Team.

David had a nice shooting touch. He was a good rebounder and defender. I was impressed with him. But Kevin made him look ordinary. Unless Kevin or Robert were in foul trouble, David wasn't going to see much playing time beyond ten to twelve minutes a game. He too belonged on the Blue Team.

The same held true for Coleman, Elijah, and Tim. They were either stuck behind better players or just not that good.

But me, I didn't belong with these guys. I was livid. Despite Jim's warnings, I hated Brian and the other White Teamers the moment I stepped onto the court. Clearly, Coach Ross had not seen enough of our pickup games during September and early October. That was normal. Coaches aren't supposed to watch their teams play before October 15th. But if he had, he'd have seen me out-play nearly everyone! There must be something going on that I didn't know about. Was Coach Ross testing me? Did he want to see how I'd respond to adversity?

Because of what Jim said about freshmen starting, I thought Coach Ross would put Coleman or Elijah on the White team and make Brian earn his spot. But it didn't happen. Sure, Brian had played well during our pickup games, but so had I. And Brian had assumed the starting job was his the moment he stepped on campus. Now that it was official, he'd be even more insufferable to live with.

In the minutes leading up to practice, I warmed up at a basket all by myself. I didn't want to talk to anyone. I wanted to play and get this blue jersey off. Alex came over. I barely acknowledged him. He could hardly walk and dribble at the same time.

"So, on the Blue Team, huh?" Alex said with a big grin I didn't appreciate. "Dude, I'm right there with you. And Brian a starter on the White Team? Please. As if his head isn't big enough already?"

He kept talking and I kept shooting, avoiding eye contact. He was so clumsy. The ball rattled around in his hands like they were metal. He had no feel for it. He broke nearly every fundamental rule of shooting. And I was on this guy's team? Where was his passion for doing things right? Where was his sense of commitment and honor for the game? It was in the simple things, like holding onto the ball. He couldn't even do that right. When I held the ball or took a shot it mattered. I took it seriously. My hands felt every dimple. They could sense if the ball needed more or less air or had the slightest bit of lopsidedness. Even if I was just warming up, I shot with a—

Coach Ross's whistle pierced the air and my thoughts. Practice was starting. I would show them, every one of them. I would prove to the coaches and Brian that I could play, that I belonged in the starting lineup.

We all huddled around Coach Ross at center court. He gave us a brief welcome to official practice, the "here's what I expect" speech and the "now let's get to it" pep talk. For the next two hours it was one drill after another. I was lights out during the shooting drills.

One final drill remained before we scrimmaged. Full court one-on-one. I hated this drill. It exposed the two worst parts of my game—dribbling under pressure and guarding someone one-on-one. If I went up against Tim Rogers or Matt Davis it wouldn't be that bad, but when I heard Coach Ross pair me up with Brian, my stomach turned. What was he doing? Why wasn't he pairing up guards with other guards and forwards with other forwards? How in the world was I going to stop Brian?

"Freshman up first," Coach Ross said.

The goal of the drill was for the defender, totally exposed with no help, to force the ball handler to slowly dribble his way up court. The person on offense was trying to get past the defender and score as quickly as possible.

I got into my defensive stance in front of Brian. Knowing how quick he was I gave him lots of room. My leg muscles jumped nervously. He started dribbling, gave a few jukes then made his move. He exploded to his right and I nearly tripped trying to untangle my feet. He blew by me like I was sitting down. I trailed him downcourt and watched him make an uncontested dunk.

The hoots and hollers from my teammates stung. "All right," Coach Ross said, "let's try that again. Thomas, you've got to give ground to someone faster. Don't play him straight up. Try and force him to change direction."

When Brian and I played one-on-one that one afternoon, no one was watching. Now the whole team was. I couldn't let him embarrass me like that again. We got back in our same spots. Brian had a cocky grin that I wanted to wipe off his face. This time I shaded Brian to his left, hoping he would be a bit slower dribbling with his off hand. It didn't work. He went right around me again.

I wanted to run and hide. Watching Robert do the same to Alex didn't help.

We ended the day with a Blue-White scrimmage. Coach Ross watched while Coach Ciancio coached the White Team and Coach Jennings my Blue Team. I redeemed myself with a number of made shots. But the long practice was getting to me. My lungs burned, the bottoms of my feet were on fire, my groin muscles were sore, and my legs felt like lead. I'd run out of gas.

The White Team hammered us. We gave up four straight baskets, the last one on another drive by Brian. As soon as his shot cleared the net, Coach Ross blew his whistle.

"All right," he said. "We're done. Great work everybody."

I could barely stand up straight. I was so dehydrated I wasn't even sweating anymore. Coach Ross said a few words and we were dismissed. Moments later I ran to the bathroom and vomited.

By the time I'd refilled my stomach with a gut busting dinner I was ready to call Jenae. I sat in our dorm room and waited for Brian to head to the john so he wouldn't hear anything.

She asked how it went and I hit all my highlights. I never mentioned anything about jersey colors or being embarrassed by Brian. She told me a bit about her first volleyball practice back in August and how nervous she had been.

"You know what," I said during one of the pauses, "we've never gone back to get ice cream."

"You're right. We should do it."

"When's your next home volleyball match?"

"This Friday."

"Great. I'll come watch you play and then we'll celebrate afterwards."

"You're on."

CHAPTER 8

A POWERFUL MINT odor hit me like a brick the moment I walked in the room. Somebody had obviously slathered on Ben-Gay muscle cream. It's an unmistakable scent, one I'd experienced many times in many smelly locker rooms.

It was funny, really, watching guys walk into the locker room and get dressed for practice. It looked more like the lobby of a retirement home. Guys were moaning and groaning, rubbing sore joints, and icing knees.

Like everybody else, I too was stiff and sore from yesterday's practice. Every year I played basketball, it was always the same. No matter how much I played pickup ball or worked out in the off season, I was painfully sore after the first day of practice. The reason was always the same—defensive slide drills. I thought I was playing good defense in our pickup games, but the intensity always rose when a coach was watching. Defense was a big emphasis for Coach Ross and he ran us through lots of defensive drills the first day.

My groin muscles were the sorest, but I felt it everywhere. I tried to ignore the pain as I put on my practice gear. What I couldn't ignore was seeing my name under the Blue Team column on the practice sheet. I vowed not to let this continue.

Just like before the first practice, Coach Jennings walked in the room and clapped his hands. "All right! Tremendous first 'practice, gentlemen. Let's have another one today!" He sniffed the air with a scrunched up nose then waved his hand. "Phew! Easy does it with the Ben-Gay. Who is that? Matt? Gotta be Matt."

I didn't know who had slathered the stuff on, but Matt was moving rather slowly. He had a banged up elbow from diving on the floor for a loose ball and one of his legs looked like a Chiquita banana it was so black and bruised.

When I got to the gym floor Jim was there warming up. He looked as fresh as a rose.

After loosening up, I had a great practice. My intensity was withering on Matt. I wore him out, hoping to make it painfully obvious Coach Ross needed to put me where I belonged. I burned him several times in our scrimmages and didn't let him even sniff an open shot on defense.

The next day, Friday, it was done. The practice sheet said it all. I was the starting White Team small forward.

White Team
1 - Barger
2 - Patterson
3 - Conner
4 - Williams
5 - Hodges

Being on the White Team, where I belonged, felt awesome. My confidence was sky high and the competitive juices flowed. I set out to dominate the scrimmages that were the final portion of practice.

On the first play Brian stole the ball from Alex and went the other way for a breakaway dunk. The next possession he stole the ball from Coleman, dribbled between the legs to get by Matt, and threw me a no look pass for a wide-open jumper. He followed that up with three remarkable moves to the hoop on three straight possessions. I could see Coach Ross nodding in approval to Coach Ciancio.

After Brian scored his fifth straight bucket Coach Ross blew his whistle and, standing next to Coach Ciancio, they conferred for a moment. He said something out of ear shot, but I clearly heard Coach Ciancio's reply. "Go ahead and do it now. Why wait?"

Coach Ross walked over to Brian and put his hand on his shoulder. Brian stood there, dripping sweat, his hands on his hips, breathing heavily.

"I was going to wait to put in these plays, but might as well here. Obviously Brian's ability to get to the hoop adds a dimension to our team that we haven't had in the past. I've got an offensive set I want to put in and it's predicated on his dribble penetration."

He proceeded to put the White Team in spots on the floor and explain how important it will be for Brian to have space to operate, how key Brian is to our offensive efficiency, and how Brian will be the primary option in this offense. We walked through the set first, then ran through it without a defense.

"Okay," Coach Ross said, "let's try it full speed now. Blue Team, you're on defense."

We ran the set and Brian's dribble penetration worked all right. It kept getting me open looks. I hit a three. Then another.

"Thomas," Coach Ross said with what sounded like a hint of impatience, "let's run the play."

I wasn't? I was open and hitting my shots. We ran it again. Brian was open for a brief moment. It would've been a tough pass. I hesitated, then fired. Swish.

Coach Ross blew his whistle. "Thomas, nice shot, but run the play, okay?" There was no hint of anything this time. He was annoyed.

I nodded but wondered what he was so upset about? Brian's penetration was setting me up for open shots. Couldn't he see that?

This was Coach Ross's fifth year as head coach at GW. His first two years produced losing records, but the last two were much better. Each year the record improved and now that everyone on the team was someone he'd recruited to GW, the pressure was on to win. With three returning seniors and a solid backup in Matt, we were going to be very good. But I got the sense he was expecting too much from

Brian and overlooking how much I could contribute. I resolved to be patient. In time, he'd see.

When practice ended I corralled Coach Jennings to rebound for me. I'd been hot all day and I wanted to milk it for all it was worth. Ten minutes later he was done.

"Not bad, Thomas," he said. "But I've got work to do in the office."

I wanted more. Plus, the whole scene with Brian being the key to our offense left a bad taste in my mouth. I had to get rid of it. While they took down the baskets and cleared the main gym for the volleyball match, I headed upstairs to the auxiliary gym to shoot. Thankfully no one was there.

I loved having the gym to myself. Just me, the ball, and a hoop. Nothing else, nobody else. As I fired up one jump shot after another I thought back to all the time I spent shooting growing up. I'd spent countless solitary hours refining my shot in the gym at the old YMCA near my home or on the basket in our backyard.

The YMCA was within jogging distance from my house. On a side street in a small town in a small state that loved basketball, I was not the first to spend hours there working on my game. Nor would I be the last. High school kids hooked on basketball was not exactly a rarity in New Jersey. Despite the popularity of basketball in my hometown, I usually had the YMCA gym to myself. The old wood floor creaked here, groaned there. It was a minefield of dead spots where the ball refused to bounce, so I perfected the art of shooting off the pass. I would toss the ball in the air to myself, mimicking a pass, then catch it and shoot. Toss, catch, shoot, swish. Hours on end.

In the summer when I was there the most, fans were set up near the doors to suck out the stifling hot air and bring cool air in. Despite this, it was still hot and muggy, and I was always covered in sweat. The ceiling lights were inefficient and the small row of windows lining one wall barely let in any sunlight.

But I didn't care that it was hot and dimly lit, that the floor was bad or the walls were inches from the edge of the court. It felt like my private gym and I loved it.

The same held true for my backyard court. It was part of the driveway that wrapped around our house and extended beyond the garage. The huge oak trees that shaded our house created a canopy over the entire court. They kept it cool on sunny days, but also slowed down evaporation after rain showers. In autumn, the court was covered with fallen leaves that crunched under my feet and the ball. When it snowed my older brother, Mike, and I shoveled around the basket first before the rest of the driveway was cleared off.

Two windows faced the court, one over the kitchen sink, the other providing the view for the dining room. I sometimes caught my mother at the sink or my father at the dinner table looking out at me while I shot baskets. My mother's flower beds, which were always in danger of being trampled by errant shots, were located along one side of the blacktop next to the house. The other side sloped away ever so slightly so rain water could run off into the grass. I loved taking fade away jump shots from the far sloping corner. Over the years it became my favorite spot to shoot from.

The court was witness to numerous games of one-on-one between me and Mike, plus plenty of impromptu games with the neighborhood kids. Add in all my shooting and we were constantly replacing worn-out nets. We even wore out the backboard one summer.

It was here where I first fell in love with basketball. I was five years old, playing with my toys in the backyard. I was into dinosaurs at that time. One summer evening after dinner, my father came out with a basketball in hand. "Thomas," he said, leaning down so he was at my eye level, "come and join Mike and I. Let's shoot some hoops." I immediately dropped my little green diplodocus and followed him. That was the very first of many moments together on the basketball court. Over the years he taught me everything he knew.

Years later I was on our backyard court when basketball greatness became my passion. I'll never forget the moment. It was the summer before my sophomore year in high school. I was shooting hoops at night and the lights over the garage and kitchen window cast uneven shadows over the blacktop. The hot summer air was thick with humidity, and the sound of crickets competed with my little portable radio and the bouncing ball.

When my favorite song "*Sweet Dreams*" by the Eurythmics came over the radio, it gave me a rush of adrenaline. I took shot after shot and they all went in. Near the end of the song, as I left the ground for yet another jump shot, something clicked. Before my feet landed on the blacktop and the ball swished through the net, I realized I could be great at this. I was already good, but I became obsessed with being great at basketball. A chill went down my spine.

Over the remaining summers of my high school years I polished the blacktop of my driveway and the wood floor of that gym with the bottoms of my sneakers and droplets of my sweat. Now I was doing the same at GW. The only thing that would make this moment better would be Jenae here rebounding for me. That, I was sure, would—

Oh no! Jenae! I'd been so lost in my thoughts, I lost all track of time and had forgotten about our date!

My shot clanked off the rim. I ran down the rebound and hustled out the auxiliary gym. Not knowing how long I'd been in there, I was hoping the volleyball match was still on. Turning the corner I saw it was! I breathed a huge sigh of relief.

The match was nearly over and in the short time I watched, Jenae didn't play much. Her team was good and dominated by seniors. Their best player happened to play Jenae's position, middle blocker. When Jenae did finally get in, the outcome of the match was all but secured. She got her only block of the night on match point. I shot out of my seat and cheered as loud as I could.

Minutes later I was downstairs in the lobby where most of the girls on the team had congregated to visit with friends and family who had come to watch the match. "Nice block," I said as I gave Jenae a high-five.

"Oh … thanks," she said with a hint of embarrassment. "I was actually out of position."

"Well, you looked good to me. So, we still on for tonight?"

"You bet." She looked me up and down then said, "Guess I'm not the only one who needs to change."

"Yeah, and I still have to shower. Why don't I meet you in front of your dorm in thirty minutes?"

"Give me an hour?"

"Deal."

Jenae went to her locker room and I sprinted across campus to my dorm. After showering and changing, I headed for Jenae's dorm. Figuring I still had a few minutes to spare, I took a detour and went to Manush's.

Manush operated the most popular hotdog stand on campus. It was located at a terrific spot, right across the street from the student union building and a block south of the most frequented bars and restaurants near campus. He did a brisk business and most weekend nights there was a line snaking past his stand.

His stand was covered and enclosed like a tiny RV, just big enough for one person to stand in. There was a door on one side and a large serving window in front. The window slid open and closed so he could stay warm during cold months. He did all his cooking in there and also used it to store everything he sold, except for his drinks. He had a cooler full of ice next to his stand for that. He couldn't leave his stand there over night, so he set it up and took it down every evening, towing it to his home behind his junky little foreign car.

I liked visiting Manush. He was short, bald, had a huge nose and was always friendly. His perpetual smile was mostly obscured by a dark black mustache. I often saw him as I was coming and going to the gym or a class. He sold much more than hotdogs. It was amazing how much stuff he sold out of that rickety little shack. Candy bars, gum, mints, muffins, beef jerky sticks, chips, lip balm, flowers, etc. It was a tiny traveling boutique for hungry, needy college kids.

Some people eat to live. I live to eat. I loved Manush's hotdogs, especially with his cooked onions on top. One of my first meals at GW was a Manush hotdog. They tasted great, but I didn't eat them often since they didn't sit well with my stomach. Alex loved them and was a regular at the stand. He was also regularly passing gas in practice. Jim always complained about Alex's invisible screens.

"Tom my friend," Manush said with typical exuberance, "you want a hot dog?"

"Not tonight, Manush. Just need a few breath mints."

"Any ting else?" Manush said. His Middle Eastern tongue was like a seven-footer that shot-blocked the 'th' sound from making its way into any of his words.

I looked around the shack to see if I did want anything else, then pointed at a vase full of multi colored roses. "I'll take the red one."

"Very good, Tom my friend." From inside his hotdog stand Manush wrapped the stem of the rose in a paper towel and handed it to me.

"How much do I owe you?"

His smile pushed his thick mustache up on his face so it wrapped halfway around his enormous nose like a wreath. "On your home," he replied.

"What?"

"Yes, on your home." He looked puzzled. "Or is it on my home? It's free."

I laughed. "On the house. The saying is, 'It's on the house.' And thanks, Manush."

"Yes, you're welcome. On de house. See you Tom, my friend!" I was always "Tom-my-friend" as if it were one word.

I popped a mint in my mouth and walked to Jenae's dorm. A minute after I arrived she was walking out the front door. "Here," I said handing her the rose. "For the best block of the night!"

She smiled and smelled the rose. "Thanks, Thomas. How sweet of you. So, should we go get some ice cream?"

"Well, if you're hungry can I take you out for dinner too?"

"Am I hungry?" she said as she grabbed her stomach, "you bet I am! Dinner sounds great. Where to?"

"I was thinking Cortellesi's."

While she talked about the volleyball match, I led the way as we walked north towards Pennsylvania Avenue. It was a gorgeous fall evening and she playfully kicked fallen leaves under her feet. The concrete jungle of D.C. didn't leave a lot of space for trees, but there were some. Brown, gold and maroon danced around her ankles. Coming from Idaho, I imagined she missed trees and leaves and nature. Not knowing if she'd be comfortable walking through dark alleys, I avoided them. I wondered if Pocatello had any alleys.

Over the years, the growth of GW had swallowed up large swaths of the Foggy Bottom section of D.C. Some of the old, brick row houses were gone, but some remained. Many of those still around had been converted to commercial use, like the building Cortellesi Pizza was located in.

I had eaten at Cortellesi's on my recruiting visit with Coach Ross and Coach Jennings. They served more than pizza and the food was fantastic—as good as the Italian food I'd grown up on in New Jersey—and that was saying something! The ancient hard wood floors squeaked, the tables were covered with red and white checkered tablecloths, and the walls were adorned with black and white photos. In the photos were celebrities who'd eaten there: politicians, athletes, famous Italian Americans. The place looked like it was straight out of the movie *The Godfather*.

Tony Cortellesi, the owner, greeted us at the door. "Hey, Jenae, Thomas. Look at you two, all dressed up." I was wearing my best khaki dress pants with a blue collared shirt. Jenae was lovely in brown slacks, lilac shirt and a denim jacket. "So, table for two?"

He seated us at a small table in a dimly lit corner near the back of the restaurant. The candle on the table gently flickered, casting shadows on the wall and nearby bottles of olive oil and vinegar.

"Thanks again for hiring Ray," Jenae said to Tony as we sat down. "Is he here tonight?"

"You bet," Tony said as he handed us our menus. "Hard at work as always. I'll tell him you're here. Enjoy." He left us, weaving his way around tables, chatting with other patrons along the way.

Jenae leaned forward, easing her smile into the glow of the candle light. "This is great, Thomas. I came here once to meet Tony and talk about Ray, but I've never actually eaten here before."

"The food's good. You'll like it." I spread my napkin on my lap and did a quick mental checklist of table manners 101. A second later I took my elbows off the table and sat up straighter.

"All right no kissing you two," Ray said as he walked up to our table. His long blue apron was soaked in dishwater and his forehead glistened with sweat. "Got a little something for you."

"Hey, Ray," Jenae and I said in unison.

He put a small vase on the table that had two inches of water in it. He stood up straight, supremely satisfied with himself. "Saw you walk in with that rose. Thought you might need this."

"Thanks, Ray," Jenae said as she delicately unwrapped the rose stem from the paper towel and put it into the vase. "So what's good here?"

Ray patted his stomach. "I like the veal parmigiana, myself."

"That's one of my favorites," I said.

Jenae closed up her menu. "Sounds good to me."

"Well, gotta get back to work. Great seeing you two again. Have fun."

Jenae watched Ray make his way back to the kitchen. "Look at him. I can tell he loves working here." She turned to me. "This is so good for him. Not just so he can earn money, but so he has purpose, responsibility, a place to be. It makes me think of the saying, give a man a fish, feed him for a day, but teach him to fish and you'll feed him for a lifetime."

Just then our waiter approached. Aloof and skinny, with a gold necklace and jet black hair that was slicked back, he spoke with a thick Italian accent. "Is good choice," he said when we ordered.

The food was more than good, it was delicious. I was tempted to lick my plate but thought better of it. It was something Alex might have done, but I wasn't with Alex.

"I'll bet their desserts are just as good," Jenae said. "Maybe we should just eat here instead of going somewhere else for ice cream."

"Sounds great."

When our waiter brought out the spumoni, he put one spoon on the table. "Here is one," he said. "I get another if you like, but this way you can put on each other's nose and lick off."

Jenae laughed and blushed. "We're not there *yet*."

Her "yet" sounded good to me, but our waiter was disappointed. "Very well. Here's another." He dropped the spoon on the table and left. I wondered, was he going to stand and watch us if we went for the one spoon option?

Jenae dove into her multicolored ice cream.

She was still blushing and it was adorable.

CHAPTER 9

I COULDN'T HELP but strut into the locker room early the next morning. Yesterday was such a great day. My first practice on the White Team then a fun date with Jenae. The only thing that could beat that was a game day.

It was Saturday, our first day with two practices. I walked up to the practice sheet to take a quick look at the schedule and could not believe my eyes. I was back on the Blue Team! What was going on? Nobody else had been moved up and down like me. But there it was, on the practice sheet. I was definitely in Blue again.

Jim sat on his chair tying his shoelaces. He'd seen me walk in and go straight for the practice schedule. "I'll bet your wondering why you're back on the Blue Team," he said. He'd read my mind, again.

"How'd you guess?"

"Dude, I told you, you read like an open book. Besides, it was pretty obvious after yesterday."

"Yesterday? What did I do wrong yesterday? I hit nearly every shot I took."

"No, you shot nearly every time you touched the ball. If coach puts in a play, run the play. Don't try and show him he needs to run plays for you. We run plays so we can score, not so *you* can score."

Exasperated, I asked, "Did you tell coach to put me on the Blue Team?"

He laughed as he stood up and turned to go. "Wanted to, but didn't need to."

I spent the morning and afternoon practice in blue. Another day on the Blue Team. For what, making my shots? As tired as I was after our second practice, I lingered to shoot. It was a habit I'd started in high school and no matter how tired I was I always stayed after to shoot.

When I was done and had made my way downstairs, Alex was the only person left in the locker room. He sat slumped on a chair in front of his locker, staring at nothing. Shoulders stooped over, his face sporting bags underneath his eyes, he looked awful. He had suffered all day. Nothing new, just another cold. He was rarely ever healthy or feeling good.

When Alex arrived on campus as a bean pole skinny freshmen, Jim joked he needed to run around in the shower to get wet. Coach Ross wanted him to gain weight and this was one edict Alex followed. He went to all you can eat buffets, ate tons of Hamburger Helper, grabbed late night Manush hotdogs, and drank lots of beer.

He gained the weight all right, most of it tucked into the tire around his waist. Now he needed to trim up more than gain weight, but he still ate everything in sight. There was no dietician on the GW coaching staff so Alex remained on the see-food diet: if he saw it, he ate it. With all the junk he put in his body it was no wonder he was constantly run down.

"You gonna sit there all night or get up and go shower?" I asked. "That is, if you can even walk."

Alex didn't bother to look at me as he mumbled, "I'll make it. Just need some time." His voice came out like a gravel and mucus milkshake.

"I'll say."

He grunted then grabbed his towel and loudly blew his nose in it. "So you in the doghouse?"

"Doghouse? With who?"

"Coach Ross, dummy."

"Why would you think that?"

"Because you're on the Blue Team again."

"That doesn't mean I'm in the doghouse."

"Hey, don't kid yourself, the Blue Team is the doghouse. And you don't belong on it."

"Well, thanks. I don't think I'll be on it for long though."

"Yeah, if you move up I hope you take Brian's spot. Now that's a guy that belongs in the doghouse." He shook his head then his whole body froze before turning to face me. "Wait. If you do that, Brian will be on the Blue Team with me. Never mind, just take Matt's spot."

"Hah, having Brian on the Blue Team with you might motivate you to get in shape so you can play better. Then you could earn your way off the Blue Team."

"Like that will happen."

"You never know. Guys get hurt, get in foul trouble. There might come a time this season when we need you."

"Hog wash. We got Robert and Kevin. I don't care what kind of shape I'm in, I ain't playing much this year."

"Well…"

Alex shook his hand at me as if swatting away my words. He then stripped and wrapped the same towel he'd just blown his nose in around his waist before shuffling out the room towards the showers.

THOSE FIRST FEW days of official practice felt like a roller coaster. From Blue to White, back to Blue. The next week was better. After a few days of keeping my head down, playing hard, and being a bit more selective with my shots, I was back on the White Team.

Even with our grueling afternoon practices, I still had energy for my nighttime shooting sessions. Tuesday nights became my favorite. I would wolf down dinner and rush through my homework so I could get to the gym by eight. Jenae had a class every Tuesday night that ended at 8:45pm. Knowing that walking alone on campus after dark made her uncomfortable, I made sure I was there to escort her home. After I got done shooting, I would walk across the street from the

Smith Center to Funger Hall where her class was. You should have seen the smile on her face the first time I showed up unannounced. She always had a glow about her, but this time her face lit up like a Christmas tree.

I saw that same look on her face right before our first game of the season. It was during pregame warmups. She was sitting in the bleachers with some of her teammates. I was already fired up to play, but when I saw her smile and wave I thought I would burst out of my jersey. It was a home game versus a team we all expected to beat easily, the University of Maryland Baltimore County—more commonly known as UMBC.

A raucous crowd had packed the Smith Center. The student section was right behind our bench and when they stood and leaned over the railing, it seemed like we were all sharing a crowded elevator. The energy and excitement of the first game of the year was overwhelming. When my name was announced during the starting lineups, I ran out onto the court, pouring sweat and shaking in anticipation, and loving every second of it.

We jumped all over UMBC from the opening tip and dominated the first half. But our big lead at half time must have gotten to our heads. In the second half we came out cold and UMBC found their passion and intensity. After picking up my third foul early in the half, I had to sit. UMBC then whittled our double-digit lead to nothing with twelve minutes remaining in the game. Our home crowd got antsy and everyone on our team suddenly got tight. Everybody except Brian. He was lighting it up. Nobody on their team could stop him. It was my first college game ever and Brain was stealing the show. I kept looking over at Coach Ross hoping he'd put me back in the game. With only seven minutes left he finally relented.

"Thomas! Get in there for Matt." As I ran to the scorers table Coach Ross slapped me on the back and said, "Hit some big shots for us, kid."

Once on the court, I saw everyone's face close up. Our two big men, Robert and Kevin, were stunned to be tied with UMBC this late in the game. Jim was concerned but calm, and Brian stood aloof, confident only he could save the day.

It was our ball. We got into our set offense but it quickly broke down as Brian tried to go one-on-one against his defender. He dribbled himself into a trap and nearly turned it over. He passed out of it and I bailed him out by nailing a three-pointer. Moments later I buried another. We were now up six.

Sensing a run, it was UMBC's turn to feel the pressure. They took a poor shot on offense. I grabbed the rebound and rifled the outlet pass to Brian who went the length of the court for a layup. Now down eight, UMBC called timeout. It didn't help them. The Smith Center crowd found their lungs again and kept the noise ratcheted up. After the timeout UMBC missed again. We got the rebound and worked the ball around on offense. With the shot clock winding down, Jim penetrated, drew an extra defender, passed to me in the corner. I hit my third straight three-pointer. That made eleven straight points for us, and I'd scored nine of them.

That run sealed the win.

Despite my big shots, Brian was the story. He led the team with 24 points. In the locker room afterwards all the local reporters crowded around him, not me.

THE NEXT DAY my father called, his voice filled with excitement. "I saw the score in the paper this morning. What a great way to start the season. I want to hear all about it."

I filled him in on the game but he immediately sensed something was bothering me. I could never hide things from him, so I told him exactly what I was thinking. "All anyone could talk about after the game was Brian. Brian this, Brian that. It was as if I'd never hit those shots."

"Thomas, you won," my father said. "You should be thrilled you won and thrilled you played the way you did. 14 points in your first college game—that's awesome. Don't be jealous of Brian. Who cares if he scored 24 points or 42 points? He's your teammate. Be thankful he's on your team and you don't have to guard him."

"Yes, sir," I replied sheepishly, knowing that if I had to guard Brian he might have scored 50.

"And remember, scoring is not everything. When you can make your teammates better with things other than shooting—like passing, defense, setting screens—then the sky's the limit. Just look at the way Magic Johnson plays. He's always making his teammates better."

I cringed. "Dad …"

"Oh, right. Well, Larry Bird does the same thing."

"That's better."

He laughed. "But the key is being willing to do the little things that don't attract the spotlight. Winning and playing your best is more important than adulation. At least it should be."

"You're right. It's silly to be jealous."

"So how's it going with you and Brian? You two getting to be friends?"

"No, not really." Not really? We couldn't stand each other.

"Why not?"

I tried to be brief but must have rambled on for five minutes. His arrogance, his sense of entitlement, his ball-hogging on the court, the way he disrespected my game, I brought it all up. I even told my dad about the time I lost to Brian in that game of one-on-one.

"Well, I encourage you to take the first step. Reach out to him. Overlook your differences. He's going to be your teammate for the next four years. The better you get along off the court, the better you'll play together on the court. Plus, from the things you've said, I get the sense he hasn't had a lot of positive influences growing up. Maybe he needs a friend like you."

Reaching out to Brian was the last thing I wanted to do. "But he's so arrogant, Dad. He doesn't listen to anything I say. Shoot, he doesn't listen to anything anyone says."

"Don't be so quick to judge him, Thomas. You know you've had your moments too."

"I know, but not like him."

"Well I don't know what Brian is like, but trying to figure out who's more arrogant is like trying to figure out who's more pregnant."

I laughed. "All right, Dad. I'll give it a shot. But how many times should I try? I could see starting a conversation with him seven times over the next week and it never ending well. I doubt he'll listen to me."

"I think you should try as many times as you need to. Be a good listener. Build a bridge. Find common ground. And when the opportunity presents itself, share what the Lord has done in your life. Do you want me to mail you an extra Bible to give to him?"

Remembering Brian telling me not to 'start preaching to him from the Bible,' I said, "No, that probably wouldn't be a good idea."

"Okay, but you'll try and talk to him?"

I took a deep breath and blew it out hard. "Yes, Dad, I will."

LATER THAT NIGHT I was sitting at my desk doing homework when Brian walked in. He flopped onto our couch, propped his feet up on the coffee table, and turned the TV on without asking if it would bother me. I shook my head but didn't say anything. Every now and then he'd make a sarcastic comment on what he was watching. I tried to ignore him but my dull history textbook made it easy to get distracted.

"Ridiculous," he blurted out. "Bunch of white jump shooters."

That I couldn't ignore. I pivoted in my chair and saw the preview for the movie *Hoosiers*. I was captivated. Small town in Indiana, underdog High School basketball team, led by a great shooter beating the odds. It seemed they'd made the movie just for me.

"Let me take a wild guess," Brian sneered. "They probably beat some all black team in the end. Please."

"Shhh!" I said without taking my eyes off the screen. To me Indiana was synonymous with good shooting, fundamental basketball. Larry Bird came from Indiana. So did legendary UCLA head coach, John Wooden. The University of Indiana was one of the best college basketball programs in the nation. No matter what the storyline was like I knew I had to see the movie.

"Bet you'd like to see that," Brian deadpanned.

A light went on. Maybe this was an easy chance to reach out. "Why don't we go see it together?" I said.

Brian laughed. "You couldn't pay me to see that trash."

I knew he'd react like this! He's impossible. If my dad could only see Brian like this, he'd know what I was talking about. The guy's head is bigger than the whole state of New Jersey! "Why is it trash?" I shot back. "Looks like a great movie to me."

"Yeah, if you're white."

"What? It's a basketball movie. Who cares what color they are?"

"I do, that's who. *Rocky. The Natural.* Now this thing, *Hoosiers.* When's Hollywood going to make a sports movie with a bunch of black stars? Hmm? I'll go see that movie."

I shook my head. "Ridiculous."

"Yeah, you're right, that movie is ridiculous!"

CHAPTER 10

BY THANKSGIVING WE had won three more games to run our record to 4-0 on the season. Other than the short bus trip we made to Fairfax, Virginia to play George Mason University, all our games had been at home.

Campus was abuzz with Colonial fever. Me and the rest of the starting five played the bulk of the minutes. Matt or Elijah were usually the first ones off the bench, followed by David Dugan and Tim Rogers. Alex and Coleman rarely got on the court. Joe was leading the team in assists, Kevin in rebounds, Robert in blocked shots, Brian in scoring, Matt in floor burns, and me in three-point shooting.

It was hard to argue with our success, but I still felt that Brian took too many shots. Sure he was leading the team in scoring at just under nineteen a game, but his shooting percentage was horrible and he was taking nearly twice as many shots as me. I was second on the team in scoring and hitting just over 50% of my attempts.

Due to our team commitments, neither Jenae or I got to go home for Thanksgiving. We went to the soup kitchen instead. I think it helped ease some of the pain of separation for Jenae, but I could tell it still hurt.

We walked to the old stone church in silence. "Thanks for coming with me," she finally said as we drew near.

"My pleasure."

She reached out and took a tight grip on my hand. "This is the first time I've ever been away from my family for Thanksgiving. I miss them."

I tried to imagine what Thanksgiving at the Swanson home in Idaho was like. Snow covered mountains, aspens and evergreens in the backyard, a warm glow from the fireplace, and everyone wearing sweaters and smiling. I could see Jenae, the oldest of the children, in the kitchen helping her mother prepare the food while her father read stories to the little ones.

At the church they skipped breakfast and served a traditional turkey dinner at noon. When we arrived the basement of the church was stuffed, just like the turkeys. It seemed there were just as many gray haired volunteers from the congregation as there were people looking for a hot meal. Ray was there as usual. The four of us— Ray, Paul, Jenae, and I—all sat together sharing stories and laughter. After another funny story was told, Jenae had tears in her eyes from laughing so hard. "You know," she said, "being here with you guys is the next best thing to being home. Thanks."

That afternoon Jenae ate dinner with her team and I went to Coach Ross's home with the rest of my team for a big Thanksgiving dinner. It was a beautiful place in Maryland set among horse properties with rolling green pastures that looked like the tops of pool tables. Miles of white fencing and towering trees provided the matting and frames for the stately homes. It amazed me that such open country existed so close to the city.

When I got back from dinner I met Jenae outside her dorm. She stood and patted her belly. "So, are you as stuffed as me?"

"Yep."

"I can't believe Coach Ross had you guys over for dinner. He must have cooked a dozen turkeys to feed all of you."

"No, just four. And besides, Coleman wasn't there. He went home to have dinner with his mom."

"Lucky him."

"You should have seen it. Alex spilled cranberry sauce all over their carpet. Coach Ross's wife looked like she'd seen a ghost. To his credit, Alex got down on all fours and cleaned it up. I kind of felt bad for him, so I grabbed some paper towels and helped him out."

"That was nice of you."

I shrugged. "Say, I've got a surprise for you. You up for one?"

"You bet."

"Come on, let's go see a movie."

"Okay. Which one?"

"That's the surprise." I stuck my elbow out inviting her to slide her arm into the crook.

She took my arm. "You lead the way."

The small movie theater I steered us towards was just north of campus. It wasn't until we were close enough to read the small marquee above the entrance that I got nervous. What if she didn't want to see *Hoosiers*? What if she, like Brian, could care less about a bunch of jump shooting Indiana high school basketball players?

"*Hoosiers*! Thomas, I've heard great things about this movie. What a wonderful surprise."

"Really?"

"Well, I had a hunch you might chose this one."

From the start of the movie to the finish, I was riveted. I had goose bumps watching Jimmy Chitwood, the star player for Hickory High School, hit the shot to win the Indiana state championship. Like me, Jimmy was a deadly outside shooter. During the climactic game of the movie, I could hardly sit still in my seat. I peeked over and saw Jenae leaning forward in her seat, caught up in the drama.

After we left the theater, I didn't walk as much as I danced on the streets of D.C., mimicking the moves of Jimmy Chitwood. I pretended to dribble the ball between my legs, behind my back, and then release a jumper that hit nothing but net. Jenae giggled at the sight. She looked so beautiful and basketball seemed such a noble thing. It was always this way with me. Basketball made me feel more deeply. It made me more passionate about everything.

"You look like you want to be the next Jimmy ... what was the guy's name again?"

"Jimmy Chitwood."

"I'll make it," Jenae said modulating her voice deeper to imitate Chitwood's key line in the movie.

I laughed. "That's pretty good. And yes, I'd love to hit game winning shots like Jimmy." As we approached her dorm building, I asked, "Say, you want to keep walking?"

"Sure. Beats going back to my lonely dorm room. Where to?"

"You'll see."

"You're just full of surprises tonight!"

"I think you'll like this one too."

We continued walking south along 23rd street. Streetlights and passing cars lit our way along uneven sidewalks. We crossed over Virginia Avenue, passed the State Department, and then ran across Constitution Avenue, dodging taxis along the way. She may have been from the country, but Jenae was no dainty wallflower. She beat me across the street, laughing the whole way!

We arrived at the National Mall. It was like stepping into a whole new world. Instead of pavement, concrete, and tall buildings we were surrounded by grass and trees and inviting walking paths. Some distance off bright lights filtered through the massive trees creating a beautiful mosaic of dark and light. "Let's go there," I said pointing.

"Wow," Jenae said with genuine awe. "The Lincoln Memorial. I've never been."

I had been to the Lincoln Memorial once before. I went out for a jog one afternoon and stopped by for a look on my way back to campus. It was impressive during the day but awe inspiring at night. Jenae and I ascended the marble steps of the building and sat just outside the building's portico. It was remarkably different at night. The view of the city all lit up, the smaller, quieter crowds. It was perfect.

We sat next to each other in silence, soaking in the view, the moment.

"It's hard to describe how different this place is from where I grew up," Jenae said after a while. She gazed to the east, then took her hand and gracefully brushed back some of the blond hair from her forehead. I was amazed at her ability to take a simple gesture and turn it into something so beautiful it should be captured in song.

"I'd love to see Idaho," I said. "I've never been out west. We should go there sometime. Maybe this summer. I could meet your family."

"Sounds great. I'll bet the historian in you loves coming to places like this. Did your love of history make you choose GW?"

"I do love the history here, but I chose GW because I wanted to play basketball at the highest level I could. None of the schools in the ACC or Big East recruited me, so I came here."

"And now you can become the Jimmy Chitwood of the Atlantic 10."

"I guess." I hesitated. I'd never told anyone my real desire, but she was different. I felt like I could tell her anything. "Actually, I've always dreamed of being the next Larry Bird."

"Really? The next Larry Bird, huh?" She was intrigued but not skeptical.

"Yeah, I guess it sounds kind of silly."

"Silly, no. Unrealistic—" Her shrug filled in the gap. "It's good to have role models. I don't know much about him, but he seems like a good guy."

That made me think. I knew Larry Bird the basketball player, but Larry Bird the man, I knew next to nothing.

"You know, Thomas, I admire your drive," she continued. "It's a gift to find what you love and devote yourself to it."

A gift. I never thought of it like that. She was right, though. How rudderless would I feel without my basketball goals? "What about you? What do you want to devote your life to?"

"Well, I love volleyball, but not enough to devote myself to it." She sighed, deep and thoughtful. "I want to do the Lord's will, but I'm not to sure what that is. Is it rolling up my sleeves and helping guys like Ray, or should I focus on getting my degree so I can be a teacher?" She paused. "Maybe I was naive, or it's the perfectionist in me, but when I first started going to the soup kitchen, I was sure I could save all those people. It didn't take long to realize that life can be messier than that. Theirs and mine."

"What do you mean by that?"

"I guess I never took the time to think about why a person would be homeless. But after hearing some of the stories, I was amazed. Drugs, alcohol, physical abuse, mental illness—the reasons run the gamut. Then there are those who come to the soup kitchen who aren't homeless. For one reason or another they're struggling and can't make ends meet. My heart goes out to all of them. They need far more help than I could give. Then I cringe when I think about the things I've complained about. And I hate complaining, but … it's still the same story with my teammates. Growing up I was taught to be mature and responsible. Here, other girls seem to think that's odd. Somehow I'm the problem because I don't complain about my weight or talk behind other girls' backs. Sometimes I wonder if GW is the right place for me and if I shouldn't just transfer closer to home."

A lump formed in my throat. All I could say was, "You're thinking of transferring?"

"It's crossed my mind. My family would love it. They're supportive of me coming here, but I know my mom and dad miss me and worry about me in this dangerous, far off city. Sometimes volleyball is great. But sometimes my teammates, professors—it can be so poisonous. I wonder how I'm being affected by it."

I couldn't imagine GW without her and didn't know what to say. I don't think she did either, so we were silent for a very long time. We watched people. An elderly man using a cane and wearing a gray suit slowly made his way around. A young couple warmly embraced and kissed once they reached the top of the steps. City lights flickered behind them in the distance and it was very romantic.

"Thomas," Jenae said breaking the silence, "transferring is not something I think about often. Has it crossed my mind, yes. But there's a lot to love about this city, this place and … and tonight was awesome. This day was awesome." She squeezed my arm. "Thank you."

I smiled back at her. "You're welcome."

It was nearly midnight and we were both tired from the long day. I walked her home and we held hands the whole way.

COACH ROSS FED us on Thursday, then ran it out of us with a long practice on Friday and two more on Saturday. I loved the feeling of putting in hours of hard work on the court. But by the end of Saturday's second practice my legs had been sapped of all their energy and it felt like I'd lost a good ten pounds of body weight. I needed sustenance.

Alex was in the same condition, so the two of us went to Leo's Deli, a small grocery store located across the street from the gym, and loaded up.

The deli was a campus institution. It opened up in 1945, family owned and operated, and had been there ever since. The owner, Leo Ambrogi, worked up front at the cash register with his sons, while his wife, Maria, made food in the back. This was no supermarket where you drove up to the parking lot and pushed a shopping cart around. There was no parking lot outside of Leo's and the aisles in the store were too narrow for shopping carts. Photos of old GW basketball teams hung on the walls and the tall shelves that separated the aisles were crammed full of an assortment of food, drinks, and toiletries.

The funny thing was, they didn't use the cash register much. Instead they just did the math in their heads. Sitting on a shelf right behind the cash register, they had four small cardboard boxes. Each box was old and worn with layers of mismatched tape reinforcing the corners. Pennies were in one, nickels in another, then dimes, and quarters. Bills sat in the open till of the lonely cash register. When checking out, they quickly spouted out prices for everything you were buying, and added it up in their heads. You handed them your cash, they plucked your change from the boxes, and you were on your way.

We bought beer, soda, ice cream bars, cereal, milk, salsa, tortilla chips, hamburger meat, and Hamburger Helper. Back at Alex and Coleman's dorm room, we spread out the drinks, salsa, and tortilla chips on the coffee table in front of the couch. I watched college football on TV while Alex, beer in hand, cooked the hamburger meat.

The place was a mess. Having seen the inside of Alex's locker, I was pretty sure the mess was mostly his. But, if living in a pigsty bothered Coleman, he sure wasn't doing much about it. Piles of laundry were everywhere. I had to move a pile to make space on the couch. When I asked Alex where I should put the clothes—I hoped they were clean—he told me to toss them on the floor. If they were Coleman's clothes, he wasn't there to object.

Over the past few months Alex had, little by little, filled me in on his background. His father was an Irish Catholic bus driver who'd lived most of his life on Long Island. When she was a young girl, his mother escaped communist Russia, along with the rest of her family. They settled in New York City where she met Alex's father in high school. They married young and Alex, the first of four children, came along nine months later. He liked to amuse everybody with the smattering of Russian he picked up from his mother. And there were times in practice when Alex would mess up and blurt out some Russian word. Coach Ross frowned on swearing so we all knew what Alex was doing.

He also told good stories. Like the one about his high school teammate who'd never been on a plane before. At the airport, waiting for his flight to go visit a university that was recruiting him, the plane was delayed. Over the public address speakers the airline told the passengers it would call them when the flight was ready to leave. So Alex's teammate caught a cab and went home. Later that day, after he'd missed his flight, he got a phone call. It was from the coach who'd been waiting for him at the other airport, wondering what happened. Alex's teammate was still at his home on Long Island waiting for the airline to call him there! There was a part of me that wondered if it wasn't really about him and not some teammate.

We had only been in the room ten or fifteen minutes when the doorbell rang. Alex opened the door and was greeted by Coleman's mother.

"Hello, Alex. Is Coleman here?" she said.

"No," Alex said, seemingly unfazed by her presence. "We've only been here a little while. Haven't seen him since practice."

She lived in a suburb of the city and was a smothering mother hen who I'd see at the Smith Center at least once a week. In high heels she stood over six feet tall. She almost seemed bigger than Coleman. She had wide hips, mocha skin, dark wavy hair, and dressed impeccably. Her smooth, strong voice filled every corner of the room, easily carrying over the sound of the sizzling hamburger meat in the kitchen.

She smiled politely then said firmly, "Let me in, Alex." Alex obliged and she strode in, scanning the room. "Hi there, Thomas."

I stood up and greeted her. Alex stood by the door, spatula in one hand. He saw my puzzled face and simply shrugged.

Mrs. Jones continued to study the room as we stood there, watching. She walked over to the TV and turned down the volume.

Alex's face expressed annoyance. "Is there something we can help you with, Mrs. Jones?" he asked.

"No, Alex. Thank you, though." She wandered into the bathroom. "Did practice go okay?"

"Practice was fine, I guess." Alex answered loudly so she could hear in the next room. He shrugged again and rolled his eyes.

She emerged from the bathroom and walked over to the bedroom, her eyes searching out every inch of the place.

"Thomas," she said from the bedroom, "have you seen Coleman lately?"

"Uh, not since practice, ma'am."

Mrs. Jones continued her search, peeking under Coleman's covers. "Hmm. That's fine." She walked past the TV and opened the door to a small coat closet near the front door. "Well, sorry to bother you boys. You have a nice—" She glanced inside and started to shut the door before stopping herself.

Swinging the door open, she put her hands on her ample hips. "Get your ass out of there!"

From out of the closet, Coleman threw off the concealing coats and uncoiled himself from the cramped space. I gawked and glanced over at Alex. He stared in disbelief. A moment later the spatula in his hand dropped to a messy landing on the floor.

"Did you really think you could hide from me?" She said it like he'd tried and failed before. "We're going right now. Your father should be here. He'd lay into your backside something fierce."

"He don't care," Coleman mumbled.

"Well I care!"

I stood watching, unable to move. Coleman stood next to his mother, his head down, shoulders slumped in defeat. What was he doing in there?

Coleman's mother slammed the closet door shut and opened the front door. "Come on," she said, flicking Coleman in the back of his ear with a long, painted fingernail. "Bye boys!" she called to us as she left.

As Coleman walked out of the room, he looked back at Alex and I, and flashed a devious smile.

After they left, I turned to Alex. "What in the world was that? Was he in there that whole time?"

Alex shook his head as he leaned over and picked up the spatula. "Yep, he had to be. And I'll tell ya what, that kind of goofy stuff happens all the time with he and his mom. Seriously weird."

"Well, now you've got another funny story to tell."

"Ain't that the truth," Alex said as he walked over to the kitchen and turned down the heat on the stove. Without cleaning off the spatula he plunged it into the pan and stirred the meat. I put my hand up, the words formed in my mouth, but it was too late.

CHAPTER 11

OUR NEXT TWO games after Thanksgiving were against overmatched, non-conference opponents. With the wins, we improved to 6-0. The school newspaper, *The Hatchet,* crowed loudly over our success but the *Washington Times* and *Washington Post* were guarded in their optimism. They wanted to see how we'd perform in the crucible of league play come January. So did I.

The Colonial volleyball team lost in their conference tournament so Jenae's season was over, but once final exams for the fall semester commenced I still hardly saw her. My life was pretty much studying, taking exams, and practice. It was the same for everyone else on the team too. Well, at least some of the guys were studying. The routine was mentally and physically exhausting, putting many in a foul mood. The seniors talked about blowing off steam over beers at their favorite local hangout, the 21st Amendment. Finals ended Friday and we had another game that evening. I wondered if the steam could wait till Friday night.

Thursday of that week I was unstoppable in practice. Every shot I took went in. Matt had no hope of guarding me. He wasn't playing that bad, I was just in a zone, like when I went shooting with Ray that one night. After I'd scored on him five straight times, Matt resorted to the one thing he did better than me, better than anyone. He started fouling. Anybody can foul just like anybody can go rob a bank and get thrown in jail. But like a deft pickpocket artist that no one sees lifting wallets, Matt had a knack for fouling and getting away with it. A little shove here, a knee there, a well placed elbow or hip—Matt knew all the tricks. It wasn't dirty and he never hurt anyone, but when the moment called for it, he could give a good whack across the forearms to prevent another shot from going in, which is what he did to me.

"Nice shooting, Thomas. Someone else want to try guarding him?" Coach Ross asked after whistling practice to a stop. "We're going to face good shooters like Thomas during league play. We need to know how to guard them."

"I got him," Brian blurted out. "Enough of this."

"Oooh … better watch out Thomas," Alex said, his voice dripping with sarcasm. "Brian is going to guard you."

"Shut up, stiff," Brian said without even looking at Alex.

Alex glared. "You couldn't shut me up if—"

"Oh, shut up both of you," Jim interrupted. "Just play."

"Oh, I'll shut you up all right," Brian said quietly as he walked by Alex. "And you," he said pointing at me, "I'm going to shut you down."

To accommodate Brian and the rest of the White Team who needed to learn how to guard a good shooter like me, Coach Ross had me go Blue.

Brian was an incredible defender. His feet and hands were the quickest I'd ever seen, and he had an amazing feel for stepping into the passing lanes at just the right time and stealing a pass. It was like he had some extra sensory gift that enabled him to read your mind. But him guarding me had nothing to do with the White Team learning to guard good shooters. It was all about him wanting to put me in my place. When I got this hot in practice I was stealing his limelight. That was something he couldn't tolerate.

Then the thought occurred to me; maybe it was time somebody put him in his place.

It was Blue ball. I tried running Brian off screens to get open, but he was stuck to me like glue. Unable to get free, the ball went inside to Alex who threw up a brick.

Running back down court Brian gloated. "See! You won't even sniff another shot today. Guaranteed!"

After the White Team scored, I tried again. I faked one way then ran the other way, right past Alex's shoulder. Alex usually played soft, shying away from contact. Not now. His big bony elbows were ready for Brian's mid-section. I could hear the collision between them as I caught the pass and hit an open jumper. Brian grunted an expletive and Alex directed some trash talk his way.

So did I. "Guess I sniffed that shot," I taunted Brian. "Did you smell it?"

Next time down it was the same thing—open jumper, bottom of the net. It continued that way. I rubbed my shoulder right next to Alex's shoulder so Brian would have nowhere to go but trail behind me or go around the screen. If he trailed me off the screen, I continued in a curl pattern. If he went around the screen trying to beat me to a spot on the floor, I faded away from the screen. If done right, either option allowed me to create distance between Brian and me for yet another jumper.

I ran him off single screens and double screens. I hit one jumper after another, sometimes with less than an inch to spare. "You got to get a hand in his face, Brian," Coach Ross called out.

Seems my stupid set shot wasn't so stupid anymore.

The collisions between Alex and Brian got worse. Alex leaned into the screens and stuck his elbows out. "You have to get around those, Brian," Coach Ross said. "Don't let him create space."

The trash talking between Alex and Brian escalated. Brian started grabbing my jersey and lowering his shoulder into the screens. I ran off screens even tighter. Brian tried pushing me away from the screen. "Quit fouling, Brian!" Coach Ross shouted.

I faked one way, like I was going around the screen of David Dugan. Brian over committed, trying to anticipate my move. I quickly ran the other way and led Brian right into Alex's chest. I brushed past Alex's shoulder. Behind me, the collision between Alex and Brian produced a painful sounding grunt from both. I was wide open and hit the shot.

"Hey, Thomas," Alex shouted as we ran downcourt to play defense, "Brian sure is shutting you down!" He was practically giggling.

That pushed Brian over the edge. I could see it in his eyes. After Alex nailed him with another moving screen, Brian abruptly stopped, turned and took a mighty swing at Alex's chin. The punch just missed landing flush and glanced off his face. Alex and Brian followed up with wild, off-balance punches that hit nothing but air before others stepped in. Kevin grabbed Alex and lifted him off the ground like a rag doll. Jim grabbed Brian and moved him away.

Coach Ross blew his whistle several times cutting off any more trash talking between Alex and Brian. Once the charge in the air settled, Coach Ross spat out his whistle. Tied to a lanyard, it bounced on his chest. "Listen, I love the competitiveness. I love the effort. But we're all on the same team. No more fighting or there'll be consequences. We clear?"

Alex nodded. Jim still had a hand on Brian's chest. He looked ready to charge Alex at any moment. The hard lines seemed to boil the sweat that rolled off his face. Brian didn't answer. Coach Ross looked Brian square in the eye and in a very clear and strong voice said, "Are we clear?"

"Yeah," Brian muttered.

Coach Ross told Alex to stop setting moving screens and then said, "Now, you two shake hands." Nobody moved. Instantly the atmosphere was charged again. "Alex, Brian, shake hands and drop it. If you don't, you're both done for two weeks. No practice, no games, nothing." He put the whistle in his mouth, folded his arms across his chest and waited.

Brian had far more to lose than Alex. Then again we all did if Brian didn't listen. Nobody would miss Alex much if he was gone for two weeks.

Alex shuffled over to Brian and extended his hand. Brian moved his hand just enough to meet Alex's for a brief moment. Was Coach

Ross going to accept *that?* Technically Brian did what Coach Ross asked of him, but his attitude stunk.

"Fine," Coach Ross said. "Thomas. Nice shooting. Go back to White."

As I took my jersey off and turned it inside out, I wondered if Coach Ross really thought he was getting through to Brian. I sure had my doubts.

THE NEXT DAY was game day. James Madison was making the short trip to D.C. to play us. I had just finished my last final exam that morning. Having those exams out of the way felt like taking off a heavy backpack. I was pretty sure I aced most of them, and as I headed to the gym for our team shoot around, I felt light as a feather.

I briskly rounded a corner a block from the gym and then stopped dead in my tracks. Aqualung. There he was, no more than thirty yards off, talking with two other bums. It felt like someone just picked up that heavy backpack and slung it over my shoulders again. I turned to head the other way when I heard my name. Looking back I did a double take. It was Jenae. She was initially shielded from my view, but now, there she was, clear as day, standing with those men waving at me.

An awkward smile accompanied my wave, and I continued walking towards them. Aqualung looked worse than ever. His dirty hair was everywhere and his clothing consisted of soiled pants and a light shirt, both shredded within a few stitches of uselessness and far too meager to survive a winter outside. The thought of a night outside wearing just that made me shiver, and I was wearing a coat. Yet, somehow Aqualung managed. He must have blankets or a sleeping bag and extra clothing stashed somewhere. Where though? Under a bush in a park, a hidden crevice in an alley?

I often saw Aqualung walking the streets in and around campus. Most times he was carrying on a conversation with himself. He would flail his arms, caress his beard, and point at imaginary conversationalists. I always avoided him; it seemed most other students did too. Except Jenae.

"Hi, Thomas," Jenae said cheerily.

"Hey. What are you guys talking about?" My effort at sounding nonchalant failed miserably.

"Oh, just life," Jenae said.

Aqualung looked me up and down, and spat out, "Bah," and then lumbered away on stiff legs.

"Huh, wonder what's wrong with him?" Jenae asked. "Bye, Al!" she called out to him.

Aqualung shook a hand in disgust, never looking back and never breaking stride. Jenae said goodbye to the other homeless men and they left too.

As soon as they were out of earshot, I grilled her. "Did he say anything to you? What were you guys talking about?"

Jenae looked at me curiously. "Al? He didn't say much, never does. Why?"

I knew I should tell her why he didn't like me but I couldn't do it. "Just wondering. I've never heard him say anything ... and how does he survive with so little clothing? Anyway, should we plan on going out after the game?"

"Oh, yes. I was going to ask you, do me a favor and hustle out of the locker room afterwards, will you?"

"You got it. Any particular reason?"

"You'll see."

POOR JAMES MADISON never knew what attacked them. After a week of finals we were ready to take our frustrations out on somebody else. We jumped all over them from the start. Alex's surprising display of toughness in practice carried over into the game. He only played twelve minutes, but in that time he picked up four fouls, grabbed three rebounds, and blocked two shots. Maybe he played so hard because he knew afterwards there'd be a few cold ones waiting for him at the 21st Amendment.

I nailed a few shots late in the game to seal the win, making up for a silly turnover Brian committed. We won by seven and were still unblemished on the season. Afterwards I lingered in the shower and locker room, relishing the victory and another solid performance on my part. Matt and I were the last two still in the locker room. He was icing his elbow and I was finishing getting dressed.

Jim strode into the locker room. "Jenae is waiting for you upstairs. She wants you to hurry up."

He said it with all the subtlety of a punch in the nose. I doubted Jenae told Jim to tell me to "hurry up." Somehow I couldn't see her waiting in the lobby of the Smith Center, arms crossed, tapping her foot. I chalked it up to Jim's translation.

When Coach Jennings poked his head into the locker room moments later and suggested I hurry, I remembered what Jenae had said. She wanted me to hustle out of the gym after the game so we could hang out. Maybe she *was* up there tapping her feet and looking at her watch.

When I bounded up the stairs and onto the blue carpet of the lobby I was dumbstruck by the sight of my father standing next to Jenae.

"Surprise!" she said.

"Hi, Thomas," my father said as he grabbed me and gave me a great big bear hug. "Great game tonight." He wore a gray business suit with white shirt and maroon tie underneath a charcoal wool overcoat. It was as if he'd just stepped out of a boardroom. He'd always commanded my respect, but, looking at him now, I was sure he did everyone else's too.

I had no idea he was at the game. Thank the Lord I had played so well. "You saw the whole game? Where were you sitting? I didn't see you by Jenae. And when did you two—"

"Meet?" Jenae finished my thought and interrupted my stream of questions. "You can thank Coach Jennings."

"She's right," my father said. "I had to come down on business so I called yesterday to see if I could get a ticket to the game. I wanted to keep it a surprise so you wouldn't be too nervous about me watching. Coach Jennings promised he wouldn't say a word and left me a ticket at will call."

"Not a word to you, that is," Jenae said pointing at me. "Because earlier today, before I saw you on the sidewalk, I saw Coach Jennings at the gym. He told me your dad was coming to the game and asked me to keep it a secret. He said he'd introduce us after the game."

"Which he just did before heading down to get you," my father said wrapping up the story.

"By the way, you did play great," Jenae said as she stepped forward and gave me a hug. "But what's up with taking so long afterwards? You were supposed to hurry." She playfully squeezed me tighter.

"Right and we should get going," my father said and started for the door. I instinctively followed.

Once outside my father explained he had to catch the 10 p.m. train back to New Jersey. We hailed a cab and drove across town towards Union Station. Jenae and I sat in the back while my father sat up front. The driver was racing through the narrow streets at ridiculous speeds. I was loving it because around every tight corner Jenae and I slid closer to each other. But it was driving my father crazy. "You know," he said to the driver in a calm voice, "we're not in that much of a hurry." It brought on deja vu as it was the same voice and nearly the exact same words my father said to me when I was learning to drive the family station wagon.

The driver, a middle aged man with dark black skin and dreadlocks, never took his eyes off the road. He nodded a slight acknowledgement and barely slowed down.

"Anyway, I had quite an interesting time in the lobby," my father said. "I met Coleman's mother. She couldn't understand why Coach Ross wasn't playing her son. She kept saying she was going to have a talk with Coach, which I don't think would be a good thing for Coleman. The little I saw of him tonight, he's just not that good. I also met Brian. I introduced myself. He was very respectful. Looked me in the eyes, firm handshake. I was impressed. I think you've got a good roommate."

"He can put on an act when he needs to."

Jenae shot me a, "Was that necessary?" look.

"Perhaps," my father replied. "He's got tons of talent but, boy is he out of control sometimes. Like that turnover late in the game. He was trying to dribble through four guys. Coach Ross has his hands full with him. Hard to figure out what he's thinking."

"He thinks he knows it all," I said.

"Why don't you find out what he is thinking? Your games are tailor made for each other. If you guys communicated better you'd probably have more success."

"We don't talk much."

"Still? Have you tried to talk to him, tried to befriend him like I asked?"

I shrugged. "A few times. Didn't go so well. Never goes well, really."

"Too bad. You know I've had the chance to talk to him on the phone a few times. I've called for you but you weren't there. He doesn't seem to have any trouble talking to me."

"Hmm. He has troubles with me."

"Well ..." my father started then hesitated. The reggae music that was playing low on the cab's radio filled the gap. "Like I said, Coach Ross has his hands full."

While Jenae listened, my father and I discussed the highs and lows of my performance in technical basketball jargon. As always his comments and observations were spot on. It was my father who engaged Jenae in the conversation by changing the subject to family and holiday plans. In a few days she was heading home to Idaho for a long Christmas break.

"I'll be back down in early January for another business trip," my father said. "I looked at your schedule. I should be able to make your home game versus Rutgers. That should be an interesting one." He took his eyes off the road briefly and looked back at me. "I saw in the papers back home that Giambalvo is starting for them."

"Really?"

Jenae leaned in and quietly asked, "Who's Giambalvo?"

"I'll explain later," I mumbled to her, then turning to my father, "Are you serious? Giambalvo is starting for Rutgers?"

"Yes," my father said, "and playing well. You've had two run-ins with him. You don't want a third."

"Don't worry, Dad. Nothing's going to happen."

"I'm glad you're confident of that, but tonight I saw some of your old habits on display."

"Like what?"

"Well, late in the game, you guys were headed back on defense. James Madison was walking the ball upcourt. As he went past, Brian said something to you. I obviously couldn't hear what you said back, but you completely dismissed him. You gave him a nasty look and he gave you one back. I don't know who else saw it, but it was embarrassing. I love how well you played tonight, but I was hoping I wouldn't see stuff like that anymore."

I remembered the moment he was talking about. It was classic Brian, complaining about me taking a shot when he was absolutely sure he was more open. I didn't remember giving him a nasty look but what was I supposed to do? Brian is always complaining, he's always demanding the ball. "He wanted me to pass to him," I said. "He's so greedy sometimes. If I passed to him every time he asked for the ball I'd never take a shot."

"He does like to shoot a lot. But as your father, I'm not concerned with *his* shot selection. I'm concerned with *your* attitude. You can do better, okay? And you really need to. If you're going to shine the light on the court you can't let Brian or anyone else bother you like that. Last time I checked, impatience wasn't part of the fruit of the spirit."

"Yes sir."

"The Giambalvo kid, Brian ... they may seem like unwanted nuisances, but I encourage you to look at them like challenges that can make you stronger, if you embrace them. Just think, James chapter one. The testing of our faith develops perseverance." He paused and looked right at the cab driver. "Just like this cab ride is testing mine."

We laughed but the cabbie said nothing. He whipped the car around another corner and we screeched to a stop in front of the train station and got out to say goodbye.

Jenae and I both gave my father a hug. It reminded me of August when he dropped me off at the train station in New Jersey. However, this time he was getting on the train and I was staying. As I watched him walk away, I was already looking forward to his return in January. I wanted to show him I could do better.

My stomach gurgled a complaint and I remembered I was hungry. Cortellesi's lasagna instantly came to mind. Jenae and I hopped back into the same cab. I didn't need to tell him to step on it.

"So, who's this Gia … what did you call him?"

"Giambalvo. He's a jerk." Tony Giambalvo played for our rival high school. What he lacked in athletic ability he made up for with his toughness. It seemed every New Jersey high school team had a Giambalvo or somebody like him: tough, feisty, smart, and not above playing dirty every now and then. He also talked serious trash. To him, the bigger they are, the harder they fall. By the time I was a senior in high school, I was the biggest big shot in our league. He must have looked at me like a top heavy redwood that needed to be chopped down.

Both times our teams faced each other the games were tight and physical. In the first contest he threw a few dirty elbows. I retaliated with a moving screen that sent him to the deck. He stood up boiling mad and the refs had to separate us. The second game was a slugfest that got real ugly in the second half. He undercut me on a layup sending me crashing to the floor. A few minutes later my elbow caught him on the chin as he scratched at a rebound that I had grabbed. Words were exchanged and he was about to cock his fist when the refs stepped in. We both got technical fouls, but all that did was delay the inevitable. After we won he came after me in the handshake line. He poked his finger in my chest then dropped a few four-letter words. I slapped his finger off of me, which triggered a brief melee. Nobody got hurt. A few errant punches were thrown but it was mostly a bunch of pushing, shoving and foul language before the coaches and refs broke it up.

I never thought he was that good and couldn't believe he was given a scholarship at Rutgers University. I was even further surprised that he was starting for them. I relished the thought of once again putting him in his place.

After I was done explaining, Jenae asked, "You said he's a point guard, right?"

"Yes."

"That means you won't be guarding him, so you guys won't have to share close quarters."

I frowned. "Let's hope so."

"You sure you don't want to go celebrate the win with the guys at the 21st Amendment?" Jenae asked as we approached Foggy Bottom.

"No, I'm sure we'll do plenty of that over the Christmas break. You and me at Cortellesi's is more my speed tonight."

"Good. Me too."

As soon as we walked through the doors at Cortellesi Pizza, Ray spotted us from the kitchen and came to greet us like he was our personal maitre d'. He tried to get the night off from washing dishes to watch my game, but they were short staffed and they needed him. He wore his usual blue apron that was soaked and green rubber gloves that went halfway up his muscular forearms. Even after he took off his gloves he still smelled like a dirty sink. He may have been the lowly dishwasher, but he acted like he owned the place. He was so happy. So was I.

CHAPTER 12

WHERE I GREW up towns bumped into each other like milk jugs in a crowded refrigerator. It wasn't city living, but neighboring houses, sometimes only twenty feet apart, could be in different towns. Everything seemed close. A long road trip in high school was a bus ride that took more than half an hour. As a result, I'd never flown to a basketball game. Until today.

We were cruising at 30,000 feet on our way to the University of New Mexico to play in their Christmas tournament. Looking out the small plane window at the vast expanse below, I wondered how far Pocatello, Idaho was from Albuquerque, New Mexico. Jenae was home for Christmas. Was she close enough to drive to the game? I didn't know since I'd never been out west, and my knowledge of western geography was sketchy at best. I probably wasn't going to get in any sightseeing either. We had two games to play over the weekend and Jim told me that in all likelihood we'd see the airport, hotel, and arena, that's it.

A tap on my shoulder got my attention. It was Alex. He was sitting across the aisle from me, crammed into his seat like a jack in the box. His left knee was wedged into the seat in front of him and his right leg was sticking out into the aisle. "What're you lookin' at?"

"Don't really know, but it's beautiful. What's up?"

"I didn't finish telling you about the hotels," he said. "The hotels are the most important part." Throughout the flight he'd been instructing me on the finer points of traveling to road games. He had advice on what to pack, how to sneak out of your hotel room without the coaches noticing, the best kind of food to order for room service, etc. "You ever seen my closet?" he asked.

"You mean the one Coleman hides in?"

Alex chuckled and rolled his eyes. "Naw, not that one, the other one. It's filled with towels."

"So?"

"Hotel towels, man. Got 'em from all over. Marriott, Holiday Inn ... smaller places in West Virginia, Rhode Island, you name it. Got a few bathrobes too from the fancier places. You should pick up a few this weekend."

"Well, isn't that—"

"And those housecleaning carts that carry those little bottles of shampoo, conditioner and lotion—forget about it! It's like a buffet table. By the end of this trip I'll have all the soap and shampoo I need for over a month!"

"Yeah, but isn't that stealing?"

"Oh, come on now! Stealing? They're practically begging you to take the stuff. Man, there are times I've seen the cleaning lady watch me take stuff off her cart and she don't say a thing!"

I scratched my head then opened up the book I was hoping to read. Alex didn't give me a chance. "There's been lots of nights in boring hotels where I've livened up the joint. Cards, videos, food, beers—you never know what I'll come up with next. One time, at this hotel in Philly, I got this urge to throw my spaghetti across the room! It was totally nuts! It was some weak takeout food that was awful. No flavor, rubbery noodles, you know. I just took the whole container of spaghetti and hucked it onto the window!"

"Why?"

"I don't know, just felt like doing it, so I did. Boom! It splattered into this huge mess on the window and started dripping down to the floor. Instead of cleaning it I just crawled into bed and pulled the covers over me. Drove Jim nuts!"

"Jim was rooming with you? What'd he do?"

"At first he just busted my chops, then he finally made me clean it up. Stinkin' captain. This was last year when I was a sophomore and Jim was a junior. Seniority, you know. All that rah-rah stuff Jim gets into. Ain't that right, Jimmy?" Alex reached across the aisle with his long angular arm and slapped Jim's shoulder.

"Knock it off, you big galoot," Jim said. "Can't you see I'm busy playing cards? And don't call me Jimmy."

Without taking his eyes off his cards Coleman said, "Busy getting his ass handed to him."

"Coleman thinks he's so smart because he can play cards better than Jim," Alex said leaning over towards me. "Well, let me tell you another story. Last fall I'm going through the class directory. You know, that printout that lists all the classes, where they meet, the time, and who teaches them. When they don't know yet who's going to teach the class it just says 'staff.' About a quarter of the classes say 'Staff' in the professor column. Coleman and some of the other guys are sitting there with me looking at it too. He says, 'Man, this Professor Staff sure is a busy guy.' I kid you not! He actually said that!" He smacked his knee and laughed.

"Don't be telling that freshman a bunch of lies," Coleman said over his shoulder. "That was you!"

"Oh whatever!" Alex blurted out. "I specifically remember you saying that."

"Sounds like something you'd both come up with," Jim said. "But I think Alex is right, Coleman. I remember you saying that."

Elijah was sitting next to Coleman and added his two cents. "I'm sure you said it. I'll never forget that. I laughed so hard my stomach hurt."

Seeing he was outnumbered, Coleman gave up the ruse and laughed. "Yeah, I guess it was pretty funny."

Alex sat back satisfied. "Just wait Thomas, you and I'll probably room together on this trip. I'll show you what road trips are all about."

I nodded and tried to look pleased. But with his coordination he might decide to huck some spaghetti at a window again, but instead hit me.

"I tell you what though," Alex continued more quietly, "Jim can be real strict, but he also knows how to have a good time. Last summer for my birthday he got me a case of beer. Drank a few himself too. Yeah, I can down them when I want to. Kind of like my old man. That guy, my dad, there's a guy who—" Alex stopped suddenly, staring at his hands. He turned them over, examining them for a moment, then said, "Well, he likes to drink."

"Does your dad ever come see you play?"

"My dad?" He looked at me incredulously. "Naw, he couldn't be bothered."

"What do you mean?"

"Aw, he's too busy hangin' out with his buddies at the local tavern getting his fill of carbs, if you know what I mean." He inhaled loudly and crossed his legs, bumping the seat in front, which elicited an annoyed look from Coleman. Watching his legs move in this cramped space was like watching a giant construction crane crash into all the surrounding buildings. "But enough of him. Let me tell you what we're going to do once we arrive in New Mexico."

He went on and on about what he was going to do when not at the gym for practices or games. This trip was all business as far as I was concerned. I got the feeling the basketball related events were simply a nuisance to Alex, an interruption to his free weekend getaway.

When we finally arrived at the hotel in Albuquerque, Coach Jennings handed out the room keys. It was two to a room with most guys being paired up with someone other than their roommate back at GW. "Thomas, you and Brian are in 214," he said.

What? Was this some kind of sick joke? My face must have shown the shock.

"Sorry," Coach Jennings said as he handed me the key. "Not my decision."

Brian took the elevator to the room, I took the stairs. So much for enjoying this road trip.

THE CHRISTMAS TOURNAMENT featured four teams: Colorado, Vanderbilt, New Mexico, and us. On Friday night we played Colorado, and New Mexico hosted Vanderbilt.

The games were played in the legendary Pit arena. It sat over 18,000 and they filled it every night. It was one of the more famous, and loudest, college basketball arenas in the country. I remembered it from when it hosted the 1983 NCAA Final Four. That was the year North Carolina State beat the vaunted Houston Cougars on a miraculous buzzer beater. NC State's best shooter, Dereck Whittenburg, hoisted a long shot that fell short—right into the hands of his teammate, Lorenzo Charles, who dunked home the winning basket as time expired. It was a huge upset win for NC State and their energetic coach, Jim Valvano.

I'd never played in an arena this big. I couldn't wait to get out onto the court. Just prior to tip off, Coach Ross gathered us together. "Out of the four teams here at this tournament, everyone thinks we are the weakest." He paused and scanned our faces. "Colorado's a big school that plays in a big conference. Deep down they probably have very little respect for a school like GW. Fine. Let's give them a reason to respect us."

We did, beating Colorado by six points. I think they were shocked. I played my best game of the season. With less than twenty seconds to play Colorado had cut our lead to three but with the shot clock winding down I drained a three and that sealed the win. I scored 19 points, my most as a Colonial.

Back in the hotel that night Brian and I settled in to watch some late night TV. The room had two double beds and one large TV on the dresser. We were lying in our own beds, the only thing illuminating the room was the light of the TV. Brian, clicker in hand, turned the channel to ESPN. SportsCenter covered the highlights of that nights NBA and major college games. After about forty minutes they finally got to our game. We both shot up in bed.

"Look at that!" Brian shouted.

I could tell our teammates in the next room over were watching it too because of the hoots and hollering coming through the walls matched the timing of our highlights. One highlight was a pretty amazing drive and finish by Brian and another was of me stroking the late three-pointer. I had goose bumps all over. After a minute they switched to another game. Outside our room I heard a door open and then slam. A second later there was loud pounding on our door.

"Did you see that?" came the shout from the hallway. Brian jumped out of bed and opened the door. I scooted forward to the edge of my bed so I could see clear to the doorway.

"Tell me you saw that on ESPN!" Coleman said standing in the hallway with nothing but his tighty-whitey underwear on. He could hardly stand still, his face glowing with childlike enthusiasm. He mimed basketball moves in the doorway in front of Brian. Even though he'd hardly played at all, he did make a pass in one of the highlights.

Brian laughed loudly. "Yeah, we saw it," he said. "I know you saw my sweet drive to the hoop." Now it was Brian mimicking a finger roll layup, his right knee raised and his right arm stretched above his head, palm up, fingers extended.

"Ha, ha! Saw it man, saw it!" Coleman put out his right hand and Brian slapped him five.

"Man, get some clothes on!" Brian said after looking Coleman up and down. Brian wasn't wearing much either but at least he had some shorts on.

"Why you buggin'? What's it to you what I'm wearing?" For a moment it seemed like they were gearing up for another long argument.

"Oh, here we go, here we go," answered Brian. "I'm just gonna let this one pass, like I never seen your chubbiness oozing out of your undies." Coleman's belly was sort of oozing over his undies.

"Whatever man. Eight and oh, baby. Eight and oh!" With that he went down the hall. Even after Brian closed the door we could hear Coleman going from room to room, having pretty much the same conversation with our other teammates. What in the world would he do if he ran into somebody in the hallway that wasn't on our team? I guess we'd hear a scream.

"Just wait," Brian said, never looking at me. "Somebody is going to get a taste of Brian Patterson tomorrow night." He sat in bed cross-legged, the covers over his lap, mimicking head and shoulder fakes, crossover dribbles, and finger rolls. He seemed to be talking to an imaginary friend or himself—anybody but me. But I was the only other person there to hear it. "A little juke, a little this, a little that and—boom—right to the hoop. Wonder if my pops saw those highlights on TV. He'd be tellin' me I shoulda dunked on that play. He's always tellin' me to dunk if I can. Easier to miss layups he says."

"You were high enough," I said as I laid back down. "How about that three of mine?"

"You can shoot it, man." Brian situated two pillows behind him and leaned back, his eyes still on the TV. "Now all you gotta do is learn to take it to the hoop. You suburban white guys are always shooting jump shots."

Suburban white guys? I shook my head. "Well, maybe you should learn to shoot better from the outside."

"Why do I need to do that?" His tone, sharp and thrusting like a knife, was instantly argumentative.

I sighed. Why didn't I keep my mouth shut? We hadn't engaged in a civil conversation, or any conversation, in weeks, and this one was going downhill fast.

"No one can stop me, so why do I need to become a jump shooter?"

I didn't answer. I stared at the highlights on TV and soon Brian was engrossed in them as well.

After a few minutes, I said, "You know, my old high school coach had a funny explanation for the way a suburban kid plays versus a city kid. He said that suburban kids shoot jump shots because they grow up in homes with driveways. And the driveway has a basketball hoop with a pole supporting the basket. But the pole is right there in the middle—in the way—so if someone like me goes in for layup I might run into the pole. But city kids grow up playing ball in the playgrounds where the basket has two poles, one on either end of the backboard. So the city kid could go in for a layup or dunk and not have to worry about running into the pole."

I looked over at Brian. He was staring at me like he could scarcely believe his ears. A split second later he started howling laughing. He convulsed up and down under his covers like someone was tickling him. "You're not serious," he said once composed.

"I am, I mean he is, my old coach. At least I think he was."

"Who is he? Archie Bunker? Some other comedian?"

"No, come on. I know it sounds silly, but you gotta admit there's something to it. I mean, I grew up with a hoop in my backyard and look at me. Look at you. You never shoot from the outside and you came from New York City."

He exploded out of his covers and practically shouted at me as he sat up in the middle of his bed. "You've got to be kidding me! I can score from anywhere on the court. And I remember plenty of courts where there was only one pole supporting the hoop. This is crazy! You're basically saying that all black guys play one way and all white guys play another way. How racist is that?"

"What?! I'm not saying that! I never said black and white. I said city and suburban. *You* said black and white. You want to read into it and make it a race thing, that's your deal."

"Man, I can't believe I'm even discussing this with you. You're one seriously crazy white guy." Brian inched back down to the prone position in his bed and mumbled. "One pole, two pole, give me a break. *New Jersey* high school coach." His voice got loud again, and he angrily gestured with his hands. "What do they know? Man, that's just the way we play in the city. We just know how to play because there's always good players around. Don't make any difference what kind of hoop we're on!"

"What do you mean 'We know how to play'? Are you saying that people like me who shoot from the outside don't know how to play?"

"What, you telling me that all the great players who came from the city don't know how to play? You know as well as I do that on any given night, a guy can be off from the outside but if you always taking it to the hoop, you either going to get fouled or score."

This was ridiculous, arguing with him. "Listen, I didn't say city players don't know how to play. It's just that you made it seem like suburban players don't, that's all." I did not want to stay up all night arguing with him, something I figured he would have loved, so I tried to end the discussion. "You and I should just be thankful that there's a place in the game for both of us. The shooter and the scorer."

He grunted. "Well, I know I'd rather be a scorer. Team needs a scorer. Shooters are fine but come crunch time you need someone who can score. Just know I wouldn't want to be standing outside all the time firing from deep." He pulled at his covers and shuddered, as if the thought of relying on a jump shot made him feel cold.

I didn't answer. I stared at the TV without really taking anything in. I was thinking about the scorer and the shooter. To get better all the scorer needs to do is improve his outside shot, which might just call for a change in his mechanics or more practice. But for a guy like me, a shooter, to become a better scorer required a lot more than changing mechanics. I'd have to change the way I thought and played the game. I always looked for my shot first, a drive to the basket was secondary. Playing like Brian, always challenging the defense rather than settling for the jumper, was something I'd never done. Larry Bird could do it. Could I?

CHAPTER 13

IT WAS SO loud it reminded me of a game I played as a child. My friends and I would suck in a big breath of air and submerge ourselves in the pool. Floating close to each other, one of us would shout out a word and everyone else had to guess what it was. Under water the gurgled word was as much a vibration to feel as it was something to hear. That's what it felt like on the floor of the Pit. The place was packed. 18,000 voices became one, all-encompassing vibration that made it nearly impossible to hear the person next to you. Standing close by, Alex mouthed something to me. It looked like he was shouting at me, but without reading his lips I would never have known he said, "Wow, it's loud!"

Lots of places get loud during the introduction of starting lineups, then things settle down a bit. The Pit never settled down.

We were playing New Mexico in the championship game of their Christmas tournament. Christmas is the celebration of the birth of Christ, who came as a sacrifice for us all. But this night 18,000 full-throated Lobo fans saw us as sacrificial lambs.

Traditionally, New Mexico's fans stay standing at the start of the game until the opposing team makes a basket. They scored on their first possession and I missed on our first two. It got louder, if that was possible. When Brian finally made a shot after two and a half minutes of scoreless play on our part, I was, for probably the first time ever, happy to see him score.

New Mexico was good. They switched defenses often from man-to-man then zone. But Brian was a tough matchup for them. Either that or he was simply having a great night. Meanwhile, I couldn't get anything to go in.

The first half was tight, but midway through the Lobos went on a big run. We needed a bucket to stay close and Jim provided it. Our whole bench stood up and cheered, but everyone quickly sat back down. To stay standing would risk the wrath of the Lobo faithful. They were savvy basketball fans and studied the game program, learning the names of all the players on the visiting teams. That way they could shout out trash talk to individual players. Back on defense I glanced over to our bench and saw that Coleman was still standing and clapping. A few guys yelled for him to sit down. When he didn't, a chant arose that was soon taken up by hundreds. "SIT DOWN, JONES! SIT DOWN, JONES! SIT DOWN, JONES!"

Still Coleman stood there, clapping.

The ball went out of bounds. The momentary stoppage in play allowed "SIT DOWN JONES!" to echo throughout the Pit.

All eyes were now on Coleman. Even the New Mexico cheerleaders, who were stationed along the baseline closest to our bench, had stopped cheering and were staring at him. Tim Rogers nervously tugged at Coleman's shorts, trying to convince him to sit down. Just then Coleman bent his knees and started lowering himself to his seat. The crowd cheered, but before he was all the way down he suddenly stood back up! After an initial "Woah!" the fans behind our bench went wild. Even the New Mexico cheerleaders broke out laughing!

"SIT DOWN JONES," was replaced with, "Hey, Jones, you're all right!" and, "Hey, Coach Ross, put in Coleman!"

When Coach Ross did finally put Coleman in the game late in the first half, the New Mexico crowd gave him a tepid cheer. However, there wasn't much for us to cheer about at half time. We trailed by a dozen and I had missed all six of my shots.

The second half was more of the same. I missed my next three shots. I'd never started a game 0 for 9! After the last miss, Brian grabbed the offensive rebound and scored on a reverse layup. Running back downcourt on defense he bristled. "Pass the ball, Tom! It ain't your night. Quit shooting!"

What could I say? It was his night to play great. The layup gave him 28 points in the game. Thanks to him, we were able to slowly whittle away at their lead and eventually tie the game with under a minute left. With twenty-five seconds left the game was still tied and it was our ball. We worked it around the perimeter of New Mexico's zone defense. Time wound down. Since I'd been so cold they didn't guard me that tight. It was Brian they were concerned about. Fourteen seconds left. They were denying Brian the ball so Jim swung it to me along the baseline. I was open from just inside the three-point line.

I hesitated. I never hesitated on an open shot. You're a shooter. Don't think, just shoot! I did and it went in, hitting nothing but the bottom of the net.

I pumped my fist in the air and shouted, "Finally!" We were now up by two points. It was our first lead of the night.

Without calling timeout, the Lobos quickly pushed the ball upcourt, catching us off guard. Their star guard pulled up from deep and swished a long three. Coach Ross immediately called timeout.

I was stunned. It only took them a few seconds to get the lead back. There were now only seven seconds remaining. We were down a point with the full length of the court to go for the game winning score.

In the huddle Coach Ross spoke quickly. "Alright run our baseline out of bounds play then press-breaker. They haven't been able to stop Brian all night so they're probably going to try and deny him the ball." Coach Ross pointed at Kevin. "Kevin, you're taking it out. You can run the baseline if you need to. Get it to Jim. Get upcourt quickly, Jim! They won't want to foul so you'll be able to move pretty freely. You're either going to have to get by your man for a layup, or if they help, feed Thomas for an open jumper. Now, if they don't pressure us full court but start out in their half court defense, all the better. Get the ball to Brian and get out of the way. We only have seven seconds. I don't care if it's a two or a three, I just want a good shot. Any questions?" We all shook our heads. "Okay, let's win this thing!"

New Mexico didn't deny the inbounds pass but played 3/4 court man-to-man defense. Brian was open and Kevin immediately passed to him.

Brian took a couple hard dribbles, blowing by defenders and, in what seemed like a blink of an eye, he made it to just inside the three-point arc. As I watched I drifted to the corner of the court near him. Without looking at the clock Brian stopped on a dime and rose to shoot just beyond the foul line. The guy guarding me rotated over to help and was right there with one hand in the air ready to block the shot. Brian hung in mid-air. Was he standing on a ladder? Somehow he fired a perfect pass to me. I was open. How much time was left? A second? Two? Another defender was running at me. I had to shoot!

This'll show Brian how important the shooter is.

My form was perfect as I released the ball, but somehow that Lobo defender that rushed over got a finger on the ball. My shot fell pathetically short of the rim. There was a scramble for the ball then the buzzer sounded followed by an explosion of noise.

We lost.

Brian stormed off the court.

After Coach Ross addressed the team in the locker room Brian confronted me. I was sitting down taking off my sneakers. He was headed to the showers with a towel around his waist and a dark cloud over his head. "Didn't you see that guy coming?"

The nerve of this guy! "Yeah," I said, "but what was I going to do? I had to get the shot off."

"You could have gone by him and scored on the way to the bucket."

"I didn't have the time!"

"Sure you did, you just can't drive. At the very least you could have shot faked and taken a dribble pull up."

"You've got to be kidding me! There was seven seconds left on the clock when it was inbounded. You passed me the ball too late. There was barely a second left!"

"No, I didn't. You had at least three to four seconds. That guy was running right at you because he knew you would catch it and shoot!"

I stood up with one sneaker still on and pointed right at his chest. "He knew I would catch it and shoot because that's all I *could* do."

Brian pointed back. "No, that's all you *can* do!"

"Oh, give me a break." I sat back down and took off my other sneaker.

"You play like a typical suburban kid, I don't care how many poles you're dealing with." His tone was mocking as he headed to the showers. "All you can do is shoot that set shot, nothing else. Even your hero Larry Bird knows how to play."

LATER THAT NIGHT, I lay in my bed in the hotel watching TV by myself. Nothing of Brian's was still in the room. When the bus dropped us off at the hotel after the game I went and grabbed some fast food nearby. He must have removed his stuff then. Who knew where he'd sleep tonight. Probably on the couch or the floor in Coleman's room. Being alone was fine with me.

As I channel surfed, I heard some of my teammates out in the hallway. They were probably headed out for some late night food too. I could clearly distinguish Brian's voice. "He sucks! He blew the game for us!" he said.

The next voice I heard was Coleman's. "Quiet man, he's going to hear you. His room is right over there."

Brian's voice got louder. "I don't care. He sucks! He lost us the game! Gets his shot blocked and wants to blame it on me! Dude had four seconds to make a move and he panics and throws up this lame set shot that gets blocked."

"Shhh! Quiet, man."

"You should have heard the crazy nonsense he was telling me the other night—one pole, two poles. Man, it was seriously stupid! I mean really loopy."

There was more, but as they moved down the hall I couldn't understand it. I'd already heard enough. I was tempted to go out into the hallway and tell him how it really was, but I never left my bed. My mind replayed the moment over and over. There wasn't four seconds on the clock ... was there? The hotel room seemed uncomfortably small.

I turned the TV off and closed my eyes. I couldn't sleep so I thought of Jenae and empty gyms.

IT WAS LATE when we got back to D.C. from New Mexico. The bus we rode from the airport pulled up along the sidewalk next to the Smith Center. Coach Ross stood up in front and addressed the team. "It's late and it's been a long day. Go to bed. No going out. I want everybody to go home. Just get your rest."

Most of the guys were so exhausted from the long day of travel that Coach Ross's instruction wasn't necessary. Everybody trudged downstairs to drop off their basketball gear—jerseys in the laundry bin, sneakers in their locker—and then left. Bill Pebble was still there, making the rounds, getting ready to close up the building. He was in charge of closing up the gym most nights. Bill was a graduate student in his mid-twenties and worked at the Smith Center to help pay his way through school. He had a well-trimmed beard and a right arm that was crooked at the elbow due to a childhood accident. There had been a few times this fall when I'd stayed after closing to shoot while Bill went and lifted weights. Once he even gave me the keys to turn the lights back on in the auxiliary gym. With his schedule of work and classes it was probably the only time he could find to exercise.

"You sticking around to workout?" I asked Bill.

"You bet," he said with his usual enthusiasm. "I was just about to get started. Did you want me to turn on the lights in the gym for you?"

"Yeah, but give me a few minutes. I'd like to wait until everyone else has left."

"You got it. Just tell me when."

I made a point to get to know Bill soon after arriving at GW. He had keys to the Smith Center and I wanted as much access to a gym as I could get. Growing up I always had access to a gym. A high school teammate of mine had a key to the local Catholic school's junior high gym, the YMCA manager let me in the gym when it was closed to others, and our coach opened up the high school gym anytime we wanted. Throw in the dozen or so outdoor courts in town and there was always a basket to shoot on.

I went back to the locker room and changed into workout clothes. In my stocking feet I waited at the bottom of the stairs until I heard the coaches leave their offices and head out the door. With the coast clear, I went upstairs to the lobby, gave Bill the okay to turn on the lights in the gym, and sat down on the floor to put my sneakers on. They were brand new black Converse Chuck Taylors, just like the ones they wore in *Hoosiers*. I'd bought them a few days after I saw the movie with Jenae.

Lacing up those shoes, I thought back to my early childhood when my brother and I wore white Converse Chuck Taylors. The moment we got home from the sporting goods store, we went out to the backyard to shoot hoops in our clean, crisp white sneakers. We would play until our mother called us in for dinner. It was a challenge to see how long we could keep our shoes white. Usually after a week the canvas started to turn concrete gray. When the newness faded and the white became gray, I challenged myself to see how quickly I could wear out the rubber soles. The faster those shoes wore out, the harder I was working at becoming a great basketball player.

As I got older and progressed from elementary school to junior high and then high school, Chuck Taylors were worn less and less. They were replaced by newer model leather sneakers, just like the ones everyone on our team at GW wore. Chuck Taylors were now antiques. If you looked at old photos from the 50's, 60's and 70's nearly all the great shooters in basketball history were wearing Chuck Taylors. When I slipped them on, it felt like I was continuing the legacy.

When I walked into the gym, the friction of my Chuck Taylors rubbing the floor produced bird-like squeaks that vanished into the darkness. Turning on the lights in a dark gym was like opening a carefully wrapped present on Christmas morning. I could hear the quiet hum of the fluorescent lights hanging from the ceiling as they warmed up. Slowly the dusty gym filled with light and I could see more clearly. The rafters were bare, waiting for us to win something so banners could be hung with pride. The baskets, suspended over the court, cast long shadows. Sometimes I wondered if anyone famous had ever played in this gym? Had Larry Bird ever shot baskets here? Would people wonder these things about me one day?

Rubbing my hands over the contours of the ball always triggered a Pavlovian surge of warmth into each finger. The first bouncing of the ball echoed loudly, shattering the silence. Uncomfortable at first, like a loud alarm clock, soon the echoing sound of the bouncing ball created a welcomed rhythm. Both the gym and I craved it. The sound of the ball swishing through the net was the exclamation point.

Shooting was my therapy, my meditation. Alone in the gym distractions faded and my thoughts became clear. It had always been this way with me. I would shoot and shoot until I slowly entered a trance. It was my most comfortable state of being. It was where troubles became less significant with each made shot. No matter what happened in my life, on or off the court, I could shoot the basketball.

To me, shooting a basketball is one of the most beautiful things in the world. I'd spent years perfecting the art. In the perfect shot, there is no wasted motion, nothing extraneous, nothing to defile it. The ball is placed on the pads of the fingers and does not touch the palm. The wrist of the shooting hand is cocked back at just the right angle to produce a wrinkle in the skin of the wrist. The shooting elbow makes an "L" shape and extends straight out from the shoulder. The eyes stay focused on the rim the entire time. The shooter's entire body moves as one. The legs flex then push upward while the arms begin the shooting motion. The non-shooting hand gently releases its grip so as not to affect the rotation of the ball. The ball is released at the apex of the jump as the shooting hand flicks the ball off the fingertips and the wrist snaps downward, creating a tight backward rotation. The shooting arm remains above the head and the wrist stays bent during the follow through, fingers pointing down. The ball makes a smooth arc toward the basket and, at just the right trajectory, it will snap the net back and hang up on the rim.

Perfection.

Despite all the good coaches I played for growing up, it was my father who really taught me how to shoot a basketball well. Often before dinner he would come out to the backyard and shoot with me, giving me pointers. He knew the game well and was a good teacher. I soaked up his instruction.

I worked at my shot so much, my body just took over and shooting became second nature. The muscle memory was so strong, shooting was as easy as breathing. But seldom, if ever, does a basketball game simulate the conditions of a lonely gym where there are no distractions and you have all the time in the world to take the pure shot. In a game there is always a defender, a hand, an elbow—someone, something— either running at you or already there to contest your shot. You have to shoot it quicker, release it higher, fade away, or absorb the contact from the defender and still make the shot. Even in the frenetic conditions of a game, the shot is still beautiful.

I usually started my individual practice sessions by shooting one hundred free throws to warm up. If I didn't make ninety, I'd shoot another hundred. After free throws I'd pick spots on the floor and shoot ten, maybe twenty jumpers from each location. Next I'd go back to those same spots and pump fake, take a dribble and shoot. Then I'd move out further and shoot three-pointers.

The three-point shot didn't exist when I played high school ball so I never played on a court with the line. If I was out past twenty feet it was simply a long jumper. Things were different now. This was the first year the three-point shot was used nationwide in college. I'd read there had been experiments with it decades ago at the college level and in some smaller pro leagues, but it was the old American Basketball Association, or ABA, that first used the three-pointer consistently.

The upstart ABA was trying to compete with the more established NBA and used whatever it could to gain more fans. It came up with the dunk contest, used the three-point shot, and played with a goofy looking red, white, and blue ball. I remembered playing with a red, white, and blue ball as a young kid in the 70's. It felt like a gimmick, like a toy gun or electric train set; it wasn't the real thing. A real basketball wasn't painted three different colors.

The league used the three-point shot until its demise in 1976. When the ABA folded, the tri-colored ball became a historical footnote, but the NBA adopted the three- point shot for the 1979-80 season.

The three-point shot was tailor-made for my game. I always had deep range, now I would be rewarded for it. Talk about low hanging fruit; for every two of my three-pointers, a player like Brian would have to make three layups to come up with the same amount of points. It's what made Larry Bird so great: He could score from anywhere, including behind the three-point line. It was something Magic Johnson, and Brian Patterson, couldn't do.

Every time I finished a shooting session I'd hang the nets. It was my calling card. I'd go to each of the baskets in the gym and shoot till the shot made the net hang on the rim. When that was done, I'd stand back, like a painter admiring his colorful canvas.

It was close to midnight when I decided to finish up by taking the same last-second shot I had against New Mexico, over and over. My hot, sweaty feet crowded into my Chuck Taylors and the pads of my fingers were so acutely tuned in to the ball I could sense microscopic variations on its surface. Each time I carefully counted down the seconds in my mind. It was just like when I was a kid in my backyard and I'd dream of taking the last-second shot to win the NBA championship. I hit the shot ten times in a row, the last felt perfect. My form was flawless and the ball hung the net on the rim. I could go now.

CHAPTER 14

WE WENT INTO the Christmas break with an 8-1 record. Coach Ross gave us three days off. I took the Metro from Foggy Bottom to Union Station. From there I hopped on a Metroliner train and left D.C. Three hours later the train traversed the basement of Manhattan and arrived at Penn Station. At street level I bought a hot salted pretzel with mustard and then joined the typical Manhattan sidewalk stampede, walking the few blocks to the Port Authority bus station. The bus made numerous stops, snaking its way through northern New Jersey before finally arriving in my hometown.

My whole family came to pick me up at the bus stop. The short car ride home was festive. My mother brought a shoebox full of her famous chocolate chip cookies. The four of us munched away while catching up on each others' news. Mike, who was attending a small college in upstate New York, had recently gone with a few of his buddies to watch a Syracuse basketball game. "Did you get to talk to Boeheim?" I asked in jest.

Jim Boeheim was the head coach at Syracuse. While in high school Mike and I dreamed of playing for the Orangemen. They were one of the better teams in the Big East Conference and played in front of huge crowds at the Carrier Dome. If someone called the house for my brother, and I picked up the phone, I'd tell Mike it was Jim Boeheim calling to recruit him. He always did the same with me.

"Nope," Mike said. "Still can't believe that guy never called for either one of us! You keep playing the way you've been playing and he'll be regretting that decision."

On Christmas morning we continued our family tradition of reading from the Bible the story of Christ's birth then opening presents in the living room with a warm fire in the fireplace. At midday we feasted on a delicious turkey dinner with stuffing, creamy mashed potatoes, gravy, beans, rolls, and cranberry sauce. I followed it up with three slices of my mom's homemade cherry pie and a couple glasses of milk. Later, we plopped in front of the TV like blobs of wet cement and watched the Celtics play while our food digested. I was riveted watching Larry Bird play another great game. I pumped my fist when he hit a big shot. I glanced over to see their reactions, but my father and brother were both sound asleep on the couch.

WHEN I GOT back to D.C. we played two home games in front of small crowds since most of the students were still on their break. The atmosphere stunk. All the money in athletics may be tied to alumni, boosters, and corporate sponsors, but students are the lifeblood of college sports. They are its heart and soul. Without many students there, it was like a morgue at times. Every big shot we hit was greeted by polite applause. I missed seeing the passionate frat guys in the stands, jumping up and down and yelling at the top of their lungs.

We won both games and improved to 10-1. Our record was the best start to a season since Coach Ross had come to GW. We even started getting votes in the national top 25 polls. The *Washington Post* and *Washington Times*, which usually gave top billing to Georgetown and Maryland, were taking a keen interest in our success. *The Hatchet* now featured us on the front page of every issue.

Come the first week of January we had one more non-conference game before the start of league play. Coach Ross decided to give us another two days off from practice—New Year's Eve and New Year's Day.

Jenae was still in Idaho with her family. We talked on the phone often and she told me about her tour of the University of Idaho State's campus. She never mentioned transferring after bringing it up that night at the Lincoln Memorial, but I was pretty sure it was still in the back of her mind. Her campus visit to ISU confirmed it.

With Jenae gone, I hung out exclusively with the guys on the team. On New Year's Eve we all went to the 21st Amendment and secured a table for ourselves. Brian was there but just like in our dorm room, he acted like I didn't exist. I returned the favor.

The 21st Amendment was a narrow brick building on a block of Pennsylvania Avenue where many brick buildings had once stood but now few remained. It was similar in style to Cortellesi Pizza and located directly across the street. The 21st Amendment had a cozy covered front porch that was often filled during the warmer months. Being one block off of campus, it was definitely a GW hangout. Since the drinking age in Washington, D.C. was eighteen, there was no need to try and sneak in. We were all perfectly legal.

I liked hanging out with the guys and grabbing a beer or two. Whenever we showed up, we were treated like kings. Everybody knew who we were. I guess it was pretty easy to figure out—a bunch of guys walking in together, the average height north of 6'5".

Tonight was cold so the porch outside the 21st Amendment was empty. Inside it was packed. Just like most nights, a layer of cigarette smoke hung over the throng of people. Some danced, their bodies tight to each other like blades of grass moving in the wind. Others bellied up to the crowded bar. Many wore party hats to celebrate the new year. Because of the loud music, most of the voices were undecipherable.

The crowd was almost entirely college aged, but at the bar I saw a middle aged man sitting by himself. I could tell it wasn't Ray but it made me think of him. What would Ray think if he saw me drinking a beer? Would he be angry? Disappointed? Jealous? Would he want to join me or lecture me? I'd never known an alcoholic until I'd met Ray. Funny thing was, he didn't seem like an alcoholic. Sure, he had told me all about his past, but I'd never seen him drink. The one who did seem like an alcoholic was Alex. One look across the table and it was obvious Alex was drunk again.

Coach Ross knew guys liked to have a few drinks every now and then, so he allowed it, within reason. Most of my teammates showed respect for their bodies and the freedom they were given and didn't drink too much. Alex, and occasionally Coleman, were the exceptions. Those two were at it again tonight. Coleman was carrying on about something, but I could hardly hear him. What I did hear was mostly slurred. I looked over at Jim and Matt. There were both quietly enjoying their beer, watching the show. Did they ever act immature?

I don't know why he did it—maybe to show off—but Coleman suddenly put his mug of beer down and punched the wall right where he was sitting. His fist went through the drywall and his arm disappeared halfway up his forearm. There was a momentary pause then everyone laughed as Coleman pulled his arm out of the wall, smiled, and took a big swig of beer.

Alex pointed at Coleman and let out a drunken guffaw. He rolled up his sleeve and shouted, "Watch this!" He reared back and punched the wall. It wasn't the first time he had done something outrageous at the 21st Amendment. I'd heard lots of stories about Alex being the life of the party. If the walls of that old bar could talk, they'd have a lot to say about Alex. But this time the wall didn't talk, nor did it budge. After delivering the blow he jerked back his right hand and cringed in pain.

Coleman burst into laughter. He examined the small dent where Alex's hand connected with the drywall and exclaimed, "Nice going stud, you hit the stud!"

More than likely Alex had punched where drywall covered up brick. Coleman must have gotten lucky and hit a spot where there was a gap of bricks behind the drywall.

After initially acknowledging the pain, Alex tried to play it off and pretend it didn't hurt, but I could tell it did. Despite all the beer he was drinking, the pain registered. "Gee wiz, guys," Matt said. "Settle down. You're not even going to last till midnight."

"Hey, man." Coleman spoke slowly, exaggerating his enunciation in a failed attempt to disguise his drunkenness. "We not going settle down. We already sittin' down on these here chairs. Last midnight is come and gone. I'm workin' on this one." His big white teeth flashing with each syllable. Matt rolled his eyes and then let it go.

Turns out I was the one who had a hard time lasting. The cigarette smoke was bothering my eyes and listening to Alex and Coleman make fools of themselves was getting old. But mostly I missed Jenae.

Midnight came with the customary countdown, shouts, and kisses. I left soon after and went home. I had just gotten into bed and turned the lights off when a loud crashing sound from the hallway jolted me awake. My room was dark except for the sliver of light creeping under the door. I heard the elevator door closing, followed by another loud crashing sound and laughter. With school out, the dorm was completely empty except for our team, so it had to be one of the guys. I threw off my covers, quickly slipped on a pair of shorts and tiptoed to the door. I cracked it open and peeked through. Down the hallway, Alex rounded the corner, awkwardly rolling a keg of beer along the floor with one hand. The keg wobbled as it rolled, intermittently banging into the walls.

A moment later David and Coleman stumbled around the corner right behind him, wearing party hats and laughing hysterically. They were all hammered. When David saw me peeking out the door he shouted, "Hey, Tommy! Let's go! We're going out again! Come on!"

I stepped into the hallway and laughed at the sight of them.

Alex stopped rolling the keg and pointed at me. "Hey, Thomas! Come on! Don't put any more clothes on, just come like that!" David and Coleman laughed and pointed too.

I shook my head. "No thanks, guys. Looks like you're having enough fun without me. Where in the world did you get that keg?"

Alex, looked down at the keg, then back at me, puzzled. "What, this thing?"

"Yeah, that thing."

"21st Amendment," he replied flatly. He cradled his right hand, the one he punched the wall with.

"How'd you get it?"

Alex looked down at the keg again. David and Coleman were both leaning on the wall. "Yeah, Alex," Coleman slurred. "How'd you get it?"

Alex turned around and responded sharply to Coleman. "I took it! They won't miss it. Besides they know I'll drink it and not waste it. Hey, wait till Jim hears about this! Bet he's never gotten away with this." He bent over and started rolling the keg again. He was headed for his room but the keg veered and rolled into the doorway across the hall from his. It crashed into the door with the unmistakable sound of cracking wood. "Shoot!" Alex stumbled over to inspect the damage. "Oh well. It's just a crack."

I cringed. I wanted nothing more to do with these guys tonight. Who knew what they were going to do next. Alex managed to roll the keg into his room and then the three of them went off again, this time running down the stairs, laughing and shouting.

I went back to bed but couldn't fall asleep right away. I lay there staring at the ceiling. How did Alex, all 6'11" of him, roll a full keg of beer down Pennsylvania Avenue in the pitch black of night and not get stopped or caught? It seemed impossible with so many cops, plus military and secret service personnel in the city. He had no car, truck, or dolly—nothing to carry that keg with, only one good hand, an incredibly clear conscience, and a fearless, if not sober, mind. And to think, only a few blocks east, President Ronald Reagan lay sleeping.

I SPENT MOST of New Year's Day on the couch watching college football on TV. Nursing hangovers, Alex, Coleman, and David all slept in past one o'clock in the afternoon. Once his hangover had dissipated enough, Alex wandered into my room and asked me if I wanted to join him at the 21st Amendment again tonight. I tried to talk him out of it. He'd already had his fun and done his damage the night before—to his hand, the door down the hall, and who knows what else. Plus we had practice the next morning. I failed to convince him, and Alex went out and got lit again.

The next morning while warming up for practice I saw Alex walk into the gym. He was clearly hungover with dark bags under his eyes.

Coach Ross was by the door and watched Alex walk in. "Alex, wait a minute," he said with a suspicious looking face. "Come here."

Alex walked over to Coach Ross who instantly recoiled in disgust at the smell of, well, stale beer I'd imagine.

"You stink!" he shouted. "I should kick you out of practice, but I have a feeling keeping you here will hurt even more!" Everybody in the gym was watching. He had a rolled up practice schedule in his hand and waved it at Alex. "I'm going to run every ounce of that beer out of you until you puke! I gave you two days off. Did you drink the entire time?"

He paused, daring Alex to answer. Alex didn't say a word. "You're here to play basketball and go to school, not drink! If you ever applied yourself you could become a decent center. But right now, you're just like some of those frat boys who do nothing but drink and waste their time."

True to his word Coach Ross ran Alex, and the rest of us, hard. I was loving it. It felt good to get a sweat going. Alex looked like he could puke at any moment. He was sweating profusely and his skin looked like green plastic. His hand had swelled up so bad it looked like four fingers and a thumb sticking out of a flesh colored marshmallow.

During one of the water breaks, Alex showed his hand to Danny, our head trainer. He cringed at the sight. "Holy smokes, Alex," he said. "Why didn't you show me this earlier? You need to get an X-ray immediately."

Coach Ross walked over. "What's up, Danny? I don't want him giving you some tale of mystery illness. He's not getting out of this practice unless he's got broken bones."

"Well, he's got at least one broken. Now, more than one, I'm not sure." Danny pointed at Alex's nasty looking hand for Coach Ross to inspect.

"What?" Coach Ross looked it over. "How did this happen? And don't lie."

Alex dredged up something from the depths of his lungs and forcefully spit into a nearby trash can. "I punched a wall at the 21st Amendment."

"Oh good grief!" Exasperated, Coach Ross tossed the lanyard and whistle he had in his hand into the air and it soared a good twenty feet. "All right, listen up everybody. I was hoping I wouldn't have to do this, but I'm going to lay down some rules. No drinking at all the day before a game. None. Every other night, two beer max. No wine, no hard stuff for the rest of the season. You got it? I didn't want to treat you like kids who can't handle a little freedom, but this is ridiculous."

He walked over and picked up his whistle then stalked over to Alex. "Two beers! Got it?"

Later that day, we got the word that Alex's right hand would be in a cast for four weeks. That night Alex had hamburger helper and beer from the keg in his room for dinner. When Jim found out Alex was still knocking back on the keg, he nearly exploded. He marched into Alex's room, poured the rest of the beer into the toilet and left without saying a word. Alex didn't dare try and stop him.

CHAPTER 15

OUR FIRST GAME of the new year was against local rival, American University. American's campus was only a few miles to the northwest of ours and the schools played each other nearly every year. And, like us, they too played in the shadows of local standouts, Georgetown and Maryland. Georgetown, which had won the NCAA championship a few years earlier, was a perennial national powerhouse that played in the Big East Conference. Maryland was another top ranked program that played in the mighty Atlantic Coast Conference. Those two teams were considered by far the best in the D.C. area and received the lion's share of the media coverage. It was as if they were the White Team and we were the Blue Team. And if we wanted to earn the respect of schools like Georgetown and Maryland, we had to beat teams like American.

Jenae flew back from her Christmas break that afternoon. I was hoping to pick her up at the airport but her flight coincided with our game day shoot around.

Our shoot arounds were usually relaxed and upbeat. Not today. It was all business. The coaches were tense, especially Coach Ross. He kept his whistle close at bay, using it quickly to snuff out any goofing off or unnecessary comments. Jim had told me earlier that Coach Ross's record against American wasn't good and he was feeling the pressure. If you can't win in your backyard it doesn't matter where else you win. A loss to American would fuel the fire for all our doubters, but a win would help validate the great start we'd had to our season.

Coach Ross walked us through our plays then Coach Jennings went over the plays American would run. "Shoot around went a little long today," Coach Ross said, "so once you've made twenty free throws go ahead and take off for pregame meal."

I missed only once and was done quickly. As usual, I stuck around to shoot some more. One of my shots missed and the rebound bounced towards the hoop Brian and Coleman were shooting at. Of course they were still trying to make their twenty free throws. I tried to run down the long rebound but Coleman grabbed the ball before I could reach it. "Hey, look at this," he said to Brian. "Tom actually missed. Must have shot a brick!"

"Yeah, Coleman, you would know what that looks like," Brian kidded.

Coleman feigned like he was insulted. "Man, why you always say stuff like that?"

"I ain't always doing that. Only when you deserve it. You just always deserve it!"

Coleman smacked my ball in his hands and exploded in laughter.

"Hey," I said. "Can I have my ball?"

"What this ball?" Coleman held the ball in the palm of one hand and pointed at it with the other.

"Yeah, that ball. Come on. I want to shoot some more."

"He wants to shoot some more, Brian. Thomas just can't get enough of it."

Brian held his hands out to receive a pass and Coleman immediately passed him the ball. Coleman's response was a reflexive move that had been ingrained in us by Coach Ross early in the year. If you are open and you want the ball don't shout for it, just put both your hands out and create a target. Nine times out of ten the person with the ball will see the target and make the pass. Of course with Jim it was ten out of ten.

Brian pounded his dribble on the floor as if he was going to back down a defender in the post. "I'll show you what he can't get enough of. Come on, Thomas. Guard me."

I shook my head. Typical Brian. Always looking for a confrontation. "Come on man, just give me the ball."

"Come on. Guard me. See if you can stop me."

"Yeah, Thomas," Coleman chimed in. "Go guard him."

"You guard him." I wasn't in the mood for this. I just wanted my ball so I could go shoot.

Coleman shook his head. "I ain't guarding him."

Brian lowered his shoulder and dribbled right at me. "Magic Johnson ... driving in the paint. Bird can't guard him! He can't guard anyone!"

I was standing right under the basket as Brian approached. He went out of his way to bump into me and flipped up some crazy underhand shot. At the last minute I swiped at the ball and hacked his left forearm. The ball spun off the glass backboard and went in the hoop like he'd done it a million times.

They both whooped it up as the ball went in. "Oh! And one!" Brian shouted.

Coleman hopped up and down one foot at a time like he was in double dutch jump rope competition. "You the man, Magic! You the man!"

"Hey, Thomas," Coach Ross called over. Brian, Coleman and I all jerked our heads towards him. "Leave them alone and quit goofing around. Have you made your twenty free throws?"

I was goofing off? I already made my twenty free throws. They were the ones goofing off! "Yes," I snapped back as I grabbed my ball.

Except for a snicker from Brian, the gym suddenly turned quiet. All three coaches stared at me. Apparently I snapped back a bit too hard.

"Didn't you hear me tell everyone to go to pregame meal once you've made your twenty free throws?" Coach Ross asked.

"Yes. I ... I just wanted to get in some more shots like I usually do."

"I'm not interested in what you usually do. I'm interested in you listening and doing what you're told. Got it?"

"Yes," I groused as I turned to leave.

"Is there a problem, Thomas?"

"No, sir."

"My butt, there isn't," Coach Ciancio muttered.

Head down, I walked towards the doors hoping they wouldn't say anymore. Coleman shot another brick and the ball bounced off the rim towards me. Brian ran to retrieve it but it got to me first. I caught it and handed it to him.

He whispered, "Bird can't guard anyone," before flashing a wicked grin and jogging back to his basket.

A HALF HOUR before tip off, Coach Ross came into the locker room, with the assistant coaches following right behind. He went straight to the dry erase board as usual and wrote down the starting five. Without the slightest hesitation he wrote down Jim, Brian, Matt, Kevin, Robert. Matt was starting? I'd started every game this year. I'd been on the White Team in practice since November. Why was Matt starting now? Was it because of the scene at today's shoot around? Had to be. Was it *that* big a deal? After writing the starters down Coach Ross addressed the team without saying anything about the lineup change.

The Smith Center crowd was full of energy. I could feel it coursing through me during pregame layup lines. I was so excited to get out there and play it was hard to sit down. At the start I sat on the bench near the coaches. Whatever point Coach Ross was trying to get across, I didn't expect to sit long. And once I got in I didn't expect to come back out.

The first few minutes of the game we built a nice lead over American, and like everyone else, I was swept up in the excitement of beating our cross town rivals. But the time was ticking away. Three minutes of the game were gone and I hadn't been in yet. The electricity that had me ready to pop out of my seat had dissipated.

Three minutes turned to five then ten.

As other guys got in the game, I moved further down the bench, away from the coaches. With five minutes left in the half, Matt missed a wide-open jumper and then, on the defensive end, let his man get by him for an easy score. I shook my head in frustration. Why wasn't Coach Ross playing me? I slumped in my chair at the end of the bench next to Alex.

"Dude," Alex said in his street clothes, "look's like Coach has you in the doghouse again. What did you do?"

"Nothing. Well, it didn't seem like anything to me. I think he's mad I stuck around and kept shooting at shoot around today."

"I don't know about that. Must be something else, cause if that were the case he'd be mad at you all the time."

In the locker room at halftime my teammates were sky high but I was flat as a pancake. We were winning big but I hadn't played a single second. I sat on my chair, warm-ups still on, my jersey bone dry. Soaked in anger and humiliation rather than sweat, I hardly heard a word of what Coach Ross said.

In the second half we continued to hold a good lead over American. Everyone was playing well. Except me. In agony, I watched the seconds tick away. Three minutes into the second half Coach Ross looked right past me and sent in David Dugan and Tim Rogers. Flabbergasted, I tried to look like I was happy we were winning. I caught Coach Jennings look over at me before awkwardly looking away. Some of the other guys on the bench did the same.

Next, Coach Ross sent Coleman into the game. Four minutes later, after two assists and three turnovers, Coleman was back on his seat next to me. Sweating profusely and too tired to smile, he wrapped a wet forearm over my shoulder. "Man, this is messed up," he whispered between breaths. "Me getting more playing time than you? Shoot, I thought it was kinda funny what happened in shoot around. Guess Coach didn't think so."

With six minutes to go in the game, and one of our guys shooting a free throw, Jim came over towards our bench and stood on the edge of the court talking to Coach Ross. Having spent the last three years together, he and Jim were very close. Jim was Coach Ross's alter ego on the court. They thought alike and acted alike. Coach Ross made Jim a better player and Jim made Coach Ross a better coach and they both knew it. So Jim coming over to talk to Coach Ross during the game was nothing new. I couldn't hear what they said but then Jim pointed over at me and shrugged.

I straightened up in my seat. Coach Ross, his back turned to me, shook his head. Jim nodded before walking away. Coach Ross didn't even glance in my direction.

I sunk back down into my seat. Alex was right. I was in the doghouse.

I looked across the court and spotted Jenae. She saw me look her way and smiled empathetically. I forced a smile in return.

As the minutes ticked away it felt like I'd sunk to the bottom of the pool. Then with three seconds left on the clock, the ball went out of bounds, stopping the clock. Coach Ross stood up and pointed towards the end of the bench.

"Thomas!" he shouted. "Hurry up! Get in there for Matt."

Instinct took over. I was getting in the game! I jumped out of my seat and ran to the scorer's table as I pulled off my warm-up top. The crowd cheered and at the sound of the buzzer I went in.

As I stood there near mid-court it dawned on me that I had no idea what to do. There were 3 seconds left. Coach Ross sat me for 39 minutes and 57 seconds. Mortification started to sink in. An American played strode past. He was soaked in sweat, his muscles warm and limber from exertion. I felt cold and limp. Somehow I'd found a deeper spot in the pool to sink to.

I now regretted running to the scorer's table like some scrub who was happy just to get in the game. It felt like everyone in the arena was staring at me and laughing.

Elijah received the inbounds pass and the three seconds began to tick off. He took one dribble then fired a long meaningless shot at the buzzer. Still stunned, I jogged off the court towards our locker room, feeling the crowd's piercing gaze on my back.

Despite the fact we won, it felt like a nightmare. I don't think I had ever played just three seconds in a game. I dressed quietly and left.

Jenae was waiting for me upstairs in the lobby. She greeted me with a curious smile. I could tell she was trying to read my face for clues that would explain what just happened. I would imagine all she could see was anger.

We went to Cortellesi's as usual but our walk there felt like a funeral procession. Cortellesi Pizza was where we went to celebrate. What was there to celebrate about tonight's game? It was a total disaster, complete humiliation.

Just past the crowd loitering outside the Smith Center Jenae tentatively asked, "So, what's going on? Why didn't you play much tonight? You're not hurt, are you?"

"No, I'm fine. Coach Ross simply sat me for the entire game. Well, all but three seconds of it."

"Did something happen over Christmas break?"

"Not that I know of. He got on me a bit in shoot around today, but it wasn't that big of a deal. It was actually Brian and Coleman who were goofing off. I just got caught in the middle of it."

"Hmm. He must be trying to send a message."

"Must be." I shook my head. "Seems like he's always trying to send me messages. Moving me back and forth between the Blue Team and White Team in preseason, and now this. Why doesn't he send Brian a message every now and then?"

"You know what I thought when I saw you run out there tonight? I thought, wow, he's still fired up to play. After sitting on the bench that long, you were excited to play. I thought it was awesome."

"Really?"

"Yes! You didn't sulk over to the scorers table. You ran. There were three seconds to play and you ran out there. You ran like every second counts. You ran like you love the game. I was proud of you."

139

She was proud of me? It was so silly to run out onto the court with three seconds left. It was my most humiliating moment and she was proud of me. "I wish I could take credit for being mature and having a great attitude, but I really wasn't thinking much until I got onto the court. By then I was totally humiliated."

"You know what it made me think of? Matt."

"Matt? Matt Davis?"

"Yeah. The guy who lost most of his playing time to a freshman." She nudged my arm. "Do you know who's first up off the bench cheering when you hit a big shot? Matt. Every time. In fact every time anybody hits a big shot he's the first one up cheering."

I shrugged. "I guess I never noticed."

"It's got to be humiliating for him, a senior, to sit behind a freshman when all the other seniors are starting."

"Yeah, but he probably doesn't see the humiliation."

"Exactly! Because he loves the game and he's a 'team first' kind of guy."

"My dad loves him. I mean loves the way he plays."

"I think your dad would have loved the way you played tonight."

"I didn't play tonight."

She smiled weekly and waited a beat before asking, "Do you love the game, Thomas?"

I was caught off guard. No one had ever asked me that. "Basketball? Of course. Why?"

"Maybe you should focus on that more. Love isn't needy. It sounds like you need so much from the sport. A need for validation and approval. Maybe, if you played simply because you love it, you'd be freer. I've seen you when you're shooting around in the gym by yourself or with Ray. It's obvious you really love the game. When you're just shooting, there's a twinkle in your eye, a real passion. I don't see that as much when you're playing with the team."

I nodded but didn't say anything. Obviously it's different when I'm alone versus playing with others. My opponents on the court aren't there to help me love the game. They're there to beat me. But it was more than that. She was on to something. But what?

Shortly thereafter we arrived at Cortellesi's. I paused as she stepped forward and grabbed the front door. It just didn't seem right to eat at Cortellesi's.

"You don't want to go in, do you?" Jenae said.

"No." I said it more to my feet than to her.

"Should we just keep walking?"

"A walk sounds good, but I am hungry. I'd like to get something."

She stuffed her hands into her pockets and pondered the situation for a moment. The night was cold but the glow from inside Cortellesi's was warm. "Hey, why don't we go get a hotdog from Manush?"

I clapped my hands together. "Now that's a good idea!"

We started to leave then I remembered Ray. I knew he had to work tonight so he missed the game. He didn't like missing home games but with his job it happened every now and then. Even though I didn't want to talk about it, I felt I should at least go in and tell him how the game went. But before I could say anything, Ray emerged through the front door. He wore a dingy white shirt that seemed shrink-wrapped over his impressive shoulders and biceps. A white towel was slung over his shoulder and, despite the long apron he wore, the bottoms of his pants were nearly completely soaked.

"Hey, saw you two standing outside," he said as he dried his hands on the towel. "Surprised to see you here."

Jenae and I looked at each other puzzled. "You are?" I asked.

"Yeah. Heard about the game from some folks who went. They told me you didn't get in until the last few seconds of the game. Coach Ross must be trying to send you a message."

Jenae spoke up. "Ray, that's exactly what I said."

"Oh yeah? Well, I've had lots of people trying to send me messages over the years. Can't say I listened that much. Trying to now, but you don't want to be my age and still trying to figure things out."

"We're always trying to figure things out, Ray," Jenae said. "Each and every day, with the Lord's guidance."

"Amen to that, darling! Anyway Thomas, I just thought you wouldn't want to be out and about. But now that you're here, you two coming in?"

"Thanks, but not tonight, Ray," I said. "How's work going? Looks busy in there."

"Work is great. I should probably get back in there. Say, Thomas, maybe you and I need to shoot together again?"

I laughed softly. "Maybe."

"You guys going to get some food somewhere else?"

"There's a couple Manush hotdogs in our future." Jenae rubbed her hands together as if relishing the prospect. "Maybe even four." She winked at me.

Ray frowned, and we both laughed as he plugged his nose. "Suit yourself. But, hey, Thomas, you and me, let's go shoot."

"You got it, Ray."

We left, walking hand in hand, taking our time. Manush saw us coming.

"Tom and Jenae!" Manush had endless enthusiasm. A smart business owner, he knew everybody's name. "How are you? Are you going to de gym?"

"No," I replied. "We just came from there. We're looking for a couple hotdogs."

"Excellent, Tom my friend. I have dis ting you are looking for!"

We got our hotdogs and sat down on a park bench close enough to hear the music playing on the little radio in Manush's stand. People came and went and we ate and watched. For me it was a welcome diversion from the memory of the game. Three seconds. It took longer than three seconds to take a sip of my soda.

From out of the shadows came a disheveled looking man. He walked up to the stand and Manush greeted him warmly. Jenae elbowed me gently. "Thomas," she whispered, "there's Al, I mean Aqualung."

In the dark I hadn't noticed him. But the beard and thread bare clothing—it was Aqualung all right. Jenae raised her arm to wave to him and I put my hand on hers. "Let's not talk to him right now," I said.

She lowered her arm back to her lap and looked at me curiously. "What's wrong?"

I turned my head to avoid her gaze. I couldn't look into her deep blue eyes knowing I wasn't being honest with her. How could I tell her what I did? I knew I should, just not now. "Nothing's wrong. I'd just rather not talk to him tonight."

Jenae studied me then quietly said, "Okay."

Manush gave Aqualung a hotdog and soda and then he walked off without seeing us, or paying. Curious, I asked, "Manush, does Aqualung have an account with you or were you just helping him out?"

"Dat guy? What did you call him?"

"Aqualung. At least that's what we've heard him called."

I looked to Jenae for confirmation. She nodded then added, "I sometimes call him Al for short, but everyone else seems to call him Aqualung."

"Aqualung, huh? Never knew dat. He don't say much, so I just call him 'my friend'. He doesn't have anything so I help him out with free food sometimes."

"Manush, I think that's wonderful," Jenae said. "He comes to the soup kitchen at Western Presbyterian Church."

"Yes, I know dat place. Run by my friend Paul. Good man."

"You know Paul?" Jenae asked.

"Yes. Paul comes from Italy and I come from Iraq. So we are both foreigners making dis place our home. And we both try and do our part for de homeless. Paul feeds dem in de morning at soup kitchen. I feed dem at night at my stand!"

"So you give out hotdogs to other homeless people?"

"Only sometimes. Ones dat come by and are polite, maybe help me out with dis or dat, yes, I give dem hotdog." He snapped his stubby fingers as he remembered something. "Say, I have dis ting I want to show you two. I tink you'll like it."

Manush crouched down out of sight within his rickety stand. Seconds later he emerged with a big smile on his face. "What do you tink? Abe Lincoln, huh?"

Jenae and I burst into laughter at the sight of Manush, who was entirely bald on the top of his head, wearing a thick black hairpiece and matching beard formed to look like Lincoln's. His enormous nose was neatly framed in the outlandish costume.

"What you tink? It looks good, right? I figure Lincoln statue not too far away, why not wear Lincoln beard?"

I was still laughing and this made Manush laugh too. As he laughed, the fake beard crept up over his lower lip. "Oh! One more ting!" He reached into his stand. "How about dis hat?" He put a on large black stovepipe hat.

"Perfect," Jenae said in between giggles.

Moments later Alex showed up and ordered two chilidogs. He was wearing worn out hightop sneakers, laces untied, with wrinkled black slacks, a maroon shirt, and a long, dark wool overcoat. The coat was much like the one my father wore, only Alex's had worn patches at the elbows and signs of fraying at the cuffs.

"Hey, love birds," he said. "Surprised you're not at Cortellesi's."

"Where you headed?" I asked.

"21st Amendment. Want to come?"

"No thanks," Jenae answered before I could.

"Suit yourself." Alex sat down at a bench next to ours and devoured his chilidogs then washed them down with a soda. After belching he stood up, said "See ya," then sauntered down the street. "Oh," he shouted back at me over his shoulder, "I'll be sure not to punch anything! One cast is enough!"

"Good!" I shouted back and laughed.

"Ah, Alex. He is good customer," Manush said. "He has long legs to fill with food, no? So, why not fill dem with hotdogs?"

We sat and watched people come and go. Two female students showed up. They instantly broke into a girlish titter when they saw Manush.

"Love the hat, Manush!" one of them squealed.

While they waited for their food, one of them looked over at us and said, "Say, aren't you on the basketball team?"

"Yes," I said as casually as I could.

"Yes, yes indeed," Manush said. "He is big man on campus. Right, Tom my friend?"

"Whatever you say, Manush." I sure didn't feel like it tonight.

"I remember you for some reason," the girl continued. "What was it?" When she looked over at her friend for help, her friend said indifferently, "I've never seen him."

"Everybody knows Tom plays on GW team." Manush handed the girls their hotdogs.

The two girls paid Manush then started to walk away when one suddenly turned around and excitedly said, "I know it! You're the guy who played three seconds tonight. I couldn't believe your coach put you in with only three seconds left. You must have been so humiliated!"

CHAPTER 16

"THOMAS," COACH ROSS called out, "come over here."

Five minutes before the start of practice, he casually stood off to the side of the court talking with his two assistants. They were in their usual practice attire: Coach Ross looked sharp in his gray GW sweatpants and crisp navy blue polo shirt. Coach Jennings and Coach Ciancio wore GW shorts and t-shirts.

I walked over knowing he'd bring up last night's game. On the one hand, I was hoping for an explanation. On the other, I was a little nervous to hear what what that explanation was.

"I imagine you're wondering why I only played you a few seconds last night."

You could say that again.

"Was it four or five?" He looked at his assistants.

Coach Ciancio shook his head and held up three fingers. He never said much.

"Three? Oh well, I didn't plan on putting you out there for exactly three seconds, but I did purposely sit you. See, there's been too many times this year where you've either disregarded what I've said or simply acted as if you're too good to be corrected. Yesterday's shoot around is a prime example. I told everyone once you've made twenty free throws to go to the pregame meal. But after making your twenty free throws you stuck around to shoot longer. You didn't listen to my instructions and you showed some major attitude. Then when we came back after the New Mexico trip, I specifically told everyone to go home and get to sleep. You stayed and shot hoops in the gym."

How did he know that?

"Bill Pebble told me, not too long ago. He said he was impressed with how hard you worked. He told me about that night we got back from the Christmas tournament ... said you were there for a few hours. Thomas, there's one head coach on this team and it's me. I need everyone listening to me and respecting my decisions at all times. Otherwise, no matter how good you are, I won't play you. We all know you can shoot, and I love the fact that you want to keep getting better. But you need to show me you can listen. And you need to show me you can follow directions."

Won't play me? Just because I like to work on my shot? I was shocked. I nodded and turned to go.

"And Thomas." I stopped at the sound of Coach Ross's voice. He pointed at my practice jersey, which had the white side facing out. "You need to go blue."

THE BLUE TEAM. I was back and I was livid. I couldn't believe I was back on the Blue Team. For what? For working hard on my game? I spent the next two days of practice wearing blue and following every single direction Coach Ross gave. Next up was the start of conference play and a visit from the Scarlet Knights of Rutgers University—and Tony Giambalvo.

Other than Jenae, nobody at GW knew Giambalvo and I had a history. It drove me nuts that he had so little respect for my game after I had already proved how much better I was than him. But I knew he would show up with nothing but disdain for me and demonstrate it every chance he got with trash talking and dirty play. The fact that he was starting and I was not would give him even more ammunition. If Coach Ross pulled another stunt like he did the other night and played me only a few seconds, Giambalvo would probably tell everyone in New Jersey!

My father would be at the Rutgers game. He was in the city on business and planned on staying afterwards to watch. He called me right before I left my dorm for shoot around. When he asked how my week was going I told him about the American game, my past couple of days on the Blue Team, and why I was there. His response was blunt. "I would have benched you too. You didn't listen. He's the coach, Thomas. It's his job to make sure everyone listens."

"But all I was doing was trying to get better."

"No, all you were doing was disregarding his instructions."

"Yeah, but you should see Brian. He never listens. I just don't get why Coach Ross is so concerned with me and doesn't say anything to Brian?"

"You should be thankful Coach Ross is concerned about you. It shows he cares and wants you to be not just a better basketball player, but a better person too. Just like your mother and I do. If we didn't keep you accountable then we wouldn't be loving you."

He was right and I knew it. But it just bothered me to no end that Brian could get away with whatever he wanted and I was under a microscope.

"Well, you've got a big game tonight. Don't worry about not starting or how much you play. Just do your best."

"Thanks, Dad. Boy, I'd sure love to beat these guys by thirty."

"Don't worry about the final score or any other players, just focus on what Coach Ross wants you to do. Play with discipline and class. Remember son. Christ says we are to love our enemies."

Even Giambalvo?

"Even guys like Giambalvo," my father said as if he could read my thoughts over the phone. "My meetings should be done soon so I'll be there for the start. Afterwards, let's you, Jenae and I go get something to eat. And Thomas, I love you and I'll be praying for you."

THE ATMOSPHERE IN the packed Smith Center felt like a playoff game. A large percentage of GW's student body came from the tri-state area of New York, New Jersey, and Connecticut. It seemed all those students who grew up in New Jersey and decided not to attend Rutgers were in the building rooting for us, like a win would prove they made the right decision by coming to D.C. to go to school.

I spotted my father in the crowd during layup lines. He was dressed in his usual understated, yet immaculate, business attire. Jenae was standing next to him along with Ray. Even Paul from the soup kitchen was at the game. They were smiling and laughing and having a great time. My father caught my eye and gave me a thumbs up.

This being the first conference game of the season for both teams the game started out with a high level of intensity. At least that's the way it looked to me from the bench. I still couldn't believe I was on the bench.

Much of Rutgers' intensity came from Giambalvo. He was barely six foot tall but shouldered a chip the size of Mount Rushmore. He was like a gnat, a cocky loud-mouthed gnat, that wouldn't go away. Watching him now, he was better than I remembered. He played his role perfectly—distribute the ball without committing turnovers, play smart defense, and be ready to knock someone's head off if it meant getting a rebound or loose ball.

We led at the start but never by more than five. Then three minutes into the game Matt quickly picked up two fouls. Coach Ross never hesitated in sending me in. I was back where I belonged: On the court playing, not sitting on the bench watching.

The game remained close throughout the first half. I was playing okay, but their zone defense was giving me troubles. They always had a hand in my face and pounced on any lazy pass. I'd hit two shots, but missed four, all of them rushed. I'd also thrown two turnovers.

I managed to stay away from Giambalvo until there were two minutes left in the first half. I tried to pass to Jim who was open on the left wing. The pass was tipped by a Rutgers defender. The loose ball bounced toward the sideline. I chased after it, and right before it fell harmlessly onto the scorers table, I collided with Giambalvo.

When we hit I took the brunt of the impact. My arms were extended reaching for the ball. I grimaced at the sharp pain in my ribcage. I knew his elbow found my midsection on purpose. The whistle blew and the ref pointed emphatically towards our basket. No foul, but since I never got my hands on it and the ball was last touched by a Rutgers player it was still our possession.

"Cheap shot," I spat at Giambalvo who was standing right next to me. Searing pain cut short my breath and I grabbed at my side. "Next time I won't go for the ball, either."

He didn't back down an inch. He stood his ground and said, "Well, if it ain't the pretty boy from Jersey. What're you going to do, pretty boy? Huh?" His eyes mocked me.

The referee stepped in and said, "Knock it off fellas and play ball."

Jim walked over and grabbed my arm. "Thomas! Let it go. Just play. It's our ball."

"That's right, pretty boy," Giambalvo taunted.

"Oh, shut up you little punk," Jim said to Giambalvo.

Giambalvo laughed as he walked away, his eyes never diverting from mine. My lungs craved air, but each breath brought searing pain. That kid has no idea—inhale, pain—how much better I am now. I'm going to—inhale, pain—rain jumpers on his head! Disrespect my game—inhale, pain—at your own risk.

As play resumed, I remembered my father. He was here watching! Did he hear what I said? No, the crowd booing Giambalvo was too loud. But did he see Giambalvo's cheap shot?

Our fans now booed Giambalvo every time he touched the ball. It didn't faze him or his team a bit. After the collision they went on a run, capped by a Giambalvo three-pointer. When the first half ended we were down two.

In the locker room at halftime, Danny felt my ribs. "Ow!" I winced at his touch.

"Just bruised," Danny said. "Ice it after the game."

The second half was just as tight. Matt started but picked up a quick foul, his third, and I went back in. With eleven minutes left in the game we were down two. Brian gave me a good pass, setting me up for an open shot. I missed. Kevin made an incredible effort to get the offensive rebound, powering his body through two Scarlet Knights defenders who were draped over his arms. He grabbed the rebound and gathered himself before going back up for a shot. The Rutgers players swarmed like bees. Two flailed about his shoulders while Giambalvo came in low, swiping at the ball held securely in Kevin's vice-like grip. With a loud grunt Kevin exploded off the floor and through the tangle of limbs and gently put the ball off the glass and in. The game was tied again. The walls of the Smith Center shook.

Then suddenly, thanks to three straight misses on our part, Rutgers went on a mini run and scored three times in a row to take a six point lead—their largest of the game. As always, Jim had his finger on the pulse of the moment. Needing a good shot, he slowly walked the ball up court and yelled out the play.

Turning to me Brian snapped. "Don't take no forced set shot! We got to attack the basket on these guys!"

I shook my head. Me taking forced shots? Now if that's not the pot calling the kettle black, I don't know what is.

We had the ball and worked it around the perimeter of the Rutgers zone. It was a huge possession. Our crowd, which had become deflated during their run, now rose to its feet like a swelling wave, ready to crash down on the Scarlet Knights. Brian passed the ball inside to Robert on the right side low block. He wasn't a big threat to score so they didn't double-team. Brian cut through the key and Rutgers defense reacted, cutting off the passing lane. A free spot on the floor opened up. I slid over, open for a three. Robert quickly kicked it out to me. The second I got it I let it fly. I was surprisingly wide open. Giambalvo was the closest defender and he ran over too late to contest the shot. I had ample time to set up, square my shoulders, and release the ball.

Right as I shot Giambalvo yelled, "Missed it!" and poked me in the ribs with his finger, something the refs probably wouldn't see. Despite the annoying poke, the shot felt great as it left my hand. I was sure it would go in. Instead, the ball clanged off the back rim. Dang it! Now that little gnat would think he made me miss.

Rutgers rebounded and quickly pushed the ball upcourt but we got back on defense in time.

Still down six we needed a defensive stop as much as we needed a score. Seconds later Brian got a steal and took off for our basket. There was only one Rutgers player to beat. The two converged on the basket at the same time. I trailed them and saw the whole play develop. If Brian missed, I'd be in perfect position for the rebound. The Rutgers defender made a great defensive play, contesting Brian's layup attempt without fouling. Brian missed and the ball headed right for me! It was just about to reach my fingertips—

Whack! I took a hard blow to the back of my head.

I wheeled around and swung. My right hand landed flush on Giambalvo's face. My back leg lifted off the ground with the force of my punch. The crushing impact of bone on bone raced through my arm all the way to my shoulder like a hot, searing pulse of electricity.

Giambalvo crumpled to the ground. I watched blankly as his teammates rushed over. The referee quickly grabbed me and led me away from the scene. It all happened so fast. I was shaking and there was yelling and shouting. The referee guided me toward our bench with one hand wrapped around my waist, the other one on guard to stiff-arm anyone who made an attempt to continue the fight.

I avoided eye contact with the coaches but I saw a few teammates faces. They were shocked.

What did I just do?

The blinding, white hot rage disappeared as confusion took its place. Time moved slowly. Sounds were muffled. My hand hurt, my whole arm hurt. My head hurt too. Two police officers moved onto the court where they were visible to the crowd.

The referee practically shoved me onto a seat on our bench. He turned and conversed with our coaches. I buried my head in my hands. Kevin walked over and placed one of his huge baseball glove sized hands on my head and tousled my hair. The uncontrollable shaking of my body lifted me out of my daze. Their trainer helped Giambalvo stand up and guided him to their bench. The crowd applauded, some lustily, some nervously. Rutgers players were cursing at me. Some of my teammates were shouting back.

Brian stood over me. "Man, you knocked him good," he said. Then his voice changed to the tone he always gave while arguing. "But I have no idea why."

The question "why" started ringing in my head. Why did I do it? What was I thinking? I had no idea. My father! He's here! Fear and regret intensified the pain in my hand and arm and head.

One of the officials told Coach Ross I'd been kicked out of the game and had to leave. Head down, I walked across the court from our bench to the hallway leading downstairs to the locker room. Coach Jennings and a policeman accompanied me. Some clapped as I left, others booed. A few fans were throwing popcorn and soda onto the court. Somebody threw a cup of soda that sprayed the three of us.

We took the winding staircase downstairs to the locker room. Coach Jennings had a hand on my back the entire time. As we arrived at the locker room door, Coach Jennings addressed the cop. "We're fine now, thanks. You can head back upstairs."

The large cop stared a moment. "I should really stay here and—"

"We're fine!" Coach Jennings snapped at him. He punched in the combo on the door and we walked in, closing the door behind us.

I sat down on the chair in front of my locker. Coach Jennings slowly paced back and forth and ran his hands through his hair. "You want me to stay here?"

"No, thanks," I said without looking up.

A moment passed. "Well, I'm going to head up to the bench then."

He left and I was alone. I waited out the rest of the game in tortured agony. The second-guessing process reached a fever pitch and I was starting to feel like the biggest fool on earth. Lord, what have I done? Did I really just punch someone because my pride had been bruised? Because I missed a few shots? Because Giambalvo didn't respect me? I had no answer. It all happened so fast. It wasn't like I thought it out.

When the team finally arrived in the locker room I was already dressed without showering. Alex, who hadn't played thanks to his broken hand, was the first one in the door. I knew immediately we'd lost. As everyone else filed in, my teammates looked at me with curious eyes. It was quiet. Nobody said a word. Rutgers had beaten us, on our home court no less. I feared having to look in the faces of my teammates and coaches.

Alex slumped onto his chair next to mine and whispered, "Lost by three. Coach ain't happy."

Lost by three points to Rutgers. The local media would have a field day with this. I could have made a difference. No, it was more than that. I'd lost the game.

Coach Ross walked into the locker room with the assistant coaches. My pulse raced. He didn't say anything for a moment or two. As he leaned on the wall next to the dry erase board, his arms were folded and his head down. The silence was maddening.

"You upperclassmen," he finally said, "I'm proud of you. You played hard and you played unselfishly." He paused before continuing. "You young players need to do a better job of observing the leaders we have in this locker room. No matter how talented you are, we won't accomplish anything if we're not all on the same page, all working towards the same goal." He looked around the room at each of us and finally settled on me. My eyes dropped in shame and the weight of regret ground me into the floor. "We're a team. We do things as a team. Individual glory means nothing here. Don't do that again. You hurt the team tonight. You hurt yourself." He paused then blew out a deep breath. "If anyone needs treatment be sure to get to the training room. We'll watch film tomorrow ... short practice. Nothing too hard. I know this stings, but tomorrow we move on." He shook his head and walked out of the room.

Nobody said a word to me. I was unsure if I should leave right away, apologize to everyone or not say a word. Finally Jim came up to me. "Don't ever do something like that again while I'm on this team, you hear me?" He walked away without waiting for a reply.

I got up and left. Just outside the locker room Coach Jennings stopped me. "Be in Coach Ross's office tomorrow at eight. I wouldn't be late if I were you."

CHAPTER 17

I WALKED UPSTAIRS to the lobby. It was full of people. I turned to head back down and wait out the crowd but stopped when I heard my father call my name. He was standing at the top of the stairs.

"Come on," he said as he nodded his head towards the door. "Let's get out of here." He turned to go and I followed, squeezing past gawkers and people mumbling, "Dumb" and "What was he thinking?"

Once out of the building we walked down the block, not saying a word. "Where's Jenae?" I finally asked.

"She went home. I asked her is she'd be willing to let me talk to you alone and she said yes."

"And Ray and Paul?"

"They left too. When you hit that guy Ray practically jumped up and cheered. Paul grabbed the back of his shirt and yanked him back down into his seat. I think everybody else was simply in shock. I know I was." With his right hand he gestured off in the distance. "Let's go for a walk. I want to talk."

He led and I followed in silence. My mind was screaming for a way to erase what I just did. If I could only rewind the night and do it over.

My father steered us south from campus then slowly filled me in on what transpired after I was escorted to the locker room. The head coach for Rutgers was yelling and screaming at the officials and Coach Ross. Players were jawing at each other. The officials barely kept it together on the court. "It was pretty ugly. Then a little later

Giambalvo shows up with a bandage over his eye and goes back in the game. He played like nothing ever happened. I was impressed. He's a tough Jersey kid. The whole incident seemed to infuse them with energy. You guys looked stunned. They led the rest of the way."

"Did you talk to Coach Ross?" he asked after another long interlude of silence.

My stomach churned. "No. He wants to meet with me in the morning. I think he was too mad to talk tonight."

"Not surprised."

We continued walking south and before I knew it we'd made our way to a spot between the Lincoln Memorial and Reflecting Pool. My father showed no desire to walk up the stairs to the Lincoln so we stood near the bottom step. It was dark and quiet with only a few people milling about.

"Impressive looking building," he said gazing up at the Lincoln's portico. "This city sure loves its monuments. Lots of them, all beautifully built. Most dedicated to freedom and Christian liberty. Yet our politicians sure do love to take away our liberty. Hypocrisy, that's what it is. It's the same thing when we claim to follow Christ and then do things that are totally contrary to His Word. Like you did tonight. Son, how did this happen?"

"I don't know. I just lost it. I got so angry at that kid that I lost it. I'm sorry."

"Lost what?"

"I don't know, my temper?"

"Are you asking me or telling me?"

"Telling you, I guess."

"You guess?"

"No, I am telling you. It was my temper."

He sighed. "Everybody gets mad on the court at one point or another. It happens. The emotions are flowing … it's a physical game with a lot riding on each shot, each play. But the Bible says in your anger do not sin. You did. And tonight wasn't just about you losing your temper."

157

"What do you mean?"

"Thomas, here you are, having a great season for a really good team. You're playing in front of a full house in an important game. It's everything you've wanted. Then you hustle down the court, grab the rebound and get fouled hard. Now, you could have maintained your composure and realized you had two free throws coming. You could have stayed in the game and helped your team win. Instead you hit that kid. You got kicked out of the game, and your team lost. It was completely and utterly counter to what you should have done. That wasn't just anger. That was your ego totally out of control. Remember what it says in Romans 8? The mind of the flesh or the carnal mind is enmity towards God. When the Lord saves us, He saves us from ourselves, from our egoic mind. Tonight wasn't Giambalvo's fault. Giambalvo and others like him aren't the enemy. Your mind is." He paused, then said, "We truly are our own worst enemy."

I'd heard this before from my father, but now it hit home. I felt tears building up as I looked down at my hand. It hurt even more.

"And your mind made basketball more important than God. Isn't that right?"

It was and I knew it immediately. I tried to follow the Lord in every area of my life but basketball. Basketball was mine, not His. I nodded as the tears flowed.

"Remember what Peter the disciple went through? Time and time again he'd made all these boastful declarations. He said he'd never stumble. He said he'd never deny Christ. But he did. Three times! And after the third he wept because he finally realized what he'd been saved from. Thomas, you need to see what you've been saved from. Do you?"

Tears poured out and I put my head in my hands and sobbed. All my arrogance and pride, trying to prove I was better than Brian, trying to show everyone how great I was, that I was the next Larry Bird; the Lord saved me from all that. He was so patient and I was so stubborn. My father put his hands on my shoulders. Once I could get the words out, I said, "I do … I do."

"Good. Then surrender it all to the Lord. Don't hold anything back. Trust in the Lord with all your heart. Not just part of it, all of it. And lean not on your own understanding. In all your ways acknowledge Him and He will direct your paths."

I ran my palms over my face, wiping away the tears. "I will, Dad."

"And trust Him with your basketball career. Abraham was willing to give up Isaac. Are you willing to give up basketball? I'm not in any way saying you should or need to, but that should be your attitude. Whatever you want, Lord. But I think He does want you to play. He gave you an amazing gift … you can shoot a basketball better than anyone I've ever seen. So play the game because you love it and because you're thankful He gave you this gift. Play your heart out every time you step onto the court and let your competitive fire burn—not because you're out to prove a point, but because you want to do your best with what the Lord gave you. You spend tons of time disciplining your body to play well. Now discipline your mind. That same chapter in Romans says the mind governed by the Spirit is life and peace. Allow the Lord to renew your mind day by day. Not only will you have life and peace, I believe you'll be a better player."

I exhaled deeply and felt a calm I hadn't had in a long time. "So, how do I do this?" I asked. "How do I discipline my mind?"

"You need to immerse yourself in the Word. I know you read it, but you need to read it every day. Don't just read it, study it and meditate on it. You need to make it more important than basketball. Make it *the* priority. And with basketball, focus more on things that help your teammates look good. Do all the little things on the court that Jim and Matt do. Of course you still need to shoot because you're great at it, but work on making the extra pass, setting good screens, playing good weak-side defense. Think about how you can make the team better, rather than how you can make yourself look better or how many points you can score. Then carry that attitude off the court into every other area of your life.

"And one more thing. You've been arrogant and hypocritical towards Brian. You've been judging him, thinking you're better. But you're not. Tonight should make that pretty obvious."

My face flushed as he spoke. Brian wasn't the enemy either. He was my teammate and yet I had made him out to be the bad guy. Worse than that, I judged him to make me feel better about myself. So what if he's arrogant? Wasn't I just as arrogant? I shook my head at the awful truth. "You're right," I said meekly.

"For you to truly serve the Lord, you need to start loving Brian. It's not all his fault you guys don't get along. You're going to be around Brian every day. He's the perfect gauge for you. You start acting towards him the way you should and you'll know you're maturing and growing.

"Tell you what. I know you're busy with school and basketball, and I'm busy at work, but you're more important than my work. Let's start reading the gospels together. A chapter or two a day, every day. Then we'll talk on the phone every few days about what we read. Okay?"

"Sounds good. Thanks, Dad."

"My pleasure, son. I love you and I'm on this journey with you. I'm learning and maturing just like you. Just because I have some gray hair doesn't mean I'm done learning or know it all. It's just that I've been on this road a little longer than you." He winked at me and I smiled.

THE NEXT MORNING I got up early to meet Coach Ross. At half past seven I was about to exit the lobby of our dorm when the student receptionist at the front desk called my name. "Got something for you. Some old guy dropped it off a few hours ago." He handed me a folded piece of paper and grinned. "Didn't know you could throw a punch like that."

"Me neither," I said under my breath as I examined the paper in my hand before opening it. I recognized my father's handwriting.

Thomas,

Good morning. I wish I could spend more time with you but am needed back home. Heading out to catch the 6am train. Thought I'd drop this off before I left.

I'll be praying your meeting with Coach Ross goes well. Accept responsibility for your actions and do whatever he says. "Whoever loves discipline loves knowledge, but whoever hates correction is stupid." Proverbs 12:1

Remember, your actions will speak louder than your words, especially with Brian. "Preach the gospel at all times and when necessary use words." Francis of Assisi

And make sure you're reading the Word every day. I'll be reading Matthew chapter one on the train this morning!

Love, Dad

I folded the paper back up and stuffed it in my pocket. I walked briskly to Coach Ross' office with thoughts of correction and discipline on my mind. Loving discipline meant loving knowledge. I got that. And if hating correction was stupid then I guess I better start loving correction too. I was pretty sure I was in for a good dose of both. What would he say? At 7:55 a.m. I walked into the Smith Center to find out.

Coach Ross was alone in his office sitting at his massive desk. A frozen image from last night's game was on the TV screen behind him. He gestured to a chair and I sat down opposite him. On the desk there was a small pyramid, about six inches tall, with writing all over it. He must have seen it caught my eye because he pointed to it and said, "It's Wooden's famous Pyramid of Success. Ever heard of it?"

Of course I knew who John Wooden was. He was one of the greatest basketball coaches ever, winning 10 NCAA titles at UCLA, but I'd never heard of any pyramid so I shook my head.

Coach Ross picked up the small pyramid and turned it over in his hands as he looked at it. "Coach Wooden developed this to help define what success is and how to achieve it. There are fifteen blocks in all that make up the pyramid. Each one is essential for success.

Poise, confidence, skill … self control. There are some you excel at. Others you need a lot of work on."

He handed it to me and I read each block. At the top of the pyramid was the block called 'Competitive Greatness.' "What is competitive greatness?" I asked.

"Wooden defined it as loving the battle, the struggle, the competition, because it gave you the opportunity to be your best when your best is required."

I handed him back the pyramid and he reached across his desk and took it.

"So about last night…"

I tried in vain not to hold my breath as I waited for him to lay into me, but he didn't scream or yell. He was very matter of fact as he laid out my punishment. I had to sit out one game per NCAA rules, apologize to Giambalvo in writing, apologize to my teammates in person, and run sprints at 6:30 a.m. for the next week.

I let out that breath I was holding. I don't know what kind of punishment I was afraid of but this didn't seem too bad. And I probably deserved worse.

"Thomas," he said, "one of the reasons I recruited you was I thought you were a high character kid. I look at your parents, how you grew up—I didn't think I'd have these kinds of problems with you. But right now, I'm wondering if I was fooled. I sure hope it wasn't an act. Because, I want to be real clear. One more incident like this and you're off the team. For good. I'd hate to do that, but I will. Am I clear?"

"Yes, sir," I said, although I desperately wanted to say more. I wanted to tell him he could trust me from now on. But I knew with the way I'd acted lately, it wouldn't matter what I said. My words would be hollow. My father was right. I had to show him.

He leaned back in his chair and tried to wipe the stress off his face. It didn't work. Deep wrinkles furrowed his brow and dark circles cupped his eyes. He looked awful. Had he slept at all last night? "My job is to help each one of you guys on the team be successful. So far I don't think I've done a very good with you freshmen. That's my fault and it's going to change. Wooden's definition of success is a good one. He said success is, and I quote, 'peace of mind which is a direct result of self-satisfaction in knowing you made the effort to become the best you are capable of becoming.' Last night was the not the best you are capable of. It was probably the worst. At least I hope it was the worst. And I hope it's all behind you."

I nodded. "Yes, sir."

"One of the reasons why I like Wooden's principles and quotes so much is they parallel biblical principles. When Wooden says your best is required each and every day it's similar to Christ saying we need to deny ourselves and pick up our cross every day. From now on I want your best every day, Thomas. I know you can do it."

CHAPTER 18

AFTER MY MEETING with Coach Ross, I walked across campus to class. It seemed everyone knew about the punch. People I'd never seen before were coming up to me or shouting to me from across the street, telling me how cool they thought it was that I decked that kid. It made me sick to my stomach. I wanted to tell them it was stupid and I'd take it back if I could. But they'd slap me on the back and walk away before I could say anything. Then I thought about my teammates. How could I face them? Rutgers beat us and I was largely to blame. It was a bad loss.

I was never comfortable speaking in public. Give me a basketball and the more people watching the better. But apologizing in front of the team in our locker room was agonizing. Here I was, just a freshman. I'd made a dumb mistake and it cost us a game. "I'm sorry," I said. "It was my fault and mine alone. It won't happen again." I looked over at Coach Ross who gave a slight nod. I sat back down.

Coach Ross went over some of the tape of the Rutgers game before everyone headed upstairs to practice.

Down the hall at the equipment room window, Kevin had paused to talk to Max, the equipment manager. The two were buddies and Kevin often hung out at Max's window either before or after practice. Leaning on the counter, Kevin said, "Hey, that was a sweet punch." Max nodded and smiled with obvious appreciation. "Don't see many white kids in my neighborhood doin' that sort of thing."

164

"No, sir," Max echoed.

"But," Kevin lowered his chin, his brow partially obscuring his dark eyes, "I was more impressed you took responsibility for it. See a lot less of *that* in my old neighborhood." He and Max both slowly shook their heads.

I was about to respond when Kevin gave Max some elaborate handshake, said goodbye, and quickly walked off. "Well, don't just stand there lookin' like a fool," Max said. "Get your butt up there so you can earn your way out of that blue jersey you got on! Believe me, I seen enough of them things. I know that jersey's got a white side to it."

MY HAND HAD been sore ever since the punch, but as practice wore on, it hurt more and more. It started to swell and obscure the knuckles. Every time it was bumped or I caught a pass I felt a pain rip through it. I had no idea it was this bad. After a half hour I couldn't stand the pain any longer.

I showed it to Danny. "Hmm ... doesn't look good. Better get this X-rayed."

Danny's words shot through me quicker than an actual X-ray. My skin went hot and my hand instantly hurt even worse. I quickly went down to our locker room and changed without showering. Twenty minutes later Danny and I walked into the GW hospital and met our team's orthopedist outside the X-ray room.

"That doesn't look good, Thomas," the orthopedist said as he gingerly felt my right hand. He was a sharp-looking man in his thirties. Glasses, white coat, tall, clean cut. He oozed credibility. My pulse sky rocketed. "There's lots of little bones in your hand and any damage in there can end up being a pretty big deal. You're right handed aren't you?"

I nodded. The burgeoning lump in my throat prevented me from speaking. Out of the corner of my eye I saw Danny shaking his head.

"Hmm ... well, the only way we can tell if this is a break or just a bad bruise is to get an X-ray, so let's get you in there. Danny, come get me when they're done." The grim faced orthopedist nodded in Danny's direction and then walked down the hallway.

I was escorted into the X-ray room where they took numerous pictures of my hand. This was my right hand, my shooting hand. Without it I couldn't play, period. Was a broken hand the Lord's way of disciplining me? Or getting my attention? I certainly deserved it after what I had done. Acute regret swept over me.

When the X-rays were done, Danny carried them into the orthopedist's office. I watched nervously while the two of them examined the images intensely. They stood inches away from the lit wall, pointing, whispering, and contemplating the X-rays like two archeologists trying to decipher some ancient hieroglyphics.

Finally, the orthopedist and Danny shared one last "Mmm-hmm." Somehow this signaled agreement. They turned to look at me. Here it comes. My heart pounded inside my chest.

The orthopedist took off his glasses and rubbed his eyes. "Well, there's no break."

I exhaled and nearly went limp as the tension left my muscles. Thank you, Lord!

The orthopedist put his glasses back on. "I thought I saw something in one of these X-rays but I think you're in the clear. It is a bad bruise though, so I'd stay off it for a few days." He looked at Danny who nodded, his marching orders clear.

When I arrived back at the gym, practice was over. Danny handed me a bag of ice. "Get started," he said. "Twenty minutes on, twenty minutes off."

The upperclassmen on the team joked that according to Danny the cure for anything, be it a sprain, bruise, break, hangover, or headache, was ice. Seeing a bag of ice resting on the back of my hand versus a cast was a wonderful relief.

6:00 A.M. CAME early. I slapped my alarm clock to stop the annoying noise. Time to run my sprints. Getting up this early was punishment enough even without the running. Head down, I slowly shuffled out the front door and headed for the Smith Center. But by the time I arrived I was actually looking forward to running. This was my discipline. I deserved it and was supposed to love it. When I arrived at 6:25 a.m. Coach Jennings, who had been assigned the unlucky task of monitoring my attendance and effort, was nowhere in sight. I decided to stretch out while waiting for him. After fifteen minutes I went to go look for him. The first place I checked was his office. The door was locked and no one answered when I knocked. Then it hit me. Then I hit myself, slapping my forehead with the palm of my left hand. My sprints wouldn't start until the next morning. I'd forgotten Coach Ross told me Coach Jennings had to leave and go scout our next opponent St. Bonaventure. He wouldn't be back until this afternoon.

Now what? Should I go back to bed? Stay and shoot? Shooting probably wasn't a good idea considering how much my hand still hurt. I stood on the far edge of the court immobilized by indecision. I watched an early riser throw up some shots at one of the baskets. He had good form. Watching him made me want to grab my Chuck Taylor's and shoot all the more, despite my sore hand.

Shooting a basketball is a beautiful thing, but it doesn't produce much that changes lives. Made baskets didn't change my life. The Lord did. Real change is when people like Jenae go—

The soup kitchen! That's where I should go. I looked at the clock. They'd be serving breakfast by now but maybe I could help clean up. I bolted out of the gym. The thought of seeing Jenae inspired me to run all the way to the church. I hadn't seen or talked to her since before the Rutgers game.

When I swung open the basement door to the church I was greeted by a mouthwatering combination of bacon and coffee. As I entered, two men left. "Better hurry if you want some grub," one of them said.

"Thanks, I will," I replied. Most of the tables and chairs were still occupied with men enjoying their hot meal. I glanced around the room and spotted Jenae and Ray eating at one of the far tables. I quickly grabbed a tray and served myself.

As I put one more scoop of hash browns on my plate Paul emerged from the kitchen and greeted me with a big smile. It was almost impossible not to smile back. He had on corduroy pants, a striped shirt that needed ironing, and a wool sport jacket that went with neither his shirt nor pants. "Thomas, what a surprise!"

"Hi, Paul." I noticed he was carrying two mugs of coffee. I pointed towards them and said, "you still serving the coffee this morning?"

"Sort of. This one is for me." He held up the mug in his right hand. "And this one is for Ray," he said indicating the mug in his left hand. "Can you believe this is his fourth cup of coffee this morning?"

"Man, he sure loves his coffee."

"Indeed. Come, let's go join our friends."

Jenae hadn't seen me come in so when I sat down next to her she turned and looked at me with eyes as wide as pancakes. "Thomas, you're here! Are you alright? Is everything okay?"

"Everything's fine." I put my hand on her shoulder. "Really. I'm great." I nodded towards Ray. "Good morning."

"Morning to you, big fella!" Paul handed him his mug of coffee and Ray took a big whiff of the aroma. "Fourth cup of the morning for me. Can't wait to talk about that punch!"

I cringed inside. Jenae eyed me warily then asked, "Where have you been and what's happened to you? Your father asked me to leave you two alone the other night. I didn't know for how long so I didn't call. I haven't seen or heard anything since then."

"I know, and I'm sorry. I've been busy and so much has happened. I have so much to tell you."

"You do? Well what were you thinking when you hit that guy? I just couldn't believe you did that, Thomas. I was shocked."

"Shocked? Man I was impressed," Ray chirped. "That guy dropped like a rock."

Paul held out his hand like a traffic cop. "Ray, please, let him speak."

"I don't blame you for being shocked. Any of you. I was too. I still can't believe I did that. But I did. And as horrible as I feel for

Giambalvo, it exposed everything. See for most of my life I wanted to be great at basketball. I wanted to be respected and admired as the next Larry Bird. Seriously, that was my goal, and it dominated my life. All my desires, dreams, goals, you name it—they all hinged on that next shot. I was obsessed and never really saw it until the other night. That guy had no respect for me or my game. And he was so in my face about it. I wanted to score on him again and again to shut him up. But I missed. And ... he just wouldn't quit. So, when he hit me in the back of my head, I didn't think about it. I just swung.

"My father and I had a great talk after the game. He really helped me see it. I talked the talk and thought I was walking the walk. But I wasn't. I was fooling myself. I wanted so badly to be the next Larry Bird, I didn't trust the Lord or my father or any coach to get in the way and screw it up. It was too important to me. I wasn't about to let anyone—even God—get in the way of my dreams. How crazy is that? So, now I surrender it all to the Lord. In many ways I was just like the disciple Peter, thinking I knew best and was doing such a great job following Him. But I wasn't, and just like Peter in the Bible, I found out that's one of the things I was saved from."

Jenae's hands were on the table and I put my hand on top of hers. "And you were right. I wasn't playing the game out of love. I was needy. I wanted to play great to impress you. I wanted the game to provide my identity rather than finding it in the Lord. I'm sorry. You have been such a wonderful example of true Christian love. Thank you. I love you."

A tear slid down her check as she slowly nodded then leaned over and rested her head on my shoulder. The table was quiet. Ray discreetly picked up a napkin and dabbed his eyes underneath his glasses. When a minute of silence had passed Jenae sat up straight and with both hands ran her fingers through her hair then let out a deep cleansing breath. She looked at me and said, "I love you, Thomas."

It was my turn to shed tears.

Paul raised his coffee mug. "Here's to the Lord's love being shared through us each and every day."

Jenae and I raised our mugs too. "Amen to that," she said.

"How about your hand?" Paul asked me. "Is it okay? That was quite a punch."

I cleared my throat. "It's fine. Thought it might be broken but the X-rays were negative."

"How did you know it was him?" Ray asked. "I mean you swung without looking. How'd you know it was the same guy that elbowed you earlier?"

"I knew. I've played the game enough. He was the only one who would have done that."

"Pow!" Ray smacked his fist into the palm of his other hand. "Yes, sir. This reminds me of the one time I mashed up my hand pretty good." He held it up as if to inspect it for any remaining evidence of the mashing. "I was in New Mexico. I think it was Santa Fe, but I'm not sure. Could'a been Las Cruces. Well, I'm riding the rails like I did back then. So, I'm in New Mexico. Could have been Albuquerque now that I think of it."

"I think I've heard this story," Jenae said. "Is this the one where you ended up in jail with the farmer who was missing a few fingers?"

Ray shook his head. "Nope, that's a different story. No jail time in this one. So I'm riding the rails. You always had to look out for railroad bulls. So, I'm on my own in this car hoping to dodge railroad bulls—that's what they call railroad police. Anyway, this one huge bull finds me sleeping in this car. Shines his flashlight right in my face and wakes me up. He tells me to get up, asks my name, trying to intimidate me, being disrespectful, you know. He just keeps yelling these questions at me. So, I stood up and took a good look at him. Didn't seem like he had a gun and I could tell he was slower than a can of glue so I just clocked him." He punched his hands together again to emphasize the point. "Man, he dropped like a sack of potatoes. My hand hurt something fierce. Swelled up like a balloon for days. Never did get an X-ray. Now, I know that's not the Christian thing to do, but darn it, the guy just wouldn't shut up. Telling me how I'm some no-good piece of trash. Man, I hate it when guys just don't know when to stop talking. I mean, he just went on and on. It was the only thing I could think of doing right then and ..." Ray stopped as he noticed Paul chuckling. "Why are you laughing? I thought you would be angry and all, me hitting that guy." Paul's laughter got louder. "What's so stinkin' funny?"

"Ray, my good friend," Paul said while still shaking with laughter, "I am not laughing because you punched that guy. I'm laughing at your indictment of his communication skills. If one were to punch us for talking too much there'd be a lot of broken noses around here!"

With a frown Ray took a long sip of his coffee. He shook his head and very slowly started to smile. Then he finally laughed. "Paul, man," he said as he pushed his glasses further up on his nose, "you always seem to have my number! I get it, I get it. I like to tell stories and I need to get to the ... well I need to get to the ..."

"Punchline?" Paul could barely get the word out as he was already laughing at his own joke.

Everyone laughed. "Yes, Ray," Paul said after we all settled down, "you've had lots of fights. Perhaps you can put your pugilistic past behind you and learn to turn the other cheek."

"I know, I know. I'm working on it."

"Me too," I said.

"Tell me, Thomas," Paul said, "did you apologize to the player you hit?"

"Giambalvo? Yes, I sent him an apology in writing. Don't know if he got it yet. Oh! That reminds me. Is Aqualung here?"

Paul shook his head. "No. I haven't seen him here in a while. Why?"

"I need to apologize to him too."

"What?" Ray nearly shouted. "Apologize to *Aqualung*? For what?"

"It's been a while, but one day I was really upset and saw him on the street. I told him to take a shower sometime this century."

Jenae snapped her fingers. "So that's why he always acts weird when you are around."

"He always acts weird! You want to apologize for that?" Ray was incredulous. "Shoot, he should have taken your advice. It probably *has* been a century since he showered!"

"Easy, Ray," Paul chided. "Thomas, what were you upset about?"

"I'd just played a game of one-on-one with my roommate Brian and lost. I was furious. I left the gym and started walking. I saw Aqualung and another guy sitting on a park bench. The other guy was about to ask for some money and I said something to him. I simply lashed out. It's exactly the kind of thing I was talking about. Being competitive is one thing, but that was something else. That was simply mean."

"Indeed it was," Paul said. "I think you should apologize to Lewis."

"To who?" Jenae, Ray and I all asked in unison.

"Lewis. Aqualung's real name is Lewis Bowman. I don't know where or when this Aqualung thing started, but everyone seems to call him that these days. I've known him for years. Do you know he used to be a successful businessman?"

Ray looked even more shocked. "No way. You're kidding, right?"

"No, I'm serious," Paul continued. "He worked nearby and often came to church. I used to talk to him quite often. Back then he wasn't so crazy. Eccentric yes, but not crazy. Then he lost his job, his relationships—his life really went downhill. He started to lose his mind. He was so consumed with his thoughts, what he thought about this or that. His thoughts became his identity. He thought he was so smart because he spent time thinking about the banking industry or philosophy. He was so prideful. He would tell me all these things to show me how smart he was, and yet he couldn't even dress himself properly. I tried to help him, but he didn't want to listen. He was too smart for the word of God. Can you imagine? Look at him now. He's like an animal. Barely wears any clothes, doesn't bathe."

"I don't care what you call him, I can't stand the guy," Ray blurted out.

"Why?" Paul asked.

The question seemed to really set Ray off. "We had this run in about a year ago," he said in a loud and angry voice. "I was in a rough spot, sleeping out under the stars if you know what I mean. Saw Aqualung all the time. One night we got to drinking together. We got drunk and then got into a fight. He's lucky I was drunk or else I would have creamed him. Anyway, I'm suffering through a hangover the next day, but I tried to do the right thing and make amends. Aqualung wanted no part of it. The dirty bastard cussed me out, spit at me—he even threw an empty beer bottle at me. I just avoid him these days, but if that thing wants to pick up where we left off, I got no problems with that."

Paul wiped his mouth with his napkin. "Well, Ray, like I said. I think it's time you retire the boxing gloves and try something else."

Ray shrugged. "Probably so." His forearm muscles rippled as he turned his coffee cup in his hands. "Still don't think he's worth it."

"Oh, hush," Paul chided. "God could have said the same thing about you and me. Instead, He loves us. And He commands us to be peacemakers."

Ray looked off across the room like he didn't want to admit Paul was right.

"One day, Raymond. One day you will have the chance to be a true peacemaker. Maybe it will start with Mr. Lewis Bowman."

CHAPTER 19

THE NEXT MORNING I was up early again. This time I knew Coach Jennings would be at the gym and I'd have to run sprints. I hated getting up early in the morning under normal circumstances, but this morning was even worse. With all that had happened in the last few days I was exhausted. If it was possible to be so tired it hurt, I was there. I dragged myself out of bed, dressed and walked to the gym in the cold, dark predawn morning.

When I showed up, Coach Jennings smiled weakly. "Get warmed up." I could tell he wasn't too happy about being there either. Living outside the city in Virginia he probably had to get up around 5 a.m. to get here on time.

The gym hummed with activity as people hustled to get in a workout before heading to class or work. I could hear the clanging of weights coming from the weight room. Two men ran up and down the stairs in the bleachers while a group of guys played pickup ball on one of the courts.

Coach Jennings ran me hard. "If we have to be here at this hour, we're going to make it worth our while." He stood off to the side, stopwatch in one hand, a huge Styrofoam cup of coffee in the other.

I had to run fifteen suicides, or guts as some call them, and each one had to be completed in under a minute. They weren't fun. I started on the baseline and ran to the first free-throw line, touched the line and ran back to where I started. Without stopping I repeated to the half court line, the opposite free-throw line and finally the opposite baseline. That comprised one gut. After seven of them I wanted to puke, but my gut had nothing to produce. I hadn't had breakfast yet, or "breafast" as Coach Jennings sometimes said, oddly leaving out the 'k'.

LATER THAT MORNING I sat in my American History class, staring out the window, my mind flipping through the catalogue of my recent misdeeds. The punch, insulting Aqualung, hating Brian—it was all so embarrassing. How could I have been so blind? It was the words of my professor that did the job and finally brought me back to the present.

"So, do I think the role of religion is at times exaggerated, yes. Every now and then I'll get some student who argues with me, saying America was founded as a Christian nation. Now, the story of the Pilgrims and the Mayflower Compact is intriguing; George Washington praying at Valley Forge, inspiring ... but, please, let's not get carried away."

My American History Professor Leo Howard was eccentric. His head was mostly bald on top, but on the sides shaggy hair framed his long face. None of his clothes matched and his hands flew about in exaggerated gestures when he talked. He had a thick New York City accent and he taught from a very liberal viewpoint. He was nothing like Benz Velo, my ancient and energetic European history professor, who had fun in class and seemed like the kind of guy that could laugh at himself. Not Professor Howard. He may have been eccentric, but he was also a classroom bully. Any student that asked a question he didn't like was liable to be verbally accosted in front of the whole class. One day he drove a girl to tears.

He contradicted nearly everything my father had taught me about our nation's beginning. I remembered the many times my father would talk about this subject. It was one of his favorites. Usually we'd be at the dinner table and a current event would start the ball rolling. No matter what it was, my father could always bring it back to the basics—the Bible, the Declaration of Independence, and the U.S. Constitution.

I thought about dropping the course, but since I wanted to major in history, I figured I better stick it out. Brian and John Hornbeck, one of our team managers, were also in the class with me. Initially my thought was I couldn't let Brian know more American history than me. Now that seemed so silly.

"I'm not here to denigrate anyone's faith," Professor Howard continued, "but I'm also not going to perpetuate this myth that America started out as a Christian nation. Nor do I think the Christian churches were really such a positive influence. Just ask all the witches they burned or slaves they held. But ..." he held a hand up as if to admit he'd gone too far, "that's just an aside. Just my opinion. Really, let's keep this in mind; We do have the first amendment and its separation of church and state, and it's a good thing. Okay. Any questions so far?"

I looked around. Nobody moved. Most were waiting with pen in hand for Professor Howard to continue. I was wondering when I should pick my jaw up off the floor. America starting out as a Christian nation was a myth? Christian churches were not a positive influence on our nation? Who was he kidding? He was trashing my faith and loving every minute of it. Should I say something? This was his class, his turf, and he was entitled to his opinions. However, the First Amendment to the Constitution was another topic my father discussed. I had listened well and Professor Howard was wrong.

"Ahh, Mr. Conner," Professor Howard said after noticing my raised hand.

I cleared my throat. "You mentioned the First Amendment and the separation of church and state. The First Amendment doesn't use any of those words. It never mentions church, state, or separation."

"That was more of a statement than a question." Professor Howard's tone was icy cold.

"Oh, right ... I guess it was. But it seems so many people get it wrong. The First Amendment was never meant to separate religion from our government."

"People get it wrong, do they?" He glared at me. "You're saying *I* get it wrong?"

I had the feeling I'd accidentally whacked a hornet's nest. To answer was to take another whack and risk getting stung worse. He wasn't about to let some student correct him. Then again, Leo Howard seemed like the kind of guy that might go after me even harder if I backed down now.

"Well, a lot of people do. The First Amendment was supposed to protect the church from the government, not keep Christianity out."

"Really ..." A switch was flipped and Professor Howard's manner changed. He smiled wryly, like a fox about to devour a chicken. "So, I'm getting the words mixed up. Let me ask you this, Mr. Conner, what do the words in the Bible say about treating our enemies? Does it recommend turning the other cheek, or does it say we should punch them in the nose? Did you get those words mixed up, or are you simply a hypocrite?"

Gasps filled the room. A few seats over Brian snickered. All eyes were on me. Although the room had quieted down so you could hear the proverbial pin drop, I couldn't hear it because my heart was pounding too loud.

A familiar indignation swelled inside of me. Who did he think he was, calling me a hypocrite? Me hitting that guy has nothing to do with the First Amendment. Angry phrases formed in my mouth but they suddenly came to a screeching halt. He was right. Claiming to follow Christ and hitting that guy was hypocritical. I was speechless.

"Well, Mr. Conner?" He waited, tapping his fingers on the lectern.

I was a hypocrite. Could I admit that here in front of everyone? In front of Brian? I took a deep breath, then realized if I didn't now, when would I? "You're right," I said. "I was a hypocrite."

There were more gasps, but these sounded uncomfortable. Out of the corner of my eye I saw Brian's mouth slowly droop.

At first Professor Howard stared at me like he was at a loss for words. He almost seemed disappointed to win the argument so quickly. His fingers stopped tapping and he cleared his throat. "Well, indeed." He paused again and looked at his notes. "Anyway, your First Amendment argument is utter nonsense and not germane to our discussion. So, does anyone else have something to say?"

He surveyed the classroom. Nobody breathed, let alone allowed a word to slip past their lips. "Fine, let's move on."

The adrenaline rush slowly started to fade but my hands still shook. I peeked over at Brian who was still gawking at me. He immediately looked away like he was embarrassed. But I wasn't. I felt ... relieved.

At the end of class John Hornbeck was right behind me as I left the room. John was a freshman like me. He also loved basketball and history so we had plenty to talk about. He came from central Illinois and had a wholesomeness that was rare on campus. While guys like Alex and Coleman wolfed down sodas in the cafeteria, John filled up his tray with glasses of milk. I never saw him out late at night and he never swore. Even when Brian treated him with condescension—"Get my water bottle," or "Give me a dry towel next time,"—John put team above himself and performed his job well.

"I can't believe the nerve of that guy," he said. "Who does he think he is? Calling you a hypocrite!"

I wasn't surprised that he too was offended by Professor Howard. I shook my head. "Unfortunately John, he was right. Not about the First Amendment stuff, about me."

"Really? I don't know. Seems Giambalvo had it coming, I mean—"

"No, John," I said. "I had it coming."

John looked at me puzzled then scratched his head.

"Listen, I appreciate you being on my side and sticking up for me, I just want to be clear. It was my fault, nobody else's. Giambalvo didn't get what he deserved. What happened in there," I waved towards the lecture hall we just left, "that's what I deserved."

DRESSED IN STREET clothes, I served my one game suspension on the bench, sitting next to Alex. We beat St. Bonaventure easily.

Over the next few days I iced my hand every chance I could. Before and after practice, in class, before bed, you name it. I think Danny enjoyed seeing me ice it so much. As the swelling and pain went away I became Exhibit A for him to extol the virtues of ice. Sitting out a day of practice before and after my one game suspension gave me plenty of time to heal.

Once I got back on the practice floor I was stuck on the Blue Team. Brian seemed to love the fact that I was back in blue. The smirk on his face made it obvious. Rome wasn't built in a day and being able to deal with all of Brian's attitude was going to take some time. But I'd get there.

Next up were the St. Joseph's University Hawks. One of the better teams in the league, they were deep and experienced, especially at the center position. Rodney Odom, a broad shouldered beast with an incredibly long wingspan, did not look like your typical center. He was a closer resemblance to some of the big, nasty power forwards of the NBA. Over the past three years Odom had eaten GW alive. We had our work cut out for us.

They started thumping us from the opening tip. They were more aggressive on defense and offensively they were on fire.

Our fans shifted nervously in their seats as the Hawks built up a double-digit lead. I shifted in my seat too because I started the game on the bench. Our offense stunk, and I knew I could do something about it. We were completely out of sync, like five guys walking to the beat of different drummers. Our spacing was poor, passes were off target, shots were rushed, and with Odom roaming the paint, our inside game was ineffective.

After ten minutes had gone by I still hadn't played. I knew Coach Ross had to send a message. After what I did against Rutgers he couldn't play me right away like nothing ever happened. I wondered if I'd even play at all that night. But as much as everyone loved Matt, he was hurting us out on the court. A minute later, after Matt picked up his third foul, Coach Ross subbed in Tim Rogers in his place. That only made things worse. St. Joe's continued to pour it on and Coach Ross was forced to call a timeout. With only six minutes left in the half, we were down by 17, our largest deficit of the entire season.

As we all stood in a huddle on the court Jim went ballistic. "Are you kidding me?" he shouted to no one in particular. "Are you? Because this is ridiculous. They're kicking our ass!" As he said it he pointed over his shoulder towards the St. Joe's bench and inadvertently knocked a cup of water out of Alex's hand. No one said a word while Jon Hornbeck quietly crawled around our ankles and wiped the court clean of the water. Standing in the middle of the loosely formed circle, Jim glared at everyone. In moments like this no one challenged Jim's role, not even Kevin who'd probably rip the head off of anyone else who dared glare at him. "No way St. Joe's is beating us on our home court," Jim continued. "I don't care what you tell yourself, but I'm telling you we're turning this thing around. They're not that good. Odom isn't that good. Quit playing scared and suck it up. On defense let's get some stops. On offense we all take good shots. Not scared shots, not rushed shots. And if we have to go right at Odom and get our shots blocked a dozen times, fine. We are not backing down. Got it?"

After a few guys nodded, Jim turned to Coach Ross and gave him a knowing look. Behind us cheerleaders shouted and tossed themselves into the air while our band banged out some awful music. I knew it was loud, but at that moment, as I waited to see what Coach Ross would do, it seemed eerily quiet.

Coach Ross scrunched his forehead then nodded my way. "Thomas. Go check in."

I blinked then for some reason looked at Jim. He hadn't said much to me since the Rutgers game. This team, this season was precious to him and I'd messed it up. But now I was needed and Jim looked at me like he was going to rip *my* head off if I didn't hurry up and check in. I extricated myself from the huddle and ripped my sweat top off.

On my way to the scorer's table to check in, a flood of doubts came out of nowhere. Could I really play without an ego, without a chip on my shoulder? Would my competitive fire still be there? I was a shooter. Shooters need to have a crazy amount of confidence. Would I still have enough?

I got back in our huddle where Coach Ross was talking about our defense. Jim still wore the look he gave me—intense and determined. Had I ever seen Jim put his ego, his glory, above that of the team? Of course not. But he was an amazing player. My ego wasn't going to help me or anybody. I didn't need it to stoke my competitive fire. The love for the game would. The love of competition, the love of using my God given talents to do something great. The fire would still be there. But without my old ego calling the shots, it just wouldn't burn me … or anyone else.

The buzzer sounded and we broke the huddle. We were down 17 points to a team on fire. Our backs were to the wall and our fans were frustrated and edgy. Plus I was as stiff as a board from sitting so long. But as I walked out onto the court, a calm confidence swept over me, the same one I got when I put on a brand new pair of sneakers or walked out onto the blacktop back home to shoot baskets.

It was exhilarating to be playing again. Running, jumping, breathing, sweating—I felt so alive! I gave every ounce of energy I had on defense, focused on rebounding, set good screens and made the extra pass. I was doing the little things that Matt and Jim did all the time, and loving every minute of it. The fire in me was brighter than ever. Jim's speech got everybody else fired up and in the final few minutes of the half we slowly cut into their lead but still trailed by ten at the intermission.

Coach Ross kept me in the lineup to start the second half. We responded with a 6-0 run during which I drew a charge, grabbed two rebounds, and set a screen that led to an open shot for Brian. I hadn't even taken a shot all night. I didn't feel like I was playing to prove a point to Coach Ross. It felt like I was playing the game the way it should be played. When a good shot presented itself, I knew I would take it.

We continued to chip away at their lead. Rodney Odom was still dominating the paint. He'd swatted one of Brian's layups and three of Jim's. He'd so thoroughly frustrated Kevin and Robert that our post game was non-existent. If we were going to win, it would be from the outside. St. Joe's had done their scouting homework. Even though I hadn't taken a shot the entire game, they knew I was a three-point shooter and played me tight. Instead of forcing shots I set good screens and dished off assist after assist.

When we finally tied the game with eight minutes left, our fans erupted. St. Joe's responded with two quick baskets: a jumper of their own and a thunderous dunk from Odom. Jim hit consecutive jumpers to tie it back up. As the clock wound down everyone got tight. St. Joe's was desperate to pick up an important road win and avoid choking after their huge first half lead. We were desperate to make our comeback stick and hold home court.

With three minutes to go Brian slashed into the lane and lofted a high arching floater that just cleared the fierce swipe of Odom. It bounced off the glass and in. We led by two.

The next three possessions no one scored. The capacity crowd at the Smith Center groaned with our every miss and cheered every one of theirs. With thirty seconds left, and possession of the ball, St. Joe's called timeout. They still trailed us by a bucket. During the timeout, Coach Ross was adamant. "No three-pointers! Got it? No threes. We're up two. The only way they can win is if they hit a three. So don't give them one! Stay on your man and don't help out in the post."

After the timeout, St. Joe's worked the ball around the perimeter and waited for the their big man to get open. Kevin and Odom bumped, grabbed, shoved, and grunted in the paint like wrestlers. At this point in the game the refs had swallowed their whistles and were letting them play. When Odom finally got open, St. Joe's point guard made a beautiful pass to him. The ball nearly disappeared in Odom's huge hands. He hesitated for a moment. Kevin had his forearm firmly planted into Odom's back.

Suddenly, Brian gambled. He left his man and doubled down on the big St. Joe's center, swiping at the ball.

In any given moment during a game there is a buffet of voices on the court. Everything from shouts and curses to mumbling and laughter. Throw in a vociferous home crowd and, at times, it's hard to hear anything. But I clearly heard Jim shout, "No! Stay with your man!"

Brian ignored him. Odom swung the ball out of Brian's reach and fired a bullet to the guy Brian was supposed to be guarding. He was their best shooter and was wide open. Of course he buried a three-pointer and put St. Joe's on top by one. I shook my head in disgust. Brian had been caught with his hand in the cookie jar and no cookie to show for it.

We called timeout with ten seconds left in the game. In the huddle Brian wiped the sweat off his face and didn't say a word. It's hard to be cocky when you've just screwed up. And he had, royally. But he never offered a "My fault," or "Sorry, Coach." Coach Ross stared at him. "You going to listen during this timeout or do I need put someone in who will listen?"

Brian nodded.

"Fine. Let's get a good shot and get this over with."

Coach Ross drew up the play. We were behind by one and had only ten seconds to score.

Standing on the sideline near half court, the ref handed Brian the ball. His inbound pass went to Jim. It was an easy pass but he took it for granted. It was lazy, not crisp. The St. Joe's defender saw the pass was soft and lunged and tipped the ball towards their basket. He and Jim raced to the loose ball. The St. Joe's defender beat Jim to it and in one smooth motion took a dribble and scored.

I was shocked. What was Brian thinking? I looked at the clock. Seven seconds left.

Down three we now needed a three-pointer just to tie and send the game into overtime!

Brian grabbed the ball out of the net and inbounded the ball to Jim who immediately sprinted up court.

Six seconds left... five seconds...

Kevin tried in vain to set a screen to get me open but my defender stuck to me like glue. Robert ran towards the top of the key to set a screen for Jim but nearly ran into him. Two St. Joe's players were running around chasing Jim. It was chaos.

Four seconds...

Jim dribbled between his legs and changed direction. Hands swatted at the ball and shouting voices filled the air. For some inexplicable reason my defender left me to help out on Jim. I ran to an open spot behind the three-point line and Jim saw me.

Three seconds ...

Jim delivered the ball right on the money.

Two seconds ...

My hands and arms were already in the proper position, cocked and ready to shoot. I felt the dimpled leather and my fingertips reached for the seams. Shooting a basketball is one of the most beautiful things in the world. I'd done it a million times. I was good at it and right now, my team needed this shot to go in.

One second ...

I let fly my first shot of the night just before the buzzer sounded. Swish!

My three-pointer tied the game and sent it to overtime. As I jogged over to our bench, I was mobbed by giddy, backslapping teammates. Alex and Coleman were jumping up and down as if they'd just sank the shot.

"Coleman!" Coach Ross's voice pierced through the sound of our crowd going nuts. "Check in for Brian."

Coleman did a double take then pulled his sweat top off, ran to the scorers table to check in, then returned to our bench.

"Brian, get up and move so Coleman can sit down," Coach Ross barked.

Brian slowly got up off the chair, disgust written all over his face, and stood off to one side. He should have been disgusted with himself, but I wondered if he was even capable of that. He was so sure of his infallibility. He probably saw Coach Ross as just another middle-aged white guy who had no business ordering him around. I think Coach Ross knew that and decided to finally do something about it. Coleman immediately sat down in Brian's chair as Coach Ross went over our strategy for overtime.

On the first possession of overtime St. Joe's went at Coleman. His man went right by him for an easy layup. On our possession they sagged off him to help guard everyone else. With the shot clock winding down Coleman was wide open. Jim had no other choice so he passed to him and St. Joe's dared Coleman to shoot. He did and the brick that he put up caromed off the rim and right into Odom's hands.

St. Joe's went right back at Coleman and got the ball into the hands of the man he was guarding. They cleared out one side of the court and let Coleman's man go one-on-one. Having been burned the time before Coleman gave his man too much space and he buried an easy fifteen footer.

We were down four. Again, the crowd nervously buzzed. They all knew Brian was on the bench and they didn't like it. I looked over at Coach Ross. He made no move to send Brian in.

Jim brought the ball up and St. Joe's sprung a surprise half court trap on us. Two defenders rushed at Jim. Instinctively Jim found the open man and threw the ball over the hands of the defense. The open man was Coleman. He caught the ball along the sideline opposite our bench. In a panic he took two dribbles towards the baseline, trying to get past his man, then stopped. Another St. Joe's player hustled over and Coleman was trapped in the corner. Sensing what was bound to happen, Jim tried to call timeout. The ref didn't see or hear Jim.

"Coleman! Here!" I shouted to him as I ran to a spot where I thought he could complete a pass.

He never heard me either. Instead Coleman threw a cross-court pass intended for Robert that St. Joe's easily picked off. Swiftly they fast-breaked the other way. They had a three on two advantage. I ran as fast as I could to catch up but it was too late. With Jim and Kevin our only two defenders back and playing to protect the rim, St. Joe's pulled up for a three-pointer and nailed it.

Coach Ross called timeout. St. Joe's had scored seven straight points in just over a minute of overtime. In the huddle Coleman was struggling for breath. I was sure Coach Ross would put Brian back in the game. Everyone knew we needed him out there. Maybe that's why he didn't. Instead Coach Ross calmly made adjustments to handle what St. Joe's was throwing at us. On defense we switched to a zone so they couldn't clear out against Coleman, and on offense he told Coleman to bring the ball up. "If they don't guard you, drive in for a layup. Make 'em pay for not respecting you."

Out of the timeout it was our ball. Coleman brought it past half court. St. Joe's practically ignored him. Coleman dribbled around for a moment hoping somebody would get open but St. Joe's denied all options. My defender was draped all over me. Suddenly Coleman made a move towards the basket. His defender was forced to finally take him seriously. As he went up for a layup Odom soared in to help out and blocked Coleman's shot, sending it into the stands. A whistle blew. Coleman was lying on the ground. Odom had hit not only the ball but Coleman too.

Coleman had two foul shots coming. His first shot clanged off the side of the rim. We were still down seven points. He made his second and the horn sounded. Coach Ross sent Brian back in the game for Coleman.

Our crowd rose to its feet. I wished it was appreciation for the effort Coleman made, but I knew better. They were thankful for Coleman's hustle, but wanted Brian in the game. After the last few minutes, I think I did too.

Down six points we needed to make some defensive stops. After taking their time, St. Joe's missed their next shot. On our end Jim scored to cut our deficit to four. St. Joe's next possession resulted in another miss. On offense I hit an open jump shot. We now trailed by only a bucket. All the momentum St. Joe's had built up from the seven to nothing run at the start of overtime had evaporated. With the crowd pumping us full of energy we were in their faces and had them on their heels.

They called timeout to try and deflate our momentum. It didn't work. They were nervous and rattled and it showed on their next possession. Nobody wanted to shoot. Fear of losing gripped them by the neck, cutting off their breath. As the shot clock wound down, our crowd rose to a crescendo. We weren't cutting off their oxygen, but we cut off passing lanes, shut down the paint, denied any open looks at the basket. They threw up a horrible shot as the shot clock buzzer sounded.

Jim rebounded the miss. It was our ball with just under a minute left in overtime. It looked like he would take his time heading up court but instead he suddenly heaved a full court pass over my head. Who was he throwing to?

I whipped my head around to see Brian streaking towards our basket. He'd beaten the St. Joe's defenders down court. It was a perfect pass. Brian caught it in stride, one step ahead of the nearest defender. He gracefully elevated above the floor and floated in the air. I was momentarily mesmerized. Only in my wildest dreams could I jump like that.

Brian soared towards the defenseless basket and attacked it. But the ball slammed off the back rim, his thunderous dunk now a colossal miss. The ball careened high into the air. The crowd gasped. Silently I scolded myself for staring at the play rather than running after it just in case something like this happened. A St. Joe's defender rose to catch the rebound, but out of nowhere Robert tipped the ball away from him. Robert jumped again, grabbed the ball, took a hard dribble and dunked home the tying basket.

Chaos ensued again. St. Joe's was out of timeouts. They inbounded and set up their offense. They could still pull out the win and we all knew it. The crowd knew it too.

They worked the ball around the perimeter of our defense. The clock wound down. They weren't taking their time; they were trying to figure out who had any nerve left to take a shot. It wasn't that long ago that they felt invincible. At the start of the second half, with their big lead, St. Joe's swaggered onto the court cocky and confident. Now they acted like frightened little lambs stuck outside the barn in the dark of night with the wolves howling.

All except Rodney Odom.

He had Kevin pinned on his back and was screaming for the ball. The pass went into him. He nearly squeezed the air out of the ball as he surveyed the situation. No one dared double-team him. Kevin was all alone.

Odom sent one of his massive shoulders on a fake to the left, then took his whole body to the right. Mountains weren't supposed to move that fast. He dropped stepped into the paint and pounded the ball onto the floor. After gathering himself he left the ground to shoot a short jump hook. Kevin went with him. The two men rose as one, well over two feet off the ground. Odom's shot went just over the outstretched hand of Kevin. It was a beautiful touch for such a big man, but it hit the front rim, then the back, then bounced off.

I went for the rebound but never came close. Odom and Kevin were off the ground so quick it was as if they'd never come back down. The ball was tipped in the air twice before Jim timed his jump perfectly and grabbed the rebound.

The game was still tied and only twenty-five seconds remained. We would take the last shot. This time Jim did take his time walking the ball up court. The entire crowd was on its feet. I tried to hide along the baseline and sneak my way to an open spot, but my defender wasn't fooled. I tried to fake and juke free of him but he anticipated where I wanted to go.

Then I gambled. I ran right towards Odom. He was guarding Kevin on the low block. I ran right towards his back then curled around him and went through the tiny gap between him and Kevin. Only at the last second did Odom see me coming, and I knew his initial reaction would be to try and hinder my movement with a subtle forearm or extended hip. But he was too late and the shove of his hip, which was meant for me, instead knocked his teammate off balance. Kevin recognized what I was doing and slid over and gave my defender another hip check. I kept curling right up to the top of the key. The gamble worked. I was open. Jim saw me and there wasn't a single molecule in my body that doubted he'd pass me the ball.

I immediately left the ground to shoot. Suddenly another defender's hand appeared in my face. I couldn't see the rim but I did see the blur of Jim streaking to the basket. He'd never stopped moving after passing me the ball and was now wide open. It was a textbook give and go situation. My pass was right on the money. Jim caught it in stride and elevated for the game winning layup. Odom flew at him for the block. In the shadow of his muscular frame Jim looked like a sparrow darting for his life. Somehow he was able to get the shot off. The ball floated gently off the glass and cleanly through the net.

A moment later the buzzer sounded.

The place went nuts. I ran over and bear hugged Jim right underneath the basket. Soon the rest of the team was there too, jumping up and down, soaking in the moment.

"Nice pass," Alex said as he clubbed me on the back with his casted right hand. "I'd give ya a hug but I don't want you sweating all over my nice shirt."

"Aw, what're you worrying about?" Coleman said. "You got wrinkles all over that shirt. A little sweat might do it some good." With that he grabbed Alex by the shoulders and rubbed his sweaty afro over the front of Alex's shirt.

The fans were still cheering as we walked off the court and headed down the stairwell to our locker room. There was something special about our team and they wanted us to know how happy they were to be a part of it. In the hallway just outside the locker room door Brian patted me on the back. "Hey, nice pass. Not bad for a Blue Teamer."

Before I could react, Coach Ross turned around sharply. "What did you say?" His tie was loosened around an unbuttoned collar and sweat trickled down an angry red cheek onto his already sweat soaked shirt. "Not bad for a Blue Teamer? He just bailed you out!" Everyone else was already in the locker room. It was just me and Brian and the coaches. "Not bad, huh? Let me tell you how bad *you* were." He pointed to the locker room door, which Coach Jennings was holding open. "Get in there."

Brian didn't move. Nobody moved. Laughter and gleeful voices emanated from the locker room. In the hallway, I sensed the walls were closing in on Brian.

In a firm tone, Coach Ciancio said, "Better get in there, son."

CHAPTER 20

I WALKED IN the locker room first. Brian and the coaching staff followed right behind me. Everyone was celebrating the win. When they saw the look on Coach Ross's face the room slowly fell quiet. Jim sat down and soon everyone else followed, including Brian who fidgeted with the towel wrapped around his neck.

I could tell by the intense look in his eyes that Coach Ross was still livid, but, like always, he managed to compose himself before he spoke. "Missed dunks and stupid passes are one thing, but it's your attitude that's awful. You think you're so good you can do whatever you want. You think you're smarter than me and don't need to listen. Well, let me be clear." He took a step towards Brian and pointed his finger at him. Brian stopped his fidgeting, glanced at the finger, then looked up and stared. "I am the coach. I have been put in authority on this team. When I tell you to do something, you do it. Period. There will be no more coddling, no more making allowances. It's my fault for allowing this to go on this long. And I don't care if you've never had a coach or relative or anybody try and discipline you. It's my job to do it and you will be disciplined. You will do exactly as I say. If you don't like it, you'll sit the bench until you do."

Nobody moved or said anything. We all waited while the words sunk in.

"Tomorrow's practice, you're on the Blue Team. Thomas," he said to me without ever taking his eyes off Brian, "make sure you show up tomorrow in White."

BY THE TIME I got back from eating at Cortellesi's with Jenae after the win, it was too late to call my father. The next morning I had a fifteen minute window between classes so I hurried back to the dorm and called. "You should have heard Brian getting chewed out after the game," I said to him over the phone. "Coach Ross got on him pretty good."

"Sounds like he sure needed it from what you told me about the game," my father said. "Good for Brian. It's his lucky day."

"Lucky day? What do you mean? He got chewed out in front of the whole team."

"He got stopped. We all need that at some point in our life. If not we'd just continue down the wrong road. Now Brian has a chance, if he listens."

"Hmm. Doubt that will happen. I overheard he and Coleman at the cafeteria this morning. He was whining and complaining about what coach said to him."

"That's too bad. Just don't join in. My old college coach used to say the two things that can get you in the most trouble are what you say about people and what you write about them."

"Brian says a lot of stuff. He just never gets in trouble for it."

"Well, just remember it's not your role to judge him or change him. Just try and be his friend. I know it may not be easy, but you can do it. He needs someone like you more than ever. On another note, I didn't get to talk to you about them when I was down there, but Paul and Ray sure are an interesting pair. I got to talk to Paul a bit during the Rutgers game. He told me about the soup kitchen. I think it's great you are volunteering there."

"I've only been there a few times. I'll probably go more often when the season ends."

"Paul seems like a sharp guy. What's the story with Ray?"

I told him how we met, what I knew of Ray's life story, and me getting him a job as a dishwasher.

"Thomas, I think taking an interest in Ray is fantastic. This is exactly the kind of thing you need. Something or someone to take the focus off your own life for a change. You've got coaches and trainers and managers all focused on you. It'll do you good to serve someone else. That's what leadership is all about. How often do you see Ray?"

"Whenever I'm at the soup kitchen or when Jenae and I go to Cortellesi Pizza he's usually there working. He always makes a point of coming out and saying hi. Oh, and we've spent time shooting at the gym together too."

"Where does he live?"

"I'm not too sure, but I think he mostly stays with friends. They're probably not a great influence on him. Jenae thinks it would be better if he were in some kind of home or shelter where he had someone looking after him."

"Hmm... I may have solution for him. I've got an old friend of mine that I'll call. He's thinking of starting a shelter for men in the city. Let me touch base with him before you say anything. Okay?"

I shrugged. "Okay."

AFTER THE PHONE call with my father I hustled across campus to my next class. Halfway there I spotted the "extenuating circumstance" guy. He was walking through the quad, pausing at garbage cans to scan the contents for something salvageable. I dug into my pocket and pulled out my wallet. I had a five and three ones. Wasn't much, but it would do.

Coming up from behind, I said, "Hey."

I startled the little man. He jerked his hand out of the garbage can then took two steps back. It was the reaction of someone who didn't like being surprised. Maybe he'd like this one.

"Here, take care of that circumstance," I said and handed him the money.

Momentarily frozen, the sight of money in his palm melted the hard facial lines that creased his face.

"Have a great day," I said as I started to walk away.

"Lewis doesn't like you," he said. "I'd stay clear."

Surprised, I turned and asked, "Lewis? You mean Aqualung?"

He looked at me like I was a fool. "Yes. The guy you told to take a shower. He hates you and can't stand you hanging around the girl."

Guess I can't blame him. So not only does he not like me, he doesn't like me hanging out with Jenae. Can't wait to apologize to him.

"By the way, nice game last night."

"Excuse me?"

"Nice game." He held up a grimy newspaper that had been folded over a few times. "Read about it in the *Post*."

BRIAN SHOWED UP for practice that afternoon in blue and I was once again on the White Team. While it felt good to be back in white I was more interested in seeing how Brian would respond playing on the Blue Team. Coach Ross watched him like a hawk and didn't let him get away with anything. If Brian sulked or pouted or barked at a teammate Coach Ross immediately stopped practice and confronted him about it. Same held true for the next two practices. For his part, Brian caught on quicker than I thought. He eventually kept his head down and mouth shut and did what he was told.

Coach Ross surprised everyone when he started Elijah instead of Brian in our next game versus Penn State. Despite being a true point guard and playing out of position, Elijah responded and played well. If starting Elijah was a surprise, it was a shock when Coach Ross sat Brian the entire game. At first Brian was stoic, like being benched didn't bother him. But by late in the second half I could see a grim reality was creeping in, and he didn't like it. Coach Ross was serious. We won the game and in so doing, Coach Ross made an important point to the team—if needed, we could win without either one of our two talented yet immature freshmen.

After that there was a little less swagger in Brian. I still had my doubts. Was it an act or was Coach Ross's message really sinking in? The next day when Brian asked to turn on my stereo rather than just doing it like he usually did, I knew something was happening. A few nights later I went to the gym to shoot and Ray joined me. When I came back to my dorm room Brian was watching TV. "Your dad called again," he said without ever taking his eyes off the screen.

"Yeah. What did he say?"

"We talked for a bit. I told him you were out shooting hoops with that bum friend of yours."

How in the world did Brian know about Ray? I'd never said a word to him. Trying not to show any surprise I tossed my keys on my desk like I usually did, and asked, "How'd you know about Ray?"

He slowly shook his head. "There's lots I know."

I sat down on a chair and took my shoes off. "Yeah, like what?"

"Like where you go all these nights. Off to the gym and lacing up them black Converse hightops like you're about to audition for the remake of *Hoosiers*. And when you sneak out early in the morning, you go to that soup kitchen. Feed a bunch of bums. I see all that, man."

"Well, I wouldn't call Ray a bum. I used to call guys like that bums, but then again I used to do a lot of hypocritical things."

He laughed. "Man, when you said that in Howard's class I thought you was just trying to butter him up. Make sure he didn't flunk you or something."

"No, it was true."

He turned and looked me over, sizing me up, trying to figure out if I was bluffing or being honest. "Yeah, I guess you were a hypocrite," was his conclusion.

"Along those lines, I know I haven't been much of a friend ... I'm not the easiest guy to talk to, and you and I don't exactly talk much. But that could change."

He pivoted in his seat to face the TV again. "Fat chance of that happening. You just keep hittin' shots on the court. Don't need to change that."

It wasn't much, but at least it didn't end in an argument. And that was a start. "Well, as long as you keep seeing me open on the court," I said, "I'll keep hitting my shots."

He let out a muffled laugh and changed the channel on the TV.

ELIJAH STARTED THE next game too, but this time Brian did get in. And he played great. He made smart decisions and sparked a second half run that sealed the win. It took more than two weeks, but Brian eventually earned his way back into the starting lineup.

We were now on a roll and carried that momentum through the entire month of January and into February. The losses were rare and the wins piled up. By late January we cracked the national top 25 polls. In mid-February we were just outside the top 10.

I was playing the best basketball of my life. I still made a lot mistakes and missed some shots, but no longer did they fester in my mind. I simply hustled downcourt to play defense and moved on. As a result I played with an incredible amount of freedom and fearlessness. It felt like I had that peace of mind Coach Wooden talked about in his pyramid of success. It also seemed like the peace of God mentioned in Philippians 4:7.

"And the peace of God, which transcends all understanding,
will guard your hearts and minds in Christ Jesus."

I wasn't the only one who noticed. "You should see the smile on your face when you play these days," Jenae said one night after another win. "You don't look stressed anymore. I can tell the game gives you real joy. It's fun to watch."

I continued to have fun in my shooting sessions in the gym too. Jenae often came to rebound and I returned the favor for her by shagging volleyballs when she went to work on her serve. Every now and then Ray joined me as well. His shot never improved but his smile lit up the gym.

Jeanae seemed happy and never mentioned leaving GW, although one time I did spot a pamphlet for Idaho State University sticking out of her backpack. When we could, we volunteered at the soup kitchen. I made it there about twice a week while Jenae was usually there four days. Ray was always there, but Aqualung never showed up. At least not that I saw. Perhaps he finally succumbed to the cold weather.

My father and I talked on the phone often. Ray was a frequent subject. My father was excited about the prospect of helping Ray. His old friend that was working on opening the shelter was Bill Pettit. Bill and my father played basketball together in college and kept in touch over the years. I remembered my father mentioning him a few times while growing up. Bill became a successful entrepreneur at an early age. Now approaching fifty, he'd recently gone through a huge life change. He sold his company and decided to open up the shelter. He refused to take government money, relying solely on his own funds or donations.

Bill's shelter was to be more than just a place for men to sleep with a roof over their head. He planned on strict rules that everyone in the shelter had to agree to in writing: no drinking, no drugs, no foul language. Each man was expected to help with the chores to keep the place running and, if work did not interfere, attend the daily Bible studies.

Bill promised my father that if Ray wanted to come, he'd get him in as soon as possible. When I mentioned it to Ray he was immediately interested. Paul thought it was a great idea too. With the shelter still a month or two away from being operational, Ray would simply have to be patient and wait.

WITH OUR SUCCESS on the court, GW became the toast of the town and started getting much better exposure from the D.C. media. I think they enjoyed covering somebody other than Georgetown and Maryland for a change. Those two schools were the local big shots and fixtures on the front page of the sports section. They were phenomenally successful programs that played in high profile conferences.

The Georgetown campus was just over a mile away from ours. Its basketball program was one of the elite programs in the nation. This was due in large part to John Thompson and Patrick Ewing. Thompson was their head coach. An intimidating mountain of a man, he stood 6'10" and won two NBA titles playing for the Celtics in the mid 60's while backing up Bill Russell. But it was his coaching that made him famous. His Georgetown Hoyas, with their suffocating defense and incredible athleticism, had already played in the national championship game three times in the 80's, winning it all in '84. Patrick Ewing was their star center. It was during his four years at Georgetown that the Hoyas made those championship games. Ewing was 7" tall and could move like a guard. Now playing in the NBA for the New York Knicks, he was still shaking buildings with his thunderous dunks.

Maryland had a storied history and their longtime head coach, Lefty Drisell, had achieved great success in the 70's and 80's. Drisell had coached future NBA players Len Elmore, Tom McMillan, John Lucas, and Albert King. But their season had been completely overshadowed by the death of Len Bias.

During the 1985-86 season, Bias had an incredible year. I remember watching him on TV, awestruck by his power and leaping ability. After the season he was picked second by the Boston Celtics in the NBA draft. My beloved Celtics had just won the NBA championship nine days earlier. With the addition of Bias, I was sure the Celtics would continue winning championships. The combination of Celtic veterans Larry Bird, Kevin McHale, and Robert Parrish, plus Len Bias would have been unbelievable. However, the day after the draft, Bias died of a cocaine overdose. I vividly remember the moment when I heard the news. I was hanging out in the hallway with some friends on our last day of high school. It was one of my basketball teammates who told me. He just walked right up to me and said, "Len Bias died."

At first I thought it was an incredibly poor joke. When he failed to smile I could tell he wasn't joking.

The news staggered the sports world and sent the Maryland basketball program reeling. When I arrived in D.C. in August, it was still the dominant story in the area. After Bias's death it was revealed that other Maryland players were associated with seedy characters and drugs. The team's academic record was also dismal. The popular Drisell was forced out by the scandal before the season started. He was replaced by Bob Wade, a remarkably successful high school coach in Baltimore. But with Drisell, Bias, and others gone, no one was surprised that Maryland was struggling this year.

And, now that the Patrick Ewing era was over at Georgetown, the moment was ripe for GW to finally step into the spotlight. Problem was, until we had success in the NCAA tournament like those schools had, we'd never get their respect. Until then, no matter how good our regular season was, we might as well be the Blue Team.

CHAPTER 21

BY THE TIME our last regular season game of the year rolled around in late February, a lot was on the line. If we won this game we'd clinch the regular season conference title. With a loss, we'd come in second. It was that simple.

Temple University, with their swagger and history of kicking our butts, was coming to the Smith Center. They were a bunch of tough, confident guys who played for an intense coach. Our four seniors had never beaten Temple and Jim made a point of reminding everybody of that fact. We'd already lost to them at their place in January. We played well but they hit some big shots in the last two minutes to pull away.

For years Temple had been one of the best teams in the Atlantic 10 and a top 25 program nationwide. This year was no different for them, but for us it was. With over twenty wins and only four losses we could now look them in the eye as peers. No longer did we need to look up to them in awe.

I headed to the gym early. I was ready for Temple. We all were. I could feel it. On the way there I was greeted by no less than a dozen students who offered their encouragement, shook my hand, patted me on the back, that sort of thing. As I rounded the corner on F Street onto 22nd I saw the Smith Center. Television crews were setting up in the parking lot on the south side of the building and students were already waiting in line to get in.

I saw what I thought was another homeless person lying down in the grass out in front of the building. Nothing out of the ordinary. But as I got closer I realized it was Ray. "Hey, Ray," I said, "Waiting to pick up your ticket at will call? It should be there by now."

As soon as he heard me he sat up. I noticed his hair was disheveled and he looked disoriented. "Hey, Thomas!" he shouted in a slurred voice. "Hey, man, I need some tickets for the game."

He was drunk. My chest sank. As far as I knew he'd been sober all winter. Why now? Why ruin all the progress he'd made? I walked to where he sat on the grass. "Ray, you've been drinking, haven't you?"

"Who said anything about drinking?" He had a hard time standing up.

"Ray, come on, it's obvious you've been drinking." Obvious, indeed. I wasn't standing that close to him but I could still smell the booze on his breath.

"Well, Conner, you got me. Yep, you got me. But it's only … I mean I've only had a few. Not many, no, not like the old day of riding the rails and clocking railroad bulls. Man, those were the good old days. Denver, Cheyenne, California…"

He could go on for hours like this and I had a game to get ready for. But I couldn't just leave him. Who knows what he'd do. "Ray, come on, let's get you to Paul's office."

"Paul? He doesn't drink. Why would I want to go there?"

Just then someone with a thick Long Island accent called out, "Yo, Tom!" It was Alex walking towards us from the same direction I came from. "Hey, getting to the gym already? You know it's …" He paused as he looked Ray up and down. "Whoa, who's this drunk? Believe me, I've been drunk enough to know one when I see one and you, my friend, are drunk."

"Well, the great Alex O'Neill," Ray slurred in contempt.

Alex looked at him doubtfully. "Tom, who is this bum? Is this that homeless guy you talk about?"

"Yeah, this is Ray," I answered. I told Alex about Ray and the soup kitchen back in January and invited him to come along one morning.

I was hoping meeting Ray and hearing his life story might be just the wake up call Alex needed. He wasn't interested at all.

"Yeah, well you want me to kick his ass and send him on his way?"

I could hardly believe my ears. "What? No, Alex. He needs help."

Ray laughed loudly. "You, kick my ass? O'Neill you couldn't kick my grandmother's ass! Heck, you'd probably swing and miss and break your hand again. Ha! Want to go ahead and punch the Smith Center? Go ahead, it's only made of concrete."

Alex glowered. "What did you say, you old lush?"

They both tensed.

"Guys, knock it off!" I shouted. "Alex, he's drunk. Ignore him. Ray, come on, let's go to Paul's."

For an anxious moment they just stared at each other. Their fists and chins clenched, ready for anything. I held my breath. Ray mumbled something and started walking away. I followed.

"Tom, where you going?" Alex asked.

"With him," I hissed.

After a minute or two of intermittent coaxing and arguing, I was able to get Ray moving in the direction of Paul's office. It was just over two blocks away but at the pace we were going it would take a while. He was talking faster than he was walking. I was getting agitated. I was going to get to the gym late! This was a huge game and I couldn't afford to let anything get in the way of my preparation. What was I doing anyway? What good was—

A hard smack on my shoulder instantly jolted me out of my private dialogue and brought me back to the present.

"Hey man, have you heard a word I've been saying to you?" Ray asked loudly.

"What?"

"Conner, I'm talking and you ain't listening. I said do you want to get a drink too? I mean … it might loosen you up a bit. You're obviously uptight about this game."

I stood there, mouth agape not knowing what to say. Then I smiled. He was right. He was drunk as a skunk, as Alex would say, and yet he was right. I was uptight. I was so obsessed with my preparation for the Temple game that I couldn't even spare a few minutes to help Ray without getting angry about it. I shook my head. It was the old Thomas Conner.

"I'm sorry, Ray, but I'm not going to get a drink with you, and you shouldn't be drinking. You know that. Now, come on, let's get to Paul's office. He'll know what to do."

It seemed as long as he kept talking he would keep walking. Thirty minutes later we arrived at Paul's office. It was located in a beautiful dark brick row house that had tall windows and a postage stamp sized front yard with an ornate metal railing surrounding it. Thankfully, Paul was there. Between the two of us we got Ray inside and seated on a couch. His office was cluttered floor to ceiling with books, magazines, and newspapers. The books haphazardly lined two walls, their different colors giving the walls the look of an impressionist painting. The magazines and newspapers were scattered about in piles on the floor.

I wove past the piles and sat down in a hard wooden chair next to the couch Ray was slouching on.

"Ray, my friend, I am disappointed. But to say anything further would be like spitting into the wind." Paul knelt down and started to untie Ray's shoes. Ray, who'd quit talking right before we got inside, offered no reaction. He simply stared out the window, hardly aware of our presence, let alone our words.

"I hope he doesn't get sick," I said, knowing that if Ray did throw up it would splatter on Paul's back.

"He is already sick," Paul said without looking up from his task. "Would a healthy person do this to himself? Of course not. His sickness is not of the liver, although that is probably very ill. No, his sickness is of the mind."

He finished taking off Ray's shoes then disappeared into his kitchen. A minute later he came back with two mugs of hot coffee. He handed me one then sat down in a high backed chair. "Ray says he wants to change. But he can't because he's still not willing to hand over control of his life."

"Sounds familiar."

"I found myself confronted with that choice of giving up or holding on not long after we moved to America. Do you have time for a short story?"

"Absolutely," I replied. Over the past few months I'd heard plenty of Paul's stories. They were all good.

"I was ten years old when we came here. I didn't want to come. I loved Italy and missed it very much. I pouted and complained and blamed my father for making my life miserable. In my mind it was all his fault. He tried to help me make friends with the other boys in the neighborhood by getting me involved in baseball. They all played baseball so he thought it would help me fit in if I played too. He bought me a bat, ball, and a glove and put me on a little league team. Now, I had never played baseball. I'd never even heard of the game until I came to this country. I had no idea how to play it. My father tried to teach me, but he didn't know much about the game either.

"When I showed up for practice I couldn't throw, I couldn't catch, and I could barely swing the bat without falling over. All the other kids laughed at me and ridiculed me. I looked different than them. I came from a foreign country, had a funny accent, and could barely speak their language. On top of that, here I was desecrating their cherished game. I wanted to quit right then. My father made me stick with it and I eventually got a little better. But I still didn't like it. I was still angry at my father. I didn't want to be playing baseball in America. I wanted to be playing soccer in Italy!

"One game the coaches asked me to pitch. They let everyone on the team have a turn and so there I was on the mound, pitching. Only I wasn't there to get anyone out. I was there to get myself kicked off the team. In my mind I concocted this devious little plan. I would just keep hitting batters until they kicked me out of the game, and hopefully off the team. The first kid up to bat I hit with my second pitch. I couldn't throw very fast so it didn't hurt the little boy. I don't think anyone was wondering if I did it on purpose. They probably just thought I was so inept I couldn't throw straight. When I hit the second batter my father knew. He called out to me in Italian, telling to me stop and play with honor. I was almost in tears. I hated this game and hated being there. I didn't care if I embarrassed myself and my father, I was that angry, that selfish. I reared back and threw as hard as I could and hit the third batter. The umpire immediately tossed me from the game but by that time my father was already half way to the mound. He grabbed me by the jersey and took me to our car.

"He was shocked I would do such an evil thing. It got worse. The father of the last boy I hit came over and berated my father. It was an ugly scene. This man was shouting and pointing fingers at both of us. As newcomers to the town and the country, I put my father and our family in a very difficult situation. Instead of just getting kicked off the team I wondered if our family would get kicked out of town! It wasn't until this moment, when I saw my father paying the price for my actions, that I finally realized the wickedness of what I had done. I felt horrible. We had a long talk when we got home that day. I saw how exceedingly sinful I was."

He pulled a handkerchief from his pocket and dabbed a moist eye before taking a sip of his coffee. "So, my friend the question now is, what will it take for Ray to come to that point?"

I looked over at the couch. Ray was asleep.

WHEN I FINALLY left Paul's office I ran all the way to the gym and got dressed as fast as I could. By the time I got my ankles taped it was almost time for our pre-game scouting report. Usually by this time of the night I had already been up to the floor and had shot for over an hour. I caught the curious glances from my teammates, wondering why I hadn't been here earlier.

I sat down next to Alex and hurriedly tied the laces on my sneakers. "Yo, Tom," Alex muttered under his breath, clearly not wanting anyone else to hear, "what do you see in that old drunk?"

"What do I see in him? I don't know, someone who needs help, a guy who loves basketball. He's a friend and unfortunately has completely destroyed his life with alcohol."

"Hmm," he said trying to pretend his curiosity was sated.

"Hmm? What does that mean?"

"I don't know. Seems kind of like a good thing, I guess ... even if the guy's a lush."

"He's not a—" Just then the door to the locker room swung open and the coaching staff walked in. My discussion with Alex would have to wait. It was show time.

CHAPTER 22

BECAUSE IT WAS our final home game of the year, it was also senior night, the final home game ever for the seniors: Jim, Kevin, Matt, and Robert. For that reason Coach Ross chose to start all four seniors and Brian. Matt would be starting in my place. I was more than happy to give up my starting spot for him. He deserved it.

Before the start of the game we honored the seniors. Their parents stood at center court, the mothers holding colorful bouquets of flowers. Three fathers clutched a large framed photo of their son in a GW uniform. Kevin's father wasn't there. He never mentioned him and, as far as I knew, he hadn't been to a GW game all year.

Over the season I'd heard tidbits about Kevin's upbringing. None of it was pretty. He came from a miserable section of the city and by all accounts was lucky to be alive. That he was going to earn a college degree and possibly make good money playing basketball overseas was remarkable.

Kevin and Coach Ciancio were especially close. Coach Ciancio grew up in the District and still lived there. With their similar backgrounds and stories they could relate to each other. Whenever Kevin had a problem learning a new play or had issues in class, he went to Coach Ciancio.

When the public address announcer's voice boomed out Kevin's name he walked straight to Coach Ciancio. They embraced like it was the last time they'd ever see each other. The entire gym was on their feet clapping. Together they walked out to center court and embraced Kevin's mother. I had chills running down my spine.

Robert was next. The crowd stayed standing. His father, tall and thin like Robert, was dressed impeccably in a pinstriped suit. His mother was surprisingly short. In heels she was barely over 5'4". How the genes of those two combined to produce a son standing 6'10" was beyond me.

Next came Matt, the classic "tweener," stuck in no man's land between guard and forward. I had come in and taken his playing time and yet he remained upbeat. He always cheered the loudest on the bench, and worked as hard as anyone in practice. The students loved him. He'd been relegated to the bench for most of his career at GW, but they knew he never gave up. They saw his drive, his passion. I think they identified with him since he wasn't supremely talented with height like Robert or athletic ability like Brian. When it came to God given talent, Matt was more like the average student.

They saved Jim for last, as they should. If we had an identity as a team, it was Jim. Hard working, talented, focused, and driven. Sure we had our goof offs like Alex and Coleman, but the vast majority of minutes were played by the four seniors and Brian and me. When it came to basketball, we were all business, and our example was Jim.

When they introduced Jim, he handled it with class, acknowledging the rabid crowd but not overdoing it. My ears were ringing from the noise reverberating off the Smith Center walls. I spotted Jenae in the crowd. Like everyone else she was standing and clapping for Jim, but when she saw me looking her way she gave me a wink and smile. Jim had the crowd, but I had the girl.

While we honored our seniors, the Temple players and coaches sat with bored looks on their faces. They made the perfect villain and our crowd lustily booed them when it came time to announce their starting five. The building hummed with the electricity of a prize fight. It wasn't Ali vs. Frazier, but it was to us.

Two minutes into the game we were down by ten points. If this was a fight, the referee would have given us a standing eight count.

Temple came out firing from behind the three-point line. While some teams were still not comfortable shooting three-pointers, Temple's coach embraced the new rule. I could tell his players all knew their roles and stuck to them. Two of his players had the green light to shoot from anywhere: Nate Perry, a talented freshman with a smooth game and accurate jumper, and Ricky Boyle, a senior from Baltimore. Boyle in particular had absolutely no conscience when it came to shot selection. If he had the ball and was past half court, he was a threat to shoot.

Between them they'd hit two three-pointers and two long jumpers just inside the arc. Matt had been burned on a few of those shots and when he picked up his second foul a moment later, Coach Ross sent me in.

Boyle was assigned to guard me. He may have been a city kid but he carried himself with a backwoods strut. He had an oily, unkempt shock of hair and thick stubble on his face. Boyle stuck so close to me that at one point we inadvertently bumped into each other and his day old stubble scraped my face, producing a tiny trickle of blood. By now everyone knew the scouting report on me—don't leave me open for a shot. With Boyle in no position to help out, Brian took advantage of a clearer path to the basket and scored. Next time down Brian did the same thing. After a Temple miss, it was our ball, and again Brian drove to the lane. This time Boyle took the bait and tried to help. Brian instinctively passed to me and I buried my first shot of the night, a three-pointer.

I hadn't seen this kind of effectiveness on offense from Brian while I was on the bench. Matt was a good shooter, but it was clear Brian didn't trust his shot as much as he did mine. With me out there the jigsaw puzzle of breaking down opposing defenses was easier for him. Maybe he'd never admit it, but when I was on the court I made him a better player, and the same held true for me: Brian's ability to drive made me a better player. While I saw this the first time we played together, I wondered if even now Brian recognized it.

Brian's baskets and my three cut into the deficit, but we still trailed. Temple's coach shouted and barked at his players incessantly but they never seemed to be bothered. They were ruthless and efficient and remained in the lead the entire first half.

Down eight to start the second half we tried to make a run but they withstood it and countered with a run of their own. Five minutes later we tried again. I hit my second three of the night and Jim followed with another. But as quickly as we scored six straight they answered with six of their own. With only five minutes left in the game we were still trailing by eight points.

Jim made a shot, Perry hit a three. Brian scored on a finger roll layup, Perry answered with another jumper. We were desperate to finally deliver a win against Temple for our seniors, but they had an answer for everything we threw at them.

With the clock winding down we pushed the pace, hoping to get some quick scores. It backfired. Brian and I took quick shots and missed. Temple fast breaked and Perry dunked on a beautiful lob pass from Boyle. Brian took another bad shot and missed. Temple scored again on their end.

With under two minutes to play and leading by double digits Temple started talking trash and hot dogging. Our fans saw it and showered the Temple players with contempt. I was irritated to the core. We had finally become a team worthy of national respect. We'd made it into the top 25 polls, beaten everyone else in the league and played well enough to earn the respect of the good teams like Temple, but it was clear they still didn't respect us. They thumped us by 14 points on our home court. Those last few minutes of the game they treated us like we were still the GW of old, a team to beat up on and pick up an easy victory. They treated us like we were still the Blue Team.

Not much was said in the locker room. Jim sat slumped over on his seat, a towel draped over one shoulder. Four years of losing to Temple made he and the other seniors look beat up and worn out.

Kevin slowly took off his shoes and tossed them into his locker. "Man, I wanna play them one more time. Just one more. Tournament time."

Robert nodded. "I hear you, brother."

AFTER THE GAME I told Jenae what happened to Ray. She said nothing at first, then spoke in a subdued voice. "I had no idea. I just assumed he missed the game for work."

"I wish it were that."

The enthusiastic skip in Jenae's step was absent. Instead we slowly made our way north on 22nd, heading for Cortellesi's. "Is he okay?"

"I don't know. He's with Paul so he's in good hands."

"He'd been doing so well," she said softly. "It's the first time he's been drinking in months. What did we do wrong?"

"What did we do wrong? What do you mean?" I looked and saw tears pooling in her eyes.

"We're his friends. We should have done more. We shouldn't have let this happen."

"You think we could have prevented Ray from drinking again?"

"I was hoping so."

"I don't know, Jenae. Ray has to want to do it himself. We can't do it for him. Who knows, maybe this is exactly what he needed, one last rock bottom experience. At least we can hope it's his last."

We rounded the corner onto Pennsylvania Avenue. Ahead of us, the neon open sign at Cortellesi's flickered. I could faintly hear the muted strains of Italian music coming from inside the restaurant.

"I know you don't want to hear this after tonight's game," Jenae said, "but I can't help looking back on my year here and wonder where it all went wrong. Am I doing anybody any good by being here? I didn't get much playing time on the volleyball court and now, after all the time and effort, thinking I was going to do such wonders with the homeless, Ray is still struggling just to stay sober. I know it's not about me, it's about Ray and the others there at the soup kitchen, but … I feel so inept."

I grabbed hold of her hand. "When we feel inept that's when we're strong, because we rely on the Lord even more. So maybe this is exactly what you needed."

AFTER DINNER I walked Jenae to her dorm and said goodnight. A big bowl of angel hair pasta covered in tomato, basil, and garlic brought back some of her spark. It was close to midnight when I started for home. The sidewalks and streets that teemed with activity after the game were now silent. Not a soul was in sight. I had just emerged from a dark alleyway when I paused. A lonely streetlight down the block cast my shadow along the sidewalk towards the front of Leo's Deli. The way to my dorm was to the left, to the right was the gym. Bill, the man with the keys, would probably still be at the gym cleaning up from the game. I could go shoot ...

I blew out an extended breath and watched it dissipate in the cold night air. I turned right.

A moment later I was startled by the sudden emergence of a hulking figure directly in front of me. Whoever it was had been sitting out of sight behind a large garbage can in front of Leo's. He stood up, took two lumbering steps towards me and into the light. Aqualung!

CHAPTER 23

I FROZE. HE'D survived the winter after all. I remembered his homeless buddy told me Aqualung hated me and I should steer clear. Too late for that. Did he still hate me? It had been months since I insulted him. Could he have a knife like that guy on the subway? My first instinct was to put my head down and walk off quickly. But I knew I needed to apologize. I hesitated. The script I'd kept ready in case I saw him disappeared in a tidal wave of adrenaline.

He stood stock still, a mere ten feet away. In the dark I could barely see his eyes through the rats nest that passed for his hair and beard. But I saw enough to know they weren't friendly.

"Listen, I want to apologize for—"

He threw his arms up in the air, and shouted, "Bah!"

Startled, I took a step back.

A deep rumble reverberated in his throat. He cocked his head back then spat at me.

Somehow I sidestepped the lougie. "Hey! Watch it!"

We stood glaring at each other for a moment. My adrenaline surged as my heart pounded inside my chest. What would he do next? Thankfully he turned and walked quickly away, his arms stiff at his sides and both hands balled in a fist.

I skipped the gym and headed home, avoiding alleys.

NEXT UP WAS the Atlantic 10 tournament, held at the Palestra in Philadelphia, PA. The City of Brotherly Love loves its basketball. From the high school ranks to the pros, some of the best players have, at one time or another, called it home; Wilt Chamberlain, Julius Erving, Moses Malone, to name a few. I was thrilled the tournament would be played there.

Practices before the tournament started were intense. In addition to physically pushing us, Coach Ross preached to us the importance of mental toughness, especially at this time of year. He said each season is really made up of three different seasons. The first is the regular season before conference play, the second is conference play, the third, and most important, is playoff time.

Were we ready for playoff time? Would our loss to Temple shatter our confidence or were we mentally tough enough to put it behind us?

I was also concerned about Ray. He slept the night of the Temple game in Paul's office, but then disappeared the next day. No one had seen him since. Whatever season in life this was for him, he'd blow the previous ones. How many seasons did he have left?

Going into the Atlantic 10 tournament we were the two seed. Our home loss to Temple gave them the one seed. Our quarterfinal game was against Rutgers. Giambalvo had recovered quickly from my punch in January, but in February he suffered a bad ankle sprain. He wasn't in the lineup when we played Rutgers in New Jersey during the regular season, and he was still out when we faced them in the quarterfinals. They weren't the same team without him and we won easily.

Our semifinal game against the Mountaineers of West Virginia was a different story. West Virginia was the only league team other than Rutgers and Temple that beat us. Both times we played them in the regular season the game was close.

This one was close too, but it shouldn't have been. With a minute to go our lead was six. All we had to do was be patient and smart with the ball and the game was ours. However, Brian, who had played great up to that point, inexplicably took a quick shot and missed.

West Virginia rebounded and scored within seconds. On our next possession Brian tried to dribble through a crowd of defenders and committed an egregious turnover. Again, West Virginia capitalized, cutting our lead to two.

Coach Ross called timeout. This was probably the fifth or sixth time this season that Brian had made consecutive boneheaded plays late in a game. His fiasco versus St. Joe's in January was not an isolated incident, but now wasn't the time for a tongue lashing. There was just enough time on the clock that West Virginia didn't need to foul. If they played good defense and held us, they could take the last shot to win the game. We needed one more score and Coach Ross drew up a play for me to take the shot. After diagramming it, he looked up at me. "All right, Jersey boy. Go hit another big shot for us."

Robert inbounded the ball to Jim and I came off a double screen. Jim gave me a perfect pass and I hit a textbook jumper. That put us up four, sealing the win.

We were on to the Atlantic 10 championship game. Our opponent? Temple of course.

AFTER OUR TEAM breakfast the next morning we gathered to watch tape of last night's game. Waiting outside Coach Jennings' hotel room, Jim nonchalantly walked up and leaned in close. "It's Matt's birthday," he whispered to me. "We're going to surprise him. Just follow my lead."

I snuck a quick glance down the dimly lit hallway at Matt. He was leaning against the wall not more than fifteen feet away, seemingly oblivious. "What are we doing?" I asked.

"You'll see," Jim said out of the corner of his mouth.

The coaches appeared around the corner and walked down the hallway towards us. Always looking to go the extra mile for his boss, Coach Jennings quickened his pace so he could get to the door and open it without making Coach Ross wait. "All right, gang's all here," he said, juggling a half eaten muffin, VHS tape, and his room key. "Give me a just a second."

He stuck the muffin in his mouth and opened the door to his room. Coach Ross and Coach Ciancio entered then Matt did. Jim quickly moved right behind Matt. A line of guys got in behind Jim and I followed. On Jim's cue everyone shouted, "Happy Birthday!" The half dozen players in the room pounced on Matt, tackling him onto the king sized bed.

Everyone was laughing, Matt loudest of all. The coaches stood and watched, smiling and shaking their heads. "Is that what you wanted for your birthday, Matt?" Coach Ross asked.

From underneath the pile Matt's voice was compressed, just like you'd expect with several two hundred pound athletes stacked on top of you like pancakes. "Never asked for a thing, Coach, but what else are these knuckleheads going to give me?"

"Ah, you love it and you know it!" Jim said from somewhere in the middle of the stack.

One by one we peeled ourselves off and everyone voiced their birthday wishes again. As Coach Jennings worked on getting the tape cued up in the VCR I looked over at Matt. Sitting on the edge of the bed with Jim, Kevin, and Robert, he quietly wiped away a tear. Jenae was right. Matt loved every minute of it. He loved being a teammate.

I HAD SOME free time after our video session, so I went to go see my parents. They were in the city for the tournament and staying in a hotel two blocks away from ours. For the tournament, Coach Ross was requiring everyone to be dressed up to go to the games. Rather than change later I put on my blue blazer, white shirt, red tie, and khaki slacks prior to meeting my parents.

As I arrived, I noticed the front of their hotel was surrounded by half a dozen police cars, TV cameras, and hundreds of yelling demonstrators, many holding signs above their head. There were police barricades zigzagging every which way. Half a block from the hotel, I stopped and surveyed the scene. There were two camps of demonstrators, one on either side of the street. Both were waving their signs and shouting across the street at each other. In the middle were the police, a few of them on horseback. The barricades created an avenue to safely enter the hotel and avoid the mayhem. Reading the signs I realized the protest was over abortion. On the side closest to the hotel was the pro-abortion crowd. On the opposite were the pro-life supporters.

I met my parents in the hotel restaurant for a light lunch. I still had my pre-game meal to look forward to so I didn't eat much. "What's up with the ruckus outside?" I asked. "Why'd they choose to demonstrate here?"

"Isn't that something?" my mother said shaking her head.

"There's a pro-life seminar going on in the hotel," my father answered. "There are some elected officials here along with leaders of some of the bigger pro-life organizations. Those people outside have been at it all morning."

From my seat I could look out the window and see the protestors, their faces contorted in anger. So much for brotherly love.

Our conversation turned to basketball and tonights game. "You guys will have to play one of your best games of the year in order to win," my father said. "Playing in the Palestra is tantamount to a home game for Temple. It's a huge advantage. You'll have to play smart and disciplined for a full forty minutes."

"That certainly wasn't the case last night," I replied. "Did you see some of those decisions Brian made in the last minute?"

"I did. It's hard to say if he's getting nervous or simply has mental lapses at the wrong time. But you can't lose faith in him. You've got to continue to trust him just like the others."

"Really? With all the dumb things he's done this season ..." I couldn't find the right words. I was surprised my father continued to show so much confidence in Brian. Sure Brian had played well early on, but his decisions at the end nearly lost the game last night. It wasn't personal; it simply didn't seem smart to trust Brian in those key moments.

"Thomas, you guys wouldn't be in this situation without Brian. He's too talented to simply be ignored late in the game. Sure he made some bad plays late in the game last night. But you still won and I guarantee you he won't make the same mistakes two nights in a row."

"I don't know …"

"Look, being a teammate is one of the best ways to learn trust. Everybody makes mistakes, especially creative players like Brian. He's constantly pushing the envelope, looking to make something happen. Of course a guy like that will have his share of turnovers. But you've got to trust each other."

"I hear you, Dad. It's not that I don't trust Brian. It's just his judgment hasn't gotten much better over the season."

"Any of the other guys feel this way?"

"I don't know. Coach Ross is clearly frustrated with him."

"But he keeps him on the floor. Have faith in your coach, and have faith that Brian can improve and make better decisions. Sure, it's easy to trust Jim or the other seniors in those spots, but they can't make every decision for you guys. You can't give up on Brian. He's a tough kid and a tough competitor. He and I have talked on the phone quite a bit these past few weeks. If I call while you're out and he answers he's always willing to talk. Never for too long but he seems grateful to have someone asking him questions and taking an interest in him. I'll bet he's going to come out and play a great game tonight. You'll see."

AFTER LUNCH I walked out the front of the hotel and after surveying the situation, decided to bypass the maze of police barricades and take a shortcut back to my hotel. I turned left, hugging the side of the building, slipped past a few policemen and stepped over a barricade. What had been the back end of the demonstration instantly became the epicenter. A surly crowd surrounded me shouting insults. I stood, towering over the mob, flabbergasted at the cacophony of angry voices. Why were they upset at me?

A squat woman was inches from my chest, pointing and viciously spewing a profanity-laced tirade. She had a big mouth and bushy eyebrows which made her a dead ringer for Oscar the Grouch.

Others were closing in. This wasn't safe. Then it dawned on me! My clothing—jacket, tie, slacks—they must think I'm part of the pro-life meeting. Sure enough out of the din I clearly heard someone call me a "fetus fanatic!" I smiled slowly which made Oscar the Grouch all the more enraged. "I'm a basketball player," I said. "I'm playing in the Atlantic 10 tournament."

The pause was brief, like the split second between the last notes of a song and the applause of the audience. In that moment their faces studied mine. Once that second had passed, and they had digested what I said, they turned and resumed shouting across the street. Even Oscar the Grouch turned and completely ignored me. It was as if I never existed.

I was just about to walk away from the crowd when, from behind, I heard a challenge. "Well, are you pro-choice?"

I turned and saw a pleasant looking older woman. It was hard to reconcile the skeptical voice with what I saw in front of me. She had long gray hair that was pulled back in a knot, wore rimless glasses, a long flowery dress, and a light green knitted sweater. A faint smile graced her face. She didn't look like she belonged in the same crowd as Oscar the Grouch.

"Ma'am," I said, "children are a gift from God, and I just can't imagine why a woman would want to kill her baby."

Her mouth dropped and her eyes grew bigger than her glasses. The others nearby, who had heard my reply, descended on me. Oscar the Grouch was right there again in my face. I could smell her hot breath and feel her spittle on my face.

The crowd closed in tighter than before. I couldn't move. Oscar the Grouch poked me in the chest. A skinny guy with a scruffy beard pointed a finger within inches of my nose and shouted, "Keep your religion to yourself you fascist, corporate pig!"

The older woman shouted, "I've had two abortions and never killed a baby! You can go to hell!"

"Knock it off!" The voice from my right was booming and commanding. At the sound of it everybody suddenly backed off a step in sync, like they'd chosen an odd time to play Simon Says. I turned just in time to see a police officer grab my arm.

"Let's go kid, you're outta here!" Everything about him was thick. His chest inside his blue police uniform, his hairy arms, his dark mustache, and his Philly accent. Squeezing tight on my arm, he led me away from the demonstrators, stiff arming Oscar the Grouch in the shoulder. "Kid, I don't know what you said, but you need to get a move on. Them people are fanatics." With him leading the way, we covered a good twenty yards in no time. "Heard what you said, kid. Got to know your audience. That old lady you spoke to? Forget about it. I've been listening to her for over an hour. She's already in hell."

"Thanks for stepping in," I said. "I was just trying to take a shortcut back to my hotel. I was starting to get nervous."

"Nervous? You shoulda been running! Anyway, what're you all dressed up for? The meetings going on in there?"

"No, I'm here to play in the Atlantic 10 tournament."

"You playing in the basketball tournament?"

"Yes. I play for GW."

He immediately dropped my arm and took a step back. "GW?" His face pinched like he'd just swallowed a bottle of cough syrup. "Kid," he pointed down the sidewalk to the pro-choice crowd, "I saved your butt from them, but you guys are going to get clobbered by Temple tonight. I can't save you from that."

CHAPTER 24

EVERYONE ON OUR team knew we'd have to play Temple in order to win the tournament. We were 0-2 versus them this year. They were back in the conference finals where they expected to be. Maybe they were overconfident. Maybe they were overlooking us. Maybe it was good to be considered the Blue Team.

This would be our third game in three nights. Some of the guys were getting tired legs and having a hard time recovering. The effects of the long season were everywhere—ice packs on knees, the smell of pain rub on sore muscles, and the groans from stiff, achy joints.

Me, I felt great. I could do this every night. Especially with the atmosphere of the Palestra. The Palestra is a jewel. Although not nearly as well known, its place in sports history and lore is similar to that of Wrigley Field, Fenway Park, or Notre Dame Stadium. It sits on the campus of the University of Pennsylvania and for decades has witnessed some great games and great players. Opened in 1927, it has hosted more games and NCAA tournaments—including the first NCAA championship game in 1939—than any other college facility. It looked and felt just like an old college gymnasium should, evoking black and white images of cheerleaders and fans in distant fashions, sneakers squeaking on a hardwood floor, dreams being fulfilled and extinguished. Made of brick, concrete, and steel, sounds within echo with forcefulness. The noises, the memories, and the athletes who spent some of the best moments of their lives there are what holds it all together.

Ten minutes before tip off there wasn't an empty seat in the house. During the introduction of the starting lineups, I wondered if the Palestra, which seats less than 9,000, could contain the noise. Jim was the last on our team to be introduced. When he arrived on the court with the non-starters right behind him, we all squeezed into a tight bundle of bodies. Elbows and shoulders bumped into foreheads and ears as everyone attempted to reach their hands into the center of the conglomeration. Jim yelled words of encouragement but I couldn't understand them in the overwhelming din. Bodies were pushing and poking. It was hot and smelly and I couldn't hear myself think. It was awesome.

At center court, a moment before the opening tip, I studied the faces of the Temple starting five. The smirk on Ricky Boyle's face said it all. They didn't have an ounce of respect for us. Did anyone else notice it? Philly was such a passionate college basketball city that the fans at the Palestra would know the game well. They would recognize a team that was overconfident or fearful. They would also recognize good basketball when they saw it, and they would be looking closely.

What did these fans think of my game? Could they see just a little bit of Larry Bird in my game? Did it matter anymore? Was wanting to play like Larry Bird simply setting lofty goals, or was I being like the disciples who argued amongst themselves as to who was the greatest?

The referee tossed the ball in the air and we were underway. The tempo was slow to start, just the way Temple liked it. They were athletic enough to run and play a full court game if they wanted, but their coach preferred a slower, methodical game where every possession was crucial. They wanted every possession to be like the declining inhalation of someone caught in the grasp of a python. Each possession they looked to tighten up their defense, be more efficient on offense, and eventually suffocate us.

This type of game was mentally and emotionally draining. Every shot was contested, every rebound produced a scrum under the basket. But despite tough defense from both teams, shots kept falling. I made my first two shots as Boyle, who was guarding me, got caught up on screens. His coach screamed at him from the bench and he answered with two deep threes of his own. Brian and Nate Perry took turns slashing past each other, making one acrobatic circus shot after another. Even our big men got in on the act. Kevin hit a nice turnaround jumper from the free-throw line and Robert banked in two shots off the glass.

Neither team had a lead of more than five, and at the end of the first half Temple led by one. Before walking off the court, I heard Boyle muttering something about getting ready to have his butt chewed out in the locker room.

TEMPLE STARTED THE second half like they started the game against us in D.C. just a week ago. They made tough shots. They raised the intensity of their defense to withering proportions. They were trying to crush our will. If we didn't respond the game would be over. We threw up two bricks and committed two turnovers while they made four straight shots. Suddenly down nine, Coach Ross called timeout.

In our huddle guys were complaining about bad shots, lack of defensive help, lack of hustle. Coach Ross silently watched, taking it all in. He looked disappointed. Why wouldn't he? We were facing our toughest test of the year and we were failing. Instead of rallying as a team we were bickering like third graders on the playground.

"Guys," Coach Ross said, cutting through the static of competing voices, "relax and take a deep breath. Realize you've been here before and you'll be here again. You were here when you were little and the schoolyard bully knocked you on your butt. You were here when you got your shot blocked for the first time. You were here when you were on the Blue Team getting beat up by the White Team in practice. And you'll be here again when you're on your own and maybe you get fired or your company goes bankrupt. Who knows what it'll be, but it'll happen. How will you respond then? How you respond now will be exactly how you'll respond when that day comes. What you do right now, with this moment, will speak volumes about your character, your resolve, your maturity … or lack thereof."

Usually in moments like this, when Coach Ross paused, somebody like Jim or Matt or an assistant coach would speak up with words of encouragement or a challenge to play harder, that sort of thing. Not this time. Nobody said a word.

"This has nothing to with X's and O's. It has everything to do with this." Coach Ross pointed at his heart. "Gentlemen, show me what you got."

It was our ball out of the timeout. We got into our set offense and worked the ball inside to Robert. He elevated for a jump hook but Perry swiped the ball out of his hands. The ball pin-balled off knees and ankles before ricocheting towards half court. Boyle was nearest the ball with a clear path to his basket. As he bent over to pick it up, Jim launched his body parallel to the ground and at the last possible second tipped the ball away from Boyle. Jim crashed to the floor like a rag doll as the ball rolled towards the sidelines. Boyle pursued the ball and was about to pick it up again when Kevin dove for it. He smothered it in his arms while simultaneously knocking Boyle's feet out from under him. It was a clear foul but the refs didn't call anything. Kevin rolled over on the floor, saw me open and, while prone on his back, passed me the ball before Boyle could reach over and force a jump ball. I took one dribble and pulled up for a jumper at least five feet behind the three-point line. It was a ridiculously long shot but I never hesitated.

The ball ripped through the bottom of the net. I punched the air and our entire bench bolted from their seats. With the veins in his neck bulging, the Temple coach screamed at the officials for not calling a foul on Kevin. He was stomping his feet and flailing his arms. One official had heard enough. He blew his whistle and gave the Temple coach a technical foul. The building exploded with booing and cheering.

I hit both technical free throws to cut our deficit to four. Temple's coach was still livid and his assistants had to restrain him on the sidelines. It was still our ball so I inbounded on the sideline, just a few feet from him. I half expected him to reach out and strangle me, he looked *that* angry. As I passed to Brian, who was guarded tightly by Perry, I saw something in his eyes. I'd seen that look before, when we played one-on-one. Brian knew we were in the midst of a run and he intended to put more wood on the fire. He got by Perry with a wicked cross over dribble, juked another Temple defender, and then rose up above everyone in the paint and threw down a tomahawk dunk.

I was so stunned I hadn't even bothered to step onto the court. Brian's dunk made it seven straight points for us. But Temple wasn't about to collapse and they answered with a basket on their end. The next few minutes were back and forth. Neither team could grab control of the game. With seven minutes left in the game we were still down two. On our next possession Perry fouled Brian, his fourth foul. He went to the bench as Brian hit two free throws, tying the game.

With Perry on the bench Temple's offense stagnated. Boyle took a bad shot and missed. We rebounded and scored to go up two. Next time down Temple threw the ball away and we scored again. We were up four. Furious, Boyle demanded the ball and ordered his teammates to clear out. He wanted to take me one-on-one, sure he could score over me, a lowly freshman from GW. He shot faked and drove to his left. I was momentarily out of position but caught up. He picked up his dribble along the baseline and shot faked again. I bit on the fake and he had me. As I harmlessly flew by him he was still on the ground, wide open. He then released his silky smooth jumper, but Robert had seen it coming and hustled over for the block. He tipped the shot and Kevin grabbed the ball. Jim quickly pushed the ball up court and drained an eighteen foot jump shot.

Temple's coach didn't waste any more time getting Perry back in the game. Our lead was six and it remained that way until there were two minutes left. Jim threw a pass into Kevin who had great position on the low block. He was about to shoot when he saw Jim cutting through the lane. He gave Jim a nice bounce pass that Jim caught in stride and dunked. We now led by eight with 1:45 left.

For the first time in three games I saw doubt on the faces of the Temple players.

They hurried downcourt and one of their big men hit a short shot. They picked us up full court and forced a turnover. Perry got it to Boyle who took a shot that was further out than my deep three and nailed it. Again they played pressing full court defense. Robert took the ball out of bounds and couldn't find anybody open. The ref whistled a five second violation. I was stunned. Temple could tie the game with a three! Our eight point lead and their doubt had evaporated in less than a minute.

Temple inbounded the ball underneath their basket and got it to Perry. He and Brian had been challenging each other all night long. Their games were amazingly similar. Their modus operandi was always attack the basket, challenge the defense, only settle for jumpers when necessary. Perry sized up Brian then made his move. Brian seemed to be in great defensive position but somehow Perry found a gap to penetrate. As he neared the basket I tried to help out, but was too late. I swiped at the ball and smacked Perry on the arm. As I did he flipped the ball towards the basket. It went in and the refs blew the whistle. The basket counted and Perry could tie the game with a free throw!

I was disgusted with myself. It was a stupid foul. Were we going to blow this game and lose to Temple again?

Perry missed the free throw, but Temple somehow got the rebound. A basket now would give them lead. In the chaos of the missed free throw Kevin found himself guarding Perry. It was a mismatch. They quickly got the ball to him before we could make a defensive switch. He immediately dribbled past Kevin and headed to the hoop. But Brian was in proper help-side defensive position, having slid over at just the right time. Perry ran right into him as he went up for a layup. Brian went sprawling onto the floor as the ball went in the basket. If it was a block they would have the lead with a free throw coming. If they called a charge it was our ball and our lead was preserved.

The nearest ref had already blown his whistle but seemed to be taking an eternity to make the call. Lying on the floor Brian craned his neck to look at him. "Charge!" The ref finally shouted as he emphatically gave the signal for a charge and waved off the basket.

Brian slapped the floor in his excitement. Jim ran over and picked him up. Our bench went nuts while Temple's went berserk.

The foul was Perry's fifth. He was done for the night. It was a huge blow to Temple. But the game wasn't over yet. We still led by just one point with 40 seconds left. We needed at least one more basket to secure the win.

From the sideline Coach Ross called the play. We ran the first part of it flawlessly. I ran off a double screen and Jim gave me another great pass. But Temple saw it coming. They switched and a quick Temple defender was right in my face. So much for getting an open look at the basket. How much time was on the shot clock? I pivoted to my right. Boyle had switched onto Brian. I pivoted the other way and saw Jim. I took a dribble to try and get a better angle to pass to him. Jim's man tightened up and closed off the passing lane. Stupidly, I picked up my dribble. Now I was really stuck. I could hear Brian calling for the ball. He was open beyond the three-point line. Boyle was playing off him a few feet. He didn't want to get beat back door and why bother denying Brian out that far. He wasn't a three-point threat. Brian clapped his hands and shouted, "Come on, Tom. We gotta shoot!" What would Brian do with the ball out there? What other choice did I have? Then I heard my father's voice: *Trust each other.* I passed to Brian. Only then did I steal a quick glance at the shot clock. It was at three.

Brian immediately ripped the ball below his knees and attacked Boyle's front leg. He was so quick! Boyle backpedaled awkwardly. One more long stride and Brian elevated from just inside the free-throw line. As he did he leaned into Boyle's body. His runner had no chance of going in but he flailed his arms just enough to coax one of the officials to call a foul.

Ricky Boyle boiled over in frustration at the referee and nearly got himself a technical foul.

The foul sent Brian to the line for two free throws. If he hit both it would put us up three with under ten seconds left in the game. But Brian was not only a poor outside shooter, he was also a poor free throw shooter.

The referee handed Brian the ball. I could barely watch.

His first free throw hit the front rim then backboard then dropped in. He swished the second.

Temple had one last chance. Needing a three-pointer just to tie, they ran multiple screens for Boyle. Brian stuck to him, trailing Boyle past every pick, just like he was instructed to by Coach Ross. When Boyle got the ball, Brian over-played him on his shooting arm, daring him to dribble in for a wide-open layup. Instead Boyle hoisted a long three. Brian avoided fouling by simply putting his arms straight in the air. The shot wasn't even close.

When the final buzzer ricocheted off the ancient walls, we had won 72 to 69. We were league champs!

Our fans stormed the court. People were jumping up and down, slapping backs, hugging and high fiving. In the mayhem I saw Jenae. I pushed through the crowd and she jumped into my arms. A moment later a wave of fans bumped into us. They were ushering Brian over to one of the baskets to cut down the net.

"Great game, roomie!" Brian shouted on his way past.

"Great game yourself! Nice job on those free throws."

Jenae smiled and raised her eyebrows at me. "'Great game, roomie'? 'Great game yourself,' huh? That's a full blown heart to heart for you two."

I laughed. "We're getting there."

John Hornbeck and the rest of our student managers bustled through the throng passing out brand new t-shirts that read "GW A-10 Champs." I grabbed two and gave one to Jenae. It was huge on her, covering her jeans down to the knees.

My parents made their way to us too and we embraced.

"You were right, Dad," I said. "Brian came up big in that last minute of the game. He drew that charge, hit those free throws. How did you know?"

My father smiled, his arm still wrapped around my shoulder. "I didn't. I had a hunch, that's all. But I knew it would be good for you to trust him. The Lord knows what we need."

CHAPTER 25

THE NEXT DAY was Selection Sunday, the day the field for the NCAA tournament is announced. I'm sure the guys on the team spent most of the day glued to the TV watching other league championship games and later, the selection show. Me, I was busy helping a middle-aged alcoholic try and piece his life back together.

When I got back from Philly I had a message on my answering machine from Paul. He asked that I come by. It concerned Ray.

While I was away Ray had resurfaced at the soup kitchen. He was in rough shape. Paul demanded that Ray stay with him and he complied. When I showed up at Paul's office on Sunday, Ray filled me in. After getting drunk the day of our last home game, he snuck out of Paul's house and wandered off and got in trouble again. He spent the next two days drinking and sleeping on heated grates. The following day he showed up at Cortellesi's for his dishwashing job, but was still drunk. In the back of their kitchen is a small storage room with a cot. It was there for employees who were either sick or tired and needed a place to briefly rest. Some of his co-workers put him in the bed hoping he would sleep it off. He vaguely remembered throwing up all over himself and someone cleaning him up.

He slept there the rest of the night and slipped out early the next morning before anyone else showed up. As he exited Cortellesi's from a back door, a police car happened to drive by at the same time. They spotted Ray and immediately gave chase. Ray ducked behind a corner and was gone. Not only did Ray know the alleys and side streets of the city better than anyone, he was agile and could run well. He ran through the shadows and around dumpsters for a few minutes and never saw the squad car again. Those cops never had a chance.

After another two nights on the street and on the bottle, Ray stumbled into the basement of the church. He'd been staying at Paul's office ever since. It was his first major relapse in a long time and Paul wasn't about to give up on him. None of us were. We all hoped the shelter would provide a bit of stability for Ray but it was still two weeks away from being ready. In the meantime Ray would sleep on a cot in Paul's living room.

THE NCAA TOURNAMENT selection committee put us in the West region as the 10th seed. On Thursday we'd play in Salt Lake City, Utah vs. the University of Alabama. I was hoping for a better seed than ten. Our coaches were shocked we weren't seeded higher. I guess we still had our doubters.

With our first round opponent set, it was time to get back to business. Since we had three straight days of games at the Atlantic 10 Tournament, it had been a while since we'd practiced. Come Monday, Coach Ross ran us like it was October. He wasn't about to let us get overconfident or be happy with just making the tournament. This was new terrain for all of us. Coach Ross had never coached in the NCAAs before and no one on the team had ever played in the tournament. Everyone was enthusiastic at the start of practice, but as it wore on, enthusiasm gave way to exhaustion. By the end Alex, whose broken hand had healed, looked like he was going to puke. The last few days had been filled with excitement and emotion. But this practice was pure hard work. It was just what we needed.

At the end I was hoping to get in some more shooting with Coach Jennings rebounding for me like he usually did. It was only then that I noticed he hadn't been at practice, so I went to the coaches' office to search for him.

His office door was ajar so I knocked and walked in. "Hey, Coach, what're you doing in here?"

He looked awful. He hadn't shaved and dark half circles under his eyes made it clear he hadn't slept much lately. His office was a mess too. Video tapes cluttered his desk and his trash can was overflowing onto the floor.

"Scouting Alabama." He tried to sound energetic but didn't pull it off. "Wasn't at practice because I've either been staring at this TV or on the phone calling other coaches."

Coordinating the video exchange and scouting opponents were some of his duties. In order to scout opponents you need video of their games. To get this you need to work with other schools and have them send you game video of the team you're scouting.

In the twenty-four hours since we found out we were playing Alabama, Coach Jennings had called the assistant coaches for the last five teams Alabama faced and asked for a copy of the game tape. Watching those tapes was the best way we could scout them. Since we were leaving for our game on Wednesday, the tight turnaround meant everything had to be done quickly, within a day if possible. Without cooperation from other schools we'd never get the tapes on time. Coach Jennings had to track down these coaches and give them our FedEx number and address so they could overnight the tapes. Getting a hold of the teams wasn't easy since, for some, their season had just ended and the coaches probably weren't hanging around the office much. No doubt Alabama's coaches were doing the same thing with some of our recent opponents.

After he'd explained all this, genuine excitement filled his voice. "So, I went back through all the scouting tapes we had from earlier this year and found one with Alabama on it. They'd played New Mexico back in early December and I got that game so I could scout New Mexico before we played them at their Christmas tournament. How lucky is that?"

"Oh, I don't know about luck, Coach. You put in the hard work and it paid off."

"Well, doing this kind of work is a far cry from where I was when I first got into coaching. I thought I was going to be the next John Wooden. Boy, were my eyes opened that first year. At first I thought all the grunt work was beneath me. Like I was too good for it. Man, was I cocky. Anyway, Coach Ross straightened me out pretty quick. He helped me realize there is nothing beneath me. None of this hard work is demeaning. It's what coaches are supposed to do. It's what leaders are supposed to do. Now I don't see all the hard work and sacrifice as a bad thing. I'm a coach. I'm supposed to put you guys first. Sitting here in this cramped office watching hours of tape, well it's part of the job. The better I do this, the better you guys look on the court."

"So, how does Alabama look on the court?"

He put down the remote control and vigorously rubbed his tired eyes. "They're good. We all knew that. But this tape is from a few months ago so I really need something more recent. From what I've seen so far, I like the way we match up. Yeah, they're all big and talented and play in the SEC, but you know what? You're just as good as them. You could easily play in the SEC."

I was taken aback. The Southeastern Conference was one of the best in the nation, loaded with talented players and coaches. It was one thing to have the confidence to think I could play in the SEC, but it was something different to hear one of my coaches confirm it. "Wow, thanks. I sure owe a lot to you and the rest of the coaches."

"At the start of the year, I probably wouldn't have said that. When you first got here you were a shooter. Now, you're a basketball player, and a really good one. You're willing to do the things that don't always show up in the box score. It's hard to say when you turned the corner but it's been fun to watch your improvement."

He paused and took a gulp from the can of soda on his desk. "You know, you were my first recruit. Coach Ross and Ciancio were the ones that worked on Brian. I was the one who tracked you."

This was only the second year at GW for Coach Jennings so it made sense I was his first recruit. He must have a lot riding on me.

"I probably wouldn't have come here if it wasn't for you. Remember what you used to say to me when you called my house?"

"Yep. I'd say, 'How's that jump shot, Conner?'" He smiled and winked.

"You got it. On one hand that seems like yesterday, on the other … years ago."

"Kind of does, doesn't it?"

"So who is Alabama's best player?"

"They've got a real good point guard. Paul Jarvis. Found out he goes by the nickname Camel." He laughed. "Funny nickname. He's a lanky kid from Indiana and knows the game well. They like to pressure the ball. So we're going to need a great game from Jim if we want to win."

"Well, I'm not worried about that."

"Nope, me neither."

"So, you think you can spare a few minutes to rebound for me?"

He slapped his thighs then abruptly stood up. "You bet. I could use the break. My eyes are bleary from watching tape."

When we finished on the main court, I heard a bouncing ball coming from the auxiliary gym. Curious, I went upstairs to see who it was. I cracked open the door and saw Brian, his sweat drenched t-shirt sticking to his body like cling-wrap, shoot jump shot after jump shot. Not once did he deviate from this pattern; flip the ball out to a spot on the floor, go grab it, turn and shoot, rebound, repeat. The scorer was working on his shot. For a brief moment I had the idea to be funny and shout, "Stupid set shot!" Then I remembered. That was something I would have said a few months ago. But not now. I quietly closed the door and left without him ever knowing I was there.

OUR FIRST ROUND game was to take place at the University of Utah Special Events Center in Salt Lake City. I instantly recognized it as the site of the 1979 NCAA final between Larry Bird's Indiana State team and Magic Johnson's Michigan State Spartans. Considered one of the most famous college basketball games ever, it was the first time Bird and Magic played against each other.

Like many watching that night, I had never seen either one of them play. The game received a 24.1 Nielsen rating, an astronomical number, which meant that nearly a quarter of the TV's in the country were tuned in to the game. It was, and still is, the most watched basketball game ever.

Indiana State was undefeated on the season and Bird, a senior, had already been drafted by the Celtics the year before, thanks to Red Auerbach. Magic, who was only a sophomore, played great in the game. Bird didn't, shooting 7 for 21 from the floor. As a result, Michigan State won 75 to 64. It was the last college game for Bird and Magic who both went on to the NBA from there.

I had always loved sports history, so I went to the school library and did a bit of research on the game. It was in many ways a watershed moment for the NCAA tournament. That year it expanded the field of teams from 32 to 40. The tournament expanded to 48 teams in 1980, and again to 64 teams in 1985. As a result of the huge ratings for the game there was a corresponding increase in the rights fees. I found out NBC paid $5.2 million in 1979. In 1982, CBS paid $48 million for the rights, and then a few years ago, in 1985, they paid double.

The NCAA Tournament was now big business and March Madness was a big deal, especially growing up in my family. Bird and Magic and that 1979 championship game had a lot to do with that.

It was also during that game that I became a Larry Bird fan. I watched the game with my father and older brother and every championship game since then. Darrell Griffith and Louisville won their first ever championship over UCLA in 1980. In 1981 Indiana beat North Carolina at the Spectrum in Philadelphia on the day President Ronald Reagan was shot. I didn't know it at the time, but immediately after the shooting, Reagan was taken to GW's hospital where they saved his life. The very next year a skinny freshman named Michael Jordan sank the game winning shot as North Carolina beat Georgetown in the Louisiana Superdome. 1983's title game ending was a shocker as Lorenzo Charles caught Derrick Whittenburg's air ball shot and turned it into an alley-oop dunk at the buzzer to give North Carolina State the win over the Houston Cougars.

In the 1984 championship game the Houston Cougars lost again, this time to the Georgetown Hoyas. The next year, 1985, Georgetown was again in the finals and the heavy favorite against fellow Big East team, Villanova. This was the last college game for the Hoyas star center, Patrick Ewing. It was to be a coronation. If Georgetown won they'd be the first team to win back-to-back championships since the UCLA dynasty of the 70's. For the Villanova Wildcats just to have a chance, they had to play a nearly perfect game. And they did. As a team Villanova shot 78% from the floor, missing only six shots all game. They hung on to win by a score of 66-64.

Last year, Louisville won its second championship under Denny Crum by beating Duke in the 86 final in Dallas, Texas.

This year's Final Four would be played at the Meadowlands in New Jersey. It was hard not to look ahead and dream about playing just a few miles from my hometown, but to get to the Final Four we'd have to win four straight games. Final Four dreams would have to wait. First, we needed to beat Alabama.

BEFORE THEY LEFT Philly, my parents told Jenae they would pay for her to travel to all my tournament games, no matter how many we played. She and my parents were to fly in to Utah on Thursday, the day of the game. What made the trip to Utah even more exciting for Jenae was knowing her family planned on driving down from Idaho for the game. I wished Ray could come too but that was out of the question.

We arrived in Utah on Wednesday, in time to practice that afternoon. When I first walked onto the University of Utah Special Events Center court I got goosebumps. It seated 15,000, about three times the size of our Smith Center, but it wasn't the size that gave me the goosebumps. It was the thought of playing on the same court as the NCAA championship game between Bird and Magic. I recognized the distinctive concrete walls surrounding the court and could picture the place packed, fans going crazy, TV cameras and photographers everywhere. I tried to imagine where Larry Bird made his shots from. It felt like stepping back in time. Like an explorer walking the deck of the Titanic or a historian roaming the White House and bumping into Thomas Jefferson.

I wondered if Brian knew that this was the site of the Bird-Magic championship game. I'll bet he had no idea and I wasn't about to tell him either. After all, Magic won that game. Maybe I could erase the memory of Bird's poor shooting night and shoot the lights out tomorrow. Better yet, maybe I could help us win.

Practice was intense. It felt good to work up a sweat after the long flight. The enormity of the moment was starting to sink in. Tomorrow we would be playing in the NCAA tournament on national TV.

After practice ended a few guys stayed on the court to shoot around. As always, I was there taking shots, but this time, instead of rebounding for me, Coach Jennings grabbed a ball and started to shoot too. After spending so much time breaking down tape on Alabama, he no doubt needed to work off a little stress.

"Hey, Brian, Coach Jennings," said Jim standing off to my right. "Did you guys know this is where Bird and Magic played the '79 national championship game?"

My shot clanked off the rim.

Brian was practicing free throws. "Really? In this place?"

"Yeah, and Magic's team won." Jim continued.

I glared at him but he ignored me.

"Yeah, now I remember," Brian said. "Magic went off. Bird's team lost. They stunk. First of many that Bird lost to Magic."

"Oh, whatever! Check the history books," I countered. "Who won the 84 NBA title, huh? Bird and the Celtics beat Magic's Lakers 4 games to 3."

They were all laughing and ignoring me. Jim dribbled out near the three-point line. "Brian, you remember the dunk Magic had in that game?"

"Oh, yeah you bet. He dunked right on Bird didn't he?"

"Ugh! No he didn't!" They weren't listing to me. Magic did have an awesome dunk in that game that later appeared on the cover of Sports Illustrated. But it wasn't on Bird.

"Yeah, you be Bird and I'll be Magic," said Jim. "We'll show Thomas what it looked like."

"Good idea," said Brian. "I'll stand here like a white guy that can't jump. I mean I'll pretend to be Bird."

It finally dawned on me that they'd planned this just to tease me. "Okay, hah, hah. Let's see it."

Jim dribbled towards the basket while Brian stood underneath it with his hands raised over his head and his eyes closed. Like he'd done a thousand times before Jim gracefully jumped up and dunked the ball while Brian laughed.

Jim let go of the rim and came back down to earth. As he did his left foot landed on one of Brian's. I saw his ankle roll as he crumpled to the ground.

CHAPTER 26

IT WAS A bad sprain. Twisting your ankle is one of the most common injuries in basketball. Every time you leave the ground there is the chance you could land on someone's foot and roll your ankle. I'd done it many times over the years too. I was surprised it didn't happen more often.

Despite icing it the rest of the day, Jim's ankle swelled up during the night. He could barely walk on it during our game day shoot around. Danny wrapped twice as much tape on it as normal, and Jim bravely hobbled around the court during pre-game warm ups. But it was obvious he couldn't play.

The Alabama players and coaches noticed too.

It wasn't until ten minutes before tip off that Coach Ross finally decided to start Elijah Gleason in place of Jim. Elijah was a good point guard, but didn't get much playing time because he played the same position as Jim. Jim hardly ever got in foul trouble and this was the first time he'd been injured all year. Elijah was only a sophomore and with Jim graduating after this year we all knew his time to shine would come. But with Jim on the bench with a gimpy ankle, we needed Elijah to shine tonight.

During warm ups Elijah looked nervous, which I could understand. But why was I so nervous? I always had some butterflies before a game, but this was ridiculous. Was it because Jenae's family was here watching? I didn't think so. I got to meet them earlier in the day. Jenae's parents couldn't have been more encouraging and positive.

"Hey, Thomas," Matt said. He came up behind me in the layup lines and slapped me on the shoulder. "Relax, buddy. When it's all said and done, it's just another game, right?"

I nodded. Unconvincingly. I could barely dribble the ball and make a layup for fear of tripping and falling. Cheerleaders, photographers, and TV cameras seemed to line every square inch along the baseline. Was Larry Bird this nervous here in '79? Was he ever this nervous?

The national anthem, starting introductions, and last minute instructions from Coach Ross came and went. It was all a blur. I told myself over and over to enjoy the moment, but it was nearly impossible. This was the NCAA tournament!

Once on the court for the opening tip I gawked at how big and athletic the Alabama players were. If we were ever going to get out of the shadow of Maryland and Georgetown, we needed to win games like this in the NCAA tournament. No one was better at wining in the NCAA tournament than Coach John Wooden. I remembered his definition of success. It was peace of mind knowing you gave your best to be your best. Okay, Lord thank you for giving me peace of mind as I give my best on the court. Thank you for the chance to play this game and glorify you. I closed my eyes for a second and took a deep breath.

That breath got cut short as an elbow jabbed me in the ribs. The ref had tossed the ball in the air for the opening tip sooner than I expected. I was caught totally off guard. One of the Alabama players grabbed the ball right in front of me.

My heart jack hammered inside my chest as I sprinted back on defense. They were fast. I ran into a screen and momentarily saw stars. They shot and missed. Kevin snatched the rebound from the rafters. Elijah pushed the ball up court. My defender was all over me. They had clearly seen plenty of game tape on me. Kevin moved over to set a back screen for me. Since my defender was so close to me he never saw it coming. I jab faked to the wing then cut back door. Elijah delivered a beautiful bounce pass which led me to a wide-open layup.

Jim and Matt were the first ones up off our bench cheering. The nervousness and anxiety melted away. I was back in the present moment. Despite the setting, it was now like any other game.

With Jim not playing, it was clear Alabama was going to try and force turnovers and run on us. But you can't run on offense unless you get stops on defense, and they weren't stopping us. Elijah jealously protected the ball, and Brian and I kept hitting shots. Alabama could never get the tempo to their liking and it showed in their faces. They were frustrated. We held the lead the entire first half and at half time were up four.

In the locker room during half time Jim huddled with Elijah giving him advice and encouragement. Jim wasn't about to let his ankle prevent him from impacting the game. I marveled at his leadership skills.

We slowly built on our lead in the second half. But Alabama was too good to go away this easily and we knew they'd make a run. It started with five minutes to play when Elijah picked up his fourth foul.

Coach Ross took Elijah out and put Coleman into the game for the first time. Alabama inbounded the ball and went right at Coleman. It was the smart thing to do, and not just because it was Coleman. Whenever someone has been sitting on the bench a long time it's a good idea to immediately challenge him on defense. He's probably stiff and certainly not in the flow of the game. Coleman was stiff all right. His man, Paul "Camel" Jarvis, the lanky point guard from Indiana that Coach Jennings had told me about, went right around him and buried a jumper, cutting our lead to seven.

They pressed full court. Coleman tried to beat his defender by dribbling behind his back. He never saw the double-team coming. The Alabama defender easily poked the ball away and ran in for an uncontested layup. Smelling blood in the water, they stayed in their press. Coleman inbounded the ball to me in the corner. I was immediately swarmed by two Alabama defenders. I tried to find an open teammate but I could barely see anything past their long arms. I threw a bounce pass back to Coleman, but it was stolen by Jarvis.

That kid from Indiana was good and gutsy. He had an open layup if he chose to take it. Instead he took one dribble backwards and drained a three-pointer.

Coach Ross was shouting instructions from the sidelines while on the court we ran around, frantic. Coleman, overwhelmed by it all, quickly grabbed the ball out of net and, trying to inbound the ball before Alabama could set up their press, passed to Brian. But Brian wasn't ready. The ball ricocheted off his hands right to Jarvis. Incredibly he was standing underneath his basket and easily flipped the ball into the hoop.

The game was tied.

Coach Ross called timeout. I walked over to our bench, shell shocked. Elijah ran over to the scorer's table to check in.

"Hey, listen," Coach Ross said calmly as we stood around him. "They've had their run, now it's over. But Jim can't bail us out. You guys have to step up, right now." He nodded at Jim who was standing next to him on one foot. "Don't let his career end tonight because we couldn't win without him. Show him, show me you guys have learned from his example."

Out of the timeout it was our ball. The Alabama players were bouncing up and down on their toes, itching to get another steal and take the lead. We inbounded to Elijah. They tried to trap him but he was too quick. He dribbled past over aggressive defenders and weaved his way up court, catching them out of position. Now presented with a fast break of our own, he faked a pass to Brian. The defender bit on the fake and Elijah kept the ball and waltzed in for a layup. It was a brilliant play.

It calmed us down. Elijah's basket put us back in the lead. On the next two possessions we traded baskets.

With under a minute to go it was Alabama's ball. They decided to post up Jarvis on Elijah. Elijah was much shorter and as he struggled to prevent Jarvis from getting position near the hoop, the refs whistled him for a foul. It was his fifth. He was done for the game. Now our top two point guards were no longer available. As Elijah walked off the court our fans gave him a standing ovation. Coach Ross gave him a hug and then, searching up and down our bench, his eyes finally rested on Coleman. He had no choice but to put him back in the game.

Jarvis hit both ends of the one and one to tie the game. It was our ball with 45 seconds to go.

How is it that, with our season on the line, we had to rely on Coleman to run our offense? Everyone on the team loved Coleman, he was that kind of guy. But none of us wanted him on the floor right now.

Jarvis hounded Coleman as he brought the ball past half court. Coleman passed to me on the wing. My defender had one hand on my hip and the other in my face. He was daring me to drive. I took one dribble to my right then stupidly picked it up. Now I had to pass. Alabama tried to deny all passes. The guy guarding me was shouting "Deny" and waving his arms, blocking my vision.

I pivoted and saw Kevin had good position in the post. I was about to pass to him when I saw Jarvis sneak over hoping for a steal. That meant Coleman was open and I pivoted again and passed him the ball.

Thirty seconds left. Plenty of time. No need to rush.

But that's exactly what Coleman did. As soon as he received the pass he rose to shoot a three-pointer. What was he thinking?

Jarvis flew out at him to challenge the shot. He didn't need to because it was a brick. As the rebound bounced high in the air the whistle blew.

Coleman lay on the floor. Jarvis had fouled him on the shot. It was an incredibly boneheaded play by their best player. He should have known Coleman was no threat to knock down a shot from that far out. With twenty eight seconds left and the game tied, Coleman was heading to the free-throw line for three shots.

Coach Ross always had us shoot lots of free throws in practice. Over the course of the season I'd seen Coleman shoot plenty of them. It wasn't a pretty sight. So I wasn't surprised when he stepped to the line and calmly knuckle-balled the first two free throws off the side of the rim. He had one shot remaining. Even if he made it Alabama would have the ball and the chance to take a game winning shot.

Coleman's third and final free throw went in.

We led by one point. Alabama called timeout. In our huddle Jim wrapped his arm around Coleman's neck and gave him a good shake. "Way to go, kid," he said. "Now go save the game for us on the defensive end."

Alabama didn't need to hide their intentions. We knew what they were going to do. They passed to Jarvis on the wing and cleared out one side of the court. Coleman would have to guard Jarvis one-on-one. If any of us helped out too much, Jarvis would pass to an open teammate, and all his teammates were good shooters.

Jarvis turned and started backing Coleman down into the post. Coleman tried to hold his ground, while Jarvis lowered his dribble and his center of gravity. A few more feet and Jarvis could shoot a short turn around jump shot over Coleman to win the game.

The seconds ticked away. Only ten remained. The entire arena was on its feet. It was man on man, their best against one of our worst. Someone had to make a move.

Only eight feet from the basket, Jarvis picked his dribble up and gave a quick shoulder fake. Coleman lunged the wrong way and nearly fell to the ground. Jarvis was open but Robert finally left his man and went to help. He pump faked, sending Robert out of position. Jarvis then pivoted and had a wide-open shot. As he raised the ball to shoot, Coleman desperately reached out and cleanly knocked the ball free.

The ball bounced off Jarvis's knee and rolled towards our bench. Four seconds left. In a mad dash for the ball, Jarvis beat Coleman to it. He grabbed it just inches from the sideline. In desperation he turned and shot over Coleman's outstretched hands.

The buzzer sounded with the ball in air. It hit the back rim, then backboard and rim again before bouncing out.

We'd survived, 71-70!

Brian was our leading scorer with 22 points, and Elijah, with his 10 assists, played fantastic in relief of Jim. I ended up shooting 9 for 12 for 18 points, one less than Bird scored in the 1979 finals. But that didn't matter. What mattered was we won. We won for Jim and the other seniors, extending their careers by at least one more game.

OVER A LONG season it helps to have a few lucky breaks every now and then. We'd had at least two in the final minute against Alabama. More luck headed our way when Marshall, the 15 seed in our bracket, won in a huge first round upset. They, instead of the 2 seed, would be our opponent for our second round game.

Jim wasn't one hundred percent, but he played nonetheless, splitting time with Elijah. Coleman spent the game in his usual spot, at the end of the bench. Marshall had shot the lights out in their first round upset, but they simply could not buy a basket against us. Kevin and Robert used their size and length to dominate the inside. On the perimeter Jim, Brian, and Elijah played great. Me, I just kept hitting shots. I shot 7 for 10 for 14 points. Brian again led us in scoring with 20 points and Kevin had a huge game with 12 rebounds and 18 points. We cruised to a surprisingly easy 80-69 victory.

Despite how well we'd been playing all year, the national media was stunned. We were GW, a team with virtually no NCAA tournament history. The local D.C. media knew we were good, but no one else had a clue. Many in the national media didn't even know how to say our names. After a post-game meal, a few of us crammed into Coach Jenning's hotel room and watched the game on tape. The TV announcers messed up on our names a number of times. Jim was called "Bar-jur" rather than "Bar-ger" with the "ger" a hard "g." I was called Tim once and Brian was referred to as Byron at least twice. But the best was when they mistakenly called Elijah by the names of two other old testament prophets, Elisha and Isaiah!

Regardless, we were headed to the Sweet 16, and everyone knew how to say Cinderella.

CHAPTER 27

THE TIME BETWEEN our first two games in Utah and the Sweet 16 went by amazingly quick. I didn't even bother to completely unpack. I found it almost impossible to focus in school, let alone do any homework. Most classes started with the professors facilitating a few minutes of question and answer about our two wins in the NCAA tournament. Only my American History professor, Leo Howard, carried on like business as usual.

Ray seemed be to recovering well. Paul had him set up in the living room that was adjacent to his office. It wasn't much and it was only temporary until the shelter opened up. He was attending AA meetings and, remarkably, Tony of Cortellesi Pizza gave him another chance at washing dishes at his restaurant. Jenae talked to my mom on the phone nearly every day as they worked on flight arrangements to our next game.

Our Sweet 16 opponent was DePaul University. The game was scheduled for Thursday in Seattle, Washington. Our coaches tried to keep practices as familiar as possible, but it was difficult with all the distractions. The campus was gripped with Colonial basketball fever, so everywhere we went we were treated like rock stars. On Monday the stands in the Smith Center were packed with students wanting to watch practice. Coach Ross walked in the gym, took one look at the crowd, then immediately went and found Bill Pebble and ordered him to close the gym. Even while they were getting kicked out, the students cheered and wished us good luck.

In addition, the local media was now at every practice. Coach Ross allowed them into the gym at the beginning of practice for a few minutes before he kicked them out too. It was such a stark contrast to the long practices in October when nobody was watching.

OUR FLIGHT TO Seattle connected in Chicago where we had a two hour layover. Some of the guys wandered around magazine stands while others played cards. It seemed everyone needed a diversion because no one was talking about our next game. We were on an amazing journey: two wins away from going to the Final Four, four wins away from being national champions. Each game represented a chance to continue the dream or see it vanish into zeros on the scoreboard. It was hard not to think about what could be.

But dwelling on future wins or loses, shots made and missed, could drive you crazy. I knew. There were times where I completely drained myself mentally and emotionally obsessing about the next game, the next practice, the next shooting session. I'd lose all touch with reality, living in a fantasy world that had yet to take place. Then there were days where I couldn't think about anything but the shots I missed in the previous game. Time would leave me behind while my mind clung to the past, vainly trying to change something I could not.

Basketball demands you be in the present moment. The game changes in a blink of an eye. You can't think too far ahead or dwell on the past. If your mind is anywhere but the present moment you lose the ability to react. One time as I was stewing over a shot I just missed, the guy I was guarding went right behind me for a backdoor layup. I didn't realize it until after the ball was already through the net.

Missed shots used to drive me nuts. But things were different now. I still hated missing shots, but they didn't stay with me and hinder my next shot. If I'd made ten straight or missed my last five, each shot had my full attention, my full confidence. No longer did

I compound a mistake by fretting about it, lose my focus, and then make another one.

My competitive fire was now fueled by an inner calm that allowed me to play the game on a whole new level. I certainly wasn't near anyone's definition of competitive greatness, but I was able to play with more of the peace of mind Coach Wooden talked about in his pyramid of success. The verses in Philippians chapter four had a lot to do with that.

"Do not be anxious about anything, but in every situation, by prayer and petition, with thanksgiving, present your requests to God. And the peace of God, which transcends all understanding, will guard your hearts and minds in Christ Jesus."

So, I had more peace, both on and off the court. While the others played cards, I read. American history was usually my preferred topic but these days I found myself devouring the Bible. I brought it with me on every trip.

After reading a while I put my Bible down and took a break. As I watched people mill about in the terminal, an elderly man caught my eye. He was patiently waiting a few feet beyond the periphery of several other men. The elderly man, in his seventies or eighties, was smartly dressed in casual dinner attire. The men who were huddled together were clad in nearly identical dark power suits. Everyone in that group was directing their attention towards one man, who was clearly a man of importance. It seemed the elderly man was waiting to meet him, but no one in the group was paying the elderly man any attention.

After a minute or two there was a momentary lull in the conversation among the power suits. The elderly man stepped forward and confidently extended his hand. He was met with a handshake and smile from the important man and, after a few short words between them, the elderly man walked away with an enormous grin. The power suits closed ranks and resumed their discussion.

I was curious who that important looking man was. I walked over and asked the elderly gentleman. "Why that's our former governor of Wisconsin!" he said with the clear satisfaction of someone who had voted for him.

"How about that," I said. "What's his name?"

He gave an initial movement of his mouth like he was going to answer immediately, and then he stopped. He scrunched his face and scratched his head. After an embarrassed chuckle, he said, "I can't remember."

I smiled and waited while he rummaged through long ignored file cabinets in his mind. And to think, I used to be obsessed with being famous for playing basketball. I dreamt of having people recognize me as I walked around airports. This man seemed to adore the ex-Governor and yet he couldn't even come up with his name.

"Well, for the life of me I simply can not remember the governor's name. That's embarrassing." He looked up at me then motioned with his hand towards my teammates. "Say, you must be on a basketball team. Seems pretty obvious with a bunch of towering, young men milling about. Who do you play for?"

"GW. George Washington University."

"You in the NCAA tournament?"

"We are. We're headed to the Sweet 16."

"Really! That's great. I guess it's obvious I haven't followed the tournament this year. So, let's see, the last time you guys won the NCAAs you had that really big fella, Ewing, right?"

I smiled. "No, that's Georgetown. We're George Washington. Both in D.C. I guess we're still not as well known."

"Oh, sorry about that, young man."

"That's okay. But you should watch the games this weekend. We're pretty good."

"I will. And good luck."

"Thank you, sir."

I shook his hand and then he walked away. "Oh," he turned and waved a finger. "If I think of the governor's name before my flight I'll let you know."

He never did.

WHEN WE ARRIVED in Seattle it was pouring rain, but by game day, the weather turned sunny. I was struck by how beautiful the city was with its lush greenery and ocean backdrop.

The newspapers in Seattle said we were in over our heads. Most of the pre-game hype was devoted to Florida and UCLA, the other two teams in our bracket. Our game was almost an afterthought. Hardly anyone gave us a chance against DePaul. Our Cinderella story was nice while it lasted but many thought the clock was about to strike midnight and DePaul would move on to face the winner of Florida vs. UCLA.

But what the local pundits didn't know is we matched up incredibly well with DePaul. Our coaching staff had done an excellent job of scouting them. They looked at the game tape of DePaul's first two round wins, found their weaknesses and told us how to exploit them. Their top two scorers were guards, but Jim and Brian played lock down defense on them. Their zone defense allowed lots of open shots for us to nail. After trailing 10-8 in the first five minutes of the game we took the lead on a three-pointer by Jim and never lost it. It seemed we all shot well. I scored 16, Matt had 14 off the bench, Jim and Brian both had 18 points. As a team we shot nearly 60% from the floor. We cruised to a twelve point win.

After our close first round victory over Alabama we'd had two convincing wins. How long we could keep this up, nobody knew.

Florida beat UCLA in the other regional semi so we would play the Gators for the right to go to the Final Four. They were loaded with talent and much bigger than us. Kevin and Robert were playing great but their backups, David and Alex, were nowhere near as good as Florida's frontline. If either Kevin and Robert picked up early fouls, it could be a long night. There was also added pressure on me. As our small forward, I would need to do a much better job rebounding and playing interior defense to help our big men.

The first half was an absolute disaster. Florida came out with the intent to expose our inside game. They consistently pounded the ball into the paint and we simply couldn't stop them. Our entire starting five got in foul trouble. Robert had three fouls, and the rest of us had two. Alex and David saw significant time but were completely overwhelmed. In five minutes Alex had zero rebounds and three fouls. I could tell he was doing his best, but he was simply no match for the Gator's center, Lester Blank. I was exhausted from trying to defend and box out my man. It took its toll on my legs so most of my shots were short. Looking for someone to provide a spark, Coach Ross even put Coleman into the game and, like everyone else, he seemed lost.

Nobody on our team, other than Jim, played well in the first half and we went into the locker room down 15 points. It could have been worse. Was this it? Were we in over our heads like those in the media thought? The silence in our locker room told me I wasn't the only one thinking this.

The coaches were meeting outside the room before they came in to talk to us, as they usually did.

As always, it was Jim who spoke up. "Guys, we can't go out like this." His tone was somber, not energetic and forceful like usual. He stood up and paused. "I don't know what else to say."

Robert smacked the wall next to him. I jumped in my seat at the loud noise. "I do!" He thundered. "This is embarrassing, man! There is no way we're going to get embarrassed like this!"

The first half was probably his worst of the year. Florida's Lester Blank was big and strong, whereas Robert was wiry and quick. So far, Blank had made Robert look silly.

"Jim is lightin' it up and no one else is stepping up. Including me. Now I'm going to tell you all right now, we are going to win this game. We're not going to just make it close, we're going to win! I'm going to shut that dude down in the second half. But we need points, man.

We need points! Brian! You, my brother, can score. Now you get your ass out there and score."

I'd never seen this side of Robert before. He usually let his game do all the talking. Now, he was on a roll and started to resemble a preacher, pacing back and forth. Some of the black guys nodded or mumbled in agreement.

"Thomas!" Robert shouted and pointed a long finger at me. "I ain't ever seen anybody shoot a basketball like you, my man. You get out there this second half and shoot! You got it?"

I nodded.

"Brother," Robert said to Kevin, "I just know you're going to grab every rebound there is."

"I hear you," Kevin replied.

"There ain't no way we come this far to lay down now. We seniors been here four years. Always watching the NCAAs on TV instead of playing in them. Now, we're one game away from the Final Four! No GW team's ever been this far. Shoot, Florida and these other teams get this far all the time. Not us. Not GW. This is my final shot. I do not want this to be my last game in college. We are going to the Final Four! If you don't think so, stay here! Don't bother going out for the second half."

He scowled, searching faces for doubt or fear.

Just like that his transformation was over. Guys were clapping and shouting. Robert sat back down in front of his locker, but the scowl on his face remained.

The coaches had quietly entered the room and were standing off to the side, listening intently like everyone else. I hadn't even noticed they came in. Coach Ross added a point or two, but we all knew what needed to be said already had.

Basketball is game of momentum and runs. Every game has them. It's one of the things about basketball that makes it so much fun to watch. Unless it's a blowout, the momentum usually shifts a few times during the game. When you know the game well, you can sense a run starting. You can feel the wave swell before it forms a wall that comes crashing down. You can see it in the eyes of the players. One set of eyes are confident and eager. The other nervous and tense. One team, gathering momentum, runs like the court is tilted downhill; the other like they're running in a pool. One team goes on a run, then the other answers. The momentum takes on a life of its own, sucking everyone in. When your team is on a run you can flip the ball towards the basket with a defender draped all over you and it goes in. When the wave has you under you can't make a layup. Back and forth it goes. In close games nobody really loses. One team ends the game on a run, while the other simply runs out of time.

Florida had all the momentum in the first half. Now it was our turn.

We started the second half like a completely different team. Robert's speech was the stiff wind that set up the wave. The crash of the wave came on the first possession. Florida went right to Blank who had good position on the low block. Knowing Robert had three fouls, Blank went right at him. It was gutsy for Coach Ross to start Robert in the second half with three fouls, but after his halftime speech there was no way he wouldn't. Blank took a drop step dribble and pump faked, trying to get Robert in the air. Robert held his ground. He gave a little shoulder shake then tried to sneak a left handed shot off the glass. Robert was ready and slapped the ball in mid air right to Jim who fed Brian for a break away dunk. Everyone on our bench jumped out of their seats.

Over the next seven minutes our entire team was in a zone. We were all on fire. As a team we missed only one shot and outscored them 20 to 6, cutting their lead to one. Brian and I scored 14 of those 20 points.

Everyone in the crowd not from Florida was solidly behind us. Maybe they wanted to see Cinderella stick around a little longer. Regardless, during the run they went nuts. Kevin did grab nearly every rebound and Robert played with much more confidence on defense despite picking up his fourth foul. After trading baskets over the next few possessions, we went on another run. I hit two three-pointers and a basket by Brian gave us a five point lead.

The game remained tight as the minutes ticked off the clock. We held the lead but it never got larger than five. Florida never panicked. With just under one minute left, they hit a shot to cut the margin to one.

They immediately pressed full court. Caught off guard, Kevin threw an errant inbounds pass. The turnover gave the ball back to Florida. When the Gators inbounded they went down low again to Blank. Knowing Robert would try for the block, Blank went to his pet move. Two dribbles, drop step to the middle, then shot fake. He got Robert off his feet, leaned in, scored and was fouled. It gave them a one point lead with a chance to go up two on the free throw.

The foul was Robert's fifth. He had played a remarkable second half, blocking four shots and grabbing 9 rebounds. He left the floor to a standing ovation. Into the game came Alex. Since Robert had played such a great second half, Alex hadn't been on the court since the first half.

"Hey, let's box out now!" Jim shouted to Alex, Kevin, and me before the free throw. Alex didn't listen so well. Blank missed the free throw and Alex's man went right around him and tipped the ball in. Florida was now up three with 28 seconds left.

Coach Ross called timeout. I could tell he was livid with Alex, but he held his tongue and kept him in the game. He frantically diagrammed our next play while shouting over the din of the crowd. "Listen up! We can't take a lot of time to get a shot off! I don't want to wait and try and tie the game at the buzzer with a three. Work fast and get a good shot. Press full court if we hit a two, and fall back into man if we do tie it with a three-pointer. If we don't get a three, we need a steal or a foul. And if we don't get a steal by 15 seconds, you got to foul! Remember, if we tie it up on this possession, no fouls! You got it?"

Before I could walk out onto the court Robert grabbed my jersey. "We need you, Thomas. You get a good look, you shoot. Got it?"

I nodded. "Got it."

We inbounded. Florida's defense was tenacious. There was no chance I was getting open. My defender was practically wearing my jersey with me. After ten seconds went off the clock Jim made an incredible cross over dribble to get open for a jump shot just inside the three-point line. It went in, cutting their lead to one and we pressed full court like Coach Ross told us to. Just like we had done moments earlier, Florida threw a bad pass. It went off one of their hands and into the stands. They had turned the ball over! We had no timeouts left so Coach Ross signaled in the play from the bench.

There were fourteen seconds left on the clock and we were behind by one point. Fourteen seconds would decide whether we went to the Final Four or ended our season with a loss in the Elite 8.

The play called for me to inbound the ball. Taking a last second shot with the game on the line was a piece of cake compared to this. I hated inbounding the ball on the sideline. I tried to calm my nerves and prayed Brian would get open quickly. I felt my legs shaking as the ref handed me the ball. Florida denied Brian. He had scored 26 points so they weren't about to let him get the ball, but Brian was supposed to get the pass.

Terrified, I looked for someone else to throw to. Out of the corner of my eye I could see the referee counting down the seconds with his arm. I did not have the luxury of calling a time out if no one got open. I had to make a pass! Finally, Jim broke free from his defender. My pass to him nearly got stolen. Florida continued to deny Brian so he cut to the other side of the court giving Jim room to operate. Our set play had been completely disrupted. It was now up to Jim to make something happen and keep our season alive.

He tried to take his man off the dribble but his defender played him well. The guy guarding me turned his head and, anticipating a drive by Jim, took a step in that direction. I saw it and instantly darted away from him to an open spot on the floor. Jim saw it too and whipped a one handed bounce pass to me. Barely open, I had no time to think or look at the clock. I caught it and immediately left the ground for what I hoped was the game winning shot. As I jumped I saw Alex wide open under the hoop. How he got so open I had no idea. Instead of shooting the ball I threw a crisp pass right on the money to him. He was so open I had to throw it to him. There was no time to think about what ifs. I made the decision in a hundredth of a second.

Alex must not have known how open he was because he rushed what should have been an easy game winning layup. The ball bounced off the glass and off the front of the rim. It seemed to hang above the rim for an eternity.

The ball bounced on the rim again and finally dropped in as the buzzer sounded. We'd won by one point and were going to the Final Four!

Everybody mobbed Alex right underneath the basket. There was so much wild celebrating going on that Jim took an inadvertent elbow above his eye and got a small, but bloody, cut. He hardly seemed to notice.

In the celebration Robert came up to me and gripped my shoulder tightly and smiled broadly. "I'm glad Alex made that shot because if he didn't, you wouldn't be standing right now. When I tell you to shoot, you shoot!"

CHAPTER 28

IT WAS PAST eight p.m. by the time the bus pulled up to the Smith Center. A rowdy crowd of well wishers, some of them carrying signs, greeted us as we disembarked. Cameras from the local TV stations were there too, their lights shinning brightly in our faces. After giving two interviews and shaking dozens of hands, I slowly made my way towards my dorm. Despite the euphoria of winning and the energy of the fans, I was tired and craving a long night of sleep.

I was just about to enter the lobby when I heard my name. I turned and there was Ray, hands in his pockets and slightly hunched over against the chilly night air. "Hey, buddy," he said. "Great game today. You must be on cloud nine."

Something was wrong. The usual enthusiasm in his voice wasn't there and his smile was forced. "Hey, Ray. What's up? Everything okay?"

"Oh, sure. Well, no not really. I'm in a bit of a jam." He hesitated and kicked at a pebble on the sidewalk.

"What? What is it?"

"Golly, I feel so stupid. Paul's out of town tonight. He's been gone all day. Had to go visit someone. Anyway, he left me the key to his place but I just can't find it. I lost it somewhere."

"So you're locked out?"

"Yep. And I got nowhere to stay. Was hoping my days of sleeping in a park were behind me so I came here. I didn't know where else to go. Got any room in your place?"

"Of course. You take my bed and I'll take the couch." The words were barely out of my mouth when the thought of convincing Brian to let Ray stay in our room made my pulse race.

"Really? Oh, man you are a lifesaver!"

"My pleasure. Can't have you back out on the street."

"You said it. But please, I'll take the couch."

"Whatever you say." With my hands full of luggage, I fumbled with my keys.

"Here," Ray said. "Let me help." He grabbed the keys and unlocked the front door to my dorm.

As we headed up the stairs and down the hall towards my room I wondered if I was doing the right thing. He was my friend and I had to help him, but should I try and get him a hotel room instead? What if Brian refused? Then what?

Brian must have lingered with the TV cameras and fans because the room was empty when we entered.

"Say, what's your roommate, Mr. Patterson going to say about this?" Ray asked.

"Good question. I don't know, but hopefully he's okay with it."

Ray headed to the bathroom and a moment later the door opened and Brian sauntered in. I couldn't remember the last time I'd asked Brian for something, but now I had to ask him to let my alcoholic ex-con friend sleep on our couch for the night. How was I going to do this? Lord, I know I've pretty much blown it with Brian ever since we met but please help me handle this well so I don't let Ray down.

Brian dropped his bags next to his desk and reached for the ceiling, stretching his travel weary muscles. "Man, what a day. Did you see the way those guys went nuts when we showed up? It's like we walking on water."

I laughed softly. I wonder if he knew the Bible story of Christ walking on water and Peter sinking because of his fear. Now wasn't the time to bring it up. Nor was it the time to act like Peter in that moment. I'd done enough of that in the past. Ray was counting on me. "Brian," I said, "I need to ask you something."

The toilet flushed.

Brian looked towards the bathroom then at me. "Who's in there?"

"My friend, Ray."

"You mean the bum?"

"He's not a bum."

"Sure he is. What's he doing here?"

"He needs a place to stay tonight."

"How's he not a bum if he's got nowhere to sleep?"

I quickly glanced at the bathroom door. It was still shut. I was hoping to have this settled before Ray came out to hear it. "That's just it Brian, I'm trying to make sure he doesn't have to sleep on the streets tonight. He lives on the other side of campus with the pastor of a local church but got locked out. He's got nowhere to go. I'm just asking if it's okay he stay on the couch tonight. Just one night. That's all he needs."

He gawked at me. "You gotta be kidding."

"I'm not. Please? Just one night?"

Just then Ray emerged from the bathroom. He didn't look like a bum to me, but his clothing was a bit old and worn. The two-day old stubble on his face didn't help his appearance either. He looked over at Brian warily and nodded. Ray started to say something but stopped, apparently not sure what to say. After a momentary pause, he said to me, "So, are we good?"

I swallowed hard and turned to Brian. "Are we?"

Maybe it was the win earlier in the day, or the fact I said please, or maybe he was too tired to argue, but the hard lines that usually creased his face were much softer. "Fine," he said then turned and walked into our small kitchenette.

I pulled out my spare pillow and a blanket from the closet and gave them to Ray. "You sure you don't want my bed and I'll take the couch?" I asked.

"Nope," was his quick reply. "I've slept on a lot worse than that there couch. I'll be just fine."

I could tell Brian was as tired as I was. We both wearily went about getting ready for bed. Ray took his shoes off and got under the blanket I gave him. For a few minutes he remained stiff and quiet on the couch. "I watched the game at Cortellesi's," he finally said. "Sure was surprised when you passed the ball to big ol' Alex at the end of the game. That shot of his was nothing more than a prayer. He just tossed it up in the air like he'd never seen a ball before."

Brian was in the bathroom brushing his teeth and I was in the walk-in closet getting dressed. "I guess I surprised myself," I called out to Ray. "But he was so open I had to pass to him."

"I don't know about that! With the game on the line I think I'd rather have you take a twenty footer over Alex taking a two footer. In fact, there ain't nobody on your team I'd rather have take the last second shot over you."

Just then Brian emerged from the bathroom. Had he heard Ray's latest comment? I couldn't tell because without a word Brian walked over to the other end of the room and got in his bed. I finished dressing into my shorts and a t-shirt. I hadn't worn pajamas since I was six.

"Well, Ray," I said. "It sure was a great game, but man, I'm tired. I'm going to hit the hay." I gave him a mock salute and headed for my bed.

He looked disappointed, like a kid at a sleepover party who was told to finally go to sleep by an adult. "You all done talking? After today's game I thought you'd be itching to talk about it."

"Oh, we already did that. Quite a bit of it. In the locker room after the game. Then to the media. Then on the bus, the plane … the media and fans when we arrived on campus. Believe me, I've talked about it a lot. Give me my eight hours tonight, and we'll talk in the morning."

Ray was silent as I turned off the lights and got into my bed. I was never one to fall asleep quickly but I could instantly feel sleep creeping up on me. "Well, I can understand you guys must be tired." Ray's voice seemed louder with the lights off. "It's just amazing Alex hit the game winner and not you. By you I mean you, Thomas." I heard Brian roll over in his bed.

"Thanks, Ray." The words lollygagged out of my mouth.

"Yeah, you've been playing like Larry Bird lately," Ray said. "No question, you are the man on that team of yours."

"Goodnight, Ray," I said wondering how much more of this Brian was going to put up with.

"Yeah, goodnight, buddy. The ol' Colonials need you well rested and ready to take over at the Final Four."

Brian's covers made a ripping sound as he flipped over in his bed and propped himself up on one elbow. "Man, would you shut up!" His voice seemed to bounce off the walls like we were in a canyon.

"Easy, Brian," I said. "Come on. Let's just go to bed." It was silent and dark and I was thankful for the darkness. I didn't want to see the expressions on their faces to know just how close this situation was to blowing up in my face. "Sorry about that, Ray. We're just really tired from the travel. Goodnight."

Some light from the street lamps outside was sifting in through the windows. It was just enough to see Brian was still rigidly leaning on one elbow. I could also tell Ray hadn't moved a muscle. If he had I would have heard the noisy couch squeak and groan.

Still nobody moved. I cleared my throat. "Goodnight, Ray, okay?"

The couch issued a muffled reply as Ray scooched himself lower down. "Yeah." A moment later I could hear him place his glasses on the coffee table next to the couch.

Brian slowly slid down to a prone position. "Dude is pushing his luck," he said in a voice just above a whisper. Thankfully Ray didn't hear it and soon all was quiet.

THE NEXT MORNING I was awakened by Ray's hand shaking my shoulder. I looked up at him then to Brian, who was still sound asleep, then over at the clock. 6 a.m. "What's up?" I said.

Ray stooped over to get closer. "Going to the soup kitchen," he whispered. "Thanks again. You're a life saver."

I kept my voice low too. "Don't mention it. Glad I could help. Tell everyone there I said hi. I'll try and get there later this week."

"Okay. See ya."

JENAE PUT DOWN her cup of tea and leaned into her question. "You're serious? Ray slept on your couch last night?"

"He did. When I got back last night, he was there waiting for me in front of my dorm. He'd lost the key to Paul's place and Paul was out of town. He had nowhere to go, so I let him sleep on the couch."

We were eating breakfast in the school cafeteria. It was a huge room located on the second floor of the student union building. All the walls were painted light blue and dozens of plain white tables were scattered about. Compared to Cortellesi's it had all the charm of a prison.

"How'd that go over with Brian?"

I shrugged. "I asked him and he agreed. I was shocked, but it went fine until right before we went to sleep. You know, Ray, he loves to talk. Well, he wanted to talk about the game but Brian and I were tired. So I turn out the lights, we're all in bed and Ray keeps talking. Brian got pretty mad, told him to shut up."

"Uh, oh."

"Yeah, that's what I thought. But it didn't go anywhere. Brian got his two cents in and everyone went to sleep."

"Thanks for doing that, Thomas. You're a great friend to him."

"Just following the example you set." I took a bite of my cereal.

She looked skeptically at the bowl in front of me. "What are you eating?"

"Cheerios," I said wiping a stray drop of milk off my chin.

"Ah, the breakfast of champions."

"Hah, hah. I'm going to make up for it tomorrow. My father is taking me out to dinner. He's coming down to visit. He'll be here tomorrow night."

Jenae looked surprised. "Tomorrow? He just got home yesterday. He must be exhausted. I know I am."

She looked it. All the travel, schoolwork, spring volleyball practices, and visits to the soup kitchen was getting to her. The smile was the same but her eyes, usually sparkling with life and energy, were tired and bloodshot. It was Monday morning. We'd spent most of Sunday traveling back from Seattle. Come to think of it, I was pretty tired too.

"He talked to his friend, Bill, the one starting the shelter. It's almost ready to open. He wanted to come down and help get Ray set up there. I think he wants to see the soup kitchen too."

She instantly perked up. "Really? That's great! Ray must be so excited."

"I'll bet he is. We're all going out to dinner to talk it over. It's going to be me, Ray, Paul, Bill, and my father. Apparently Paul knows of some really good Italian place near the shelter."

"Sounds great."

"Oh, shoot!" I smacked my forehead. "I'm sorry, Jenae. I didn't think to ask if you could come too. I'm sure it would be okay."

She gently waved her hand. "That's okay, Thomas. I wasn't even thinking about that. You and the men will have fun. I'm looking forward to getting to bed early these next few nights. Tonight I'm going to turn off my alarm clock, unplug my phone and collapse into my pillow."

"Now that sounds good," I said.

She yawned then smiled. "You know, your parents are so proud of you. And sitting with them at these games is such an eye opener. It's fascinating seeing all the looks and gestures your dad makes. You're just like him."

"Really?"

"Oh, my goodness. Very much so. Especially when he does this." She made a fist then rubbed her chin with the shallow cup that is created as the thumb overlaps the index finger.

I smiled. "Yeah, I've seen my father do that. Didn't know I did it too."

"Not often, but I've seen it. Your father's like a kid in a candy store watching you play. Maybe that's how he's getting all this energy."

My father. Did all sons grow up wanting the approval of their father? Is this one of the reasons why I had always wanted to be great at basketball, to please him?

It was obvious my father was enjoying the ride through the tournament. That we were going to play in the Final Four was probably beyond his wildest dreams too. Instead of talking on the phone once a week we now talked nearly every day. It wasn't just basketball. We talked about the Gospels and faith and maturing.

"Well, they won't have to travel far for the Final Four," I said. "I can't believe we're playing in the Final Four, and it's in Jersey. It's hard to comprehend."

Jenae reached across the table and put her hand on mine. "You know what's great about your parents? They love you regardless of how you play basketball."

I smiled. "Just like you, right?"

"Yep."

"Can you believe a few months ago that would have bothered me?"

"Yep."

THE TUESDAY BEFORE the Final Four, I went out to dinner with my father, Paul, Ray, and Bill Petit. I felt like I knew Bill from listening to my father tell stories about their old college days, but I'd never actually met him. When I finally did at the Italian restaurant it was clear Bill was just like my father had made him out to be. Confident and no-nonsense, he also had a warmth about him. Before we even sat down at the restaurant, he grabbed the wine list off the table and put it out of Ray's sight.

The plan was to have the shelter open and running by the end of the week. Bill had spent the past few weeks hiring a staff and jumping through hoops dealing with bonding, insurance, inspections, building codes and a host of other government regulations. Ray was to be the first occupant. Paul assured Bill he could fill the other beds with equally qualified men in need.

"Don't worry about losing keys, Ray," Paul said. "Bill tells me he won't be handing them out."

"That's right," Bill said. He had been reading the menu but stopped, took his glasses off, and continued. "For now, we've got one key and it's in my pocket."

"That's fine with me," Ray said. "Gosh, I still feel like such a dope for losing the key, but I must say it was fun hanging out in Thomas's dorm room."

"It was fun having you over," I replied as I lifted my glass of root beer.

"Well, that was the closest I'll ever come to going to college, that's for sure."

My appetite was through the roof thanks to the smell coming from the kitchen. When the owner came over to our table, he and Paul embraced heartily and spoke to each other in Italian like long lost brothers.

I pigged out. I had a huge plate of spaghetti with clam sauce and six pieces of bruschetta. The food was as good as Paul said it was.

"Thomas," my father said in a low voice as he leaned towards me, "I bet you recognize that man over there by the door."

I turned and looked across the restaurant. The lighting wasn't the greatest and I had to look over people's heads at multiple tables to see the front door. All I saw was a man wearing a heavy overcoat and the back of his bald head. "Not really. Who is it?"

"Red Auerbach."

The man turned slightly and I saw a large cigar protruding from his mouth. Of course! It was Red Auerbach, the great Boston Celtics coach. I elbowed Ray and nodded towards the front door of the restaurant. "That's Red Auerbach by the door."

"Really?" Ray turned to look and adjusted the position of his glasses on his nose. "Well, I'll be. That's him all right. How about that."

Red was the Colonials' most famous basketball alumnus, having played at GW in the late 1930's-early 40's. He kept a residence in the area and maintained close ties to the school. He had been to a few of our games and even came to a practice early in the season. He said a few words to the team at the beginning of practice, watched a bit, then left. I'd never talked to him or officially met him but I couldn't wait to. I wanted to pick his brain, hear all his stories. I wanted to know what Larry Bird was like, how the Celtics managed to win all those titles in the 60's, and what I needed to do to become good enough to make the NBA. I figured it was a lot but I might as well know what I needed to work on rather than be in the dark. Being in the dark was no fun.

Not only was Red a great coach, he was also a brilliant general manager. He was the one who gambled and drafted Larry Bird in 1978 when Bird had a year left of college ball to play. Bird could have gotten injured in his final year at Indiana State, or if the Celtics couldn't sign him before the 1979 NBA draft, they would have lost his rights. It was a gutsy move by Auerbach, one of many he'd made over the years.

I watched as Red shook a few hands and then left the restaurant.

"Say, maybe ol' Red will draft you too, Thomas," Ray said.

"Ha. Don't know about that. He's already got Larry Bird. He doesn't need a wanna be." Still, I couldn't help but wonder what he thought of my game? Did he think I was just an outside shooter like Brian did? If I asked him what I needed to improve upon to make the NBA would he simply laugh or give me serious suggestions?

After I was done eating, Paul convinced me to try their coffee. "Trust me," he said. "You've never had anything like this."

"Not even at your office?"

"No, that was just coffee. Good coffee, but just coffee. This is different." He stirred in a spoonful of sugar and handed the large cup to me.

I took a sip. "Wow," I said after licking the foam off my upper lip. "What is this?"

He smiled and chuckled. "It's a latte. Steamed milk and espresso. You like it, huh?"

"You bet I do." I took another drink.

My father reached over, putting his hand on my shoulder. "I just hope that's decaf. We've got an early morning coming up."

"What's decaf?"

CHAPTER 29

EARLY THE NEXT morning, the Wednesday before the Final Four, I met Jenae on campus and we walked over to the church together. That latte I drank the night before was decaf but I still had a hard time falling asleep. I was exhausted and Jenae assured me that's how I looked. How she was able to tell the blunt truth so lovingly amazed me. Then it occurred to me: saying anything other than the truth isn't very loving.

My father met us there promptly at six. He was clean shaven with a cup of coffee in one hand and a newspaper in the other. I wondered what time he woke up this morning.

"Good morning, you two," he said with a spark in his eye that matched Jenae's. "Are we ready to make some breakfast?"

"You bet!" Jenae said then gave him a big hug.

"Excellent. I'm looking forward to seeing this."

Paul and Ray were the only ones in the basement when we arrived. Ray was already working on the coffee. Since he had moved into Paul's office-residence Ray was no longer just a guy coming for a free meal. He was now an assistant cook with responsibilities. Seemed to me with his duties at the soup kitchen in the morning and his job at Cortellesi's at night he'd be too busy to get in trouble again. Only time would tell.

I rolled up my sleeves and went through my routine of scrambling eggs. Paul handed my father an apron decorated with pastel colored chickens and roosters and gave him the task of frying hash browns. He held up the apron for inspection then put it on. "If only your mother could see me now," he said smiling.

Other volunteers trickled in and soon the kitchen was filled with the sounds and smells of breakfast. Bacon and hash browns sizzled while mouths watered with all the wonderful aromas.

Jenae stood on one side of me, my father on the other as we served breakfast. I savored the smiles on the faces of the men as they saw their plates filled with hot food. It was such a simple thing, providing food to a hungry man, yet so profound that Christ often filled the bellies of those he was also filling spiritually.

As was our custom we sat down to eat once everyone else had been served. The food was good, much better than what they fed us in the school cafeteria. Ray was the last one to sit down. His plate was piled high with bacon, eggs, and hash browns. He saw me looking at it and smiled. "I'm planning on doing a big push-up and pull-up workout later today. Got to fuel up."

"You've worked hard this morning," Paul said. "You deserve a big plate of food. I'm just happy the rest of the men don't eat like you. I don't think there are enough chickens and pigs that could keep up with the demand!" He and Ray both laughed. "Now when it comes to the Word of God, we should all seek to fuel up. His supply is endless."

"Amen to that," Jenae said.

"Paul," my father said, "it seems to me you're keeping up with the demand quite well. I'm impressed. You feed a lot of people here. I see some hard faces, but mostly soft ones. The ones with the humble faces, they're the ones that are truly broken. When they finally realize they can't do anything to change their situation without the Lord, then they're ready. To those people, this is much more than a meal."

Paul gave a slight bow of his head in acknowledgement. "Thank you, my friend. The Lord is good."

"I for one can tell you it sure does mean a lot," Ray said. "Yes sir, lot of men here are getting their only meal of the day. I'm the fortunate one. I've got other meals coming. I've got a job, and I've got friends.

I've got all of you. Each one of you means a lot to me. What you're doing for me …" Ray's voice silently trailed off as his emotion bubbled to the surface. "Well, it means a lot. I'm very thankful." He quickly wiped away the tear that had just begun to fall down his cheek.

"We're thankful for you, Ray," my father said.

Jenae put a hand on his shoulder. "Yeah, Ray. We love you."

"Thank you," Ray whispered, "thank you." He breathed deeply then, like a scoreboard buzzer sounding the end of a game, he smacked his hands together and said, "So, you guys going to stick around and help with the dishes this morning?"

"Ray," Paul said, "it's enough that they've come to serve. There is no need for our friends to work on the dishes. There are plenty of other helpers here for that. Besides, with your breakfast fueling you, you should be able to clean all the dishes in a few minutes."

"Ha! I'm good at dishwashing, but don't know if I'm that good."

"If it's all the same, I'd love to stay and wash some dishes," my father said.

"Me too," Jenae chimed in. "Maybe we could all learn from Ray, the master dishwasher."

"You mean pearl diver," Ray corrected mildly.

Jenae looked puzzled. "Pearl diver?"

Ray's smile was ear to ear. "That's right."

"What's that?" my father asked.

"Sort of working man's vernacular for a dishwasher. Pearl diver. Got a better ring to it than dishwasher. That's what we in the kitchen call ourselves anyway. Maybe one of these days instead of pulling up a dirty fork I'll pull up a pearl necklace."

"Now that would be a surprise," Jenae said.

"You bet it would! Of course if I did I'd have to turn it in and hope we could find the rightful owner. Yeah, the chances of that happening are pretty slim. But I don't need to find some pearl or diamond ring in the dishwater. It's all worth it to me. Gives me lots of time to think. Like the other night, when I was up to my elbows in dirty water, I thought about that story you told me, Paul, from the Bible. The Old

Testament story about that soldier who wanted to be healed and the prophet told him to go wash in the Jordan River."

"The story of Naaman, the leper."

"Yeah, that guy. Here he is, a hot shot commander and he's told to wash in some dirty river. He can't believe it. Wash in that thing? So he walks off in a prideful rage—something I know all about. But eventually he swallowed his pride and got in the river. Sure enough, he got cleaned, or should I say healed. See, when you first got me that job, Thomas, I didn't want to do it. I thought, man, I'm done washing dishes. What's a guy my age doing washing dishes? I'm better than this. But that's just like Naaman saying, what's a guy like me doing washing in the river? So, I took the job. Now I get in my pearl diver mindset and focus real hard. Yeah, I keep thinking if I work hard and keep washing them dishes, it'll happen. The Lord will give me the key to kicking the habit and being the man He wants me to be."

"You already have the key, Ray," Paul said. "Besides, the Lord's door is not locked. He's waiting there, patiently waiting for you, my friend. You want to be washed clean like Naaman? Just surrender your pride and trust in Him. Naaman completely surrendered his pride and obeyed the prophet. You of all people, Ray, know, it's a lot harder to sin and disobey than it is to obey the Lord."

Ray rubbed his chin then took a gulp of coffee. "That's true."

"The Lord used a dirty river to reach Naaman. Look what it took to get Thomas's attention. Perhaps the Lord is using dirty dishwater to get yours, Ray? Or maybe something else?"

"Could be. I'd like to think He's already got it, it's just—"

Ray stopped and froze, his muscles tightened as he glared at something or someone over my shoulder. I swiveled in my seat to see Aqualung standing just a few feet behind me and my father. I hadn't seen him come in. He must have entered the room late, after we'd finished serving.

"Hi, Al," Jenae said to him warmly. He looked like he needed some warmth. As always his clothes were a nasty, tattered mess—meager scraps draped over boney shoulders.

He gestured oddly at me, then Ray and mumbled what sounded like, "Pack of rats," but it was hard to be sure.

Ray stood. "Hey, you grease pit, can't you see we're having a conversation here?"

"Ray, please," Paul said, "remember your place. He's welcome here just like you."

"Have you eaten yet, Al?" Jenae asked.

He didn't answer. The tension rose as he and Ray stared at each other.

"There's still some food left," Jenae continued, trying to diffuse the situation. "I'll go make you a plate." As she rose to stand, Aqualung took a step forward.

Alarm bells went off in my head. "Jenae, I don't know if that's such a good idea."

Aqualung reached out his hand and put it on her shoulder. She froze. My father stood up and I bolted out of my seat.

Ray took a menacing step forward. "Get your hands off her," he growled.

"It's okay, Ray." Jenae's voice was anything but okay. Her face was white like the day I met her on the subway. She was terrified and no amount of courage could mask it.

Aqualungs dirty fingernails clutched Jenae's shoulders like the grim reaper. I reached out to remove his hand. Suddenly Aqualung whipped out a knife in his other hand.

Ray lunged at him. I threw my arms around Jenae to shield her as she screamed. A hand on my shoulder shoved me off to the side. Aqualung took a wild swipe at Ray. Ray's boxing instincts took over. He stopped on a dime and ducked the knife. It whistled overhead and landed with a thud.

There was a painful grunt. Ray leapt like a cat and knocked Aqualung to the ground. Sitting on top of him, Ray pinned the hand with the knife in it to the ground and with one powerful blow to the forehead, knocked Aqualung out.

I looked and saw my father lying crumpled on the floor, clutching his chest. Blood oozed out from between his fingers. His white shirt blossomed red. My father blinked and mouthed, "Don't worry," before losing consciousness.

CHAPTER 30

WHEN RAY SAW the blood from the stab wound on my father he started hitting Aqualung again and didn't stop until he was yanked away by Paul. Jenae quickly grabbed a stack of napkins and pressed it against my father's chest. It was chaos with people running and shouting. I tossed aside a nearby chair and knelt by my father's side. He never moved.

Although it was probably only minutes, it seemed like hours before the cops came and slapped cuffs on Aqualung and the paramedics rushed my father to the emergency room at George Washington University Hospital. President Ronald Reagan was taken here when he got shot. His life was saved at this hospital. Would they save my father's?

Jenae and Ray came with me. Ray was a teary eyed wreck. His hands shook as he paced back and forth across the lobby outside the emergency room. I was in shock, wondering when this nightmare would end and I'd wake up.

When the doctor entered the room and told me my father was gone, Ray stormed out. My first thought was to follow him but then Jenae started sobbing and collapsed into my arms.

The rest of the day was a blur. I vaguely recalled talking with doctors and policemen and calling my mother. At some point the coaches and my teammates showed up at the hospital. I'm pretty sure I held Jenae's hand through all of it.

It was nighttime when I finally left her and everyone else. When I entered my dorm room I stood near the door without turning on the lights. The darkness and silence of the room was stifling. I was completely lost as I groped the wall, making my way to the chair by my desk. As I sat down the walls closed in on me and I started crying.

"You all right?" Brian's voice came from the other end of the room. In the darkness I had no idea he was here.

I had to get out. I stood up, knocking something over on my desk. Whatever it was spilled loudly onto the floor as I hurried out of the room.

At first I just wandered. My father was dead. Killed by a knife that was meant for me. How could this happen? How could life change so suddenly? I didn't understand. Then Proverbs came to mind.

"Trust in the Lord with all your heart, and lean not on your own understanding; in all your ways acknowledge Him, and He shall direct your paths."

I walked on, pulled to an unknown destination. Whenever I stopped, a wave of anxiety and sadness crashed down on me and started me walking again. I walked to Jenae's dorm and looked up to her room on the eighth floor. The lights were off. I hesitated. Should I wake her up and have her come walk with me? No.

I moved on, walking past the library and the Smith Center. Despite the light from the occasional passing car and street lamps, it was dark enough for me to stumble a number of times on the cracks and bumps of the sidewalk along 23rd Street. As I approached Constitution Avenue the familiar glow of the Lincoln Memorial through the surrounding trees pulled me there even faster.

It was very still with only a few people quietly milling about. Instead of sitting on the front steps as I usually did, I walked down towards the Reflecting Pool and sat facing the water. People curiously looked my way, but nobody bothered me. I thought back to that night when my father and I came here. How long had it been? It may have only been a few months but it felt like years. So much had changed since then. Now what do I do?

"Trust in the Lord with all your heart ..."

I had probably been there about an hour when I felt a hand on my shoulder. I looked up hopefully. Jenae? How did she know I'd be here?

Then a voice, not Jenae's but a man's, deep and soulful, said, "Come on, we should go back now."

I recognized the voice, but was still shocked to look up and see Brian. He stood over me, his hand still on my shoulder. He must have recognized the shock in my face.

"I followed you from the dorm."

"You did?"

"When you started crying and left, you didn't seem so good. So I got up and followed."

"How ... how did you know? About my dad, I mean?"

He shrugged. "I found out like everyone else did. I was at the hospital this afternoon, but you probably never even saw me."

I rubbed my eyes with both hands and looked up again. He was still there, standing over me. "You've been here this whole time?"

"Yep. Right over there. Figured I should stay. Your dad ..." His voice caught. "He, uh ... he cared. My dad never did."

I turned on the cold hard floor to get a better look at him. He wore a solemn expression I'd never seen before. This wasn't a gimmick or some kind of twisted joke he was playing. This was genuine. "What do you mean? I thought you said your dad went to all your high school games."

He slumped down and sat next to me. "I lied. I haven't seen him since I was six. He ain't too busy to come to the games or sitting up in the stands where you can't see him. He simply ain't coming."

"You mean he hasn't been to any games this year?"

He shivered and pulled his knees into his chest to ward off the cold. I wore the same warm clothes I'd worn to the soup kitchen at the start of the day, but he was dressed in nothing more than jeans, a t-shirt, and sneakers. "Man, he ain't seen a game of mine since I was in grade school. He could care less. Probably don't even know I'm in college. I kept lying about it because I didn't want nobody knowing. Your dad, Coach Ciancio, Coach Ross—they're about the closest I've had to a dad."

I was astonished. My dad was the closet thing to dad *he* had? I didn't know what to say. "Well, my dad did a lot of things better than I did," I finally said when the words came to me. "Sorry for not caring like he did."

"For who, me?"

"Yeah. He was always encouraging me to be a good roommate and teammate. Most of the time I was too busy trying to be better than you. Guess I didn't listen very well."

Brian looked off in the distance. "Sometimes listening ain't easy."

"You're here, so you must have listened to my dad." He answered with a nod. "Thanks for coming," I said.

"Sure. Let's go."

We didn't say much on the walk home. It was well past midnight when we finally got back to our dorm.

SLEEP WAS HARD to come by. I was exhausted, but my mind wouldn't stop racing. I prayed and thanked God for the time I had with my father. Come 5 a.m. I had done little but toss and turn. I didn't want to call Jenae and wake her up, nor did I want to disturb Brian, so I quietly got out of bed, put on thick cotton sweatpants, my hooded sweatshirt, and sneakers and went for a jog.

It was cold and quiet in the predawn darkness. The city was still waking up. Even though I was exhausted, it felt good to run. At a light jog I headed for the Mall. Streetlights illuminated my breath. Before long my body warmed up and sweat formed underneath the thick layers of my clothing. I ran past the Lincoln Memorial and Reflecting Pool where I'd been only hours earlier. I continued east towards the Washington Monument then turned north.

After a while the sun started to warm the eastern sky. At sunrise it spliced through the uneven horizon of the city's skyline with a glaring light. I ran past the Ellipse and caught sight of the early morning sun hitting the White House. I enjoyed the movement, having my mind distracted, and seeing the sun. I headed back towards campus zigzagging on the empty city streets.

A block from campus I spotted a settlement of homeless men crowded onto a metal grate that spanned the width of the sidewalk next to a small grassy park. Big clouds of steam belched out from the underground vents, warming the men lucky enough to secure a spot on top of the grate. Every inch of the heated grate was valuable real estate and not to be wasted. The men all laid inches apart from each other, the steam nearly obscuring them. As I took a closer look I noticed that one of the men was Ray. He was laying on the edge of the grate, the steam grazing his rigid frame as it exploded skyward.

I turned and went to where he lay. One man watched me approach but Ray was sound asleep. Ray wore a thin jacket over a sweater. There was a paper bag next to his body with the cork-less stem of a wine bottle poking out the top.

"Ray?" I said tentatively, still not one hundred percent sure it was him. I leaned over and gently shook his shoulder. "Ray?"

"Hey man, what do ya think you're doing?" It was an irritable fellow camper laying close by. He wore a grimy hooded sweatshirt and numerous layers of tattered jackets and shirts. I could barely see his face through the onslaught of steam.

"He's my friend," I said.

"My ass, he is. You're some kind of cop." He said it so matter of factly, utterly convinced of himself. "You're some kind of cop or military guy. Well, he ain't doing nothin'. Neither am I, so just beat it."

"Be quiet," I said with a firmness that surprised me. "He is my friend and I'm concerned for him. I'm not a cop." The man just grunted and slumped back to the ground, pulling his hood over his face.

Ray hadn't moved one iota. I knelt down next to him and shook his shoulder again. Alarmed at his lack of response I shook harder. Finally he stirred, showing signs of life. "Ray, it's me, Thomas. Are you all right?" I repeated this a few times until Ray made eye contact with me.

"Oh, it's you, Thomas Conner. I always liked you, Thomas. Man what a shooter. Not as good as Larry Bird and me, but still pretty good." He was still drunk.

I squatted down into a catcher's pose. "Ray, what are you doing here?"

He stretched out his limbs and yawned loudly. "Well … I just had to go get a drink. I mean, it's my fault … I could hit him sooner … should have hit him sooner."

"Ray it's not your fault. Is that why you're here? Does anyone know you're here?"

Done stretching, he slumped back into a fetal position and closed his eyes. "You do."

True. But what was I going to do? "Ray, we need to get you to Paul's office."

"Man, I'm staying right here. Can't drink there. But I sure do appreciate you coming here to see me."

"Ray!" I said loudly.

A chorus of shouts, insults and threats from the other men filled the air. Not knowing what else to do, I ran straight to Paul's home office. On my way there I remembered, at this hour, he'd be at the church getting ready to serve breakfast. I turned the corner and ran straight to the church, past all the men lined up waiting to get in and bounded into the kitchen. I nearly bumped into Paul who was carrying a tray of sausage patties.

"Whoa! Good morning, Thomas," Paul said. "That was quite an entrance. You look like you've been running. Are you okay?"

"Yes," I panted, still catching my breath.

"I get the feeling you're not here to help cook. Did you want to talk?"

"Not now. I just saw Ray."

"Where?"

"On a heated grate. He's been drinking." I told him the exact spot. It wasn't far away.

"We better go." He put down the tray of food, took off his apron and reached for his coat and hat.

"Right now? What about breakfast?"

"The rest of the help knows what to do," he said while putting on his coat. "They're veterans. They won't miss me."

We walked briskly in the cold morning air and quickly came upon Ray and the other men. It was all quiet now except for the hum of the escaping steam. We couldn't see Ray on the edge of the group. He'd either moved into a warmer spot or left.

"Ray?" Paul said. The only answer was more cussing and shouts for quiet. "Oh, be quiet, all you men!" Paul continued. "You can go back to sleep as soon as I take Ray. Ray, wake up and come here."

Out of the steam crawled Ray on all fours. "Hey guys," he slurred. "Wish you would quit shouting."

"Ray, we're not shouting. We're going to take you with us," Paul said.

Completely out of the path of the steam, Ray flopped onto the concrete at Paul's feet. The protests from the other half dozen men on the grate deflated to a murmur. Paul stood over Ray like a triumphant fighter with his coat buttoned up to the top and his knitted hat pulled down low over his ears.

Ray's eyes were closed and after he rolled onto his back he murmured, "I should have swung sooner … should of hit him sooner …" The heat his body had absorbed from the steam was now venting off him in the crisp air. I was sure if it were bottled, that vapor would look just like red wine.

Paul looked down at him and slowly shook his head. "I don't know if Bill will be able to take him now or not. We'll see. I appreciate your help, Thomas, but I can handle it from here. You must have a million things to do. Aren't you scheduled to leave for New Jersey with the team today?"

"Yes, but I feel like I should stay. I just hate leaving Ray like this."

Paul put his hand on my shoulder. "I know you do, Thomas. Ray will be with me. I will do everything I can to keep him in my sight. You on the other hand have to get ready for this weekend."

"Ray's more important than this weekend. Besides, I don't know how I'm going to focus."

"Indeed. Please know that you can call me at any hour of the day. Okay? I am here for you. And I am confident in you, Thomas. Remember, we are more than conquerors through Him who loves us. No matter what happens this weekend, you are victorious. Having the mind of Christ, you already have the victory."

Despite being weary to my bones, my smile felt ear to ear. "Thanks."

"Now, you know what you should go do?"

"What?"

He smiled. "Go win that championship."

CHAPTER 31

LATER THAT DAY our team rode the train to the Final Four. It was the same train route that I took from New Jersey to D.C. when I started college. Upon arrival in New Jersey, the Meadowlands would be a short drive away from the train station as well as my hometown.

Named after the former governor of New Jersey, the Brendan Bryne Arena was located in the Meadowlands Sports Complex. Next door was Giants Stadium, a race track, and lots of swampland. Growing up not too far from the Meadowlands, the surrounding swampland had a mysterious and colorful quality to it as the rumored graveyard for many unlucky mafia figures. The racetrack and football stadium opened in 1976, but the arena didn't until 1981. Of course the first event held there was a Bruce Springsteen concert.

Being so young, Brendan Bryne Arena didn't have decades of history like the Palestra. Nor did it have any charm. Even our gray little Smith Center, nestled in among colorful row houses and places like Leo's Deli, had more charm. The only thing snuggling up to Brendan Bryne Arena were acres of parking lots. If the Smith Center could be represented by Leo's Deli, then the Meadowlands was symbolic of a huge shopping mall. Even the inside was bland.

Growing up we hardly ever called it Brendan Bryne Arena. It was simply known as the Meadowlands. My favorite memory there was watching the 1982 NBA All Star game with my father. I was thirteen and already a huge Larry Bird fan. Julius Erving was a big star then. At one point in the second half, the West All Star team was putting on a run and the East All Stars coach, Bill Fitch, summoned for Dr. J to go in the game. The moment he got up from his seat on the bench and started walking to the scorers table, the crowd, mostly Eastern Conference fans, started to cheer. Chills ran up and down my spine. I'd never seen a basketball player cheered like that simply for walking to the scorers table to check into the game. But it was Bird, who scored 19 points, grabbed 12 rebounds and dished out 5 assists, that was named the game's MVP. My dad bought me a hotdog and souvenir program. It was a great day.

In addition to the All Star game, we went to lots of Nets games growing up. Sometimes I went with my older brother, other times with high school buddies. We'd always go to a diner afterwards for some good Italian food.

I didn't play that many games there, but the Meadowlands felt like my home court. This was Jersey, Northern New Jersey where there were hundreds of gyms to play in. This was my territory, my backyard, and it was hosting the Final Four.

It was Thursday. On Saturday afternoon Indiana would play UNLV in one semifinal and we would play North Carolina State in the other. After the train ride, there would be practices, media sessions, and film sessions. Plus I would do what I could to help my mother plan for my father's funeral which was scheduled for Sunday. Saturday's semifinal game seemed weeks away.

It also seemed like weeks since I last slept. We were barely out of Union Station in D.C. when my eyes started to get droopy. The gentle rocking of the train quickly put me to sleep. I didn't wake up until we were just pulling out of the station in Philadelphia. I enjoyed riding trains. It was less stressful than flying and more comfortable than riding on a bus. Looking out the window of a train was like wandering through the closets and hallways of a town. We bisected brief areas of countryside, squalid patches of inner city, and the many small towns in New Jersey. They all told a story: some exhibited decay, despair, and want while others radiated renewal, hope, and prosperity. It was intimate and fascinating.

It wasn't until I let out a big yawn and stretched my stiff muscles that Alex came over and sat in the seat next to me. At first I thought he was going to start cracking jokes, try and cheer me up, but he was very serious. That was rare for Alex.

"What's up?" I asked.

"Sorry about your dad. You know we'll all be at the funeral with you." He'd said this earlier in the day. So had all my teammates. I could tell none of them knew what to say, but they said what they could and it made me love each one of them.

"Thanks."

"Can I tell you something?"

I shrugged. "Sure."

"You know, I've been thinking about that drunk friend of yours," he said rather quietly. Another rarity. Usually you could hear him if you were anywhere in the same room. Now, I could barely hear him over the noise of the moving train.

"Ray?"

"Yeah, Ray." He looked around to make sure no one else was listening in on our conversation then continued. "Well, my dad's an alcoholic. Naw, he's just a plain old drunk. Has been for years, ever since I can remember at least. Notice how he's never at any of our games? He's too busy getting hammered at his local bar. Everyone tries to pretend it's not that big a deal. My mom figures he's not going to listen to her, and all his old fart buddies are drunks too so who's going to say something, you know? Anyway, Ray reminds me a little of him. But here's the thing, no one has tried to help my dad. At least not that I know of. So, I see what you're doing with Ray and, well, I appreciate it. It's cool. I wish someone would step in and try and help my dad."

"Why don't you? Drunk or not, he's still your dad, he's still around. Do something before he's gone."

"What could I do? I'm here in D.C., my dad's on Long Island. He's not going to listen to me. I'm just his big goofball son. Besides," he said with a smile as he slapped my knee, "me telling him not to drink is like the pot calling the kettle black, if you know what I mean."

"Maybe all you need to tell him is you love him and still believe in him."

"I don't know about that." He scratched his head and I could tell he didn't know how to respond to my statement so he changed the subject. "I've toned it way down this year, my drinking that is. Especially after screwing up my hand. Shoot, if anything I should be drinking more beer to keep my weight on."

"Whatever. Why don't you try eating some steaks like Kevin? He eats them all the time. It's obviously put the pounds on him, and the right kind of pounds, too."

"Kevin could eat whatever he wants and still look like a linebacker. I think I'll stick with the hamburger helper."

"Suit yourself. Is your dad coming to the Final Four?"

He shrugged. "Don't know. My mom is. There will be two tickets waiting there at will call. How about Ray, is he coming?"

"Unfortunately not. I just saw him this morning sleeping on the sidewalk, passed out drunk."

"Fell off the wagon, huh? Bummer. Is he alright?"

"Paul, the man who runs the soup kitchen where I met Ray, is taking care of him. He'll be fine, I hope. It's just hard to see someone you care about ruin his life."

"Tell me about it. Well, at least you tried."

"Yeah. Why don't you try with your dad? Maybe a little love and respect from his big goofball son will go a long way."

He thought about that for a moment and then muttered, "Maybe, maybe." He gently punched my knee, his way of signifying he enjoyed the conversation but it was now over, and got up and left.

THE STARTING LINEUPS reverberated into every square inch of the Meadowlands. From my seat on the bench I looked down at my sneakers and saw "Proverbs 3:5-6" written in black ink on the rubber heels of my sneakers. Earlier in the day Matt asked if I thought it would be okay if we all wore a small black band on our jerseys in honor of my father. It just didn't sound right to me. Instead I asked if everyone would be willing to write one of my dad's favorite verses on their sneakers. Jim made it happen. All my teammates had "Proverbs 3:5-6" written on their sneakers and the coaches had little strips of white athletic tape affixed to their dress shoes with the verse on it.

We were moments away from the tip-off of our semifinal matchup versus the Wolfpack of North Carolina State. I was the last player to be introduced. I closed my eyes and recited the verse in my mind.

"Trust in the Lord with all thine heart and lean not unto thine own understanding. In all thy ways acknowledge Him, and He shall direct thy paths."

How could I understand all that had happened? Without Him there was no way. I had to trust Him. Right now and for the next forty minutes.

"And starting at small forward ..."

Brendan Bryne Arena was packed with cameras and people and anticipation. We were already the feel good Cinderella team of the tournament, but after my dad died, I became the story of the Final Four. It seemed everyone was rooting for me. Everybody wanted a piece of my time. Coach Ross and the assistants had done a good job of shielding me from the relentless media over the past few days. Now there was no more hiding. For better or worse, my talents and emotions would be exposed for all to see.

"Wearing number 33 ..."

I remembered the moment in my backyard when I fell in love with basketball.

"... a 6'6" freshman from New Jersey ..."

I could see my father standing at the kitchen window, watching, smiling.

"... Thomas Conner!"

The building rocked with noise as I jumped off my chair and ran out onto the court, high fiving my teammates as I went. Twenty thousand people gave me a standing ovation. I remembered my father clapping for me when I made my first shot.

North Carolina State was not interested in my life circumstances and didn't like the press casting them as Goliath and us as David. They'd tried to avoid it all week to no avail. It was only a few years ago that they'd been in our shoes, playing the role of David, and came away with a miraculous upset win over then Goliath, the University of Houston. But I thought the role of Goliath—arrogant and doomed—suited them. They were bigger and had more talent than us. They were good and they knew it.

I also thought we made a great David. We'd been in this role ever since the NCAA tournament started. But the first minutes of the game didn't play out like the Bible story, at least not on our end. Whether we were nervous or not, we all played like it. All our shots were short, passes were tentative and on defense we were a step behind. My first shot was an air ball and on defense I was beaten badly as my man went right around me for a dunk. After Brian and I threw consecutive turnovers, we were quickly down 8-0. The NC State players, led by their mouthy small forward, Bobby Gregory, were talking serious trash.

Coach Ross called timeout. "Hey guys, we have to relax and play. We've come too far to get tight now. After the start we've had, it's obvious NC State doesn't respect us. They think they'll walk all over us. They're already looking ahead to the finals. They think we're too inexperienced, too overwhelmed, and not ready for this. Well, I'm ready and I know you guys are too. Now they need to know."

He scanned our faces as he spoke. Then he settled on Matt, who was standing next to me. He pointed at him. "Matt, you check in for Thomas. We need to send the message that we came to play, that we're not scared. Get in there and set some hard screens and if one of their big men is about to score, foul him hard."

He paused for effect. Eyes drifted towards Matt who never stopped looking at Coach Ross.

"Don't do anything dirty and don't get anybody hurt," Coach Ross continued, "just send a strong message. Lay into somebody good like you so often do. Got it?"

Matt nodded and let a smile crease his face. "Got it."

"Good. And when you're done, if he's on the floor, help the guy up."

"Coach," Kevin said. "Can I do it?"

"No!" Coach Ross shouted in exasperation. "You'd probably send somebody to the hospital and that's not what I'm trying to accomplish."

A few anonymous laughs quietly bounced around the huddle. Jim shook his head and smiled while Robert's face glowed with an easy grin. When Coach Ciancio failed to muffle his laughter, Coach Ross finally let his guard down and smiled too. "Good grief. Could you imagine? Kevin knocking guys over like bowling ball pins."

We all laughed. I could almost see the tension melt off everyone's shoulders.

Coach Ross put his hand on Kevin's muscular shoulder. "Kevin, you just play like you've been playing for the past four years. If you have to foul, make sure the guy doesn't score."

When the timeout ended I sat down next to Coach Ross on the bench. "Thomas," he said, "you may be one of the best shooters I've ever seen, but when it comes to fouling, nobody holds a candle to Matt. I need him out there for this. I'll get you back in soon."

I nodded then leaned back and wondered if Matt would really do it. Could he do it without making it look obvious? Then, as I remembered all the times he fouled me in practice, I was pretty sure he could pull it off.

The laughter in the timeout was just what we needed to relax. First, Matt set a great pick for Brian who curled off the screen and hit a runner in the lane for our first points of the game. At the other end of the floor North Carolina State missed a shot and Kevin cleared out three of their players as he hauled in the rebound. Back on offense we scored again. Then, after another miss, NC State's center grabbed the offensive rebound over Matt. As he went back up to score, Matt went for the block but missed and instead sent the guy sprawling to the floor. It was perfect—hard, but not dirty or flagrant. When Matt extended his hand to help him up, it was angrily refused.

Knowing there was a good chance TV cameras were on him Coach Ross put his hand over his mouth to hide his smile. Turning to me he said, "See what I mean? Nobody does that better."

"I know. He's done it to me a few times too."

"You and everyone else. Okay, now they know we're not going to lie down for them. Get back out there. Go in and give Kevin a breather and have Matt switch over to the four. We're going to go small for a few minutes and see how they respond." He half shoved me to the scorers table.

Matt's thumping of their center was not only the shot in the arm we needed, it was also just what I needed. Watching Matt send that guy sprawling gave me even more appreciation for him and what he stood for. Day in and day out—year after year for all I knew—Matt would do whatever Coach Ross asked of him. Even after I took most of his playing time in this, his final year, he never complained, never stopped working hard. It was so clear to me now that Matt wasn't necessarily better than me at setting screens or diving for loose balls. It's not like diving for loose balls is some complex skill that takes years to master, it just takes a willingness to do it. Matt was always willing because he loved the game more than he loved the spotlight. In addition, he loved his coach and he loved his teammates. That's why he did all the little things so well.

Here on this enormous stage Matt was once again willing to do whatever Coach Ross asked. Judging by the smile on his face, I was sure he loved doing it.

As soon as play resumed Gregory started mouthing off again. He was an excellent defender and, unfortunately, his trash talking was even better. The first time I touched the ball with him guarding me, my first instinct was to do whatever it took to score on him. That's what I always did with a trash talker—scored on him. It was the only sure fire way to get them quiet. But then I saw Matt set his man up for the perfect backdoor cut. It wasn't very athletic or graceful but with NC State overplaying to get a defensive stop, it was the perfect move. I smiled as I made the easy pass to Matt that led to a wide-open layup.

"See, Conner," Gregory said moments later. "You can't score on me." It was our ball again and he was playing me tight. "You're just an overrated, one dimensional stiff hangin' on the coat tails of your teammates. That Patterson kid, now he's good. He's the real star."

"You're right," I said knowing it would surprise him. It did. I could see it written all over his face, but he didn't miss a beat.

"Of course I'm right! You stink. You'd barely get off the bench if you were on our team. Shoot, we got managers better than you. Cheerleaders too!"

On our next possession, out of the corner of my eye I saw Brian beat his man and a clear lane to the hoop open up. The play developed in a split second and I saw it, but Gregory, because he was so obsessed with showing me up, didn't see anything. If I moved too soon he might turn his head and see Brian. So I camped out near the low block and pretended to ready myself to run off a screen. Only at the last moment did I head out towards the wing. Brian waltzed in for a wide-open layup and nearly landed on Gregory's back when he came back down to earth. Gregory's teammate chewed him out for not playing any help defense.

With our last few baskets we'd tied the score. The game see-sawed back and forth for the next few minutes. With Gregory a bit more focused on helping out on defense I got two open looks and hit both shots. That got him angry, which turned his trash talking vile.

"I don't care if your dad or your dog died," he whispered in my ear. "You're not that good. All this hype they're giving you, please. You're just a story, you're not a player."

My ability to live and focus in the present moment had become so strong over the past few weeks that I'd been thinking about nothing but the game. I wasn't worrying about Ray or missing my father. I was just playing. But Gregory's comments opened up the floodgates and all the anxious thoughts came rushing back. My palms started to sweat and I hoped no one would pass me the ball.

"Do not be anxious about anything, but in every situation, by prayer and petition, with thanksgiving, present your requests to God. And the peace of God, which transcends all understanding will guard your hearts and your minds in Christ Jesus."

As soon as I was done saying that in my mind I was back, ready to play. It was just what my father wanted for me.

Gregory grabbed a small wad of my jersey and pinched a bit of flesh in the process. He was trying to bait me, get me to lash out, lose my focus and make a mistake. But he was the one making the mistakes. Again, his focus on stopping me put him in horrible defensive position. Instead of giving his teammates space to get around my screens, Gregory was practically hugging me and thus setting a double screen. Brian recognized it and used it perfectly. First Brian ran his defender into Gregory, who wasn't looking, before he ran his defender past me. By then he was wide-open and hit the shot.

Again, Gregory's teammate lashed out at him, telling him to call out the screens and get out of the way. "Hey, my man ain't scoring," he shouted back.

Minutes later I found myself tangled up with Gregory underneath the basket. We were both jockeying for rebounding position, pushing and grabbing and leaning. Robert took a shot from just inside the free throw line that bounced off the front rim. I had inside position on Gregory and the ball headed right for me, but I could barely get off the ground with him leaning on me. With one arm pinned under Gregory's grip I grabbed the ball with my right hand. As soon as I tried to leave the ground to score, Gregory hacked me, sending me to floor. I knew it was coming and braced for the fall.

All three refs blew their whistles. It was an obvious foul on Gregory. Unhurt, I rolled over and saw a smirking Gregory standing over me. Matt immediately stepped in and offered me his hand while pushing Gregory out of the way. That got the two of them yapping at each other.

Referee Ernie Huggins blew his whistle and jumped in to restore order. "Knock it off guys! I'm not going to put up with any nonsense in this game. Come on now! No more hard fouls. Enough!" Middle age may have been somewhere in his rearview mirror, but Huggins was still an excellent ref. Short with thick stubby arms and close-cropped gray hair, he'd completely taken control of the situation. He'd worked a number of our games this year and I was glad to have him working this one. Only the best got to work the Final Four and he was one of them.

After Matt helped me up, I stood just a few feet away from Gregory. "What're you going to do," Gregory said in such a taunting tone it was almost a parody. "Take a shot at me? Huh?"

"Hey," Huggins snapped at Gregory, "any more of that and I'll 'T' you up. I mean it." He pointed one of his stubby fingers right at Gregory for good measure.

The horn sounded. NC State subbed in a player for Gregory. As he walked over to the NC State bench, Jim came our way and said something to Gregory that elicited a sharp turn of his head. Huggins kept an eye on it as Jim kept walking and Gregory, after a momentary pause, continued to his bench.

"Barger," Huggins said in a drill sergeant tone as Jim approached us, "what'd you say to him?"

"Ernie," Jim said, "you're the last person I'm going to tell. But don't worry, I'll behave myself."

"Hah!" Huggins laughed heartily. "Barger, I've refed a lot of your games over the years. Let me tell ya, you got guts. If I ever get in a fight in an alley, I'd want you on my side."

Jim laughed. "Thanks, but let's hope we don't get in one!"

"Good point. And Conner," Ernie said while slapping my shoulder, "sorry about your dad."

"Thank you, sir."

Ernie nodded and walked off.

Jim turned to me. "Look at this, Conner. We travel all over the country. Win four games in the NCAAs, make it to the Final Four. The Final Four! And where are we? Right back in Jersey. Can you believe it? We're at the stinkin' Final Four, and we're playing in New Jersey. Unbelievable."

The foul on Gregory gave me two free throws, which I made, giving us a two point lead which we held until halftime. The first part of the second half was tight but with seven minutes left in the game we got hot and pushed our lead to eight.

It was our biggest lead of the game and North Carolina State called timeout.

The timeout worked for them. Our momentum came to a complete stop and NC State slowly chipped away at our lead. There are no eight point shots in basketball so they simply tightened up their defense and cut the lead to 6 then 4 then 2. I was amazed at their poise. Their players and their coaches never panicked, they never gave up. I even caught myself admiring Gregory who passed up a jumper to hit an open teammate for a better shot.

With three minutes left we started trading baskets. A minute later one of their guards hit two clutch shots in a row to cut our lead to one. Coach Ross called time.

In the huddle Jim shouted from his seat right next to me. "Hey, we can't get tight now! We still have the lead. Be confident! If you've got a shot, take it!"

Coach Ross hesitated, silently ceding the floor to Jim to talk as long as he wanted. I could tell Coach Ross was enjoying this. Although it was hard for me to imagine Jim ever being immature, I'm sure he'd done a lot of growing up in his four years at GW. Coach Ross had invested a lot of time and energy in Jim and it was paying off handsomely.

Jim continued. "We know our roles, we know our jobs. We're up one and it's our ball." He nodded at Coach Ross who nodded back. The ball was back in his court.

Coach Ross was amazingly serene given the situation. He'd been coaching nearly his entire adult life, but never in a moment like this. Being in a Final Four was new to all of us, but he acted like he'd been here many times. "Okay," he barked. "Run our sideline out of bounds and don't worry about taking too much time off the clock. They're not going to foul you. More than likely they'll be gambling, trying to get a steal. Don't let the clock run all the way down and then huck up a bad shot. Work for a good shot and take it."

As I left the huddle Coach Ross grabbed my elbow. "Hey, I can see that jerk Gregory is still talking trash. Some guys just don't know when to quit. You want me to say something to Huggins and the other refs about it?"

"Naw, I'm okay, Coach."

He smiled. "You know, with coaches, it's not all about the X's and O's. Part of the fun of all this is seeing guys grow up."

"You mean coaches like you?"

He laughed and wrapped his arm around my neck. "I'm proud of you, kid. I know your dad was too. What'd you say we beat these guys?"

"Sounds good to me."

We got the ball inbounds, ran our offense and got an open look. It just so happened the open look was mine. It was a wide-open three deep in the left corner, just where I liked it. At the last second an NC State defender flew out to try and block my shot but it was too late. I let it fly and it hit nothing but net! We went back up by four.

NC State quickly pushed the ball up and scored to cut the lead to two. Our next possession we took some time off the clock but Jim missed a tough fifteen footer and the Wolfpack answered to tie the game. I could tell I wasn't the only one on our team that was stunned. Coach Ross called another timeout, unfortunately our last. He drew up a play for Brian. When the game resumed Brian got the ball on the wing, gave a nice pump fake which his defender bit on ever so slightly, and took two dribbles into the lane and hit a high arching floater.

Now NC State called timeout with us leading 72-70. Coach Ross implored us to get a defensive stop, which could clinch the game.

There were twenty-five seconds on the clock. It was Wolfpack ball with the full length of the court to score. They inbounded, ran their set offense and got it to Gregory. Brian was guarding him. Gregory had a height advantage but Brian was quicker. Brian smartly played him tight to deny a three-point shot. But Gregory made a great one-on-one move, drove into the lane and hit a tough finger roll just over the outstretched fingertips of Robert. There were nine seconds left. The game was tied. The crowd noise was deafening.

With no timeouts remaining Jim tried to inbound to Brian but he was covered. The ball came to me and I immediately started upcourt. The clock was winding down. Gregory guarded me tightly. I had to shake him. This was my moment, the one I'd dreamed about. All those times I hit the game winner alone—now I needed to do it here, with defenders in my face, with millions watching.

I crossed half court and changed directions with a cross over dribble. Gregory moved his feet perfectly and never lost a step. I'd have to shoot over him. Or did I? I had other options. My dreams were never the exact same thing, nor is basketball. Being a basketball player is not like being a dancer who can choreograph the moves to a particular song. In basketball the music is never the same. It's always changing.

One more dribble and I was at the three-point line. I pulled up and gave a convincing head fake. Gregory flew in the air. Another defender flew at me. Brian was open. I rifled him the ball and he shot the best looking jumper I'd ever seen him take. It went in.

I looked at the scoreboard clock. It showed zeros. The refs were jogging off the court. We won! I jumped up and down and shouted at the top of my lungs. I ran to Brian and mobbed him with the rest of our teammates.

We were headed to the national championship game!

CHAPTER 32

SUNDAY AFTERNOON THE sky was blue and cloudless. Freshly blossomed trees swayed to a gentle breeze. Bees hummed and flowers proudly showed off their colors. The day brimmed with the new life that comes each spring. It was the day I buried my father.

The funeral service was held in the same old stone church that my parents had been married in thirty years prior. It was elegant and gut wrenching at the same time. My dad was gone.

One thing in the service stood out. More than the courageous eulogy my mother gave, more than having my teammates and coaches there or the sight of the dark stained wood coffin, I knew, more than anything, I would remember the bagpipes.

There to pay homage to the Scottish roots my father inherited from his mother, the bagpipe player stood off to the side in his tartan kilt, squeezing out mournful notes. I imagined my father slowly walking away, hands casually clasped behind his back, thinking about tomorrow's game. It was haunting and beautiful.

Afterwards, the team went back to the hotel, but I went home. Jenae, my brother, and I sat around the kitchen table with my mother, telling our favorite stories of my dad. Mike told the one about Dad spending the entire day rigging a rope swing for us boys to play on when we went camping at a small lake. I brought up the early morning Constitution classes he used to run in his office. He brought me along for the first time when I was eight. I felt like such a grown up sitting there with the other men. He even let me have a small cup of coffee, although it was probably two parts milk and one part coffee. My mother re-told the story about how she and my father met, fell in love, and married. I'd heard it many times before, but this time my eyes misted over.

"Thomas," she said after a moment of quiet reflection. "You should go. I'm fine. Take this wonderful girl with you and go. I know it's where you want to be."

Shooting baskets in a gym was where I always wanted to be when life's tough moments came. So I did go. The old YMCA wasn't very far away. The sights, sounds, and even smells were all the same. It was a quiet Sunday afternoon with no one in the gym except me and Jenae.

Jenae stood underneath the basket and rebounded while I shot. She had on the same clothes she wore to the funeral: heels, dark slacks, white blouse and brown sweater. She took off the heels and sweater once she started rebounding. I had changed into an old pair of high school sweats and a t-shirt from home. We were silent at first. The only sound came from the ball bouncing off the floor or swishing through the net.

"I met Alex's parents at the game yesterday," Jenae said out of the blue.

I almost dropped the ball. "His dad was there?"

"Yeah, they were both there. Why?"

I smiled. "Well how about that. It's probably the first game Alex's dad has been to all year."

She frowned. "Really?"

"Yeah, he's had his issues. Hasn't been much of a father to Alex. Maybe this means things will change."

"Hmm. When I think of change, I think of all the change in my life over the past eight months. I was a sheltered country girl from Idaho with this idea that I was going to change the world. But now I'm just thankful for the opportunity to impact one life at a time. Whether it's Ray or someone else at the soup kitchen or even a teammate. If Ray has a relapse or a teammate still hates me, well, it's all in the Lord's hands. Ray knows I'm trying to help. I think the men at the soup kitchen understand I'm trying to help. Isn't that enough?" She had one hand planted on her hip the other held out, palm up, as if holding the evidence of her words in her hand.

"It's more than enough. It's beautiful. It's you."

"I know I haven't said much about it, but I don't have any plans to transfer, Thomas. I thought about it and well, the mountains, Idaho … they'll always be there. I know GW is where the Lord wants me to be. I want to be here. I talked about it with my parents and they agree."

I'd forgotten all about the possibility of her leaving. It had been so long since she said anything about it. "I'm glad. I couldn't imagine GW without you. But just know in my mind, what you're doing with Ray and those men at soup kitchen is far more important than shooting a basketball. So no matter what you decide, I'm behind you one hundred percent."

"Thanks."

I took another shot. Swish.

"It's so amazing you guys are playing for the national championship tomorrow. Are you nervous?"

I shrugged. "Not really. Not yet at least."

"Good. You didn't look nervous yesterday. You should have seen how well you and Brian played. You guys are awesome together. I'm sure you've heard that before, but you really are. He opens up the court for you and you do for him too. It's really fun to watch. Do you guys still not talk to each other much?"

I caught her pass and held onto the ball.

"The night my father died, after I left you, I couldn't be still, I had to keep walking … I had to keep moving. So, I walked alone to the Lincoln Memorial and the Reflecting Pool … he followed me."

"Who did?"

"Brian."

"What do you mean he followed you?"

"Just that. I was sitting there by the water, had been there about an hour when he comes up to me, puts his hand on my shoulder and says we should go. At first I thought it was you. I had no idea how you'd know I was there, but I swore it was you. Then I looked up and saw it was him. He'd followed me and waited out of sight."

She raised her eyebrows, stunned. "Wow."

"He really appreciated my dad caring for him. They spoke on the phone a lot more than I realized. My dad would call for me and when I wasn't there and Brian answered, they'd talk. That kind of thing has been missing in his life. His father hasn't been around much."

"You're blessed to have an amazing father who did care and was there for you."

"I know. Believe me, I know. I look at my teammates and see what they go through, see what they're like. Coleman's dad—never heard a word about him. Brian's dad was never around. Alex's dad wasn't much of a father. Then you see Matt and Jim and Robert's dads at every game. It all makes sense."

"I'll say it again, you're a lot like your father. Ever since the day we met, you've been there for me and others. You rescued me from the guy with the knife on the subway. You walk me home at night from class. You got Ray a job. You protected me at the soup kitchen. You've always been there for me, Thomas, and I love that about you."

I caressed the ball in my hands and soaked in her words.

"I wish he could be around to see all this. I was just getting to know him, your father. I wish I could have known..." Her lips quivered and her voice trailed off.

I finished her thought. "Known him better?"

She nodded.

"Well, here's a story that might help." I took a deep breath and slowly exhaled. "When I was young we used to go as a family to this small lake in upstate New York. My grandparents had a little cabin there. My grandfather built it himself back in the 40's. We'd always go there during summer so we could enjoy the lake. In the middle of the lake was this small island. It was the coolest thing. It was probably about an acre or two, covered with trees and paths and places to have a campfire. I remember it had large rocks on the water's edge to jump from. My grandfather had an old beat up metal rowboat that my brother and I would use to get to the island.

"One day, when I was eleven, my brother and I went to the island. It wasn't that far away, maybe a half mile, but at that age it seemed like miles. Anyway, it was late afternoon when I told my brother I was going to swim back to the cabin. It was something my father allowed us to do if we stayed together. When Mike swam, I rowed the boat along side of him. If I swam then Mike rowed next to me. When we got tired we could grab hold of the boat and rest. As long as we stayed together we were okay.

"Well, this one time I wanted to go on my own. At first Mike didn't want to leave but I told him I'd be fine. So he said good luck and took off in the boat. For some reason I hesitated and waited until he was nearly out of sight. When I finally jumped in the water the sky was turning orange. I was a pretty good swimmer so I was sure I could make it. But about half way home I got tired. I started to realize I'd made a dumb decision. The sky was dark and cloudy and I started to panic. I was far from shore and from my vantage point, inches above the water line, it seemed completely black. Usually I could see the lights from other cabins along the shore, but not this night. It was so dark and it started to drizzle a little. I was going to shout for help but I didn't. I thought I'd sound like a little helpless kid, but the thing is, I really needed help.

"I don't know how close I was to drowning but I was really starting to panic. My arms and legs were exhausted, I was cold, and I was having trouble catching my breath. That's when I heard slapping sounds in the water. It was so dark and scary and I couldn't see anything. I didn't know who or what it was. When I turned around in the water, my father's arm was nearly on top of me. He grabbed one of my arms and practically flipped me into the old rowboat. He tossed me a towel and said, "Longer than it looks." A few minutes later, after I'd warmed up and wasn't so scared, he asked why I'd doubted him, why I'd disregarded his instructions. I didn't have an answer. He saved my life that day. I know it's the Lord who saves us, but without my father ... I wouldn't be here."

My voice on the verge of cracking, I paused, then said, "I told him I loved him, but did I ever tell him he was the kind of man I always wanted to be? Larry Bird is a great basketball player, but my father was my real hero."

"I think he was a hero to a lot of people," Jenae said quietly. "You can honor him by showing the world tomorrow that, no matter what happens in our lives, our strength comes from the Lord."

It was late. Time for one last shot. I wiped the tears out of my eyes with my shirt. I walked over to the top of the key and fired off a three-pointer. The ball swished through the net, hanging it on the rim. As I turned to leave, I could hear the bagpipes playing.

CHAPTER 33

INDIANA BEAT UNLV in the other semifinal so the 1987 championship game was set. The powerhouse Indiana Hoosiers versus the underdog Colonials of George Washington University.

In the locker room before the game I sat on a chair in front of my locker, trying to absorb the moment, the season, the last few months. The last few days. So much had happened so fast. So many people seemed to be joining in on this magical ride to the NCAA championship game. Who were all these people that were now everywhere we went? Media, GW alumni, GW administration, friends, agents? I had no idea. It was a relief to be in the locker room where all the faces were familiar.

Suddenly the enormity of the moment crashed on top of me like a wave. I was hours away from playing for the national championship. At nineteen years of age, one of the most important chapters that would color my life story would soon be written. The pen was in my hand but I wasn't ready to write.

I closed my eyes and prayed. *Lord, help me to have peace of mind so I can play my best tonight. Help me to have fun, play hard, not get hurt. Help me to play for my teammates, my coaches, for the love of the game, for my dad. Help me to play for Your glory, not mine. Amen.*

I looked up. It was mostly quiet as guys got dressed to play. Were they getting nervous? As I looked around only one set of eyes caught mine. Brian was sitting a few feet away and looking right at me. He

302

had on his black leather Kangol hat with a white shirt, straight black tie and black pants, no jewelry. He was never a flashy dresser, but he was dressed ready to celebrate, and these were his celebration clothes.

His face was taut, but it wasn't the usual challenging look I was used to. What was it? Nerves? Fear of failure? His face nearly always dared me into an argument, or a game of one-on-one, or ... something, anything to force a confrontation. I thought back to our first few days at GW. One night after playing in the gym I decided to run the stairs in our dorm, all ten flights. The city was hot and muggy and the stairwell was sweltering. Alex and Coleman opened the door to the stairwell and watched in amusement as I passed them by. Brian put on his sneakers and joined me. He wouldn't dare let me out work him or run to the top without him.

From day one I viewed him as a threat. But the chemistry and synergy of our talents was so good we somehow found a way to thrive on the court, despite being at odds off the court. How much better could we have been if we became friends like my dad recommended? What would those first few months have been like if I had walked the walk instead of just talked the talk?

Brian leaned forward resting his elbows on his knees and quietly said, "You need to be ready to play tonight. Your game is tailor made to score on them. If you don't take the shots you're supposed to, we got no shot at winning. You hear me? I know you miss your dad, but you got to be focused on this game, period. It's tough, I get it. He was a good Christian man. I get what that means."

"Do you? I sure thought I did. But it wasn't until I fully surrendered to the Lord what I cherished most—basketball—that I really understood what it meant to be a believer. And I'm still learning."

"What?"

"Listen, Brian, this may not be the time or the place, but if you want to know what I believe and what my father believed, then read this." I reached into my gym bag, pulled out my bible and handed it to him. "Here. I promise I won't preach to you, but I suggest you start reading the gospels. They're the first four books of the New Testament."

He looked over the book in his hands and let out a long frustrated exhale. "Okay, man. But not until later. After we're done celebrating our win. Got it?"

I nodded. "I hear you."

After putting the Bible down on the empty chair next to him, he took off his hat and started to untie his shoe laces. "Do you think your dad will be watching tonight?" I asked.

"Don't know," he replied without ever looking up, "but I know your dad will."

THE INDIANA HOOSIERS were a dominant force in one of the most dominant leagues in the nation, the Big Ten Conference. They were used to playing in front of huge crowds and TV audiences night after night. They played fundamentally sound basketball. On offense they moved well without the ball, set good screens, made the extra pass, and could knock down the open jumper. On the other end of the court they played tough, physical, man-to-man defense.

Their style of play was similar to mine, at least the style I tried to play. Focus on the fundamentals with a heavy emphasis on shooting. Was I as good as them? Was I as tough? I was about to find out.

Not many people knew this, but Larry Bird first went to the University of Indiana to play ball before becoming a star at Indiana State. He didn't even last a semester at Bloomington. The team was loaded with talented upperclassmen and Bird, still a teenager, was perhaps unnerved by the new setting.

I too was still a teenager. Bird didn't make the NCAA Championship game until he was a 5th year senior. The thought then occurred to me, perhaps for the first time ever; while I'd always wanted to be as good as Larry Bird, I could now finally see I wasn't even good enough to untie his shoelaces. Was I okay with that? Couldn't I just concentrate on being the best Thomas Conner?

As the higher seed Indiana wore their traditional home white jerseys with red trim. We wore our dark away jerseys. We were in blue.

The game was incredibly intense from the start. The guy guarding me was all over me. At every opportunity he was grabbing and bumping me—nothing too dirty just tough basketball. I knew he was trying to get in my head and throw me off my game, perhaps make me lose my temper. It's not like the death of my dad or the punch back in January were secrets. Everyone knew about them by now.

They contested everything. It wasn't like they just contested shots, they tried to prevent passes, hinder our movement without the ball, neutralize our screens, you name it. It was the exact opposite of my time alone in the gym. There I could do whatever I wanted. Here everything I did was challenged. They completely dictated the style and pace of the game and built an early six point lead.

My first shot, with a defender's hand in my face, went in. It felt good. So did my second. The harder they guarded me the harder I worked to get open. I ran along the baseline trying to smear my defender into the shoulders of Kevin and Robert. The second I was in open space past Robert, Brian zipped a pass to my outside hand. I cocked my right hand, planted my pivot foot, squared my body to the basket and, without hesitation, let fly another jumper. It sailed just over over the fingertips of an Indiana defender. It went in too. I was entering a zone.

Next trip down on offense I never stopped moving, weaving through the tangle of bodies looking for the slimmest of openings, my defender frantically chasing me. Every blue jersey that I ran by, he ran into. It was as if I was racing through the forest unimpeded and behind me the trees were reaching out and grabbing him. I caught a pass from Jim, top of the key, behind the three-point line. I knew it was going in before it left my hand. I was so far deep into my zone I could feel my fingernails flick the surface of the leather ball as it left my hand on its way to its destination. Bottom of the net.

We traded baskets. Back and forth it went. We couldn't stop them from scoring and they couldn't stop us. The game was moving incredibly fast since there were few fouls called and hardly any turnovers. It was being played the way a championship game should be played. Every basket earned, nothing coming easy.

My fifth shot went in. I hadn't missed yet. The Indiana players were furious. I could see it in their eyes. Who was this freshman raining jumpers down on us? They switched their best defender off of Brian onto me. He was lightening fast, twice as quick as me. Trying to get open on the wing I rubbed shoulders with Robert. The Indiana defender was right there, so close his sweat was dripping on me. I kept moving. I tried the other wing. Jim saw what was coming. I could tell he knew what I was thinking. I made a strong "V" cut away from the basket then immediately went backdoor. The Indiana defender over committed. Jim threaded the needle with the ball and I had an easy layup.

Six made shots in a row built to seven, then eight. Still, Indiana maintained a slim lead. With sixteen seconds left in the first half they were up three. It was our ball. Jim brought the ball past the half court line. I stood next to the imposing frame of Kevin, my jersey being held by two defenders. I faked left, went right. The clock wound down. Twelve, eleven, ten… I ran so tight past Alex, who had just checked in, that I nearly knocked him off balance. His boney elbow got a piece of me. I was sure it got more of the man right behind me. Nine, eight… I was open, barely. Jim passed me the ball. I had an Indiana jersey right in my face. I heard my dad's voice; *The screener is always open.*

Alex was open. The ball barely touched my hands as I caught it and passed it almost simultaneously.

Seven, six…

Alex jumped and caught the ball high over his head. My defender turned his head to follow the ball and I moved. The moment Alex landed he sent it right back to me. It was the right play and I was surprised he recognized it.

Five, four…

I caught it in my favorite corner. The spot where I hit the big shot the other night. The same spot I loved to shoot from back home, where the blacktop sloped away from the basket towards the large oak tree. It was a shot I had taken a thousand times.

Three, two...

Wrist cocked, shoulders squared, eyes on the rim, I elevated and shot, just over the branches of Indiana.

One... buzzer... swish!

Tied at the half. I'd taken nine shots and made them all, scoring twenty points.

It was bedlam in the locker room at halftime. Guys were slapping each other on the back, shouting encouragement, and high fiving. Passionate and precise with his words, Coach Ross stoked the flames even higher. We were twenty minutes away from being national champions.

WE STARTED THE second half with the ball. Indiana played their hand right away. They were going to deny me the ball all over the court. Coach Ross had gone over this fundamental with me, but in the moment it was my dad's voice that I heard; *If the defense denies you the ball then set screens. With your man so close to you it'll be like setting a double screen and you'll get your teammates open.*

I immediately screened for Brian. Sure enough, it was like a double screen. He was open and nailed a fifteen footer. After an Indiana miss we scored again. We were up four.

On the next possession Brian anticipated a pass and made a clean steal—his third of the game. In the blink of an eye he was going the other way with the ball. I followed, sprinting as fast as I could. With only one Indiana defender back on defense we had a two-on-one situation. Brian dribbled straight at him as he backpedaled into the lane. The defender finally committed to stopping Brian. Without looking Brian delivered a perfect bounce pass to me. I thought I'd have a wide open path for a dunk but surprisingly the Indiana defender recovered. He stood under the basket, knees flexed, ready to block my shot. For a millisecond my old default thought of not confronting the defender entered my consciousness. I ignored it. Without ever hesitating I caught the ball in stride and elevated towards the rim. The defender, long and lanky vaulted skyward. I tenderly released the ball at the apex of my jump, just over his outstretched finger tips. The ball kissed the glass and fell in.

We'd scored the first six points of the second half. Indiana immediately called timeout to try and take the momentum out of our run.

Out of the timeout Indiana hit a three-pointer. Like I said, they could shoot. They responded to our 6-0 run with an 8-0 run of their own. But all runs in the second half were short lived. The pendulum never swung far in either direction. Neither team had a lead of over 6 points.

After making my first ten shots I missed my next two. I made my next shot at the ten minute mark, a three to tie the game. I hit another three to tie with just over five minutes to play. It stayed that way for a few minutes as both teams failed to score. Robert made two blocks, Indiana made two steals.

With three minutes to go and the game still tied, Indiana hit two straight threes. Would we run out of time before we could counter? With under two minutes to play Brian cut the lead to 4 with an amazing reverse layup in traffic. We traded baskets the next two possessions and then, with less than twenty seconds on the clock, I cut the lead to two with a clean look from the wing.

It was Indiana ball with 14 seconds to play. Down by two points we were forced to either get a steal or foul. They inbounded the ball and Jim quickly committed a foul. Only two seconds went off the clock. Once again it was a smart play by Jim as he fouled their worst free throw shooter. But this was Indiana. Everybody from Indiana could shoot free throws. I shot mine by the hundreds in a small gym in New Jersey. I imagined this guy for the Hoosiers practicing his on an outdoor court surrounded by cornfields. If he made both the game would be nearly out of reach. If he made one we'd need a three just to tie and send it to overtime. If he missed both we had a good chance to win.

He clanked the first free throw off the front rim. Half the arena groaned, the other half cheered.

Once again, referee Ernie Huggins was working the game. "One shot, gentlemen," he barked. "Wait till the release."

He tossed the Indiana player the ball. I saw his eyes. He was scared to death of this shot. His release looked good but he overcompensated from his earlier miss and hit the back iron. An Indiana player reached over Kevin's back and tipped the ball high in the air. He and Kevin quickly vaulted off the ground again and reached for the ball. This time Kevin cleanly grabbed the rebound and Coach Ross called timeout. We were down two with 10 seconds left and the ball at the opposite end of the court.

With all our assistant coaches huddled around him, Coach Ross got down on one knee in front of us. His drawing board was resting on his knee. "All right, listen up. Here's what we're going to run!" With all the emotion, noise and tension of the moment he was shouting at us even though we were all very close. "Let's get it in to Jim. Jim, move it up court quick. I want us to take the last shot of the game. You've got time so no need to rush. Thomas and Brian, cut through the paint and rub your defenders off on each other. Robert, you're here, top of the key like you're setting a high screen, but once Jim crosses half court you down screen for Thomas. Thomas, you continue up to the three-point line and set the screen for Jim. They'll be playing you tight. There's no way they're going to give you an open look. If your defender doesn't help, then we'll hopefully get an open look for Jim. Jim, I want you going off the screen towards Brian's side of the court. Thomas, you roll out to the other side to the three-point line, not into the paint. Jim, they're going to stay tight on Thomas—they don't want him taking a game winning jumper. This should free you up. You'll have options—drive to the bucket and score, kick it out to Brian if his man doubles, or swing it to Thomas if they try and hedge the screen too aggressively. Whatever happens, make sure we get a shot off. We don't need a three! A two can tie it and we'll win it in overtime!" He paused and looked at each of us and then settled on Jim.

"This is your moment, Jim," Coach Ross said as he tapped him on the knee. "You're the senior, the leader. Take us home."

A chorus of encouragement followed from nearly every one on the team. "You the man, Jim," and "Yeah, you got this, Jim."

As we walked out onto the court Jim came up next to me and whispered, "Be ready. If they double me, be ready."

He walked away and I stood at center court, soaking in the moment. How many times had I dreamed up this scenario in my backyard or at the YMCA? How many times had I counted down the clock in my head or called it aloud—three, two, one, Conner shoots, he scores, they win! But, this wasn't me, alone in my backyard, shooting hoops with my dad watching from the kitchen window. This was different. Yet the goal was the same. Hit one last shot. The skin on my right hand tingled.

I scanned the crowd looking for young kids here with their father. There must be several, watching me, wanting to be the next Thomas Conner. I wished I could tell them don't bother. You don't want to be the next anybody. You don't want to put your identity in what you do or how you play a game. Basketball is the best game in the world and I've gotten pretty good at it, but my identity is in the Lord.

Indiana came out in the same physical man-to-man defense they'd played all night. Matt, who was in for Kevin just in case we needed an extra shooter, barely got the ball inbounds to Jim. Jim immediately raced up court, hounded the whole way. Brian and I sprinted downcourt and crossed under the basket—not really stopping to set a screen for each other, just trying to create space in the midst of traffic. A moment later there was Robert with his elbows sticking out setting a screen for me. I slid past his shoulder and headed to the top of the key where Jim dribbled past my screen. The Indiana defenders played it perfectly. Jim's defender did his best to get over the top of my screen and my defender helped a bit on Jim, all the while keeping sight of me in the corner of his eye.

Jim was somehow able to turn the corner and get a step on his defender. The man guarding me now hesitated for a brief moment, not sure if he should commit to helping on Jim or stay with me. Jim was open as Brian's defender stayed put. I never saw the clock. Were there five seconds left? Less than that?

Jim took one more hard dribble and stopped on a dime. He bent his knees to rise up and shoot near the free throw line. Just then the Indiana defender guarding me made a quick, albeit belated, move to help. Everyone on our bench was yelling at Jim to shoot. The lanky Indiana defender who left me got to Jim quicker than I thought possible. His hand extended way above the ball. In mid air Jim twisted and made an incredible pass. To me. Was I open? Was there enough time? No time to think, just shoot!

I shot as soon as I caught the ball. My form, the follow through, it was all perfect. I knew it the moment it left my hand.

I held my follow through and watched it go in, touching nothing but net!

Then I noticed the Indiana players were celebrating and we weren't. I saw Ernie Huggins waving his arms. My shot was too late. I had released the ball a split second after the buzzer sounded. Coach Ross argued for a moment to no avail.

I had hung the net again. But we lost.

The moment after the game ended seemed like a dream. It was incredibly noisy. TV cameras were everywhere, confetti streamed down from the rafters. Happy people were running around. Everyone seemed happy, except us. After shaking hands with some of the Indiana players I stood near the edge of the court staring through the scene, unable to fully process the moment. I heard a familiar voice. It was Jenae. She was still in the stands unable to get past security and onto the floor.

I walked into the stands where we embraced for a long time.

CHAPTER 34

LESS THAN A week after the Final Four, Ray's first letter from prison arrived in the mail. He got sent back to prison the Thursday morning Paul and I found him drunk on the heated grate.

After I left that morning, Paul took Ray back to his office. Still suffering from all that cheap red wine he immediately fell asleep on Paul's couch. Unfortunately, police investigators looking to interview more eyewitnesses to my father's murder, showed up at Paul's office shortly thereafter. They started asking questions about Ray and quickly ascertained that he'd violated his parole by getting drunk. They took him into custody on the spot, and Ray had been locked up in a Maryland prison ever since.

Ray's letter to me was five pages long, handwritten on both sides of yellow legal paper. It was vintage Ray: energetic, honest, and rambling. In a visit with Paul only days after his incarceration, Ray finally came to the end of himself. The last remnants of the alcohol were leaving his system at the same time he repented and received the Lord. He was still in prison but no longer a slave to his ego, pride, and addictions. Some of the sentences bled as my tears dropped onto the pages. His last sentence though, remained clear. He wanted me to come visit.

I was a little worried about bringing Jenae with me, but she insisted on coming. I sent Ray a reply telling him we'd visit soon. In the next five days, two more of his letters arrived in the mail before

Jenae and I borrowed Alex's beat up station wagon and drove towards the Maryland countryside.

Having never been in a prison before, I wasn't sure how I'd react. At first I was nervous as I approached the tall chain link fence that surrounded the facility. It was a good fifteen feet high, topped with menacing razor wire that glistened in the midday sun. Then, when I walked through the entrance and heard the gate lock shut behind me, I felt a jolt of fear. A robust prison guard with a superhero-like belt full of handcuffs, mace, and other gear pointed to a picnic bench and table. "Wait here," he instructed then disappeared through a door in the drab gray prison.

The prison was classified as minimum security, but it still had all the things you'd expect to see at a prison: guards, guns, locks, and prisoners. The dented metal bench where we sat and waited was located in a large courtyard adjacent to the prison building. Other benches and tables were spread out over the neatly trimmed grass. A few tables away an older couple chatted with a gaunt young man in prison issue clothing. It was hot and muggy and my shirt stuck to my sweaty back like cellophane.

When Ray emerged from the building in his garish bright orange jumpsuit, he strode over with a big smile on his face and hugged us both. A patch with his inmate number was sewn onto the chest of his jumpsuit. That number was also written on every one of Ray's letters to me.

Ray gestured to the table as he sat down. "Sit down you two, sit down. Get comfortable."

At first he talked about his friends at the prison and those he had to steer clear of, the food, the guards, and what he did with his time. As he spoke, he leaned forward with his elbows on the table. "I'm supposed to finish up a two year sentence, but with early parole I think I got a good chance of getting outta here just before your next season starts."

"Where will you live when you're released?" Jenae asked.

Ray smiled and winked. "Oh, I'll probably move into Thomas's dorm and sleep on his couch."

I laughed. "I don't know if Brian would go for that. One or two nights, maybe. But a semester ..."

Ray sat back surprised. "You going to room with Brian again next year?"

"Probably. The better friends we are off the court the better we'll play together on it."

He slowly shook his head. "Well, how about that? Now, in answer to your question, Jenae, I really don't know where I'll live, but I'm not worried. As long as I stay dry, I don't care where the good Lord puts me. Shoot, this place has got nothing on the darkness of being chained to the bottle. Now that I've broken them chains, I can't tell you how free I feel, even in here. Shoot, I'm more free now in here than I was on the outside. Yes, sir. The Lord finally got my attention and the old man, the old Ray that was trying to kill me, is crucified and dead. See, I used to think the bottle had this vise grip on me. It seemed so strong, like it was unbreakable. Well it's broken, and man, let me tell you, the Lord's grip on me feels a thousand times stronger."

"Ray, that's music to my ears," Jenae said as she wiped away a tear. "I'm so happy for you."

"Well, I'm happy too. I got so much to be thankful for. Nothing you can see here." He swept his hand to his surroundings then smacked his chest with a closed fist. "It's all in here. So don't cry, sweetheart. Don't feel sorry for me."

A laugh escaped Jenae's mouth. "I'm not. I'm crying because I'm happy."

"Good. That's what I want to hear. Now look here, I've been gabbing on about me this whole time. I want to hear about the Final Four and the national championship game. I told the guys in here I know you, but nobody believed me. I don't care. I was jumping up and down watching it on TV."

It must have taken over an hour to fill him in on everything that happened after my father died. "I wish he was there at the Final Four," I said, "but I know he was watching."

"Your father was a great man," Ray said after a long pause. "I never knew my old man very much. I can't blame him for my failures, but lots of guys in here do. They all tell the same story. No dad around, started getting in trouble the moment they discovered how. Thing is, no matter you're upbringing, where you come from and all that, we all make the bed we sleep in." He jerked a thumb at the building behind him. "I'm probably the only guy in here who knows that."

"Hmm. I wonder how many on the outside know that?" Jenae said thoughtfully.

"Good point, my dear," Ray said.

"Well, you look as fit as ever," Jenae said. "I imagine you get to workout in here."

"You bet! Let me tell you about my workouts. They got a good set of weights here. Lots of free weights. And they got a good heavy bag too, but no speed bag. I figure I'll be okay without the speed bag, just load up on the heavy bag, hit the jump rope hard—that should do it. I got a pretty good routine. All free weights one day with a little jogging, then heavy bag and jump rope the other days. Say, Thomas. You see that sorry looking thing over there?" He pointed to a corner of the courtyard where there was a concrete slab and a neglected looking basketball hoop. "What do you say we shoot some hoops?"

I shrugged. "Sure. You got a ball out here?"

"No, but I'll get one. Just a minute."

Ray went inside and moments later emerged with a rubber outdoor basketball with the initials of the prison prominently stamped on it.

"You got to see this, Conner," Ray chirped with glee. "I've been working on my shot. In addition to watching you, I've been watching Larry Bird on TV. Got lots of time to do that. See, he keeps his hands high when he shoots, like this."

He put the ball in his hands and set up to take a shot, hesitating for a moment to make sure I was watching. When he shot the ball it twisted awkwardly in the air and clanged off the rim. His form was as horrible as always, and I wondered just which Larry Bird he was watching.

"Hold it. Let me try it again." He took aim again and missed again. "Okay, Conner, I know you're itching to shoot. Here."

He passed me the ball and I caressed it in my hands. Looking up at the rickety hoop silhouetted by the tall prison fence, I let it fly.

"Swish! Man, Conner, you sure can shoot. Just like Larry Bird!"

"Larry Bird? Hardly," I replied. "I'll tell you one thing though. It's a beautiful thing, shooting a basketball. It's a beautiful thing."

THE END